RISE
OF THE
JAGUAR
WOMAN

Other Books by Lee E. Cart

Born in the Wayeb: Book One of *The Mayan Chronicles*
The Cracker Book: Artisanal Crackers for Every Occasion
The Paper Trail: Useful Charts to Organize Your Writing

The How to Do Anything Series ™ Kindle books
How to Revise Your Writing
How to Lose Weight without Much Effort
How to Save Hundreds in Editing Fees

RISE
OF THE
JAGUAR
WOMAN

BOOK TWO
OF
THE MAYAN CHRONICLES

Lee E. Cart

Ek' Balam Press
Wellington, Maine

Ek' Balam Press
15 Taylor Cemetery Road
Wellington, Maine 04942

Cover design by Lee E. Cart

Printed in the United States of America
LCCN: 2016920233
ISBN: 978-0-9906765-1-5

To my grandson, Jenson Aiden,
thank you for bringing such joy into my life

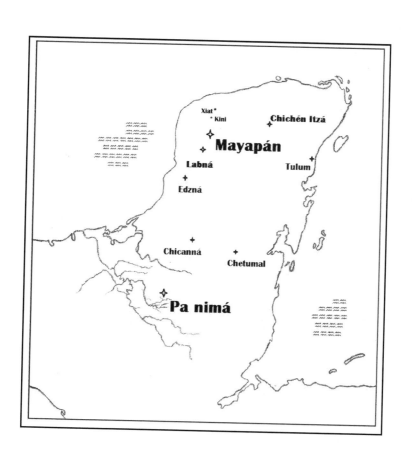

Xiat *
* Kini   Chichén Itzá

✦ Mayapán

Labná   Tulum

Edzná

Chicanná   Chetumal

✦ Pa nimá

Cast of Characters

(Note: Each character's name is an actual Mayan word, whose meaning is included after the character's description.)

The city of Chichén Itzá

Ajelbal: Member of the Xiu tribe betrothed to Satal, died of old age; a flutist.
Alaxel: Chachal's secret lover; a prince.
Chiwekox: One of Satal's personal shamans; a boa constrictor.
Ch'o: One of Satal's personal shamans; a rat.
Ixtzol: One of Satal's personal shamans; a centipede.
Kämisanel: Head of the warriors; a killer, murderer, assassin.
K'oy: One of Satal's personal shamans; a spider monkey.
Koyopa: One of Satal's personal shamans; lightning.
Pataninel: One of Satal's personal shamans; a servant.
Sachoj: Great-grandmother to Satal, reduced to a shrunken head; a viper.
Satal: Leader of the city, wife of Q'alel, mother to Chachal, member of the city council, presumed dead after falling into Mayapán's cenote; a black wasp.
Sina'j: One of Satal's personal shamans; a scorpion.
Tewichinel: One of Satal's personal shamans; a priest.
Yuxba': One of Satal's personal shamans; to bow.

The city of Mayapán

Alom: Mother to Yakal, second wife to Q'alel; a servant.
Binel ja': Younger sister to Yakal; a river or brook.
Bitol: Commander of the Gates and uncle to Yakal; a builder of ancient pyramids.
Box: Young man who works at pottery workshop; to build a fire.
Ilonel: Lead raider employed by Satal, killed in the attack on Pa nimá; a spy.
Imul: Younger sister to Yakal; a rabbit.

Kubal Joron: A member of the city council and partner to Matz'; a water jug.

Kux: A member of Ilonel's group of spies; a weasel.

Mayibal: Infant son of Yakal and Uskab; a miracle or marvel.

Masat: Younger sister to Yakal, worked as servant to Satal; a deer.

Matz': A member of the city council and partner to Kubal Joron; an ear of corn with few grains.

Memetik: Houseboy to Kubal Joron and Matz'; to bleat like a goat.

Najtir: Shaman who helps train Tz'; ancient.

Nil: Son of Q'abarel, works at the Silowik Tukan; a waterfall.

Nimal: Head of the regiment; a leader.

Q'abarel: Owner of the Silowik Tukan bar, father to Nil; a drunkard.

Puk'pik: Owner of the pottery workshop; a person with a pot belly.

Q'alel: Father to Yakal and husband to Satal, died of suspicious circumstances; a military leader.

Tarnel: Owner of the slave market; a bodyguard.

Tikoy: Younger brother to Yakal, died in the attack on Pa nimá; a frog.

T'ot: Cook and seller of seafood in the marketplace; shellfish.

Uskab: Second wife to Yakal, mother of Mayibal; a honey bee.

Xik': The fletcher of fine arrows; a feather.

Yakal: Father to Na'om, son of Q'alel and Alom, half-brother to Chachal; a stonemason.

The village of Pa nimá

Ajchak: Husband to Tzalon, father to Tuney, a new member of the village; a peasant farmer.

Ajkun (Ati't): Grandmother to Na'om, the village midwife and herbal healer; a witch who heals.

Ala: Infant son to Witzik' and K'ale'n, twin; a young boy.

Ali: Infant daughter to Witzik' and K'ale'n, twin; a young girl.

Banal Bo'j: A village member, died in the attack on the village; a pot maker.

Chachal: Mother to Tz', wife of Chiman, died in the attack on the village; a necklace of colored stones.

Chiman: Father to Tz', husband to Chachal, leader and shaman of the village; a shaman.

Ek' Balam: Black jaguar, friend to Na'om; a dark or black jaguar.

K'ale'n: Husband to Witzik', father to twins, Ali and Ala, a new member of the village; a bundle of firewood.

Kemonel: Mother to Mok'onel, Poy, and Tze'm, died in the attack on the village; a weaver.

Kab: Infant son of Xoral and Tzukunel; sweets or candy.

Kon: Young friend to Tz', died in the attack on the village; a stupid person.

Lintat: Grandson to Noy and Mam, befriended by Na'om; a young boy between three and eight.

Mam: Grandfather to Lintat, husband to Noy; a grandfather.

Mok'onel: Older daughter to Kemonel, stays in Mayapán after the attack on the village; a robber or thief.

Na'om: Granddaughter to Ajkun, daughter to Yakal, presumed dead after falling into the cenote in Mayapán; to have felt or sensed something.

Noy: Grandmother to Lintat, wife to Mam; a grandmother.

Pempen: Wife to Setesik, mother to Sijuan; a butterfly.

Potz': A village member, died in the attack on the village; a blind or one-eyed person.

Poy: Younger daughter to Kemonel, died in the attack on the village; a doll.

Setesik: Husband to Pempen, father to Sijuan; a large round basket.

Sia': Female jaguar who lives near Ajkun's hut; a cat.

Sijuan: Daughter to Pempen and Setesik, friend to Mok'onel; a female friend.

Tajinel: Husband to Ajkun, died of old age; a farmer.

Tu'janel: Mother of Na'om, first wife to Yakal, died in childbirth; a new mother.

Tzalon: Wife to Ajchak, mother to Tuney, a new member of the village; a gladiola flower.

Tuney: Infant daughter to Tzalon and Ajchak; a dahlia flower.

Tz'ajonel (Tz'): Son of Chiman and Chachal, friend of Na'om; a painter.

Tze'm: Newborn son of Kemonel, died in the attack on the village; to laugh.

Tzukunel: Husband to Xoral, father to Kab, a new member of the village; a hunter.

Xoral: Wife to Tzukunel, mother to Kab, a new member of the village; a flower garden.

Witzik': Wife to K'ale'n, mother to twins Ali and Ala, a new member of the village; a cornflower.

In the countryside

Alixel: Daughter to Kärinik and Chapal Kär, mother to Mial and Ukabal; a princess.

Be Anim: Twin brother to Tik Anim in the village of Xiat; to run.

Chapal Kär: Husband to Kärinik, father to Alixel, presumed dead; a fisherman.

Ch'awinel: Shaman and leader of the village of Xiat; a person who talks a lot.

Josol Che': The carpenter in the village of Xiat; a carpenter.

Jumumik: Twin brother to Jututik in the village of Xiat; to run fast.

Jututik: Twin brother to Jumumik in the village of Xiat; to run fast.

Kärinik: Mother to Alixel, aids Na'om on the beach; to fish.

Kunaj: Grandmother to Kärinik, died of old age; to cure, to heal.

Mial: Granddaughter to Kärinik, daughter to Alixel; firstborn daughter.

Tik Anim: Twin brother to Be Anim; to run.

Tikonel: Husband to Alixel, father to Mial and Ukabal; a sower, a farmer.

Ukabal: Grandson to Kärinik, son to Alixel; a second child.

The Mayan Gods

Acan: The god of wine, belching, and intoxication.

Ahalgan: The god of pus.

Ahalpuh: The god of pestilence.

Ah-Cun-Can: A war god related to snakes and serpents.

Ah-Pekku: The god of thunder.

Buluc-Chabtan: The god of war, violence, and death who likes to roast people on skewers over a fire.

Camazotz: The god of bats and friend to Satal.

Chac: The god of rain and lightning.

Hunahpu and Xbalanque (The Hero Twins): The twin ball players who were able to outwit the gods of the Underworld and survived the numerous trials set before them so they could return to the world of the living.

Hun-Batz: The god of howler monkeys.

Itzamná: The supreme god of the Maya who taught the people to grow maize and cacao.

Ixchel: The jaguar goddess of midwifery and medicine.

Kukulcan: The plumed serpent god.

One Death: One of the gods of the Underworld who protects the sacred fire.

Poxlom: The god of diseases.

Seven Death: One of the gods of the Underworld who protects the sacred fire.

Tlacolotl: The god of evil and dark places.

Xaman Ek: The patron god of travelers and merchants.

Yum Cimil: The god of death.

Na'om

It was the first day of the Wayeb, and Na'om had one last glimpse of the blue sky before the cool water of the *cenote* closed over her head. As she plunged toward the dark bottom of the freshwater well, she opened her eyes, and in the deepening gloom, she saw Ek' Balam, her pet black jaguar, swimming toward her through an explosion of bubbles. He turned his tail to Na'om, and she grabbed hold, letting him pull her through the darkness toward one of the many openings in the limestone walls. She concentrated on kicking with her feet and used one hand to paddle, as the two friends swam steadily upward and into a fissure in the well. Pressure built in Na'om's lungs, and the need to breathe threatened to overwhelm her. For a split second, she thought she might have made a mistake and should have tried to reach the surface. *Perhaps someone would have helped me out of the cenote, maybe thrown me a rope.*

Just as Na'om was ready to turn back, despite the intense pain in her chest, she found she was able to put her feet down and stand. Her head popped above the water, and she gulped deep breaths of the cold, damp air. In the semi-darkness, she saw Ek' Balam continue to paddle forward until his paws touched the ground, and he scrambled up out of the water. He shook from head to tail, sending a spray of water up onto the sides of the cave. With her wet shirt and skirt clinging to her limbs, she staggered upward and stood beside Ek' Balam in the dim light. "Well, boy, now what?" she said as she bent down and gave him a quick hug. She turned and looked back toward where they had come from and knew she didn't have the energy or courage to return to the surface by that route. The only access to the outside lay in front of them.

She stepped out of the water and stripped off her wet clothes, wrung them out as best she could, and then put the cold clothing back on. She shivered and knew she needed to keep moving if she wanted to stay warm. She glanced again at the weak light coming from the watery tunnel and then toward the blackness that stretched ahead of them. *This must lead somewhere,* she thought as she slowly walked into the deepening shadows. The ground was rough under her bare feet, and several times, she stubbed her toes on small rocks. As the shadows grew ever darker, Na'om stretched her left hand out to the side and touched the wall while she kept her right hand in front of her. By trailing her fingertips along the coarse limestone, she was able to move in a straight line, deeper and deeper into the fissure.

Ek' Balam padded along next to her, matching his steps to her own, and Na'om was glad to feel the warmth and softness of his damp fur whenever he bumped into her bare leg. At one point, she sensed he had stopped in the gloom. She turned around. "Hey, come on, no leaving me to do this on my own." She heard him pad toward her, and they both continued walking. As the blackness grew thicker, Na'om became more hesitant, slowing her pace until she was hardly moving at all. Finally, she laid her right hand on Ek' Balam's shoulder and instantly felt electric energy rush through her fingertips and into her body as their two spirits intermingled. That very morning, the pair had joined their life forces to confront Satal, the witch of Mayapán, when Satal had shape-shifted into a giant black wasp and tried to kill Na'om with her stinger. When Satal had tried to escape, all three of them had fallen thirty feet into the well.

At least Satal is at the bottom of the cenote, along with that awful shrunken head she talked to. Neither one of them will be able to harm the inhabitants of Mayapán again, Na'om thought. *And I know Chiman and Tz' will take care of Ajkun until I can return to our village of Pa nimá.* With her fingers still tingling, she leaned toward Ek' Balam and said, "I can't see anymore, you lead." She felt the cat take a few quick steps and twined her fingers into his coat. "Not so fast, remember I can't see in the dark like you," she cried as she felt his fur slip through her fingers. The last thing she wanted was to lose him in the murkiness.

Together, the two advanced deeper and deeper underground, and Na'om kept her left hand touching the wall, even though her fingertips grew sore from rubbing over the rocky surface. Gradually, she noticed that her hair began to catch on rocks protruding from the roof of the fissure, and she stopped long enough to place her hand over her head. The ceiling was just a few inches away. Keeping her leg against Ek' Balam's side, she continued to walk forward, and in just a few steps, she found she needed to crouch down to avoid banging her head. Ek' Balam stopped, and Na'om heard him lie down in the dirt. She took another few steps and bumped into a wall. She brought her left hand around in a semi-circle to meet her right one and groaned.

"No, it can't be!" she cried as she stretched both arms out to either side and stepped backwards. Her fingers caressed rock on all sides. She patted the walls in front of her from the ceiling of the tunnel down to the floor and knew she had reached a dead end. She knelt down in the dark and placed her forehead on the dirt. Tears dripped off her nose and into the dust, creating a tiny puddle of mud. She felt her chest tighten at the thought of being trapped, and she took a few deep breaths of the cool, moist air to calm her nerves. *There has to be a way out of here,* Na'om thought as she wiped the smudge of mud off the end of her nose. *I must have missed an opening someplace. If I follow one wall and run both hands along it while I walk back to the water, I should find the gap.*

With renewed determination, Na'om stood up and headed back the way she had just come, with Ek' Balam staunchly by her side. She dragged her right hand above her head along the rocks, heedless of the many minute cuts she was creating in her fingers, and kept her right hip so close to the wall that she banged it several times on rocky protrusions. The blackness gradually gave way to the dusky light near the cenote, but Na'om didn't stop walking until she felt the water close around her ankles.

She turned away from the light and could see Ek' Balam lying down deep in the tunnel, a black silhouette against the shadows. She faced the right wall and moved quickly along it using the same technique as before. She hurried past Ek' Balam, who only turned his head to watch her move deeper into the blackness. Within minutes, she felt her hair catch on the ceiling and then ran into the end of the fissure once again.

"There must be a way out of here!" Na'om cried as she ran her hands all over the limestone surface in front of her. "How can I have missed it?" she said. *Maybe the opening is lower than where I had my hand.*

Reluctantly, Na'om turned around once again. This time she crawled along the right wall back to the water's edge. But there was no sign of a crack, gap, or hole anywhere. She crawled into the cool water and drank deeply before washing the grit and dirt from her bleeding palms, fingertips, and knees.

"Itzamná, I beg you, help me find the way," Na'om pleaded as she slowly crept along the far wall, away from the light one more time. She paused when she reached the spot where Ek' Balam lay with his head on his paws and scuttled over to lie down beside him. She leaned back against his stomach and rubbed him gently in his favorite spot behind the ear. His purr filled the fracture in the limestone and echoed up and down. "I just need a few moments' rest, then I'll continue," Na'om said. She closed her eyes and forced herself to relax.

My dreams have always shown me what's going to happen, she thought as she listened to Ek' Balam purr. *The last dream I had was of falling into the cenote and then entering this fissure in the limestone, so there must be a way out.* She winced as she rolled onto her bruised and bloody knees. As she leaned over to give Ek' Balam a quick hug, she noticed a slight draft on her bare legs. She scooted around in the dark until she felt the wall, then she ran her hands up and down it in ever-widening circles.

Suddenly, her right hand touched air. She moved her fingers back to the left and found the rock wall again. By placing her hands side by side, Na'om was able to keep her left fingertips on the rocky wall while her right hand floated in empty space. She reached up while still kneeling, continued searching, and realized the opening was only a couple of feet high, but big enough to squeeze through.

"*Maltiox*, Itzamná," Na'om cried as she collapsed on the ground.

Ek' Balam padded over to her and licked her gently on the face.

"You knew the opening was there all the time, didn't you?" Na'om said as she hugged her pet cat. "No wonder you didn't keep following me back and forth in this place. From now on, I have to pay more attention to you," she said as she struggled to her knees once again.

Placing her hand gently on his tail, Na'om said, "All right, lead the way."

Ek' Balam lowered his big head, crouched down, and crept through the opening, with Na'om crawling on her knees just behind him. After a few short wriggles, they were both through and Na'om found herself in another tunnel, this one wider and taller than the last. She pushed herself to an upright position, used some water to wash off her knees and hands again, and turned to Ek' Balam, who was already padding deeper into the gloom.

"Wait for me," Na'om shouted and her voice ricocheted around and around before disappearing. She ran and caught up with Ek' Balam, placed her left hand on his shoulder, and together the two of them entered the pitch black.

SATAL

As Satal sank through the cold water, she kept her eyes tightly shut. She didn't want to see the walls of the cenote sliding past her as she dropped deeper and deeper into the gloom. It was only when she felt the soft, muddy bottom under her feet that she opened her eyes and looked around. The water was murky with stirred up dirt, but she was just able to make out the shapes of some old animal bones jutting up from the silt. She quickly glanced around for her great-grandmother Sachoj's shrunken head, but couldn't see more than a few feet in front of her. Her lungs began to ache with the need for oxygen, and she almost opened her mouth when she heard Sachoj's voice.

"Wait!" Sachoj cried. "It's the first day of the Wayeb; call to Camazotz and the other gods of the Underworld to help you through this test."

Satal closed her eyes and imagined the giant bat, Camazotz, hanging upside down with a thousand other bats in his underground cave. *Help me, dear friend, and I will be indebted for my life*, she thought. Instantly, she felt a burst of energy flow through her body and sensed she was shape-shifting in the water into her spirit form of a giant black wasp. She quickly pushed upward with her six-foot wings and burst forth onto the surface of the well. She inhaled deeply as she floated on her back in the deep shadows cast by the cenote's tall, straight walls. She stared up at the bright blue sky so far overhead and blinked her multifaceted eyes at the brilliance of it all. As best she could, Satal searched the perimeter of the cenote for signs of human life, but no one was around. It was the first day of the Wayeb, and most of the men of Mayapán were dancing near the base of Kukulcan's pyramid to keep the evil spirits of the Underworld at bay, while the women and children stayed indoors and prayed for their safety. Satal knew no one would come near the cenote for the next five days, and she was glad she'd decided to jump in, taking the girl, Na'om with her.

I wonder what happened to the girl, she thought as she drifted around in circles. *I didn't see her or her cat in the murk at the bottom.*

"They've entered their own journey into the Underworld," Sachoj said. "Time will tell if they survive the trials that lie before them."

Satal grimaced. She had hoped they'd died only moments after entering the water. But perhaps, if they were alive, there was still a way for her to take Na'om's powers and make them her own.

Satal tried to swim, but the weight of the water on her wings weighed her down. She was only able to drift on the surface, pushed about by the tiny ripple of breeze that flowed across the water. For hours, she stayed like this, just floating and drifting, unable to really move, until she suddenly felt one of her wings brush the rocky surface of the well. Satal scrabbled as hard as she could, twisting and spinning about, until she managed to touch the wall with her bug-like feet. She gripped the rough rocks and struggled with every remaining ounce of energy to break her wings free from the tension of the water's surface. With a great pop, audible only to herself, she felt her wings release, and she hugged the wall. Water dripped off each wing tip, and slowly she was able to fan her wings back and forth, drying them in the late afternoon shadows.

Just as quickly as she had shifted into her wasp form, Satal suddenly found herself back in her four-foot human body, barely clinging to the craggy rocks at the edge of the water. *Camazotz,* she thought, *you old bat, you couldn't wait until I got out of this hole to shift me back?* Holding tightly to the rocks in front of her, she tilted her head and just caught a glimpse of the edge of the well directly above her. *Thirty feet or more to climb, I'll never make it.* She balanced precariously on a rocky protrusion and thought of her options. *Either I climb, or I die by dropping back into the water and join my ancestors in the Underworld.*

A deep voice rumbled inside her head. "You owe me," Camazotz said. "I expect you to pray at your altar and open the doorway to the Underworld tonight so my brothers and I can gain access to the outside world."

Satal sighed. Climbing the cliff wall would take all her strength and then some, but she knew she owed her life to Camazotz. As the shadows grew deeper, she slowly began to scrabble upward, taking one cautious step at a time. Fortunately, the limestone walls were pockmarked with tiny holes that gave her an abundance of places to jam her fingers and toes. Inch by inch, she clambered up the rocky surface until she clung within a few feet of the edge. She glanced around for signs of life, and seeing none, thrust herself up and over the lip of the well. For several minutes, she lay on the dirt, worn smooth by the passage of thousands of feet, as she felt her arms and legs relax after the strenuous ascent.

The beating of the drums that marked the pace of the men dancing at the pyramid reverberated throughout Satal's body, and her heart began to pound in rhythm with them. She knew she needed to move, but it felt so good to do nothing, just feel the cool earth pressed against her cheek, with her blood pulsing through her tired limbs.

"You're a wanted woman now," Sachoj said, her voice echoing inside Satal's head. "If Yakal and the other council members find you here, you'll be sacrificed before sundown tomorrow. Go now, get out of the city; abandon everything and start anew."

Reluctantly, Satal pushed herself to her knees and then slowly stood. She swayed on her feet as the blood rushed from her head, and she bent over until the dizziness passed. She wrapped her wet black shawl tightly around her head, covering most of her face, and slipped away from the cenote. Hugging the shadows that lined the streets, she hurried through the deserted alleyways toward the small gate tucked into the corner of the south wall. From the safety of the alley, she watched the guard who tended the gate. He leaned against the twelve-foot wall, chewing on a six-inch-long piece of sugar cane, but Satal noted he was not one of her paid sentries. She wouldn't be able to leave the city that way.

She shrank back into the shadows, trying to decide what to do. She needed to open the portal to the Underworld and let Camazotz out; she had made a sacred promise to him and didn't want to anger the god. "All the gates will be heavily guarded for the next four days," she muttered.

"Any attempt to get out and I'll be stopped immediately." She crouched low to the ground when she heard footsteps approaching, but they faded away before entering the alley where she was hiding.

Then it came to her, the one place she'd be safe for the next several days. She laughed as she hurried through the deserted streets. *No one will think to look for me in my own home! And once the Wayeb is over, I can mingle with the crowds out celebrating the new year and then slip through any of the city gates.*

Once inside the relative safety of her own house, Satal breathed a sigh of relief. She was unwilling to light a single candle for fear of it being seen, but moved easily in the darkness across the front courtyard and into the main room. She shuffled down to her bedroom, removed her damp clothes, and put on another outfit. It felt good to be back indoors, away from everyone. In the deepening gloom, she could see the vague outlines of darker shapes in the room with her. The cage that had held the jet-black jaguar was still in the corner, the ropes that had bound Na'om still dangled from the wall, and Satal found it hard to believe that she had lost everything she'd spent years searching for in a single day. Suddenly, she was exhausted and wanted nothing more than to sink into her hammock and sleep. But she still had two more acts to perform.

Her favorite knife and copper bowl had been seized by Yakal at the cenote, so Satal cautiously made her way back out into the courtyard, to the kitchen area, where she kept a few utensils. She selected the sharpest knife she could find, a large ceramic bowl, and a gourd half-full of water and went back to her room. She grabbed a few herbs from her wooden cupboard and dumped them into the bowl, then added a cup of water. Then she pulled out her tongue and with one swift slash, cut the tip of it, letting the drops of blood drip into the water. She stirred the mixture with the point of the knife, then lifted the bowl and drank.

She sat on the floor, closed her eyes, and imagined she was in her small cave outside the city walls. She pictured the altar where she performed her sacrifices, the pool of water nearby, and the many tunnels that led deep underground. She concentrated her attention and saw the passageways filled with a million bats, with Camazotz in the lead. She ducked as the hordes of mammals flew rapidly by, heading to the opening that led above ground.

"Well done, Lady Satal," Camazotz said as he paused near her.

Satal opened her eyes and could see the giant bat god above her. The stench of his musty fur filled the room, and she flinched as if someone had struck her.

"Come with us," the bat said as he hovered in the air.

"Ha, not a chance," Satal replied as she inched away from the foul creature. "I'd be instantly recognized and thrown back into the cenote."

"Not if you shape-shifted; then you could fly about the city with impunity."

"Hmm, tempting idea, but it would take all my remaining strength. No, I'll cast a few spells tonight and then lie low and leave the city as quietly as possible once the Wayeb is over."

"Suit yourself," Camazotz replied. He flitted about the room, brushing his wingtip on the empty cage before heading to the outdoors.

Satal quickly gathered more herbs from her cupboard, reopened the wound on her tongue, and made another concoction in the ceramic bowl. She visualized Yakal, Kubal Joron, Nimal, Bitol, and the many other men who had accused her of treason at the edge of the cenote dancing around the bonfire in front of the pyramid. Then she pictured them doubling over, grasping at their heads, falling to the ground. As they writhed in indescribable pain, blood flowed from their noses and ears, and weeping sores appeared all over their bodies.

The imagery made her smile, and she opened her eyes before wearily making her way to the hammock where she quickly fell into a dreamless sleep.

AJKUN

Ajkun stopped chatting with Alom and looked up from the shirt she was embroidering as a shadow fell across her lap. "Chiman, what are you doing here, what's wrong?" she said as she looked at his face. She stabbed the stingray needle into the white fabric and reached out to grasp her old friend's hand.

Chiman squatted next to Ajkun, tears streaming down his lined face. "Na'om, she was here . . ."

"What do you mean 'here,' in the city? Well, where is she? I must see her." Ajkun twisted onto her knees and began to rise.

"Ajkun, wait, there's more," Chiman said as he placed a hand gently on Ajkun's back. She sat back down on the packed dirt floor of the hut. He swallowed and continued, "She's gone, fallen into the cenote with Satal."

Ajkun drew in a deep breath and held it for the longest moment, before finally letting the air escape in a gasp. "Tell me exactly what happened." She closed her eyes, willing her heart to slow its rapid pounding as she listened to Chiman describe how Yakal and the others had found Satal with Na'om and Ek' Balam near the city's well. Yakal had accused Satal of treason and witchcraft against the people of Mayapán and discovered a shrunken head and various herbs in her basket that proved her guilt. Then he'd shown the gathered men arrows and a large green obsidian knife that Na'om had brought with her, which linked Satal to the attack on Pa nimá.

Ajkun drew in another deep breath. Ever since the raid on the village, she'd suspected Satal was behind it. What Chiman was telling her just confirmed it. His words burrowed into her heart and she placed her hand on her chest to ease the pain. "How did they fall?"

"Satal started to run, Na'om grabbed at her skirt, and they both went over the edge. Ek' Balam jumped in right after them." Chiman paused and wiped his eyes. "I waited for many minutes, but none of them surfaced."

The three friends sat in silence for several minutes. Ajkun thought of the numerous times she'd worried about Na'om, left alone in Pa nimá after the assault. The raiders had bound Ajkun's wrists together, led her to their war canoes, and brought her here to the city, but the whole time, she had feared more for Na'om than herself. She never suspected that the girl might try to follow them and actually make it to Mayapán on her own.

And now she was gone, swallowed into the depths of the cenote, with no hopes of ever being seen again. Ajkun felt the tears welling in her eyes as Chiman squatted next to her.

"Help me up," she said as she held out her brown, arthritic hand to him. He stood and pulled her gently from her spot. Alom reached out to hug her as she passed by, but Ajkun shook her head at her new friend. "Maltiox, Alom, but I need some fresh air right now." She continued to hold Chiman's hand, and the two quickly left the hut.

The rhythmic pulsing of the tens of drums being rapped near the pyramid filled the air as the couple slowly walked through the empty streets of Mayapán. The able-bodied, young, and old men were dancing around the bonfire, striving to keep the gods of the Underworld at bay while the doors of the Wayeb opened wide, and the women and children hid behind their closed doors. No one hurried here and there on business, no groups of young girls ran errands for their mothers, and no middle-aged women with numerous children walked slowly to and from the market, yet Ajkun still felt trapped. "I need to get outside these walls," Ajkun said. "I can't breathe in here."

Despite the protests of the guard, they passed through one of the smaller gates and stepped into a planted cornfield. The green sprouts were almost knee high, and the deep green leaves brushed against Ajkun's calves as she hurried down the row. She took a deep breath, grateful for the fresher air and the lack of the noise that had pressed on her ears. She glanced skyward as thunder rumbled in the distance and noticed dark clouds building on the horizon, but didn't stop. In silence, the couple walked to the end of the row and continued, wandering farther and farther from the city. The ground sloped downhill, and they entered a small ravine, which was sheltered from the wind and the eyes of any passersby. Ajkun found a large boulder, sat down, and only then allowed the tears to freely fall onto the dirt beneath her feet.

Chiman sat down next to her and placed his arm around her shoulders. Ajkun leaned her head into his chest, and together, they cried for their loss. After a time, Ajkun sniffled and raised her head. "There's something I have to tell you, something you should have known long ago." She pulled a small cotton cloth from her skirt pocket and wiped her eyes. Knowing there was no easy way to break the news, she just stated the truth. "Na'om was your granddaughter." She waited for Chiman to react, but was surprised when he didn't say anything. "Well?"

Chiman smiled briefly. "I've suspected that ever since she was born, which is why I've always tried to shield her from the villagers who wanted to do her harm. And lately, I've been working hard to persuade Tz' to find someone else to marry. Being my son, he can't wed my granddaughter. But I guess that doesn't matter now." He hung his head. "I'm not sure if anything matters now."

"Of course things matter," Ajkun automatically replied as she placed her hand gently on Chiman's thigh. But in her heart, she felt hollow. The desire to see Na'om again had given her the strength to endure the arduous river trip and forced march to the city. Once Yakal had rescued them from the slavers, she'd been filled with hope and longing, eager to return to the village and see Na'om. But all that had changed in an instant, thanks to the evil ambitions of Satal. The thought of the woman stealing her granddaughter away made Ajkun angry and she felt a bitter root begin to grow in the emptiness of her heart. *Itzamná, someday I'll make that woman pay for what she's stolen.* Ajkun straightened her spine and faced Chiman. "There's something else you need to know, but you must bear in mind that I don't have actual proof, just conjecture based on certain dates." Again, she decided not to coat the truth with anything to sweeten it. "Tz' is not your son."

"What?" Chiman demanded as he stood up abruptly. He turned and glared at Ajkun. "I don't believe you."

"As I said, it's only a theory, and unfortunately, Chachal and now Satal, the two women who could have provided real answers, are both dead. I suspect Chachal was pregnant when you married her. Based on the dates she gave me for your first intimacies, Tz' should have been a sickly baby, not even fully formed perhaps, at the time of his birth, but he was a strong infant the moment he arrived in the world." Ajkun reached out to Chiman, but he stepped away from her.

"You've known this all these years and never thought to tell me?"

"Would it have made any difference? Certainly, you would have continued to raise Tz' as your son—or would you?" Ajkun demanded. Thunder crashed again, closer this time, but she ignored the threat of imminent rain.

"Yes, of course I would have, I think," Chiman faltered. "But I might not have remained with Chachal, since she was lying to me the whole time. I could have sent her back here, to Mayapán, to her mother, Satal, and then none of this would have happened." A quick wind whipped down the gully, blowing dust and small branches in a swirl, and causing Chiman's black hair to blow into his eyes.

Ajkun reached out to smooth his hair. "Whether Chachal had lived here or in Pa nimá would have made no difference to Satal. She was always after Na'om, who would still have been born, because Yakal would still have married our daughter, Tu'janel, and the whole sequence would still have unfolded as it did. You're the shaman and should know this best of all; the gods have our fates in their hands long before we appear in this realm, and what we do often has little effect on the outcome." She looked skyward as the first heavy drops of rain began to plop into the dirt, onto her shoulders, and into her face. She blinked rapidly as water landed in her right eye, and she swiped at her face with the sleeve of her *huipil*. She started to walk back toward the city, and Chiman fell in step with her.

"Unless you're someone like Na'om, born with a touch of the gods still left inside." Chiman stepped in front of Ajkun, blocking her way, and hugged her. "Forgive me for being angry with you. I'm glad you've told me the truth, all of it."

Ajkun felt her shoulders relax into Chiman's chest and could smell the remnants of copal smoke on his skin. She lifted her head and looked at him. "What do we do now?"

"I need to go back and tell Tz' what's happened. He's still at the bonfire with the other men."

"He's going to need your support now more than ever. You do realize that?"

"Yes, of course, he's my son, my only son. I'll do whatever I can to help him, and you, through all of this." Chiman held out his arm and Ajkun slipped her elbow through his. "And as soon as the rainy season is over and the rivers are safe to navigate, we'll head back to Pa nimá and pick up our lives again."

The rain pelted down in earnest, and the couple walked as quickly as the uneven ground allowed back toward the city gates, their heads bent down against the wind and stinging raindrops. "Maltiox, Chiman," Ajkun shouted above the wind. "Now more than ever, I need to return home." Chiman nodded his head and helped her up the side of the ravine. The full force of the wind and rain hit them when they entered the cornfield, and their clothes were quickly soaked through. They ran as lightning struck close by, followed by a clap of thunder that blocked the sound of the drums inside the city. Ajkun felt her heart jump at how close the strike had been, and for a split second, the pain in her chest for her sweet Na'om disappeared. But she knew that ache would never truly go away and that she would never love anyone as much as she had loved Na'om. She let go of Chiman's hand as they reentered the city. "Go find Tz'. I can make my way back to Alom's hut on my own."

"Are you sure?"

"Yes, go, I'll be fine." But Ajkun knew nothing would ever be fine again.

Tz'

The rain was coming down in a steady torrent when Chiman tapped Tz' on the shoulder, pulling him from his thoughts. He stepped away from the circle of men dancing in the slippery mud around the giant bonfire at the base of Kukulcan's pyramid and followed Chiman to a spot where they could talk above the pounding of the drums nearby.

"*Tat axel*, what's wrong?" Tz' said as he looked into his father's face. His father was soaking wet, as if he'd been outside for quite some time.

Without saying a word, Chiman stepped forward and grasped Tz' in a big hug. Tz' felt his father sob as he tightened his grip on his shoulders. "Tat, what is it? What's happened?" Tz' demanded. He pushed away from Chiman and watched tears slide down his father's cheeks. *I don't think I've ever seen him cry,* Tz' thought. *Even when Chuch was killed, Tat didn't shed any tears; at least not in front of me.*

"I don't even know where to begin," Chiman said as he wiped his face with one hand. "Yakal and I found out that Na'om was here, in Mayapán and . . ."

"She's here, where?" Tz' said. "I must speak with her, Tat, you have to take me to her."

"I wish I could, Tz'." Chiman stopped and drew in a deep breath. "We found out Satal had her, and we followed them through the streets, until we met them near the cenote." Chiman drew in a breath again. "Yakal accused Satal of witchcraft, she started to run, Na'om tried to grab her." Another sob escaped. "They—Satal and Na'om—they both fell into the cenote. They're gone, Tz', they're both gone."

Stunned, Tz' couldn't speak. He sank to his knees in the reddish mud and leaned forward to catch his breath. The sound of the drums pummeled his body from all sides, and he braced himself with his hands in the rocky, mucky soil.

He sensed Chiman squatting next to him and turned to look at his father once again. "She was the one, Tat, she was the one I was going to marry." He picked up a handful of small rocks and pebbles and threw it. "I should have told her when we first arrived back in the village after the trading trip; I should never have waited to say anything. If we'd gotten married, we'd have been on the other side of the river at the time of the attack, and she'd be safe at home now instead of de—" Tz' sobbed. The weight of his loss pressed into his chest, and he leaned forward again, resting his forehead on the ground as a wave of nausea swept through him. He felt his father place his hand on his back.

"Shh," Chiman said. "Come, we must go and be with Ajkun and the others."

"You go, I can't see Ati't right now," Tz' said as he straightened up again. He looked around the vast plaza, at the shamans chanting at the base of the pyramid, the hundreds of men in loincloths circling the fire, and the drummers seated in front of their deer-hide drums. The rain continued to pummel them, but none of the men showed signs of tiring. "I have to get out of here," he said as he quickly stood and swiped at the mud on his knees and hands. He grabbed a water jug from one of the boys and started to run.

"Tz', wait!" Chiman cried. "Where are you going?"

"Somewhere, anywhere away from here," Tz' cried. He ran through the deserted streets, past the empty marketplace, its stalls all closed for the five days of the Wayeb, and toward the main gate of the city. The guards leaned against the walls, trying to find some shelter from the rain.

Tz' ran to the double copper doors that covered the wide entranceway, yanked one open, and slipped through the gap before the guards could stop him. He paused for just a moment to catch his breath and then took off running again, through the stubble of the nearby cornfields and into the brush and undergrowth far beyond the city walls.

For hours, he wandered through the wet and muddy landscape, oblivious to the thorny bushes that scratched his bare thighs and calves as he pushed through the dense underbrush. Exhausted, his body covered with mud and odd bits of leaves, he dropped down into the dirt and drank the last few gulps of warm water in the gourd. He threw the empty vessel into the small shrubs nearby and then screamed with all his might. He yelled until his throat was hoarse and he had no more strength to shout. Then the tears came, blinding him with their intensity, as giant sobs convulsed his body, tearing at his stomach muscles until he fell on his side, his energy spent. Tz' curled into a tight ball, his knees drawn up to his chest, and drifted into an exhausted sleep. He woke only when he felt the cool night air caressing his tired, wet body.

He sat up slowly and looked around. He had no idea where he was, and he was too far from the city to hear any drums. *I'll have to wait until the stars come out to find my way back to Mayapán.* He shivered as the shadows deepened, and he began to hear creatures stirring in the growing darkness. *I need to keep moving,* Tz' thought. Grateful that the storm was over and the clouds had cleared, he peered into the deep indigo sky and began to see the brightest of stars appear. He searched until he found the North Star and started to walk. After a short time had passed, he paused to listen and could just barely discern the rhythmic thrumming of the drums.

Within a few hours, lit torches in brackets next to the many gates in the city walls were visible, and Tz' headed toward the nearest one. He hesitated as he approached and tried to brush the muck and twigs from his hair. He knew he was covered with reddish mud, his face tear-streaked, but he hoped the guards would be lenient and let him in.

He needn't have worried, as Nimal was on duty at the small door.

"Itzamná," Nimal said as he gave Tz' a quick hug. "It's good to see you again. Yakal and the others just returned at dusk; they've been out looking for you all day."

Tz' nodded his head. "Where are they now?"

"They all went to Alom's hut to be with Ajkun and the others." Nimal prodded Tz' with his hand. "Go; they need you now, and you need them."

Tz' took a deep breath, nodded, and hurried off into the dark. *I have to be strong, for Ati't and Mok'onel and the other villagers,* Tz' thought as he trotted once again through the barren alleyways and past the empty plazas and marketplace.

One torch was lit outside Alom's hut, and Tz' could hear numerous voices coming from inside. He walked across the small courtyard and pushed aside the blanket covering the doorway.

The single candle that burned in the corner flickered as he entered the small hut. Chiman and Yakal turned and stepped aside, allowing Tz' to enter the room.

"Tz'!" Ajkun exclaimed as she saw him. She hurried to him and wrapped him in a big hug.

He bent over slightly and hugged her back, despite the filth on his bare chest.

"I couldn't bear to lose you, too," Ajkun said as she stepped away from Tz'. "Come child, sit and have something to eat," she said as she motioned to the plate of cold tamales nearby.

"No, Ati't, thank you, but no," Tz' said. "I came to tell you I'm back, but right now, I should return to the dance by the fire."

"You've been through a lot, Tz', you don't have to continue," Chiman said.

"No, Tat, I do; I have to keep moving or, or . . ." He paused and swallowed the lump that appeared in his throat. "I have to keep moving, that's all," Tz' said as he turned to go. He stopped and hugged his father and patted Yakal on the forearm. "Thanks for looking for me," he added as he stepped back into the night and began to run toward the drums.

SATAL

The tiniest patch of sunlight drifted in through the window high in the far wall, and the drums outside continued to pound, but Satal knew they would end as soon as the sun was just a bit higher in the sky. She needed to move, to leave her house, but was reluctant to get up and face any new dangers. She felt safe knowing everyone believed she was dead. She'd managed to stay hidden for the past four days, sneaking out into the courtyard at night to eat what little food remained in the storage cupboard and hiding in her room during the day.

To pass the hours, she'd continued to perform black magic rituals. By squeezing the last drops of water from her clothes and mixing them with herbs and blood drawn from her left earlobe, she cast a spell of fever and chills that would infect the cenote. *As soon as the women in Mayapán draw water from the well today, hundreds in the city will grow ill and possibly even die.* The idea brought a smile to Satal's face. *That will help repay some of my debt to old Camazotz,* she thought as she stretched, yawned, and began to drift back to sleep.

"What are you doing? Get up!"

Started awake by Sachoj's strident voice, Satal tumbled out of the hammock and landed with a plop on the hard tiled floor. The eerie voice reverberated in Satal's head. "How are you still able to talk to me when you're underwater?" She stood up and shook her head, hopping up and down, hoping to dislodge the voice that was stuck like a drop of water in her ear. She was tired of listening to the old woman, tired of taking her advice, something she'd done her entire life. "Quiet, woman," she whispered, and her voice echoed in the large room.

"You can't get rid of me that easily," Sachoj said with a laugh. "What's your plan?"

"I'll pack my things into a basket and leave tonight, after everyone's been drinking and celebrating all day. Even the guards will be relaxed after their strict vigilance of the past several days." She yawned and stretched before removing her nightshirt. She pulled on her black huipil and skirt that had dried over the past several days and stuffed an extra set of clothes into the bottom of her pack basket. Then she reached into the lowest shelf of the cupboard and one by one pulled out eleven large leather sacks full of cacao beans. She lined them up on the floor, trying to decide what to do.

"You won't be able to take them all," Sachoj admonished gleefully. "All the years you've spent hoarding beans, and for what? Now you'll be destitute before the next Wayeb!"

"Quiet, old woman, let me think." Satal chewed on her bottom lip. She knew her great-grandmother was right; she'd have to sacrifice a great deal of her fortune if she was going to escape the city. She picked out the four largest bags and stuffed them into the bottom of the wicker basket, then picked up another, and hung it around her neck, but it was far too heavy to carry that way.

She poked around again in the cupboard and found a small cotton satchel full of old marigold blossoms, which she dumped out onto the shelf. She filled the cloth with cacao beans and put the small pouch over her head. "Much better." Reluctantly, she closed the leather sack and stuffed it back into the cupboard. She arranged the other bags on the shelf as well, knowing there was no other safe place to hide them. *Once I'm outside the city's wall, I'll find someone to fetch the bags for me.*

"Fool! Anyone you send will only keep them for himself," Sachoj hissed.

Anger surged in Satal as she realized Sachoj was right once again. She rummaged around in the wooden cupboard again, debating over taking several cotton bags of dried herbs, a couple of stubby candles, and the knife she had used on the first night of the Wayeb to slash her tongue. Then she pulled out her incense burner of Yum Cimil, the death god. The kneeling skeleton peered at her with bulging eyes, his black-spotted arms outstretched and his palms open and ready to receive an offering of any kind.

"Sorry, my friend, you'll have to stay here," Satal muttered as she gently replaced the ceramic piece on its old black monkey skin. "I must take more cacao beans instead." Yum Cimil glared at her as she quickly filled the basket with the leather sacks.

She tried lifting the full basket onto her back and was just able to crouch under the weight of it. She took a step and then another and felt the strain of the load in her knees, back, and shoulders.

"How do you expect to leave the city with all of that?" Sachoj asked. "You can barely walk across the room!"

"I'll manage," Satal replied as she dropped the basket back on the tile floor. "Once I'm outside the gates, I'll hide most of this in my cave where no one will find it."

Sachoj didn't answer. "Nothing to do now but wait until dark," Satal said as she slipped back into the hammock. She closed her eyes and suddenly grew conscious of the silence. The drums had stopped. After the constant pounding, the hush felt eerie and unnatural. Satal opened her eyes again, as if that would help her hear better. She strained to catch any sound beyond the beating of her heart. Then she heard the people next door begin to stir, and she imagined the thousands of women and children who had remained cooped up in their homes now heading outside. As rapidly as the sun rose in the sky, the silence was broken by the movements of the multitudes of citizens eager to start the new year. After five days of cold food and the inability to bathe or perform any work, the city soon bustled with activity.

Satal continued to sway in the hammock. The scent of wood smoke and charring meats drifted through the window, and Satal's stomach grumbled in response to the tantalizing smells. She had nothing left to eat, though. Even her water gourds were empty.

Irritated now, her peace ruined by the gnawing hunger that made her belly ache, Satal got up and shuffled down the hallway toward the courtyard. *Perhaps there's enough commotion outside for me to leave now,* she thought as she cautiously approached the front door. She laid her hand on the wooden doorknob and was just about to gently pull on it when it swung roughly open. Satal scooted behind the thick door, praying to Itzamná that no one would notice her bare feet just visible under the edge of the door.

"Stay here in the courtyard," a voice said, and Satal gasped as she recognized Yakal when he stepped into the big room. His voice bounced around the almost empty space. Kubal Joron and Nimal were just behind him.

Satal sucked in her sagging stomach, praying no one would notice the door had not fully opened. "Your curse against Yakal and the others didn't work," Sachoj whispered in her head.

Quiet, woman, or they'll hear us, Satal admonished silently as she pressed her back even harder against the stucco wall.

"Oh, what an awful smell in here," Kubal Joron said as he quickly pulled a scented cloth from the inside of his indigo sleeve and held it to his nose. "Whatever could that stench be?"

"Who knows?" Nimal said. "Perhaps that black muck over there," he replied, pointing to the wall. Smeared across the mural painted on the white stucco was a large patch of black goo. Nimal approached it and sniffed, then coughed and backed away. "Don't go near that," he said as he wiped his tear-filled eyes.

"Come on, you two," Yakal said. "We're here to inventory the contents of the house for the council, not go around smelling whatever foul thing Satal has done to the place." He headed toward the hallway and the two large bedrooms. He paused at the doorway to Chachal's old room. "Why don't you catalog things in here while I do Satal's room?"

All three men disappeared into the bedrooms. Satal could hear Kubal Joron and Nimal as they talked to each other in her daughter's room. She knew she had just seconds before Yakal figured out she was there. She peeked into the courtyard and saw the sentry had his back to the entryway. He was standing with Bitol, and both men were absorbed in the sight of several young women sauntering down the alleyway. She glanced back over her shoulder and saw Yakal in the hallway. She knew she'd been seen and began to run.

"Stop!" Yakal shouted.

Satal dashed out into the bright sunlight, past Bitol and the guard, and rushed toward the group of girls who filled the street. She scurried around them as fast as her arthritic knees would carry her.

"Grab that woman!" Yakal shouted as he bolted into the lane, with Nimal, Bitol, and the guard right behind him.

Satal kept running, down one street and into another, quickly making her way toward the marketplace. She knew the crowds would be large this morning, with people eager to buy and sell after five day's absence. If she could make it there before Yakal caught her, she had a chance of escaping.

Her side ached from the effort of running, but she didn't dare stop. The streets grew more crowded as she pushed her way through the groups of people, elbowing children and their young mothers out of the way in her haste.

She could hear more shouting behind her and quickened her pace again. Then just ahead, she saw several men carrying heavy wooden platforms toward the central square where the dances would be performed that night. The mass of people moving toward the marketplace stopped to let the men go by. *If I can get lost in that crowd, Yakal won't be able to find me.* Satal hurried along and slipped into the jumble of people. She saw someone's shawl dangling from the edge of a basket and snatched it while no one was looking. Clutching the fabric to her chest, she pressed deeper into the crowd and quickly wrapped the deep brown shawl over and around her head. She glanced behind her, but no one was in pursuit. As the crowd began to move again, Satal stayed with the pack. One young woman just ahead of her was struggling to carry a large basket full of blankets on her back while holding on to a little girl with each hand.

Satal sidled up to the girl and smiled. "Headed to the market?"

The girl nodded and quickly reached out to grab her five-year-old son by the shoulder before he could get too far ahead.

"Come, let me help you with all of these children," Satal said as she slipped her hand into the boy's hand. She looked down at the child and smiled. Together, the five of them continued to the market.

Satal kept watching for Yakal and the others as she helped the girl find an open spot to spread her wares. She smiled again and then rapidly headed toward the far side of the marketplace. There was still no sign of

Yakal or Nimal.

They'll have alerted the guards at the gates, Satal thought. *Now what do I do?*

"Use the same ploy you just used to get outside the city," Sachoj said.

Grinning once again, Satal quickly found another young woman overburdened with purchases who was struggling to control her children. They were headed toward the small south gate. She offered to help carry several bundles, freeing the girl to hold on to her children.

What luck, Satal thought as she looked at the guard on duty. He was one of her paid sentries. But the man barely glanced at her as she walked past with her packages of fruits and vegetables, and she laughed as she stepped through the open doorway to freedom.

Once outside, Satal quickly gave the bewildered girl her parcels, then cut diagonally across the old cornfield just in front of her, and dropped down into a small ravine. After glancing behind her to make sure no one had followed, she made her way to a small opening in the ground. Once on her knees, she felt around with her feet, and descended the small wooden ladder propped against the wall. She hurried through the black underground passageways by habit, finally emerging into a small cave.

Although she had no light, she knew where her altar was and scuttled toward it. She found a jagged rock and slashed her inner arm, letting the blood drip onto the flat rock in front of her. As a small puddle formed, she prayed. "Ahalgan and Poxlom, gods of pus and diseases, I present you with this small offering so that you may infect the men who have robbed me of my house, my seat on the council, and my fortune." One by one, she pictured Yakal, Kubal Joron, Nimal, and Bitol, covered in sores, with blood draining from their noses.

"Don't worry, Satal, I'll make sure they suffer," Sachoj hissed.

Satal grinned in the dark. Her great-grandmother had always had an affinity for snakes of every shape, color, and size and had kept baskets of them inside her hut. As a very young girl, Satal had been warned many times not to lift the woven reed covers, but she often had peeked inside the baskets while Sachoj was busy elsewhere. The slithering, shifting shapes had made Satal shiver, but she was drawn to them nonetheless.

When the images of the sick men finally faded from her mind, Satal left the cave. It was near dark, which made it easy for her to blend into the shadows. Weary and hungry, she walked away from Mayapán toward the only place she could think of that would now be safe, her childhood home of Chichén Itzá.

YAKAL

"Yakal, stop," Nimal said as he caught up with his friend. They were in the crowded streets near the marketplace. Ignoring the hand on his arm, Yakal kept searching the area for sight of the woman he had seen run out of Satal's house.

"Who are we chasing?" Nimal said.

Yakal turned to him, a frown on his face. "I swear by the power of Itzamná it was Satal."

"Satal, but how could that be?" Nimal asked. "You watched her fall into the cenote days ago." He peered closely at his friend. "You've been through a lot lately; perhaps the grief over your daughter. . . ." Nimal let his words die on his lips. "Let me help you back to your hut. Then Kubal Joron and I will finish inventorying Satal's palace."

"I know what I saw," Yakal muttered. "It was Satal."

The two friends walked in silence back to Yakal's house where Uskab was sweeping the small courtyard.

"Yakal, are you all right?" she asked as she hurried over to his side. "You look so pale. Let me fetch you some fresh watermelon juice." She hurried into the hut and returned with two dark green ceramic mugs and a large brown pottery pitcher. She poured the juice into the cups and handed them to Yakal and Nimal.

"Maltiox, Uskab," Nimal said. He grinned at the young woman. "How long before the baby arrives?"

"Two more moons," she replied as she rubbed her hands gently over her rounded belly. "It's a boy, I'm sure of it, and strong as can be," she said as she winced. "He likes . . . to press . . . his foot up . . . under my ribs," she gasped as she pushed with her hand against a bulge visible in the fabric of her tightly stretched blue huipil.

"He'll make a fine warrior one day," Nimal said.

Yakal spoke up. "Unless he follows in *my* footsteps and becomes a stone mason."

"And you both know the gods and the shamans will decide his occupation," Uskab said as she took the empty cups from the men. "Better?" she asked Yakal.

"Yes." Yakal turned to Nimal. "I know what I saw; promise me you'll post extra guards at the gates."

"Rest easy, my friend. If Satal *were* still alive, she'd be caught before she ever left the city. But we both know there's nothing to fear."

"I'm not so sure. Please, just do as I ask," Yakal said.

"All right, if it will make you feel better, but we're wasting our time," Nimal said as he hurried off in the direction of the main gates.

"You saw Satal?" Uskab said. "But how is that even possible?" Uskab shuddered and placed her hands on her belly as the baby began to kick. "Where was this and when?"

"Earlier today, when we were in her house. She was hiding behind the door and bolted when we entered." Yakal sat down on a stool and rubbed his forehead where a dull throbbing pounded behind his eyes. "Nimal says I imagined it, but we gave chase to a woman who looked just like her. I lost her in the crowds headed to the market."

"Shh, my love," Uskab said as she rubbed Yakal's strong, bare shoulders. "If Satal is alive, Nimal will find her. Come now and rest. You're worn out from dancing for the Wayeb."

Yakal reached up with one hand and gently tugged on Uskab's arm, forcing her to bend over his upturned face. He kissed her on the lips, then nibbled on her neck, and into her swelling breasts. "I'm feeling better already," he said as he stood up and led Uskab to the hut. He let the deerskin hide fall over the doorway, blocking out any unwanted visitors, and gently pulled Uskab to the large multicolored hammock hanging in the room.

"You're supposed to rest," Uskab giggled as she lay down in the swaying netting.

"So are you," Yakal replied, "so, we'll rest together."

The sun was setting when the couple woke and went back outside.

"Ohh, it's so late," Uskab cried. "We'll miss all the dances if we don't hurry." She went back in the hut and grabbed her dark blue shawl, as the evening air was already turning cooler. She looked at Yakal who stood staring up at the sky. "You still want to go, don't you?"

Despite a persistent throbbing behind his eyes, Yakal said, "What? Oh, yes, of course." He rubbed his forehead rapidly with his fingers and then forced himself to smile. "I was just thinking about Satal, wondering if anyone had seen her." Uskab frowned at him. He shook his head and held out his hand to her. "I'm sorry, my love, you're right. I must have imagined it was Satal. But we did chase someone through the streets."

"Probably a beggar looking for food after the Wayeb ended," Uskab said. "With the market closed for five days, there's been no help for those in need." She tucked her arm into Yakal's elbow. "Let's go watch your mother dance."

They joined the groups of people converging at the base of the large pyramid. The men and boys who had swayed and stomped around the bonfire to the incessant beat of the drums had been replaced by women, eager to dance in celebration of the new year. Wooden platforms that stood several feet off the ground lined the area in front of the pyramid, stretching thirty paces or more in each direction. Lit torches on long poles had been tied several feet apart to the sides and back of the stage, illuminating the dancers so the crowds could see them.

As Uskab and Yakal pushed their way closer to the stage, they saw a group of young girls, wearing brilliant green dresses and sunshine-yellow ribbons braided through their hair, step off the platform after finishing their dance.

Uskab tugged on Yakal's arm. "Look, there's Alom, with the other women, just ready to begin." She hurried forward and raised a hand to wave at her mother-in-law.

"I'm surprised she came," Yakal said as he helped Uskab find a spot where they could both see. "After learning of Tikoy and Na'om's deaths, I thought she might remain at home this year, with Ajkun and Chiman."

"They wouldn't let her," Uskab said, "not once they heard she was one of the best stilt dancers in the city." She patted Yakal's arm. "Life must go on, even after death." She paused as she looked at Yakal's tired face. "I'm sorry about your brother. Tikoy was a good man. But this daughter of yours, you didn't even know her. I'm sorry the girl died, but . . . ." She stopped and placed Yakal's hand on her pregnant belly, "You have a new family to think about, a new life here, right here." She pressed his palm deeper into her belly.

Yakal nodded, but didn't say anything as he felt his son wriggle under his hand. *Uskab is right, I didn't know Na'om, yet I feel as if I've lost someone dear to me. I should have done more all these years, somehow managed to protect her better, trusted my instincts, and done away with that old witch Satal when I had the chance.* He breathed in deeply, trying to lift the heavy weight he felt, and the cool evening air pulsed in his head. He sneezed and was surprised to see blood on the back of his hand, which he hastily wiped away. He looked up when the sounds of bamboo flutes and copper bells filled the air, and the crowd cheered as the group of older women took the stage, their three-foot-high wooden stilts in their hands. Stilt dancing was a right reserved for those who had passed their childbearing years, but still had the strength and agility of women many moons younger. Yakal's heart ached as he watched his mother nod to the gathering. Despite her age, she was still the most beautiful of the dancers.

Alom leapt onto her stilts in time with the music, and she twirled and pirouetted with the twenty other elders in the dance troupe. The women were dressed in deep red huipils and matching skirts that spun around their ankles as they danced. Alom's long gray and white hair was braided in a tight swirl and pinned to the top of her head by bunches of orange hibiscus flowers. As the music increased in tempo and Alom's leaps and jumps grew bolder, Yakal watched as the flowers came loose, landing on the stage, and her long braid slashed about like a snake on the end of a rope. The sight of it sent shivers up and down his spine, and once again, his thoughts returned to Satal and the possibility that she had survived the long fall into the cenote.

What evil powers has she called upon to aid her? he wondered. *And if she's alive, is there a chance Na'om is as well?* That thought gave him hope, but he knew better than to say anything to anyone, especially Ajkun, Chiman, and Tz'. *No sense raising anyone's expectations when there are none,* he thought as he clapped with the hundreds of others when the women stopped dancing.

All of a sudden, he was bone tired and wanted nothing more than to sleep with his arm wrapped around Uskab's soft form. He sneezed again and there was blood on his hands.

"Yakal, what's wrong?" Uskab said as soon as she looked at him. She pulled a clean cloth from a skirt pocket and handed it to Yakal, who wiped his face and hands. "Come; let's get you to bed."

Yakal nodded, and he helped Uskab maneuver through the crowds waiting eagerly for the next group of dancers. As he entered their hut, he thought, *Tomorrow, tomorrow, I'll try to find some answers.*

But in the morning, Yakal could barely sit up in the hammock. "Uskab," he called. His head rang with the sound of a hundred hammers pounding on stone, and the room spun in slow circles around him. When he closed his eyes, the nightmare he'd been stuck in reappeared. Large brown, green, and orange-colored snakes kept talking to him in a language he couldn't understand. Yakal rubbed his eyes and was startled to find Uskab standing next to him.

"My love, what's wrong?" Uskab asked. She placed her hand on Yakal's forehead. "You're burning with fever."

"That's not all, I'm afraid," Yakal said as he pulled down the blanket and pointed to his torso, arms, and legs.

Uskab gasped. Tiny open sores had appeared across his entire body, seeping clear fluids into the hammock and blanket. "What's happening?" Uskab cried as she placed her hands over her belly and took a step backwards.

"I'm not sure; you must find out if Kubal Joron, Nimal, and Bitol are ill as well." Yakal arched forward, coughed deeply, and blood appeared on his bottom lip. He collapsed back into the hammock.

"I'm going to fetch Ajkun and have her bring you some medicine."

Yakal nodded and closed his eyes. He felt Uskab's soft lips barely brush his cheek and heard her sandals scuffle on the dirt floor of their hut as she hurried back outside. As soon as he was alone, the snakes in his mind returned, whispering to him as they slithered over and under each other on the ground. Yakal shuddered and opened his eyes, quickly checking to make sure there was nothing below him. The room swirled as he moved about in the hammock, making his headache worse, so he tossed his blanket onto the floor and lay down on it. The ground was hard and cold, but at least it didn't move. Yakal stared up at the wooden beams and palm fronds that formed the roof of the hut, but quickly looked away when he thought he saw a snake among the rafters.

When Ajkun arrived with Uskab, he obediently opened his mouth to slurp the bitter tincture of yarrow and marigold flowers on the wooden spoon held in front of him.

"Two more and I'll leave you to rest," Ajkun encouraged him as he turned his head away from the medicine. Reluctantly, Yakal swallowed again and again, then gratefully sank back down on the bedding. Uskab hovered near the doorway of the hut, and he patted the blanket beside him, motioning her to join him.

"Best if Uskab stays away for now until we get rid of those sores," Ajkun warned Yakal as she tucked the blanket in around his chin. "We want no harm to come to that baby she's carrying."

Yakal nodded, but remained silent. What was there to say? He knew Ajkun was right. He closed his eyes, trying to remember the sequence of events leading to this illness. The headache had begun shortly after he'd seen Satal in the house and only grown worse as the day progressed. Before then, he'd felt fine. He'd danced through much of the Wayeb ceremonies, only taking a few breaks, as was allowed for a man of his age, even though he'd suffered the loss of Na'om on the first day of the Wayeb. As he pictured that morning, he felt the ache for Na'om return to his heart. After he'd rescued Chiman, Ajkun, and the other villagers from Pa nimá from the slave pits run by Tarnel, he'd learned Na'om had been taken by Satal. He'd sold his young, one-legged friend, Memetik, to Kubal Joron and Matz' for the cacao beans he needed to purchase the broken arrows and his father's green obsidian knife that Na'om had been carrying, and that proved Satal had had a hand in the attack on Pa nimá. Then he and the other men of the council had found Satal fleeing the city with Na'om and the jaguar. When Satal had pushed Na'om toward him, he'd felt his daughter in his arms for the briefest of moments before she'd turned and lunged for Satal's skirt. Then both women had fallen into the well. He opened his eyes and looked about for Ajkun.

"Bring me Chiman," he said as she hurried to his side. "It will take more than herbs to rid me of this pestilence." He sneezed and more blood flowed from his nose, which he wiped on the blanket. "And keep Uskab away from here. Have her bathe and burn her clothing and don't let her back until I'm well."

Ajkun nodded, and Yakal closed his eyes once again. But he quickly reopened them when he sensed Chiman was in the room.

"Satal is behind all this," Yakal said as he waved his hand up and down his body.

"She's dead, Yakal. We saw her fall. Her magic can't harm you now." Chiman squatted beside the young man, but refrained from touching him. He adjusted his loincloth and plucked out a piece of straw caught in his braided leather sandal. "You've caught some strange disease, that's all."

"Remember what she said before she fell into the cenote, 'May blood and pus run from all your orifices!'" Yakal pushed himself upward and experienced another gush of blood from his nose. Chiman handed him a clean rag, which he pressed to his face. "I saw the witch yesterday morning, when we went to her house." His voice was muffled behind the cloth and he tilted his head back to stem the blood. "Check on Nimal, Kubal Joron, and Bitol. They were all there, too. If they are sick, then there's dark magic behind this."

"Many in the city are ill, Yakal, not just you," Chiman replied as he stood and began to pace the small room. "But if you saw Satal . . . ." He turned to Yakal. "That woman has caused enough problems. I must consult with some of the other shamans. I'll be back."

Chiman hurried away, and Yakal quickly fell into a restless sleep. He stirred only when he sensed Chiman's return late in the afternoon. He stared up at his friend who stood backlit by the open doorway, the outline of a large basket clearly visible on his friend's back. "What have you discovered?" Yakal said weakly. The sores on his body itched as if a thousand ants were crawling across him, and it took much of his energy to fight the urge to scratch.

Chiman stepped into the room and placed the pack basket on the floor. "Those with fevers and chills were the same men who traveled with you to the south to collect tribute. When you camped along the river, were there swarms of mosquitoes in the region at night?"

"*Utzil*, yes, vast clouds so thick we had to have the slaves tend to smudges all night long to keep the horrid things away. Even still, we all came home with hundreds of bites." Yakal rubbed at his right forearm and winced as pain shot up his arm.

"We have this same illness in the south. I've spoken to Ajkun and she's helping the local midwives and healers prepare teas that will slowly cure those afflicted." Chiman came and squatted by Yakal. He pulled back the thin blanket covering the younger man's body and winced at the sight of him. "This, though," he said as he gently replaced the blanket, "is a different matter altogether." He sighed, wiped his hands on his loincloth, and slowly stood up. "Nimal, Kubal Joron, and Bitol have similar symptoms, just as you said they might."

"Can you heal us?"

"If Itzamná is willing, yes." He moved to the basket and laid several cloth bags on the floor. Carefully unwrapping a brown cloth, he took out a deep green ceramic brazier in the shape of a monkey's head, and set it near Yakal's feet. He went outside and returned with a water gourd and a small copper bowl from Uskab's cooking area, which he also placed near Yakal.

Yakal stared at the monkey's two round eyes that protruded from its face and the blackened hollow interior where incense and other herbs were burned. He watched as Chiman poured a mixture of red, black, and yellow dried corn into the brazier, then added several clumps of golden copal resin. Chiman set this mixture on fire, and the thick smoke quickly drifted toward the ceiling of the small hut. Yakal lay back on the bedding, too weak to sit up any longer.

Chiman poured red-tinted salt from a leather bag into the copper bowl and added a few drops of water to it, which he stirred into a thick paste. He lifted Yakal's left foot and began to smear the mixture on his sole. Yakal jerked his foot at the older man's touch.

"Sorry, that tickled," Yakal said. He fought the urge to move as Chiman continued spreading the salt on his other foot.

"Here, the shamans use salt to draw out any disease or ill winds," Chiman said as he poured dry salt from the same bag in an oval around

Yakal's body. Once the ring was complete, he crouched over Yakal's body and placed his hands just inches from Yakal's face. "Close your eyes and tell me what you see."

"It's all black, like the darkest of nights, and now, now something is writhing and moving, the blackness is shifting, sliding, into snakes, hundreds of them, of all shapes and sizes . . . ." Yakal jerked his eyes open and clutched at the blankets.

"Shh, relax," Chiman said as he dabbed wet salt in a circle on Yakal's forehead. "Close your eyes again and imagine the salt driving the snakes away," he said as he smeared more of the mixture down Yakal's cheeks and along his chin. He pulled the blankets back and gently dropped clumps of salt up and down the young man's body.

Yakal twitched every time another cool lump hit his hot skin and winced when some of the salt landed in one of his open sores. It burned with a fierceness unlike anything he'd experienced, and he tried to envision the salt burrowing into his body, forcing the snakes from deep within.

Chiman blew on the censor, encouraging the embers to flare higher, and then he tossed in a handful of the dry salt. He carefully picked up the hot ceramic brazier with a piece of leather to protect his hands and moved it up and down Yakal's body, covering him in thick smoke.

"Breathe in, feel the smoke throughout your body," Chiman whispered. He put the censor to one side, crouched at Yakal's head, and leaning down, blew with all his strength down the length of Yakal's body. Breath by breath, the dense smoke moved from Yakal's head to his shoulders, then his chest, his groin, down his legs, and finally to his feet.

Yakal sensed the snakes inside him were writhing and squirming, moving from his torso and into his legs, and he cried out with pain. As each serpent entered his feet, the salt on his soles burned with intense heat, and he thrashed and shouted as the snakes popped like pieces of corn in a fire when their heads touched the salt paste.

A cool wet cloth on his right foot forced him to open his eyes. Chiman was wiping the salt mixture, now a deep black, from his sole.

"How do you feel?" Chiman asked as he gently picked up Yakal's other foot.

"Better, I think," Yakal replied. He looked down at his body, which was still covered in sores. "But what about these?" he said as he pointed at the wounds in his skin.

"Ajkun has ground up flaxseeds with cornmeal and made a paste with water blessed by the highest shaman in the city," Chiman replied as he held up a coconut bowl. "We'll spread that over your skin, then cover you with thin slices of prickly pear leaves. The combination will draw the last of the poisons from your body." He began to smear the mixture on Yakal's shins before covering him with the cactus leaves.

"And how long do I need to stay like this?" Yakal said, as Chiman motioned for him to lie still. The prickly pear slices were slippery and wanted to slide off onto the blanket.

"We'll change the mixture every few hours, and in a day or two, we'll know whether the treatment has worked."

"And then you'll go heal the others?" Yakal sighed as felt the weight of cactus pressing down on his ribs and stomach.

"They're already receiving the same treatment from other shamans," Chiman said. "Close your eyes and rest. There's time enough for talking later."

Yakal nodded, but his eyes refused to close. As long as Satal was still alive, her magic would always hold power, and he didn't want to face her army of serpents and snakes again any time soon.

Two mornings later, Yakal walked outside slowly, like a man many moons older, and took a deep breath of the cool air. It felt good to breathe something other than the smoky air that still filled the hut. He lifted his arms toward the rising sun and felt the dried cornmeal crackle on his skin. Ignoring the pull of it on his body, he thanked Itzamná he was alive to see the sky shift from a deep purple to a brilliant flame red to a golden yellow. He turned back to the hut, noticed the fire in the fire pit, and was surprised to see Uskab wrapped in a blanket on the ground near it. He hurried over and tapped her on the shoulder. "How long have you been here?"

Uskab struggled to stand, her large belly making it difficult to rise gracefully. "Since you fell ill," she replied, looking into Yakal's dark brown eyes. Yakal reached out to hug her, but she sidestepped his embrace.

"First, you must bathe," Uskab said. She quickly removed a water pot from the embers and poured the warm water into a turtle shell basin. She handed him a dish half full of passionflower-scented soap and a soft rag.

It was only then that Yakal realized the sickly sour smell he'd been inhaling was coming from his own body. In the deep shadows that still filled the courtyard, he dropped his loincloth to the ground, kicked it into the fire, and washed quickly. The water was invigorating, and as Yakal dried himself with a rough towel, he realized it had been many days since he had felt so good. His stomach grumbled and he grinned at Uskab as she handed him a bowl full of hot broth. The liquid glistened with fat globules that floated on the surface, and Yakal cautiously drank a bit of the clear soup. The liquid was salty and tasted of turkey, and Yakal felt energy quickly flow through his body. "Have you seen Chiman?" he asked as he placed the empty bowl on the ground and motioned for Uskab to come sit next to him.

"Now that you're on the mend, he's helping Tz' and Ajkun with their grief," Uskab replied.

Yakal flinched. *Of course, I'm not the only one who misses Na'om.* His face burned with sudden embarrassment. *Once again, I've abandoned her,* he thought as he stared out into the brightening sky. *And what of Satal? If she's still alive, I must do everything possible to find her before she inflicts any more harm.* The turkey broth roiled in his stomach, and he took a deep breath, hoping to quell his sudden queasiness. *I know Satal was responsible for this sickness, just as she's been the force behind all the evil my family and I have endured over the years. How can I find this woman who has inflicted so much pain?* He sat in silence, watching Uskab rub her belly in a slow circular motion. Her white shift, embroidered with purple morning glories along the shoulders, was taut around her waist, and her black hair fell gracefully down her back. *So beautiful,* Yakal mused, *I'll give my life before I let harm come to her or my unborn son.*

Uskab slowly shuffled toward the doorway to the one-room hut. "Ajkun said we must burn all the blankets and even the hammock," Uskab said.

"Uskab, stop, let me deal with all of that. I want no harm to come to you or the baby," Yakal said. She hesitated outside and turned back to Yakal when he spoke. Although he was tired, he gathered all the bedding into a bundle, which he placed near the alleyway that ran in front of the hut. "I'll take it outside the city later and burn it in one of the many ravines."

Uskab didn't lift her head to look at him. "But if you do, what shall we sleep on?"

The realization burned like an ember in his belly. Once again, Satal had the upper hand, as he certainly had no extra money for new bedding. Yakal groaned as he remembered he was in debt to Kubal Joron as well. The only thing that would help them was to find Satal and destroy her for good. He had to act quickly, as too many hours had already been lost to this debilitating weakness when he should have been out searching for Satal. He would find her and kill her with his bare hands, a promise he had made many moons ago, back when Satal had caused Uskab to lose the first of many pregnancies. He looked sideways at his wife, her silhouette one of rounded shapes, her belly the largest curve of them all. He had failed as a father to his first child, Na'om, and his first wife, Tu'janel, had been taken from him too quickly, but by all the gods, he would not forsake this new family.

And just as quickly as his ire had risen, it fell, leaving Yakal suddenly exhausted, eager only for a deep and dreamless sleep, with his arm curled protectively around Uskab. "Don't worry, my little honeybee, we'll manage." He reached out and wrapped Uskab in his arms. She nestled her head against his shoulder and the two sat together in front of the fire, wrapped in their one remaining blanket.

Yakal thought of the day he'd seen Satal in her palace, of how he'd quickly inventoried the contents of the room and been stunned when he'd unpacked her basket and discovered the bags and bags of cacao beans stuffed inside. Suddenly, he grinned. *No one will notice if I take a handful or two to repay my debts and purchase the things we need.* He hugged Uskab again. "All will be well, you'll see."

Tz'

In the pitch dark of late night, his eyes wide open, Tz' swung in his hammock in the hut he was sharing with his father. He was afraid to go back to sleep, afraid he'd return to the dream of black-blood-filled snakes wriggling through his veins. In the dimmest of moonlight filtering through the doorway, he scrubbed at his arms and legs, hoping to erase the awful images. But he knew it would take something far more powerful to get rid of them. He was Satal's grandson, and he sensed the snakes were her blood moving through his body. The Wayeb was closed, the Mayan people were safe, protected from the evils of the Underworld for another year, yet Tz' felt anything but safe. He stared down at his bare arms and legs, still able to feel the slight squirms and twists of the tiny serpents as they inched their way through his frame. He shuddered and forced himself to get up.

A thorough cleansing is what I need right now, he thought as he dressed quickly and stepped into the deserted street. The public steam baths were empty at that late hour, but some of the larger rooms were still warm from fires kindled hours earlier. Tz' stripped off his loincloth and sandals and stepped onto the tile floor. Heat radiated from the thick stucco walls, and he felt beads of sweat form on his naked body. Using a stiff peccary bristle brush normally used to scour the wooden benches, he attacked his skin, leaving red streaks up and down his limbs. Then he rubbed jasmine-scented soap on his body. It burned cruelly, but Tz' welcomed the pain, for it blocked out the incredible ache he felt for Na'om in his chest and heart. He finally rinsed off with several buckets of tepid water standing nearby. Even if the water had been cold, Tz' would have used it, so determined was he to scrub away the taint of his kinship with Satal.

Only as the last drops dried on his skin did he begin to feel somewhat normal again. *I must speak to Tat axel and ask him what else I can do to get rid of these dreams*, Tz' thought as he returned to the hut and settled back in to sleep.

In the morning, the marks he'd made with the brush were still red, and many of them had opened in the night, leaving small trails of dried blood on his skin.

"Utzil, what happened to you?" Chiman asked when Tz' stepped out into the courtyard. He hurried to offer Tz' their one stool before holding up the young man's arm to examine it. "We'll need some of Ajkun's calendula salve for all these marks; otherwise you'll be scarred for life."

"I had another bad dream, far worse than the others," Tz' said as he poked at the fire with a long stick. "I guess I got a little carried away trying to get rid of it." He coughed out a hollow laugh and attempted to smile. "Tat, I don't know what to do; Na'om is gone, and I did nothing to stop her dying. And even worse, my own grandmother caused her death! I want to rip that half of me right out of my body, and I would if I could."

"I know you're in pain, Tz'. We're all grieving, but you must remember that it's not your fault that Na'om died. And yes, Satal's related to you by blood, but in between is your mother, who, in her own way, was a sweet woman who loved you very much. Your chuch is in the Underworld now, but I believe she's still watching out for you and would want you to have a good life, despite all the hardships you're facing." Chiman crouched down near Tz' and put his arm around his shoulder. "For now, we have to take it one moment at a time and stay busy, so our minds don't have time to wander into that awful space where the loss of those we love overwhelms us." He reached forward, picked up a bowl of iguana stew from the fire pit, and handed it to Tz'. "Eating will help; the food will give you the strength to carry on."

Tz' nodded silently as he took the bowl and spoon. He sipped at the rich, meaty broth made from roasted peppers and tomatoes and sighed. The food did taste good. *Just concentrate on the flavors, that hint of garlic, the bit of salt, that tiny glob of fat floating over there,* Tz' told himself as he swallowed one mouthful and then another. When he was done, he placed the empty bowl on the ground and smiled at his father. "Maltiox, that was good."

Chiman smiled. "I'm glad you're feeling better." He shifted his weight on the bare ground and moved the empty bowls to one side. "I'll speak to the shamans here in the city and see if we can use one of the temples for a proper purification, which should rid you of your dreams. And it's beyond time when you should have met your spirit animal, a ritual we would have performed in Pa nimá if events hadn't unfolded the way they did."

Tz' nodded. "If you think it will help, I'm willing to go through the rites."

"Satal was a powerful woman in the city and certainly knew how to manipulate the spirit world, but now that she's dead, I don't think you should fear her essence." Chiman drank from his cup of watermelon juice and smiled at Tz'. "There's something else I've been meaning to talk about with you, something that might help lessen your grief. While you were dancing with the other men at the pyramid during the Wayeb, Ajkun told me the truth about an issue that I've long suspected was true." Chiman paused and took another sip of juice. "Na'om's mother, Tu'janel, was really my daughter, born to Ajkun from the many hours we spent together in the jungle. Because my mother didn't approve of Ajkun, we never married. Instead, to hide the pregnancy, Ajkun married a farmer she didn't love, and she convinced everyone that Tu'janel was his child."

"But, Tat, then that means Na'om is your granddaughter, which makes her my blood relative."

"Yes, and therefore, you couldn't have married her. I'm not sure why the gods hid this fact from me all these years. In any of my spiritual trances, I always saw the two of you together, but I know Ajkun wouldn't deceive me."

Tz' didn't know what to say. The girl he'd loved for so long was really his half-sister. He had wanted to marry her, to kiss her, to make love to her. The rush of thoughts was suddenly too much, and he pushed himself to his feet. He stood for a moment, letting the swirling blackness that flooded his mind drift away.

"Tz', where are you going?" Chiman asked as he also rose.

"I don't know. I need to be alone to think about all of this."

"I understand. It's a lot to contemplate all at once," Chiman said. "I'll go and check on Yakal and the others and leave you to rest." He pointed to a pot of lukewarm water. "There's water to wash with. I'll be back later."

Tz' nodded and moved by rote to wash his face and then his dishes. When he was done, he sat by the fire again, pondering the odd twist his life had just taken.

Now I've lost a sister, rather than the woman I intended to marry. Memories of Na'om filled his mind—the two of them swimming in the river, Tz' playing his flute and watching Na'om try to teach Ek' Balam to dance on his hind feet, the days they'd spent building Na'om's hut and the constant thought that one day they'd live in it together. His eyes watered, and he felt the tears run down his cheek and into his ear. He swiped the wetness away with his fingers. *Mother didn't want me to wed Na'om; perhaps she knew who she really was all along. Which means I probably shouldn't have ignored Mok'onel, the girl Mother did want me to marry.* Tz' thought back to the night when Mok'onel had come to his room, smelling of vanilla oil, eager to make love to him. He had pushed her away, determined to save himself for Na'om. *If I had said yes, what would my life be like now?* Tz' wondered. But he couldn't see any immediate future in that direction, for his heart still belonged to Na'om, even as his body craved intimacy with a woman.

Restlessness drove Tz' to his feet, and he headed straight for the nearest gate in the city wall. He found a narrow footpath that meandered through a lime orchard and another that led past a planting of young avocado trees. He walked for hours without direction, avoiding eye contact with the few individuals working in the groves, while he tried to accept the new information.

Hunger pains finally drove him back toward Mayapán, but he stopped outside the city to watch as a group of young male slaves laden with pack baskets full of salt stepped off the *sacbé* and approached the main gates. The leather straps of their tumplines pressed deeply into their foreheads, and their backs and calves were covered in pink salt dust. Two older men cracked their leather whips to keep the slaves plodding forward.

If Yakal hadn't rescued us from the slave market when we first arrived here, I could be carrying salt right now, too. Tz' shivered at the thought. Behind the slavers came merchants lugging baskets full of corn, avocados, limes, tomatoes, wild garlic, and other produce destined for the market. The sight of all the food made Tz's stomach grumble. Then a group of boys much younger than Tz' scurried past, each clutching the feet of a recently slaughtered turkey in either hand. The headless birds dripped blood in the dirt, and a swarm of flies buzzed about the thin trail. Next came two men, each carrying on his back a stack of bamboo cages filled with songbirds of every color of the rainbow. The men staggered under the weight of their loads that towered far above their heads. Tz' stared after them, mesmerized by the brilliant teal, vibrant yellow, crimson red, and sky-blue feathers that wafted down as the men passed. He stopped to pick up an iridescent blue-black feather and tucked it behind his right ear before following the men to the market, where he purchased several venison tamales.

His hunger satiated, Tz' spent the next several hours wandering up and down the narrow streets and alleyways of the city in areas that he'd never been before. He passed shops filled with hanging bunches of dried herbs, and baskets of dried flowers and roots used for every sort of ailment or divination. Their pungent, astringent smells filled the narrow streets, making Tz's nostrils burn. A display of ceramic pipes and censers in the window opening of one store caught his eye, and he stepped inside. The long, narrow room was packed with stacks of copper bowls in a variety of sizes, incense burners shaped like giant toads, turtles, snakes, and fish, and cotton bags of copal and various herbs Tz' couldn't identify. He nodded to the old shopkeeper sitting on a stool in the back of the shop, who watched him closely as he browsed through the store. One long table was filled with a selection of knives, and Tz' stopped to admire them. He smiled as he touched the longer, wider blades made of obsidian that were the length of his forearm and then picked up a small blade the length of his hand made of green jadeite. The handle was carved to look like it had been wrapped with braided strands of twine. He ran his fingertip over the intricate design before closing his fist over it. The knife fit comfortably in his palm, and he wished he had enough cacao beans with him to purchase it. With reluctance, he set the blade back down and continued to poke around in the shop, pausing to look at the rows of old journals that filled several shelves on the far side of the room. He'd never seen so many books in one place and wanted to open them, but one glance at the old man made it clear to Tz' that he was no longer welcome if he didn't intend to purchase anything. He hurried out into the street, squinting in the bright daylight after the dim interior of the store.

In another alleyway, old men dressed in plain black cotton loincloths lingered in many of the doorways. Some had their bare chests covered with deep blue geometric designs representing intertwined arrows, double spirals, and dots and bars, while other men had black images of the gods etched into their leather-like skin. Tz' noticed that the men's fingertips were permanently stained blue or black from years of carving ink-filled drawings into the flesh of men and women alike. Sketches of the scarifications the men were capable of reproducing were pinned to the stucco walls, and Tz' paused to look, wondering if one day he'd have the strength to endure the intense pain that accompanied this popular type of beautification. Having his earlobes pierced so they could hold the obsidian ear flares he wore had been painful enough. One elderly man covered in ink gripped Tz's forearm and tried to pull him indoors, but he pried the man's fingers off and hurried on his way.

He wandered past the palaces of the elite, the lavish buildings hidden behind high stone walls, where the sounds of laughter echoed out into the streets, and he stopped to watch the guards training in the plaza in front of the Temple of the Warriors. The hours passed in a blur, and it was late evening by the time he headed back to the hut. As he edged past the lines of women still waiting to draw water from the cenote, the sight of the area startled him. He'd been so absorbed in seeing all the different sections of the city that he hadn't thought of Na'om once in the past few hours. *It's almost as if I'd forgotten her.* He looked around, wondering where exactly she had last stood before falling over the edge and then realized it didn't matter. She was gone, and nothing was going to bring her back. The knowledge clutched at his heart, and he staggered a few steps, feeling suddenly sick to his stomach. He swallowed several times, trying to dispel his nausea. As he continued through the streets, he looked down at the scratches on his forearms and picked at a scab of dried blood, reopening the wound. The pain felt good; it forced him to focus on the moment and not on what might have been if things had been different.

Chiman was tidying up his dinner dishes when Tz' arrived at the hut. "Sorry I'm so late," Tz' said as he stepped into the courtyard.

"I'm glad you got back before I went to bed," Chiman said as he dried his hands on a towel. "I spoke to the shamans and have made arrangements for us to use one of the smaller temples for an evening, but you'll need to fast before we can begin, so consider that bowl of stew you had earlier as your last meal for a day or two."

Tz' nodded. He didn't mention the tamales he'd eaten. "All right, I'm ready whenever it's possible to perform the rituals."

Chiman handed him a list of supplies he'd written on a small scrap of fig bark paper. "These are the herbs and other materials we'll need. I think it's a good idea if you purchase them yourself. You're old enough to take more responsibility for these things." He handed Tz' a deerskin pouch full of cacao beans.

Tz' quickly scanned the items and nodded. "I found several places today that probably sell these things, so I'll get them tomorrow. Maltiox, Tat, for helping me with all of this." He headed to his hammock, but sudden hunger made it impossible to sleep. His thoughts bounced from food to Na'om to Satal. From every description he'd ever heard, Satal was an evil and controlling woman with no room in her heart for affection. *But she was my grandmother; perhaps if I'd lived nearby, she would have been different.* He tried to imagine Satal being like Ajkun, someone who had always been kind to him, and then shook his head. The two women were as different as night and day.

Restless, he rolled over in the hammock and set it swaying. He had no use for Satal's palace or most of her fortune, but the power Satal had commanded intrigued him. *Even though she used it for her own ill intentions, what would it be like to have the whole city doing my bidding? Why, I could have anything I wanted if that was the case . . .* Tz' drifted off to sleep, his dreams filled with lines of the privileged city members paying homage to him, bringing him offerings of food, clothing, and cacao beans in exchange for his benevolence.

Two full days passed with no food, and Tz' could feel the weakness in his legs as he climbed the steep stairs up to the platform and the small temple room where Chiman was waiting for him. The sun was low on the horizon, casting long shadows, and Tz' had trouble seeing Chiman's face as he set down the pack basket full of supplies.

A small fire burned outside the shrine room, illuminating the hieroglyphs and images of the gods inscribed into the stone. Chiman motioned for Tz' to unpack the basket, and he hurried to follow his father's orders, as he was eager to get the task underway.

Chiman tossed several balls of golden copal resin into the fire, which instantly sent up a thick blanket of smoke. He motioned for Tz' to sit in it and waved a bundle of pink flamingo feathers up and down and around his body, pushing the smoke toward Tz', making him cough.

"Take short breaths, then it won't hurt to breathe the smoke," Chiman instructed. He packed a clay pipe with locally grown tobacco, lit the bowl with a piece of burning straw, and drew several quick puffs on the stem before handing the pipe to Tz'. "One deep inhale and hold it," Chiman said. "Good, now another just like the last one. And one more time."

Tz' breathed in a third time and felt the tobacco burning in his lungs. His head spun, and the fire before him shimmered and shifted. He knew his father had done this thousands of times, but he'd never used tobacco before and wasn't sure he liked what it was doing to his body. Chiman placed a copper bowl on the stones next to him.

"Imagine Satal's blood flowing through your body, then envision it moving down your arms, down your fingertips, and dripping into the bowl," Chiman said.

Tz' stared at the flames, watching them flicker and dance, and tried to envision what his father had told him. But he was edgy and restless. He took a deep breath and let it out slowly, then looked beyond the fire to the darkness all around him. In the distance, he could see the faint outlines of treetops, the movement of torches as people left the fields for their homes outside the city walls, and beyond them, the vastness of the night sky filled with stars. He could feel the heat of the fire on his face, his chest, and his bent knees, and the cold of the evening air on his back. He closed his eyes and concentrated. He imagined his blood as different strands of colors moving up and down his legs and arms. Green was for his father, blue for his mother, and black represented Satal. He envisioned pulling on the black threads, tugging on them at his fingertips, so the blackness drained down first his right arm and then his left. He let the cords coil and spool in the bowl he held in his hands. The bowl filled quickly, and yet, there was still more blackness in him—in his head, his chest, his legs—but he had nowhere else to put it. He didn't want it to spill out of the bowl, so he stopped tugging and imagined tossing the contents of the vessel into the fire. He opened his eyes when the flames sputtered and sparked, as if he'd squelched them with a bowl of water, and an acrid smell filled the immediate area. He looked up at Chiman who was standing nearby.

"Well done, Tz'," Chiman said as he held out his hand and helped pull him to his feet. "That should take care of those dreams you've been having."

Not wanting to disappoint his father, Tz' didn't mention that he still felt half full of Satal's energy.

"Now it's on to the more difficult task of discovering your spirit animal companion." Chiman handed Tz' a gourd full of water to drink and pointed to the temple room where Tz' could see several pillows and a blanket spread out on the floor. "It's best if you do this next ritual inside, where you'll be protected on three sides by solid stone. I'll block the doorway with my body so you'll feel safe and able to fully relax into the experience."

Chiman tapped the burnt tobacco out into the fire and repacked the bowl of the pipe with something black.

"Is that the dried toad venom you had me buy?" Tz' asked. He could feel his heart pounding in his chest, and his lungs tightening from the exposure to all the smoke.

"Yes, it's a powerful hallucinogen and should bring you strong visions." He handed the pipe to Tz'. "Once you're inside and have arranged everything so you're comfortable, just take a couple of quick puffs of this, no more, all right?"

Tz' nodded, suddenly nervous about the whole endeavor. "Maybe we should wait. I could do it another time when I haven't already done one ritual."

"No, you'll be fine, Tz'. In fact, this will work better now that you've already had some tobacco. Drink some more water, relax, and enjoy the experience. I'll be right here the whole time."

Once Tz' was settled on the blanket with his back against one wall, his body supported by the multiple pillows, he took the pipe and lit straw from his father and rapidly inhaled twice before handing them back to Chiman.

Almost instantly Tz' could see the blazing sun in the room, and then it was a warmth rapidly spreading through his body, traveling from his head to his toes, and he laughed. *He* was the everlasting sun bursting outward into the room in an explosion of brilliant light that tingled up and down his spine. An overwhelming sense of love and peace filled his heart with such joy that tears ran down his face. He saw his father and his mother and Ajkun and Na'om, his dear sweet Na'om, and his heart stretched and stretched, filling up with all the love he held for her. He was all the colors of the rainbow, swirling in a wild dance that bounced and leapt around the narrow room, and he laughed again as he felt the wonderful sense that everything was just and right and good in the world. He looked down toward his legs and discovered he was floating high over the city. He could see his body inside the temple and his father in the doorway and the last few people as they made their way home and the guards as they closed the city gates. And then a strong buzzing filled his ears, invading his head, as if a thousand bees had attacked at once, pulling him back into his body. He felt the hard stones under his buttocks and against his back, and the colors in him and around him shifted and changed and ran together, blurring into a deep, dark blackness that engulfed him, swallowing him whole. Tz' felt his body flowing and morphing, stretching and pulling in multiple directions at once. He looked down with horror as his arms and legs shortened, and dark brownish rosettes appeared on his skin, surrounded by thick yellow fur. His fingers and toes turned into claws, each hand and foot a thick padded paw. He felt his forehead flatten and broaden, his eyes narrow at either end, and his jaws grow thicker, heavier, with a full set of upper and lower fangs. A craving for warm, fresh meat rushed through him, and he wanted to rip and tear at a bloody carcass, gorging on the soft innards of a deer or a peccary until his belly was full. He licked his lips, salivating as images of hunting prey filled his mind.

Suddenly, he was running on all fours on a winding path through the jungle, his nose to the ground, following the scent of something intoxicating, something he yearned for with every muscle in his feline body. The path widened into a clearing, and he could see a small hut built inside a ring of mahogany trees. His prey's aroma filled the area, making him dizzy with desire. His blood pounded in his veins, matching the pulsing of the bees that still thrummed in his ears. A roar grew inside his chest, and with a whoosh, Tz' let it out, filling the night sky with its fierceness. The energy pushed him against the wall, and he struck the back of his head with such force that he snapped out of the hallucination.

Tz' rapidly took inventory of his body. Other than the stinging pain and small cut on his skull, the rest of him appeared normal. He looked up and saw that Chiman was still seated in the doorway, undisturbed by the events that had just transpired.

He held up one arm and stared at it, expecting at any second for it to change once again. But it remained his normal, scratch-covered arm. He gently leaned his head back and closed his eyes again, concentrating to remember every detail of his transformation. Tz' had no idea what creature he'd just become, but he hungered for the feeling of energy and desire that it had instilled in him. No matter how hard he tried, though, he couldn't return to that state of being. He kicked a pillow near his foot, which bounced off Chiman's back.

His father turned and smiled at Tz'. "You're back. How did it go? Did you see any animals?"

"Yes, but instead of seeing an animal, I became one," Tz' said as he struggled to stand up. "I transformed into a jaguar, but larger and stronger than any I've seen in real life. Is that what's supposed to happen? I thought I'd *see* an animal, not become one."

"I'm impressed! Usually the gods do just *show* you an animal companion; your mystical abilities run much deeper than I ever imagined," Chiman said. He looked with pride at Tz', who fidgeted under his father's stare. Chiman bent down and packed up the pillows and other supplies. "Changing into a jaguar is a good thing, though, since it's the most influential and commanding animal we know and is associated with the gods on many levels." He paused while he stuffed the last few items into the pack basket Tz' had brought. "Actually, I'm not surprised this happened," he said as he swung the full basket onto his back. "When I was younger than you are now, I had an encounter with a jaguar during my own vision quest, which is why I have the jaguar spots tattooed on my back and shoulders."

Tz' wondered if his father had wanted to rip and tear into the warm flesh of an innocent animal or had had such a deep and intense craving for something that he couldn't quite identify. He shook his head and shivered, knowing what he'd become had not been any ordinary jaguar. "So, now what do I do?" he asked as he wrapped himself in the blanket. He followed Chiman down the steep temple steps and walked beside him toward their hut.

"You'll probably notice jaguars appearing more frequently in your life in a number of different ways, perhaps in your dreams, or you'll see a statue or other item shaped like a jaguar, which you might not have noticed before. For now, just take note of where and when this happens. And I'll borrow a few books from the shamans so you can continue your studies, focusing your learning on jaguars. Beyond that, we wait until the rains end and then we can head home."

Tz' suspected any books the shamans had on jaguars wouldn't help him identify the creature he'd become, but he didn't know where else to find answers. Then, when they approached their hut, he thought of the shop he'd been in days earlier, with its numerous ceramic censers, books, and knives, and he knew he had to go back there; he just didn't know quite why.

Na'om

As Na'om moved deeper and deeper underground, the little light that had seeped through from another spot in the cenote disappeared until she was walking in complete blackness. She closed her eyes and then opened them again and discovered there was no difference. As she stood still, she felt bits of dirt fall into her hair and face. She reached high over her head, and by standing on tiptoe, she was able to place her fingertips on the roof of the tunnel. The ground vibrated against her skin. "I must be directly beneath the city," she said to Ek' Balam, who stood patiently by her side. *The feet of all those walking overhead are causing the dirt to sift down on to us*, she thought. *Itzamná, I hope this cave doesn't collapse.* The thought of being buried underground spurred Na'om to continue moving.

She touched Ek' Balam's back and felt a quick jolt of energy race up her hand. She closed her eyes again and imagined a shield of white protective light covering her body from head to toe, extending out to include Ek' Balam. As soon as the two of them were connected by the energy field, Na'om discovered she could see vague shapes in the pitch black. She turned her head from side to side and could distinguish the rough walls and ceiling of the fissure, Ek' Balam standing by her, and the small pebbles and stones near her bare feet.

She pulled her hand away and her sight went black; she touched Ek'

Balam, and it came back. "I guess that settles it," Na'om said. "We walk together or not at all. Come on; let's try to find a way out of here."

For several hours, the two meandered up and down slight slopes and around corners that curved right and left as they followed the main tunnel. Occasionally, smaller openings appeared in the rocky walls, but Na'om was afraid to investigate them and leave the large passageway they were in. She knew the entire area around the city of Mayapán was saturated with a labyrinth of burrows and channels, and she continuously prayed to Itzamná she was headed in the right direction, toward the surface. But despite how far they had come, there was no sign of a way out.

Exhausted, hungry, and thirsty, Na'om sank down to the dry, cool dirt. "What have we done?" she cried as she bent forward and pressed her forehead into the ground. "Will I ever get out of here and see Ati't and Tz' again?" Images of her grandmother drifted through her mind, and Na'om sobbed at the thought of never seeing her. Weeping, she rocked back and forth, and felt her black jade jaguar necklace swing free from inside her shirt. She grasped it firmly in her dirty hand and begged for a sign from the gods. Several minutes went by. Please, Itzamná, someone, anyone help me.

"Have faith in yourself," Tu'janel said.

"Chuch, are you there?" Na'om said as she heard her mother's voice in her head. She sat up and pressed the carving to her lips. "Chuch, if you're there, I need your help, now more than ever. I don't know where to go or how to find my way out of this warren of tunnels. I need to get back to Ati't and Tz'." Her eyes watered again, but Na'om brushed the tears away. "I will see them again," she said fiercely.

"Yes, my daughter, you will see them again, but you have a long journey ahead of you before you do," Tu'janel said. "You're nearing the gates of Xibalba and must be prepared for whatever mischief the lords of the Underworld throw at you. Remember, you were born in the Wayeb and have great powers, far greater than the skills of the tricksters that lurk here in the Underworld. Call on all your allies, above ground and below, to help you through the trials you'll face."

"Allies, what allies, who can help me other than you?" Na'om said.

"Ajkun and Chiman will hear you if you call for help, as will others. Be strong, my child, and you will persevere."

"Chuch, wait, don't go," Na'om cried as she felt her mother's spirit slipping away. "What are these tests? How many of them are there?" But the air was empty of any presence.

Na'om leaned over to touch Ek' Balam and instantly could see him sprawled on the dirt. "I guess we have to keep going," she said. In response, Ek' Balam stood up and stretched, first leaning forward and then back. His tail curved upward slightly at the tip, and he turned his head to look at Na'om.

She struggled to her feet again and felt a bit dizzy as the blood rushed from her head. "I'm ready," she said as she touched his back. They continued to shuffle forward for a few minutes and then Na'om noticed a sudden change in the air around them. A warm draft brushed against her face, and she shivered as she felt the heat caress her bare arms and legs.

Ek' Balam stopped and sniffed the air.

"What is it?" Na'om asked. "What do you smell?" She tried to identify a scent in the warmth, but she could smell only dirt and her own sweat mingled with fear.

She took a few more steps forward and then felt the ground tilt sharply downward. She tried to peer into the blackness, to gain a sense of what lay ahead of them, but even with Ek' Balam's help, she couldn't see anything. "I don't like this," Na'om said as she sat down. She stretched her legs out in front of her and felt the ground drop at a sharp angle beyond her feet. "You can walk, but I'm going to scoot on my bottom," Na'om said.

Cautiously, she hitched her way through the darkness. The ground was solid beneath her body, but continued to slant downward at a steep angle. For over an hour, Na'om inched her way down the precipitous slope until the ground leveled out again. She could hear running water someplace up ahead and stood up. She winced as she brushed the dirt from her skirt. She'd ripped the fabric in several places, and she felt blood trickling from several small cuts in her buttocks.

The air at this lower level was warm and moist, and thick with the smell of rotten eggs.

Ek' Balam padded over to Na'om and nuzzled her hand. "Hey boy, I'm here," she said as she gripped his fur. With his vision linked to hers, Na'om could see the source of water, a small stream several feet in front of them that burbled and gurgled over a series of rocks. "At least we can get something to drink," Na'om said as she hurried with Ek' Balam to the brook.

She knelt down and gasped. The water wasn't water at all, but a steady river of scorpions that tumbled and flowed over one another. Hundreds upon thousands of glossy black ones scuttled over desert yellow and deep brown ones, while dark green scorpions crawled on top of blood-red ones. Pearl white scorpions that glowed despite the lack of light wriggled and arched their tails as the throng skittered and marched their way over the rocks in front of Na'om. The river of insects extended deep into the darkness to Na'om's right and left, and she could see they stretched out in front of her for twenty feet or more. Na'om watched as the scorpions began to crawl up the sides of the dry riverbank toward her, as if they had sensed her presence.

She scurried away from the mass, until she bumped into the steep bank she had just come down. With her back against the dirt, she watched as the river of arachnids advanced. They slowly puddled around her, only inches from her feet, a thick wall of snapping claws and slashing tails. Afraid to move, she watched out of the corner of her eye as streams of scorpions climbed the wall on either side of her, silently encircling her with their poisonous bodies. She held her breath as first one and then another scorpion crawled across her bare feet and started to climb up her shins. She could feel their sharp feet grasping for purchase on her smooth skin, but she didn't dare move for fear of being stung.

But as one scorpion and then another reached her inner thigh, Na'om shrieked. She swiftly lifted her skirt and swatted the bugs away, then wrapped her skirt tightly around her body to prevent any more insects from crawling inside her clothes. However, more scorpions quickly converged on Na'om, scrabbling up the outside of her clothing. "Chuch, help me," Na'om cried. But there was no answer from her mother, just a quick growl from Ek' Balam as he scrabbled against the embankment away from the scorpions. Na'om shook her arms and stamped her feet, but the insects clung to the fabric and continued to crawl closer and closer to her face.

Just as two scorpions reached her neck and were prepared to strike with their poisonous tails, Na'om envisioned a bubble of white light enveloping her and heard two distinct pops as both scorpions were blown off her and landed upside down at her feet. She felt the air vibrate as the dying scorpions waved their pincers and flicked their tails forward and back. Na'om shivered and hurried to extend the protective white light out around her feet and around Ek' Balam, who by now was also covered with the stinging creatures. Scorpions sizzled and hissed, flailing limbs and tails as the white light blasted them away. Mesmerized by the continuing advance of scorpions, Na'om watched as they piled one on top of another until the ground beyond her protective circle was several inches thick with them. But the minute one of the scorpions touched the edge of her circle of white light, it snapped and popped, flipping in the air before landing on top of its neighbors. Time and again, the scorpions tried to reach her, but her energy kept her safe from their waving claws and arching, stabbing tails.

Tentatively, Na'om took a tiny step forward. The circle of light blasted the scorpions in her path, creating an opening through which she could move. She held tightly to Ek' Balam and, inch by inch, the two moved through the onslaught of scorpions. They reached the teeming dry riverbed and cautiously stepped down into the silt, dirt, and rocks. Na'om concentrated, sending the light out farther, where it flowed up and over the rocks, incinerating any scorpions that tried to sneak toward them. Gaining confidence, Na'om hurried through the river of scorpions with Ek' Balam, leaving a trail of crisp bodies in her path.

They gained the opposite bank and clambered up the side. As soon as they stepped away from the riverbed, the creatures stopped progressing toward them and turned back to the dry waterway, where they once again flowed like water, tumbling and crawling over one another, oblivious to the hundreds of dead bodies that lay all around them.

Na'om shivered and hurried into the darkness of the tunnel in front of them. Only when she was several hundred feet from the scorpions did she let the white circle fade. Exhausted, she sank to the ground. She reached over and rubbed Ek' Balam behind his ear. "We survived the first test, boy."

Ek' Balam purred in response.

After she had rested for several minutes, Na'om stood up to continue their journey. Although lightheaded from lack of food and water and drained of energy, she knew she had to keep going if she was ever to return to the surface.

"Let's hope we pass any other tests quickly and find our way out of here," she said as she held onto Ek' Balam's fur.

Within minutes, Na'om heard the sound of running water again. "Oh no," she cried, "not more scorpions." But as the couple approached the riverbed, she could see that it was filled with liquid. It was only when she dipped her hand into it and brought a scoopful up to drink that she realized the liquid was not water, but blood, warm, dark red blood. She let the fluid drain through her fingers and stared at her stained hand in disbelief. She rubbed it on the dirt beside her, but only managed to collect dust and tiny pebbles in the thick wetness. In the dim vision she shared with Ek' Balam, she could see this river burbled out of a configuration of rocks at the base of the left-hand wall of the tunnel and disappeared back underground where it touched the right-hand wall. She would have to cross this stream if she wanted to continue.

"I'm so thirsty," Na'om complained as she lay down beside the river of blood. She curled up on her side, her head cradled on her right arm, and she felt Ek' Balam lie down beside her. "I just need to rest, then we'll go on," Na'om said. She shifted restlessly on the gravel, trying to get comfortable, but she soon gave up and ignored the pebbles that dug into her shoulder.

She had no idea how long she'd been walking. In the blackness, there was no concept of time; it could have been hours or days. She didn't know whether it was daytime or nighttime up on the surface; nothing made sense any more. The only things she could concentrate on were the dull headache she had behind her eyes and the griping pain in her empty stomach as she drifted in and out of consciousness.

As she lay on the rough ground, her mind took her back to Pa nimá and to the life she had shared with her grandmother. It was a bright, sunny day, and she was gathering herbs to take to Ajkun. She wandered along the riverbank until she found another patch of nettles, which she stopped to pick. As she plucked the leaves, she heard voices and recognized Tz's as he called to one of his friends. She smiled, eager to see her good friend. Just when she was going to stand up and say hello, the group of boys appeared, stripped off their loincloths, and jumped into the river to bathe. Na'om blushed at the sight of the naked youths, and quickly ducked lower into the nettles, wincing as the stinging leaves burned her hands and face.

She hesitated and then backed away from the area. When she was sure no one could see her, she stood and ran to another section of the river. But the nettles still stung her skin, and she hurried to dangle her hands in the flowing water to ease the pain. She scooped up a handful of the liquid to wash her face and drank deeply. But instead of cool, soothing water, it tasted warm, salty, and coppery.

Na'om came to and hastily moved away from the stream of blood. She felt her stomach churn, and she tried to imagine it was anything but blood that she had just swallowed. Somehow, she managed to keep from throwing up. Surprised, she felt the blood begin to course through her body. It warmed her from the inside out, filling her belly, and spreading outward toward her fingers and toes. She sensed Ek' Balam beside her in the dark and listened as he too took a long drink from the blood-filled waterway.

"Not so bad, eh boy," Na'om said. Eagerly, she leaned down and scooped handfuls of the thick fluid into her mouth. As she swallowed, she felt the blood pulsing through her system, replacing the emptiness with energy. She knelt in the dirt, the fingertips of one hand barely touching the rough gravel and sand as the vitality of the earth flowed through her body. Tiny electric shocks vibrated through her knees, and the force of the earth throbbed in time with her own heartbeat.

"Itzamná, I never expected to feel this good," Na'om said as she stood up and stretched. She wiped her bloody mouth on the hem of her shirt and smeared her hands across her skirt. Ek' Balam sat beside her, licking the blood from around his muzzle.

"Now, how do we cross this?" Na'om asked as she peered into the darkness. The dark red river flowed smoothly past them, with no rocks to walk on. "Looks like we have to wade," Na'om said. Gingerly, she stepped into the warm liquid, which oozed around her toes and ankles. Na'om took another hesitant step. "It doesn't appear to be too deep, at least," she said as she took two more steps away from the riverbank. Then suddenly, as she placed her weight on her left foot, she sank up to her knees in soft mud.

Scrabbling backward, Na'om clutched Ek' Balam with one hand and used him as a crutch so she didn't fall down. She staggered back to the riverbank and climbed up on the dry ground.

Blood drained down her legs and pooled at her feet. With a sigh, Na'om removed her skirt and shirt. She rolled them together into a ball, which she placed on top of her head. She held it there with her right hand and clutched Ek' Balam with the other. "Looks like we might have to swim," she said as the two stepped in unison back into the stream.

Within a few feet, the blood was up to her thighs. The warm fluid was soft against her skin, and Na'om shivered despite the heat. When she was waist-deep, she felt Ek' Balam begin to paddle next to her, and then she found she couldn't touch bottom, either. She held onto Ek' Balam with one hand and let him pull her through the warm fluid as he had done so many times in the cool river that flowed past Pa nimá.

Finally, after ten more feet, she was able to feel solid ground again and hurried to the opposite shore. Ek' Balam scrabbled up beside her and shook from head to tail, sending sprays of blood in all directions. Then he sat down and groomed himself. Na'om just laughed. "No sense worrying about what I look like now," she said as she felt the blood dripping off her in the cool air. She rubbed dirt all over her body and then used the sharp edge of a stone to scrape most of the bloody mixture from her skin. The remaining coating was scratchy and dry and pulled at Na'om's skin as she unrolled her clothes and put them on.

She touched Ek' Balam, and the two continued wandering along the main passageway, ignoring the small holes and crevices in the limestone walls that might have led to other, larger tunnels. She had to have faith that she was headed in the right direction. Chuch had told her there would be many trials, and so far, she'd passed two of them. *I just hope there aren't too many more.*

Almost as if the spirits of the Underworld had heard her thoughts, she was suddenly confronted with yet another stream. A vibrant green, the fluid burbled and gurgled, as it flowed from one side of the tunnel to the other. Large gaseous bubbles covered its surface, and when one exploded, it sent a thick noxious stench of rotten meat into the air.

Na'om quickly pulled her shirt up to cover her mouth and nose. "There's no way we can step into that muck," Na'om said. She looked around in the gloom for any rocks she could step on to cross the river, but nothing poked up through the sludge that burbled in front of her.

Ek' Balam took one glance at the riverbed, turned, and headed back the way they had come.

"Wait, we can't go back," Na'om cried. Dispirited, she sat down on the rough ground several feet away from the toxic stream. Suddenly, all the energy she'd gained from drinking at the river of blood was gone and every muscle and bone ached for fresh food and water. Griping pain hit Na'om in the stomach, and she doubled over, clutching at the ground as waves of nausea flowed through her. She took several short breaths and curled onto her side, which eased the throbbing in her empty stomach. From that angle, she tried to watch Ek' Balam as he paced around the narrow passageway, sniffing and turning his head from side to side, but the farther he stepped from her, the less she could see. "What is it, boy?" she asked as he stopped, came over to her, sat down, and looked straight up. She touched his back and followed his gaze.

Ten feet above their heads was a narrow ledge that jutted out from the tunnel wall. It hugged the curvature of the passage, arching out over the roiling stream of rotten green pus, before ending abruptly just a few feet short of the other side of the riverbed. As Ek' Balam moved away from her side again, her vision dimmed, and it was only when she heard his paws running quickly across the ground that she recognized what he was about to do.

She gasped as she heard him leap and crash into the shelf, but the scrabble of claws on hard rock let her know he had safely climbed up onto it. She listened with her whole body as his paws moved along the rocky protrusion, then sighed with relief when she heard him land safely on the other side of the stream.

And then she understood she was alone in the dark, with no way to see to cross the river of secretions. She rolled onto her knees, put her hands on the ground, and knelt in prayer. "Itzamná, if you can hear me, help me once again, I beg you," she cried. There was no answer. "Chuch? Are you there?" Silence was her only answer.

Unable to hear Ek' Balam over the noise of the stream and fearful of being left alone, Na'om stood and shuffled in the direction of the rock wall. She held her arms out in front of her as she moved and was grateful to feel the pitted limestone under her fingertips within minutes. She paused and covered herself with white light, which provided a tiny amount of vision, enough to see the tiny cracks and holes just inches in front of her face. However, when she stepped backward to look up toward the shelf, she lost all sense of sight.

Na'om stepped to the wall again and searched the surface in front of her. She found a deep crack several inches above her head, placed her fingertips in it, and pulled. The rock held her weight, so she pressed her toes against the wall, grasped the crack, and lifted off the tunnel floor. She hung there for a moment, not sure if she had the strength to continue, but knew she had to if she ever wanted to see her family again. She scoured the rock wall for another handhold and then a spot for her foot, slowly crawling upward, edging ever closer to the narrow ledge. Just as the muscles in her legs and arms began to cramp, Na'om managed to scuttle from the wall onto the irregular overhang. She twisted her body until she was able to sit with her back against the wall, her feet dangling ten feet above the bubbling, toxic stream below. She took several deep breaths despite the fetid air and then hitched sideways across the ledge. She used the palms of her hands to help steady her movements, knowing anything sudden might plunge her into the green, suppurating river. The ragged rocks of the rough shelf caught on her skirt, tearing more holes in the fabric and scratching her buttocks again and again. But she gritted her teeth and slowly continued.

Suddenly, she felt empty air beside her and knew she had come to the end of the ledge. However, she couldn't see how far she needed to leap in order to reach dry ground. Trembling, she carefully stood up, took a deep breath, and launched herself into space.

She hit the ground with a thud, landing on her hands and feet. She rolled over and lay on her back, breathing deeply. Bits of gravel were embedded in her palms, and she winced as she started to pick them out. Warm breath on her face told her Ek' Balam was near, and she reached out and touched his soft fur. Instantly, she could see again and was surprised to learn she was several feet from the pus-filled riverbed. *Guess I didn't need to leap so far*, she thought as Ek' Balam tried to lick her palm. She pushed him away slightly so his rough tongue wouldn't slide over the tiny cuts.

"It's all right, I can take care of these," Na'om said as she hugged him around the neck. Dusting off her skirt, she ripped two strips off the now-ragged hem and wound the pieces of fabric around her hands to stem the bleeding. Then she lay back down, too weary to continue. Ek' Balam nudged her shoulder with his big head, and when she didn't respond, he did it again. "Stop that, I need to rest," she cried as she pushed Ek' Balam farther away. She heard him twist around and then lie down in the dirt next to her, pressing his body up against hers. The warmth emanating from him was soothing, and Na'om quickly drifted off to sleep.

She was back in Pa nimá, following Tz' through the jungle as he cut a path with his new obsidian knife. She watched his muscular arms swinging in unison, hacking at the scrubby bushes, grasses, and thick liana vines that lay in their way. When he had a pile of brush, he bent and threw it to one side, then continued to slash his way forward. Na'om followed, tossing any remaining branches out of the way. At one point, Tz' paused and arched his back, and Na'om longed to place her hands on his shoulders and knead away the tightness, but she quickly pushed the thought away. They had work to do. They were making a shortcut from the river to the cornfields so that water could be brought to the tiny green sprouts poking out of the dry ground. It hadn't rained in many days, and the villagers were in danger of losing their entire crop. Na'om wiped sweat from her brow. The air around her was hot and moist, and she longed for something to drink. She swayed on her feet and dropped to the ground. Everything grew black, and just like the new corn, she felt in danger of dying. Vaguely, she heard Tz' calling her name, but she wasn't able to speak; she could only roll over on her side, nestling into the warm body that lay beside her.

Na'om opened her eyes and became conscious that her face was buried in Ek' Balam's belly. She sat up in the dark, and the images from her dream quickly faded as she breathed in the noxious smell of the river just a few feet away. She was terribly thirsty but struggled to her feet. She had to see Tz' again, and that meant moving forward.

What do the gods of the Underworld have for me next? Na'om wondered as she turned away from the stream. Ek' Balam fell into place beside her, and Na'om was grateful he had remained by her side throughout her sleep. "I promise, I won't push you away ever again," she said, patting him on the head.

The pair had walked just a short distance when Na'om thought she saw a flickering light in the distance. *Must be my eyes playing tricks on me.* She took her hand from Ek' Balam's neck, closed her eyes, and opened them again. The wavering glow was still there. She rubbed her eyes, blinked, and looked again. Yes, there was definitely a sparkle in the distance.

Na'om laughed. "We did it, we did it, we've found a way out of here," she shouted to Ek' Balam. And the two ran toward the light.

YAKAL

It took several days for Yakal to regain enough strength after his illness to return to work, and even then, he was only able to chisel at a sculpture for a few hours before needing to rest. He was leaning against the base of the pyramid, resting in the shade of the canvas canopy that fluttered over his head, when he saw Nimal, Bitol, and Kubal Joron approaching. Yakal's heart beat a bit faster. *They can't have discovered that I took some of Satal's cacao beans already, but why else would the three of them be coming to see me?*

Shortly after he'd burned the bundle of infectious bedding outside the city, he'd returned to Satal's palace. After checking to make sure no one was watching, he quietly opened the heavy wooden door and headed straight to Satal's bedroom. He pulled out one of the many sacks of cacao beans in the basket and scooped a handful of them into the pouch he carried at his side. It was tempting to take more, but he didn't want anyone to realize the bag had been tampered with, especially since the council had yet to decide what to do with all of Satal's possessions and her house.

Yakal had used a few of the beans to purchase two new gray-, white-, and black-striped woolen blankets, a sturdy dark purple hammock woven to hold three people, and a new dress for Uskab. Yakal grinned as he remembered the surprise and delight on Uskab's sweet face when he'd held up the emerald green dress with pink and white hibiscus flowers stitched all around the neckline.

"And you said he wouldn't be pleased to see us," Kubal Joron said. His voice brought Yakal back from his daydream.

Even from a distance, the three men looked pale, despite their brown skin, and as they came closer, Yakal could see traces of their recent illnesses on their arms and legs. He carried the same spots on his own body, tiny pairs of reddish dots, almost like bites, and he shuddered as the image of a snake popped into his head.

"*Saqarik*," he said as the three stopped in front of him.

"A good morning, yes," Kubal Joron replied as he patted his lips with a richly embroidered jade-green cloth. "We've just been enjoying some delicious turtle stew at the market. We should have invited you to come along." He tucked the cloth into a dark brown leather bag slung across his shoulders.

"I know you must have something more important than breakfast to discuss with me," Yakal said.

Nimal stepped forward and touched Yakal briefly on his bare forearm. "We do, but here is not the place for such a conversation." He nodded toward the other stonemasons, many of whom had stopped chiseling geometric designs into the sides of the pyramid to stare at the four men. "Too many eyes, too many ears."

"Let me grab my water," Yakal said as he slung the gourd over his shoulder. "I know just the place where we can go." He led the others toward Satal's palace and was the first to enter the quiet main room. The air still reeked of something moldy and dead, and Yakal avoided looking at the black spots high on the wall.

Kubal Joron hesitated in the open doorway. His gold-colored shirt glistened in the sun. "Must we talk inside? The last time I entered this palace uninvited, I spent the next five days as ill as I've ever been, dreaming that hundreds of ants and spiders were crawling inside my skin. Poor Matz' spent hours swatting at them to no avail. I don't care to have that happen a second time."

Yakal spun around. "Ants and spiders? For me, it was snakes and serpents." He turned to Nimal. "And what did you see?"

Nimal frowned, his deep brown eyes almost disappearing into

the multitude of wrinkles that covered his face. "Bats." The older man shuddered. "They sucked on me like I was a piece of sugar cane." He moved to stand beside Kubal Joron. "I say we talk out here, in the daylight."

Bitol placed his hands on either man's shoulders and peered at Yakal from behind them. "I must agree with my friends. I'd rather not enter Satal's house ever again. But we do need to discuss what will happen to this place now that she's gone."

"Fine, but before you say anything, I'll be right back." Yakal turned and headed down to Satal's private bedchamber. He hefted the pack basket by one leather strap onto his shoulder and hurried back to the main room. He plopped the heavy load on the floor in the doorway. He nodded at Bitol. "Before I show you this, what did you see during your illness?"

"Termites burrowing into my skin and clouds of wasps stinging me."

Yakal studied the men standing in front of him. "Who else could have caused these sicknesses other than Satal?" No one said a word until Bitol finally broke the silence.

"You say you saw her, and we all gave chase to someone, but I'm still not convinced it was Lady Satal."

"Even after all you've been through?" Yakal laughed.

"She's gone to the land of the ancestors; we were all there to see her fall," Kubal Joron said. He dabbed at his forehead with his green cloth, wiping away the beads of sweat that had appeared. "But whether she lives or not is beyond our control. Only the gods know for sure." He pointed at the basket sitting on the floor beside Yakal. "What did you want to show us?"

Yakal reached into the basket, pulled out several of the bags, and plopped them on the tiles next to his feet. He quickly untied one, shoved his hand inside, and held out the cacao beans for all to see.

Bitol stepped forward and peered into the basket. "Itzamná, do all those satchels hold the same?"

"Quite the sight, isn't it? She's obviously been hoarding her wealth for years." Yakal let the beans dribble back into the sack and retied the piece of twine around its neck. "After all we four have been through, I say we each take a bag as payment for our illnesses."

Nimal took a step backward. "I could certainly use them, Itzamná knows I don't make much, even being leader of the regiment, but I want no part in any of this. Those beans are tainted with Satal's evil. I can feel it emanating from these bags."

"Dear Matz' and I don't really need them, either," Kubal Joron said. "The gods have always blessed us with good fortune in all our trading endeavors." He smiled at Yakal. "On the other hand, you, dear boy, will soon have a family to take care of and certain debts to repay. I doubt any of us will tell the council if a few handfuls of those old dried beans happen to land in your pouch."

Bitol stepped forward, picked up a bag in each hand, hefted them, and set them back down. "A fortune, just sitting here, while there are those in the city who go without food or a blanket to sleep in. If I ever see that witch again, I shall gladly run my knife into her black heart." He turned to Yakal. "Your father was my brother and part of this wealth is from him, I'm sure of it. When Q'alel died, Satal took everything, the money, the palace, his place on the council. Satal's only child, Chachal, was killed in Pa nimá, which leaves you as Q'alel's firstborn heir, so I say all this belongs to you," he said as he waved his hand to indicate the bags of beans and the palace behind them.

Yakal felt a sudden rush of blood in his veins at the thought of so much wealth being his.

"No, you're wrong, Bitol," Nimal said. "Chachal had a child by Chiman, Tz'ajonel, making him Satal's grandson. Everything here should rightfully go to Tz' since the laws of the council state that everything passes from mother to daughter and then to the firstborn granddaughter. In this case, the only grandchild was a boy, but Tz' is still related to Satal by blood, so he is the rightful heir."

Yakal kicked at the bags, unable to hide his frustration. Just when he thought he'd found a solution to his money problems and he'd be able to repay Kubal Joron, releasing Memetik from being his houseboy, it was all taken away again.

"Well, then we must speak to Tz' as soon as possible," Bitol said. He placed a hand on Yakal's arm. "I suspect your nephew will be only too happy to give you some of this. You have a pretty young wife and a baby on the way, while he's a simple country boy who probably has never had more than two cacao beans to call his own."

Yakal nodded. He knew the others were right, but it still felt unfair. *I should have taken more when I had the chance. No one would have cared. What a fool I've been.*

"Shall we go find this boy and find out what he wishes to do with this sudden wealth?" Kubal Joron said. He glanced at the sky. "If it grows any later, I shall be obliged to buy another bowl of that delicious turkey stew." He patted his round belly that protruded over the tight band of his loincloth. "Matz' promised to broil some deer steaks this afternoon, and I don't want to spoil my appetite, but I do get hungry so easily when I've had to do hard work."

Nimal, Bitol, and Yakal all shrugged. *Work, what work, the man has never had to lift a finger in his lifetime,* Yakal thought angrily as he dropped the sacks of cacao beans back into the basket. "What do I do with all of this?"

"Put it back inside, someplace where no one will find it," Bitol said.

"And I'll post guards to stand watch outside the courtyard," Nimal added. "Until we sort all this out, we don't need anyone to know there's a fortune inside, waiting to be taken."

Yakal hurried back indoors, searching for someplace to stow the bags. He finally decided to shove the satchels of beans inside the battered wooden cupboard that stood against the wall in Satal's room. He draped an old monkey skin full of holes over the bags and prayed no one would find them until Tz' had made a decision.

The four men quickly headed to Alom's hut where Chiman and Tz' were staying nearby. Yakal stepped into the small courtyard that defined his mother's space, leaving the other men waiting patiently in the street.

"Yakal, what brings you here during the day?" Alom asked as she looked up from her weaving. She quickly untied the back strap loom from around her waist and went to hug her son.

"Tz' and Chiman, are they here?" Yakal inquired as he looked around the small enclosure. "There was no answer when we stopped at their hut." He noticed the only wooden stool near the fire pit was held together with bits of sisal twine wrapped around one leg. *With the extra cacao beans, I could buy Chuch anything she could possibly need.*

"They've gone for a walk, but should be back any time, as I've invited them for lunch." Alom glanced at the men nearby and leaned in to whisper to Yakal. "Is everything all right? Why are Nimal and Bitol here with

Kubal Joron? He's never seen in this part of the city."

"Everything's fine, Chuch. We just want to talk to Tz', that's all." Yakal gave his mother a quick hug and was relieved to see Chiman and Tz' arriving at the house. Chiman's indigo blue jaguar spots tattooed into his skin were highly visible in the bright sunlight, and Yakal marveled again at the older man's ability to withstand the pain that had surely been a companion to such a design.

After introductions were made among the men, Yakal spoke to Tz' and to Chiman. "Now that Satal is dead . . . ." He glanced at Nimal and the others and continued, "Or presumed dead, there's the question of what to do with her palace and its contents." He held up a hand to stop Chiman from saying anything. "Before you speak, you must know that we've found many large, very large, satchels of cacao beans among her possessions."

Chiman drew in a deep breath and let it out slowly. He placed his hand on Tz's shoulder. "Do you understand what Yakal is saying, son?" He looked at Yakal, who nodded for him to continue. "You've inherited a vast fortune and with it enormous amounts of power."

Tz' looked from his father to Yakal to the three men who hovered nearby. "I never knew my grandmother and care nothing for her things, her house, or her cacao beans. Do what you wish with it all; the only thing I want is for Na'om to return. If I thought throwing everything you've mentioned into the cenote would bring her back, I would gladly sacrifice it all." Tz' scuffed his feet in the dirt as all the men continued to stare at him.

"Perhaps the boy needs a bit of time to think about all of this; after all, it must come as quite the shock to learn he's suddenly one of the wealthiest men in Mayapán," Kubal Joron said. He looked up at the sun high overhead and everyone heard his stomach grumble as he moved into a tiny patch of shade cast by the hut across the street.

"No, it's all right," Tz' said as he looked at the older, heavy-set man. "Thank you for your concern, though." He turned to Yakal. "Uncle, as you know, we all plan to return to Pa nimá once the rivers are navigable again, so I have no need for the palace or any of its contents. Some of the cacao beans will be useful to help rebuild our village, but the majority of them would only be spent on items we don't need. So, I put you in charge of deciding what to do with this fortune. Use some of it for yourself and for your family and give the rest away if you like."

"Well said, Tz', I couldn't have expressed it better myself," Chiman said as he hugged his son with one arm around his shoulder.

Yakal could see the pride on Chiman's lined face and felt his own face flush with sudden shame. His first thoughts had been to take as many of the beans as he could, and yet, Tz', a mere youth, was only too eager to give his wealth away. "You're much too kind, Tz', and I thank you for it. Itzamná knows I could use a bit of help with the baby on the way."

"Perhaps some of the beans could be used to purchase food for those in the city who go without on a daily basis?" Bitol interjected.

"Yes, yes, of course," Yakal said. "We shall set up some kind of special kitchen where those in need can have a free meal. And the rest of the beans will be placed under guard at the Temple of the Warriors, so no one may steal them."

Nimal nodded at Yakal and then at Tz' and Chiman. "We'll keep it safe and if you should need any of it at any time, just send word, and I'll send some of my guards to bring it to you."

Kubal Joron appeared next to the group of men standing in the sunlight. "Well, then, it appears that's all settled. If there's nothing left to be decided, I must go. My poor Matz' will be so worried about me. I don't want him to overcook those lovely deer steaks he bought."

"Go, Kubal Joron, we'll know where to find you if we need you for anything else," Nimal said.

"Wherever there's food," Bitol said in a whisper, and the group of men laughed as they watched the older man waddle away into the crowd.

"Maltiox, Tz', for your generosity," Nimal and Bitol said as they both left as well.

Alom padded up behind Yakal, Tz', and Chiman. "There's plenty of vegetable stew left over from last night's meal, if you care to eat," she said as she pointed to the pot balanced on three large stones in the fire pit.

"Maltiox, Chuch, a meal cooked by you is always a treat," Yakal said as he bent down and kissed his mother gently on the cheek. She hurried to gather several empty coconut shells from a shelf inside the hut.

"Tat axel, I'd like to give Alom some of the beans. She's been very kind to us the whole time we've been here. It feels only right that we repay her," Tz' said as he watched the older woman return with her hands full of bowls. He hurried to help her before she dropped one.

"Bitol is very concerned with helping the poor," Chiman remarked as he blew on a spoonful of the thick stew to cool it.

"Hmm, yes," Yakal replied. "He's often told me stories of how he had little to eat as a child, so his idea of feeding the hungry comes as no surprise."

Alom turned from the fire pit with her own bowl of soup and sat down, but sloshed some of the broth on her white skirt when the stool collapsed under her weight. Yakal and Tz' jumped up and helped the woman to her feet.

"Chuch, are you all right?" Yakal said as he helped her settle on the ground. Tz' handed her a clean bowl full of soup.

"Yes, I'm fine, just annoyed that I've ruined my skirt," Ajkun said as she pointed at the reddish spots that covered the lower half of the fabric. "These stains won't ever come out."

Yakal grinned. "Never mind, Chuch. After we eat, we'll go to the market and buy the finest skirt we can find. And a new stool or two, too."

"But how, with what? I have no cacao beans, and I know you need everything you have for Uskab and the baby." Alom put her bowl of stew on the ground and shifted her weight on the hard ground.

Tz' looked to Yakal and then Chiman. "May I tell her, Tat axel?" he asked. Chiman nodded. "Yakal and the men who were just here say I've inherited a great fortune from my grandmother, but I have no need for it. I've told Yakal to use as much as he wants to make you and the rest of his family as comfortable as possible."

"Is this true?" Alom asked Yakal.

He nodded as he slurped the last of the stew from his bowl. "Satal must have saved every bean she ever earned serving on the council. Your worries are over, Chuch. And my dear sisters and wife shall want for nothing as well."

"Huh, take those beans and get rid of them," Alom said. "They're tainted with Satal's magic and nothing good will ever come from spending any of them." She looked closely at Yakal. "You've already used some, though, haven't you? I can tell from the look on your face." She shook her head rapidly. "Ah Yakal, my sweet son, you'll never be safe from Satal if you crave the power that comes with such wealth. Promise me you won't use any more of it."

"Chuch, it's all right. I had to buy new bedding after my illness, and you've seen how tight Uskab's clothing has gotten because of the baby," Yakal paused, unwilling to make any vows regarding the beans.

"Well, do as you wish, but I want nothing from that woman," Alom said as she put her half-eaten bowl of soup on the ground. "Tell me more about Bitol's idea to feed the hungry."

"He's suggested a place where those in need can receive a free meal; we'd use Satal's beans to buy the ingredients and ask for volunteers to cook it."

Tz' looked from his uncle to his father. "Could the place be named after Na'om? Satal took her from us, so I'd like to honor her if we can."

Chiman smiled at Tz'. "I think that's a wonderful idea."

"I'd be willing to find volunteers," Alom said. "And even cook there myself once in a while. But I'd need to stop once Uskab has the baby as I'll be too busy helping her."

Yakal glanced at the sky and realized it was later than he liked. "I need to get back to work," he said as he kissed Alom on the cheek. "Thanks for the soup, Chuch, it was delicious." He nodded to Chiman and Tz' and headed back toward the pyramid.

But he couldn't stop thinking about the bags of cacao beans stuffed into Satal's old cupboard and he changed his direction, heading to the palace instead. He nodded to the guard standing duty at the entrance to the courtyard and slipped inside the house.

The air was cool inside the large main room after the heat of the noonday sun, and despite the mildewed smell, Yakal stopped long enough to let the tiny beads of sweat on his chest dry. Then he headed to Satal's bedroom, where he selected the largest of the sacks of beans. *Tz' did say to take as much as I wanted or needed.* He balanced the sack on his shoulder as he searched the house for something to carry it in. Finally, he found an old basket near the outdoor kitchen area. Even though many of the reeds were broken, it was still strong enough to use. Yakal stuffed the satchel of beans inside. *Best not let anyone see what I'm carrying,* he thought as he covered the bag with a ragged cloth.

Once outside, he headed straight home instead of back to the other stonemasons. *With any luck, Uskab will be at the market, which will give me time to hide this.* Sure enough, Uskab was gone when Yakal arrived. He quickly entered the small one-room hut and found several unused rags he'd planned to take to work for polishing his stone sculptures. He poured some of the beans into each of them, tied them shut, and then shoved them up into the rafters, tucking the dark cloth bags behind some of the palm fronds so they weren't visible. One pouch he shoved into his work satchel, and he still had a large amount left in the original bag. He looked around, trying to find a safe place for it, when Uskab appeared in the doorway.

"Yakal, what's wrong?" Uskab asked as soon as she saw him. "Why are you home so early?" She hurried to his side. "You're not ill again, are you?"

"No, no, I'm fine, I just felt like coming home early to see you," Yakal said. He dangled the satchel behind his back with one arm and reached out to hug Uskab.

"What're you hiding?" Uskab said as she tried to peer around Yakal's body.

Yakal sighed. "Oh, sweet one, I should know better than to hide anything from you." He held out the open satchel.

Uskab squealed when she dipped her hand in and realized it was full of cacao beans. "I don't understand; where did this come from?" She searched Yakal's face. "You're not in any trouble, are you?"

"No, my little honeybee, no trouble at all. Tz' has inherited a fortune from Satal, which he doesn't want. He told me to take as much as I might need for you and the baby, so here you go." He pressed the bag into Uskab's arms and was relieved to see her grin again. "You're not mad that I accepted it?"

"Mad? Of course not. That woman was a painful blister that never went away; it's only fair that she finally repay us for all the difficulties she's brought us through all the years." Uskab dipped her hand into the sack and let the beans run through her fingers. "I can't believe our good fortune!" She kissed Yakal on the cheek and spun around the small room. "You do know the larger house across from your mother's place, where Chiman and Tz' are staying, is still for sale."

"But we have a home, right here," Yakal replied as he spread his arms wide. He could almost touch both sides of the room with his fingertips.

"Yes, but a very small home, one that will only grow smaller once your son arrives." Uskab felt the baby kick and placed her hand just below her ribs. "Even he agrees that we need a larger house. Please, Yakal, we do have the money now . . . and just think how convenient it will be for me to have your mother living right across the street." Uskab looked at Yakal with her big brown eyes.

He felt himself caving in to her desires. "All right, all right, I'll talk to the owner tomorrow after work. But we won't be able to move in until after Chiman and Tz' have gone back to Pa nimá."

Later that evening, Yakal lay awake long after Uskab had fallen asleep. He could just see the places in the ceiling where he'd hidden the other bags of beans. *Uskab doesn't need to know there are more beans; she'd only find a bigger house to buy if she knew.* He grinned in the darkness. *I'll use the money to buy some things for myself; after all I've been through, I deserve it as much as the next man does, maybe more, since I had to live with Satal all those years.*

SATAL

For over two weeks, Satal followed the sacbés across the countryside toward Chichén Itzá, where she hoped to find allies in her quest to redeem her powers and her money. Barefoot and dressed in the simple black clothes she had put on before fleeing Mayapán, she looked like a thousand other old women who walked the limestone causeways headed to neighboring villages along the route to see relatives, to trade goods, or to find an herbal cure for an ailment.

Satal didn't cluster together with these other women at night when they gathered around a communal fire and shared bits and pieces of food, along with a steady supply of gossip. She preferred to remain in the shadows, wrapped tightly in her stolen brown shawl to ward off the cool night air. It was safer that way. If anyone had really noticed her ragged earlobes and numerous scars on her lips and tongue, they would have known she was of noble birth and questioned why she was alone and so far from any city.

Every night when anyone nearby was fast asleep, Satal removed the small cotton pouch from around her neck and dumped the cacao beans into the palm of one hand. She'd started out with thirty and had spent two to purchase a large package of tamales filled with venison and figs and a water gourd full of warm, brackish-tasting water shortly after leaving

Mayapán. She had eaten the last few bites of tamale a day ago and knew she needed to spend another bean for more food. But she loathed to do so, knowing what she held in her hand was all that remained of the vast fortune she'd spent so many years accumulating. Hunched over so no one could see her, she tucked one cacao in her skirt's inner pocket, slowly placed the remaining beans back in the pouch, and rehung it around her neck.

I never should have put the big bag in the basket, she grumbled as she thought of the wealth she'd left behind. *All those years of skimping on luxuries, and for what, so Yakal and the others can now spend my money? All my possessions, even my house, are probably now in the hands of the council. Who knows what they'll do with the place,* she mused, as she tried to find a comfortable position on the rocky ground.

"Perhaps Yakal will live there," Sachoj whispered in her ear and she laughed. "Q'alel would have wanted his firstborn son to have the place."

"Over my dead body," Satal muttered as she shifted yet again. "Chachal was the legal child of Q'alel, and therefore, the next in line, not Yakal."

"But Chachal is dead, thanks to those incompetent men you hired to attack Pa nimá," Sachoj said. "And Yakal is still alive."

"But that's not possible. I cursed him and the others with blood magic. They should have traveled to the land of the ancestors by now."

"A simple midwife from the south saved them with a mixture of herbs and roots," Sachoj hissed. "You're growing weak and old. If only you'd killed the girl when you had the opportunity, then none of this would have happened." Sachoj sighed. "Yakal can easily take over your house now that you're not ruling the city."

The whispered words rankled; Satal knew her great-grandmother was probably right. "Yakal's the first one I'll have killed once I return to Mayapán with my army." The thought that Yakal could now be living in her palace chafed at Satal all night, causing her to toss and turn more than the tiny sticks and twigs strewn on the hard-packed ground where she lay.

As soon as signs of dawn appeared on the horizon, she moved off the sacbé and followed many others into a small village. A street market was set up in the central plaza, and her empty stomach growled as she caught a whiff of roasting meats and the thick spicy scent of some kind of soup. She pushed through the crowds gathered around the vegetable stalls and finally found a small booth selling bowls of turkey stew. Reluctantly, she handed over her cacao bean, but as she breathed in the heady aromas of chilies and tomatoes and scooped up the hot mixture filled with chopped bits of turkey, she focused on the pure pleasure of eating. She was unable to eat more than one bowlful, however, and was still owed change, so she picked out ten turkey tamales to take with her.

It felt strange to wander among all these people and not know anyone, and more importantly, not have anyone know her. *In Mayapán, no one would have pushed and shoved me as they did back there,* Satal thought as she returned to the limestone causeway. *At least in Chichén Itzá, I will be shown more respect.*

The sacbé grew more crowded each day as Satal got closer to the city. Finally, sixteen days after her terrifying run from Yakal and the others, she saw the four-sided pyramid dedicated to Kukulcan rising above the scrubby bushes, ceiba trees, and nearby buildings. Her heart quickened at the thought of seeing the place again; it had been too many moons since she had last stood at the base of the pyramid and gazed upon the stones carved into feathered serpents that lined the sides of the steep staircases leading to the temple at the top.

She had just passed her fourteenth name day when she and her love, Ajelbal, had stood near those serpents, saying their vows, when Q'alel and his warriors had raided the city and stolen her away from her betrothed. Over the years, she had often wondered what had happened to Ajelbal, whether he had married another and raised a family, or been killed in the ambush that day.

"Soon, I'll know and soon, I'll make Yakal and the others pay for what they've stolen from me."

A man herding a small group of oscellated turkeys jostled Satal with his walking stick as he hurried past, snapping her out of her memories. She glared at the man's back, willed him to stumble, and within a few feet, the man slipped and fell backwards, cracking the back of his head on the smooth limestone.

Satal smiled as the turkeys squawked and flew about, causing a moment's panic among the crowd. She hurried past the man, lightness in her step. She might have lost all her material things, but she still retained her power, which seemed to have grown in strength after her swim in the cenote. *Maltiox, Camazotz,* she thought. She was convinced that the great bat god had given her some of his abilities as well.

Unlike Mayapán, Chichén Itzá did not have a wall surrounding the city, and from what Satal remembered from her youth, she needed to pass through large tracts of open land used to grow corn and beans before reaching the city proper. But the outlying areas of houses and small gardens simply grew more congested until Satal realized she had walked through the cornfields of her youth, which were filled to overflowing with the populace that lived and worked in the city.

The pyramid dedicated to Kukulcan sat several hundred paces off to her left. *If Ajelbal is still alive, he'll most likely be near the Hall of the Thousand Columns,* Satal thought as she got her bearings. *He often played his flute for the regiment after they were done training for the day.* She turned to her right and headed in the direction of the large stone building that sat atop a flat platform twenty feet from the ground. It was flanked on three sides with distinct groups of stone columns, over a thousand in number, many of which were carved with the images of warriors who had proven themselves worthy in battle. The pillars supported the thick roof overhead, but there was little room to maneuver between the colonnades, which gave the Hall of the Thousand Columns its purpose. The men trained in hand-to-hand combat among the tight quarters, using the pillars to hide behind to launch surprise attacks on their fellow warriors. And the grassy courtyard in front of the building was the perfect place to practice large-scale mock battles.

Satal pushed her way through the large number of young men and boys gathered on the outskirts of the large plaza to watch the military leaders drill their combatants. She could see that most of the older men were dressed in full battle gear and had black and red zigzags painted on their faces, with bare upper arms and thighs. They wore deep brown leather vests over their bare torsos. The hide was stretched over a thin wooden frame and padded with ceiba fluff to absorb the impact from an arrow or spear, and the vests hung partway over their loincloths to protect their groins. Strips of tanned hide were wrapped around their shins from their ankles to just below the knees, and similar coverings encased their arms from their wrists to their elbows. The younger men and those from poorer families just wore loincloths and cotton wrappings around their legs and arms, leaving their bare chests fully exposed. Each man carried a large circular shield made of tanned hide stretched over a circular wooden frame in one hand and a spear tipped with obsidian or a long dagger in the other.

They parried and thrust to the commands of the leaders, one man against another, or two or three pitted against a single soldier, who often succumbed when a spear point was gently pressed against the flesh in his neck, groin, or chest.

Satal tapped on the arm of a young man who was standing beside her. "Who's in charge here?" she asked.

The youth looked at Satal and frowned. "Who wants to know?" he said as his gaze returned to the battlefield.

"Just tell me the name of the man in charge," Satal said as she tugged at the boy's arm, "and I'll leave you alone."

"Kämisanel," the boy said, pointing toward a group of men who stood in the shade cast by the roof of the Hall of the Thousand Columns. "He's the one wearing the large feather headdress, in the middle of those men."

"Maltiox," Satal said and hurried away. She skirted the group, watching the men train and eventually approached the gathering of leaders. But before she could climb the few steps that lead up to the group, her way was blocked by several armed men.

"No women allowed here," they said as they stood at attention and prevented Satal from advancing.

"I just wish to speak to Kämisanel," she said.

"You'll have to file a request with the council and wait your turn for a reply," one of the guards said. "Besides, Kämisanel never attends to business here on the field."

"I don't have time to waste," Satal replied. "I'm looking for someone, an old friend, perhaps you've heard of him? His name is Ajelbal; he's a flutist and often entertained the troops in the evenings."

"Never heard of him," the guard answered. "Hurry along now; you'll find no one by that name here." He stepped forward, forcing Satal to take a step backward.

Annoyed that she was being turned away, Satal drew herself up to her full four feet. "Do you even know who you're talking to here?"

"An old woman who can't take 'no' for an answer," the guard said, and his companions laughed. "Go on, now; go find someone else to annoy back in the city proper." He stepped forward again and tilted his spear just slightly in Satal's direction.

"Be careful, young man," she replied, "you could hurt yourself with that thing."

She could hear the men laughing as she turned back into the crowd that watched the training session and then she chortled when she heard someone shout. Glancing back over her shoulder, she could see the rude soldier had somehow thrust his spear tip right through the top of his foot, pinning it to the ground.

Unsure of where to find Ajelbal, Satal wandered through the city, which had grown tremendously since she had lived there as a child. She found the steam baths and thought of joining the long line waiting to bathe, but was loath to put her clothes or small bag of cacao beans anywhere that someone might find them. The last thing she needed was to have her few possessions stolen. She followed the numerous narrow sacbés that crisscrossed the city, past the great ball court where men battled to be the first to send a rubber ball through a stone hoop set high on the ball court wall, and stopped at the *tzompantli*. The stone wall was higher than her head and carved with a repeating pattern of human skulls. This was where the heads of those who lost the ball game and any other sacrificial victims were impaled on spikes and displayed for all to see.

Satal ran her finger along the carvings in the stone, tracing the shapes of human skulls, and the bas-relief jaguars and eagles that pecked at them, as she slowly wandered along the length of the tzompantli. *Looks like they need some new sacrifices*, Satal thought as she paused and watched a few vultures jab at the heads that still contained flesh. Most of the spikes were filled with skulls, baked white from the hot sun high overhead.

She saw the start of the large sacbé that stretched toward the sacred cenote where the ceremonial sacrifices to the rain god, Chac, were performed, but knew from her childhood that there were no buildings in that area, just the sinkhole where so many had been put to death. There was another, slightly smaller cenote in another part of the city, which was used as its water source. A third sinkhole, the smallest of the three, was adjacent to the *Akab Dzib*, or Red House, the building where the shamans trained in the mysterious arts of reading the stars and planets, foretelling the future, and interpreting the signs given to them by the gods in their spiritual trances. Eventually, she found herself near a building that had still been under construction when she'd been stolen from the city by Q'alel. It was covered with intricate geometric stonework on each façade along with multiple images of the rain god, Chac, whose curled large stone nose protruded a foot or more beyond the walls and corners of the building. Many people, old and young, hurried in and out of the numerous stone doorways, and Satal ran to catch up to one young man before he entered.

She managed to grab the strap of a leather satchel he wore over his shoulder just before he disappeared into the shadowy interior. "I'm trying to find someone," she said as the man turned around. "He's an old friend, but I've been gone for many years and don't know where he lives anymore or even if he's still alive."

She watched the man sigh and glance quickly at the sky, as if checking the time of day by the angle of the sun. "Name?"

"Mine or his?"

"This friend of yours, of course," the man replied impatiently.

"Ajelbal, he's a flutist, or was," Satal said.

"Never heard of him, sorry," the man said, then glancing once again at the sky, he hurried inside.

"Wait," Satal cried. "Where do I go to find him?"

"You've come to the right place," a stranger said as he brushed past Satal. "All the people of the city are registered here; go on inside and speak to the man in the first room to your left. Give him the details and he'll be able to help you."

"Maltiox," Satal said as she watched the man walk away.

After giving the older man every detail she could remember about Ajelbal, including her own name and the date of their wedding day, Satal returned to the outside. The clerk had said it might take weeks to locate the correct files since so many years had passed.

Discouraged, Satal headed back into the city proper to find some food and a place to rest. She was determined to get answers within days, not weeks, and decided the best course of action would be to return to the Hall of the Thousand Columns. It was where Ajelbal had spent so much of his time; surely, someone there would remember her old lover.

She spotted Kämisanel still standing in the shade of the hall. But this time, he was not surrounded by a group of men. The training exercise had ended for the day, and most people had left the area in search of food and a good night's rest. As she approached the man, she could hear the beating of a lone drum as someone practiced a rhythm. Then she spotted a young boy seated near Kämisanel. He appeared to be offering advice to the youth, who continued to tap the small hide-covered log that he held between his knees. His drumming quickened, and Kämisanel nodded and smiled.

"Good," Satal heard him say. "That's the pace we want when we march into battle, a quick-fire beat to let our enemies know we're coming."

He turned when Satal stepped up next to him. "Who are you and what are you doing here?" He frowned at Satal, then nodded to the boy, who quickly picked up his drum and ran off.

Satal glared at Kämisanel. "My name is Satal; I used to be a citizen of this city, many, many moons ago, until I was stolen by the Cocom of Mayapán. My husband-to-be used to play the flute for the regiment. I'm trying to locate him and also need help in retaliating against the Cocom."

"We haven't had any raids by the Cocom for years. Why should we attack now, simply because you say so? I doubt the council will listen to the demands of an old woman," Kämisanel said as he started to walk away.

"Stop!" Satal ordered, but had to hurry after Kämisanel when he refused to. She grabbed him by his left arm, forcing him to slow his pace.

He shrugged off her hand. "I don't know who you think you are," he said as he brushed at the leather armband where she had touched him, "but you'd better run along now, before I grow angry."

"I was a member of the council in Mayapán," Satal said as she stepped in front of Kämisanel. "People obeyed my orders without hesitation."

"Well, you're in Chichén Itzá now," Kämisanel said, "where people usually obey *my* orders. And I'm telling you to go away or face the consequences."

"Ha!" Satal said with a snort of laughter. "As if anything you could do to me would harm me. I'll give you until tomorrow to reconsider what I've been saying, but when I return in the morning, I shall expect you to be ready to call your men to arms and wage war on Mayapán." She turned her back on the warrior and marched off to find a safe place to spend the night.

Outside the city proper, she found a small ceiba tree growing out of a bunch of thorny bushes and spent the night tucked under the leaves and branches, her back firmly against the base of the tree. The next morning, Satal brushed dirt off her clothes before eating the last tamale in her possession. She drank a bit of water to wash it down, and used the last few drops to wash her face and hands. She knew she needed a bath and new clothes, but there was time enough for all that once she had convinced Kämisanel that he should attack Mayapán. She pushed through the throngs of people headed to work and to the market as she made her way back to the plaza in front of the Hall of the Thousand Columns.

"You, back again?" Kämisanel said as she approached. He was seated on the grass, and several other men formed a semi-circle around him. Spread on a blanket among the men were several ledgers filled with glyphs and drawings showing various warriors in conflict with others, slashing at each other with knives, which dripped blood onto the steps of a temple similar to the one that stood behind them.

"Didn't I warn you not to come back?" Kämisanel said as he and the other warriors stood up. He adjusted his leather loincloth and the one quetzal feather that was stuck in his shoulder-length black hair.

"Have you considered my demand?" Satal said.

"Demand, what demand, who is this woman?" one of the other men said as he turned to Kämisanel.

"She claims to have been on the council in Mayapán," Kämisanel replied.

"Hard to believe, considering the rags she's wearing."

"She says we must attack the city, to extract revenge from those who have wronged her."

Satal glanced from man to man; none of them appeared to take her request seriously. "It's too bad news of my powers have never travelled this far to the east," she said.

"Humph, as if you could even hurt a fly," Kämisanel said. He and the others laughed. "Go on now, we have work to do." He nodded to his friends and they began to sit down again.

Satal glared at the men, but they continued to ignore her.

"Leave them for now, Satal," Sachoj whispered in her ear. "Come back tomorrow, when they've had time to consider your suggestion."

Thoroughly disgusted with the men's treatment of her, Satal walked quickly away. She fingered the small pouch that hung around her neck and contemplated buying the necessary supplies to perform a small curse on them. But she was reluctant to part with any more beans since she had so few left. She wandered aimlessly throughout the city, jostled by the crowds that moved from place to place, and finally decided to return to her little spot under the ceiba tree outside the city proper.

Every day Satal returned to talk to Kämisanel, and every day he sent her away, without acknowledging her requests for retribution. Reluctantly, Satal spent more cacao beans to purchase food, and due to the extreme heat, she bought a second water gourd. The lines at the large cenote were long, and she spent hours waiting her turn to fill her two gourds. Satal's irritation at being denied what she wanted grew and grew as Kämisanel and the others in charge continuously dismissed her whenever she approached the training ground. *There must be another way to convince them of my powers,* she thought as she pushed her way through the multitudes of people moving about the city. She had only two cacao beans left, but didn't want to spend them on yet more food, even though her stomach cramped as she caught whiffs of roasting meats and spicy soups as she walked past the large market. Wishing to find some privacy in the vast crowd, she stepped onto the sacbé that lead to the sacred cenote, which lay a thousand paces or more to the north of the city center. She knew no one used the pathway unless a sacrificial ceremony was to take place. But the white limestone avenue had hundreds of people on it, who were busy setting up a variety of cotton tarps and blankets along the sides of the causeway.

She tugged on the sleeve of a young woman who was spreading a green blanket on the ground. "What are you preparing for?" she asked.

"Why the sacrifices tomorrow, of course," the woman replied. "We want a good seat to see the volunteers as they pass by."

With a quick grin and a mumbled thank you, Satal turned away from the young woman. She knew how to convince Kämisanel and the other members of the council that they needed to listen to her and to respect her abilities.

She hurried back to the Hall of the Thousand Columns.

Kämisanel groaned when he saw her. "Itzamná, you can't take a hint, can you!"

"I want to be a sacrifice in tomorrow's ceremony," Satal said.

Kämisanel laughed. "You're too late. They've already been chosen, selected from those who were captured in local raids, and a few volunteers from the elite houses of the city."

"Just tell me where to go to prepare," Satal said. She stared straight into Kämisanel's face, forcing him to look at her. She could feel his eyes moving slowly over her body from head to toe, finally taking in details that he had overlooked before. Despite the ragged clothes she wore and the dirt on her face and body, there was no way to hide her tattered earlobes, scarred tongue, or the noble lines of her nose and cheeks.

"The Akab Dzib," Kämisanel said, as he pointed in the direction of the building. "The shamans there will carry out the purification ceremony on you." He stood up and looked closely at Satal's scarred face. "You're sure you want to do this? What about finding that friend of yours, what was his name, Ajelbal?"

"I have people searching the city records for him, but I suspect he died many years ago," Satal said. "I'll see you after the sacrifices." Kämisanel and the other men shook their heads, and Satal grinned as she turned and left.

The Akab Dzib or shaman's temple was built on a large stone platform that rose twenty feet in the air, and Satal climbed the steep steps that lead to the three entranceways. She nodded to a young boy who sat near the middle doorway, playing a melancholy tune on a small bamboo flute. Inside, the walls were painted a deep blood red and carved with numerous glyphs. A tall, older shaman dressed in a leather loincloth and jaguar skin cape hurried to Satal's side.

"You mustn't be here," he said. "No visitors are allowed to see the sacrifices as they prepare to enter the Underworld in tribute to the rain god, Chac."

"I'm not here to see anyone; I'm here to volunteer," Satal said.

"But the ceremony is tomorrow," the man said. "The others have been honored for a week or more; they've been fed lavish meals, given the finest clothes to wear, and are mentally prepared to join Itzamná, Chac, and the other gods."

"I'm ready," Satal said, "more than ready."

The thin old man shook his head. "It's most unusual to have a volunteer arrive this late, but if you're certain, my friend, then I can't say no. I admire your desire to help the city with this great sacrifice. We will be assured of bountiful rains and a great harvest in the fall." He held out his arm, and Satal slipped her hand through the crook of his elbow.

"Tonight, we'll bathe you in jasmine-scented waters and give you a long massage, like the others. Then, at first light, we'll adorn you with ceremonial paint and the gold jewelry you shall carry to the sacred cenote."

"Perfect." Satal laughed. She could hardly wait for the festivities to begin.

NA'OM

A thousand thoughts raced through Na'om's mind as she ran toward the flickering light with Ek' Balam by her side. *I can't believe we survived all the tests . . . . I need water and food and a bath . . . I can't wait to see Ati't and Tz' and go back to the village . . . .* The light flashed and sparked in the distance, a tiny spot of hope that grew larger with every step they took.

Then, all of a sudden, it vanished. Na'om was plunged into impenetrable darkness again, and she stopped abruptly. "No!" she cried. "What happened, where did the light go?" She felt all her optimism slide away as tears rolled down her cheeks. She sensed Ek' Balam next to her and touched his back, and she immediately could see her surroundings through the haze their combined spirits created. She peered into the blackness, praying to Itzamná that the glow would return, that it hadn't been a figment of her imagination. "Or worse," she said out loud. She wondered if the traces of light had been just another test by the gods of the Underworld, encouraging her to believe she had survived her ordeal.

Na'om leaned against the rocky wall and forced herself to take several deep breaths. She hastily wiped away her remaining tears and wiped her hands on her dirt-encrusted skirt. Wearily, she plodded ahead, touching Ek' Balam ever so gently on the top of his head as the tunnel continued in a straight line for several hundred feet.

Then, just as suddenly as it had vanished, the light reappeared, bigger and brighter than ever. It glowed and twinkled with an eerie greenish-blue light, but Na'om shouted with joy at the sight of it.

She ran, determined to find the source of the glow before it had a chance to disappear again. *Perhaps someone is walking in this very tunnel, carrying some kind of light,* Na'om thought as she hurried along. But the light remained fixed in one spot and grew ever larger the closer Na'om got to it.

She dashed ahead and staggered into a large cavern. The source of the light was a fire built in the center of the cave, surrounded by a two-foot wall of rocks and stones. Na'om ran to the flames to warm herself. She held out her hands, but the fire produced no heat, just wavering blue-green flickers of light.

"Ah, you've arrived, wonderful," a voice said and Na'om whirled around to see who had spoken. There was movement in the shadows and Ek' Balam growled as something approached.

"Who are you, what do you want?" Na'om cried out as she gripped the nape of Ek' Balam's neck.

There were more movements in the shadows, and Ek' Balam backed up, growling deeply as he moved toward the tunnel again.

"Please, have a seat," the voice said as the owner stepped into the circle of light cast by the fire.

Na'om gasped. A skeleton with bulging eyes stood before her. Scraps of fabric hung off the ancient bones, and a headdress of tattered and filthy feathers sat on its bare skull. The skeleton was pointing one bony finger toward a seat carved into the nearby rocks. Na'om took two steps away from the creature, but was afraid to turn her back on it so she could run with Ek' Balam back the way they had come.

"She's going to run, I told you she would," another voice said, and another talking skeleton stepped into the dim glow sent out by the fire. Then a third and a fourth skeleton, both shorter than the first two, appeared from the shadows. They also had eyes that protruded from their death-white skulls and shreds of clothing hanging from their limbs.

"She can't go back," the four skeletons whispered in unison.

A tiny breeze of cool air brushed across Na'om's back and shoulders, and she turned around, fearful something had touched her, and was horrified to see that the tunnel she had traveled through was now gone. Only a rough rocky wall confronted her.

"NO!" she cried as she ran to the barrier and tore at the rocks with her hands.

"It's no use, Na'om, that path has closed forever," the leader of the skeletons said. "Come now, sit with us; it's been so long since we've had any visitors." He pointed his bony finger to the seat near Na'om as he sank into one himself. The other three skeletons climbed onto chairs, too, and waited patiently for Na'om.

With extreme reluctance, keeping her back to the wall, Na'om edged toward the nearest stone chair, her hand still steady on Ek' Balam. She sank down onto the rough rock, only to leap up in an instant. The chair was burning hot, although it was nowhere near the fire.

"Ha, ha, ha, good one," the skeletons chuckled to each other. They slapped each other on the clavicles, and their bones rattled from skulls to toes.

Na'om felt a deep anger forming in her belly. She was cold, tired, hungry, and just wanted to get home to the ones she loved. "Who are you and what do you want?" Na'om demanded.

"Oh ho, One Death, she sounds upset," one skeleton said as he poked a bony finger in the rib cage of the first skeleton who had appeared.

"Quiet, Seven Death, let me handle this," One Death replied. "We are some of the lords of the Underworld; there are others, but they're busy with various tasks elsewhere." He gestured around the large cavern. "This is our home, and we want you to share it with us."

Na'om glanced around the large cave. The ceiling was high overhead, and Na'om shuddered when she realized it was filled with bats, which clung to the hundreds of small stalactites that studded the rough limestone. "I would rather die than live here with any of you," Na'om said as she stood up and backed away from the horrible talking skeleton.

She held tightly to Ek' Balam, closed her eyes, and concentrated on envisioning the blue sky and green leaves of the many trees that grew along the riverbanks near Pa nimá. She felt a tingling in her hands and feet and pushed outward, forcing a circle of white light to appear around them.

"Look, look," Seven Death said excitedly, "it's just as Satal said, she can project her energy outward."

"Quiet, idiot," One Death said as he hit Seven Death in the jaw. A loose tooth tumbled from Seven Death's mouth and landed with a plop in the dirt at his feet.

"Ow, that hurt," Seven Death said as he bent down, picked up the tooth, and shoved it back in his mouth.

Na'om opened her eyes as she held the protective light around them. "Satal, what do you know of Satal?" she demanded.

"See what you've done," One Death hissed, and he smacked Seven Death again. This time, Seven Death's tooth went flying, and was lost in the darkness beyond the firelight. "Now keep quiet, all of you." One Death picked a piece of rotten fabric off his elbow and threw it into the fire where it hissed and sparked, before he turned back to Na'om.

"Satal is a dear friend of ours, of all the lords of Xibalba, actually. We've been helping her for years in all her various endeavors, but most of all in her quest to find you. She knows, as we all do, that if your power is combined with hers, there'll be no one to stop her from ruling Mayapán and the rest of the Mayan world any way she wants."

Na'om grinned at One Death. "Well, I guess you haven't heard the news; Satal is dead. She fell into the cenote just as I did and drowned."

The three skeletons snickered, but stopped when One Death glared at them.

"Ah, dear, sweet, innocent Na'om," One Death said. "I'm afraid you're the one who hasn't heard the news. Satal is alive and more importantly, above ground, where she continues to hurt those who attempt to stand in her way, including your father, Yakal, and all the remaining residents of Pa nimá."

Shocked at the news, Na'om lost her concentration and her protective light flickered and went out. "No, that's not possible, I saw her sink to the bottom of the cenote with my own eyes," Na'om cried.

"Ah, but what you didn't see is what matters. With help from all of us, including her favorite Xibalba god, Camazotz, Satal managed to escape drowning and now wreaks havoc everywhere," One Death said. He plucked another scrap of cloth off his right kneecap and threw it away. "So, you see, you really should just remain here with us."

"Yes, stay, Na'om," Seven Death pleaded and the others chimed in as well.

Biting her lip, Na'om pushed with all her might, and a rapid burst of white light blasted out from around her body and hit Seven Death in the ribs. He exploded into a hundred pieces of bone, and his skull landed upside down several feet from his toes.

The bats overhead swooped about the cave as One Death and the other two skeletons jumped to their feet and ran deeper into the cave. But Na'om launched another jolt of energy toward them and caught the two shorter skeletons in the back. They blew into several pieces, their bones crisscrossing with one another as they landed in a jumble among the rocks and stones.

One Death crouched behind a large boulder and held up a bony hand. "Wait, stop, before you hit me, let me say something."

"Speak then," Na'om said as she watched the shadows for any sign of movement. She lurched to one side as bats flitted back and forth in front of her, and she heard Ek' Balam smack one with his big paw. It landed with a thud in the dust, and she turned her head away as Ek' Balam swallowed the bat whole.

"The only way out of this maze of tunnels is to continue through the trials we've set before you," One Death said. He pointed with his index finger toward an opening in the cave wall. "There's the tunnel you must take," he said. "If you survive the tests, you'll eventually reach your world again."

"Why should I trust you?" Na'om cried as she dodged another bat. "Maybe this is just another one of your tricks." She heard a clicking sound and watched as the bones of Seven Death crawled toward one another.

"If you won't stay here with us, then we want you to reach the world of the living," One Death said. He lowered his voice and added, "So Satal can find you once again."

Ignoring the talking skeleton while keeping her eyes on the other sets of bones that were beginning to reform into bodies, Na'om decided she had to leave while she had the chance. She sent another bolt of light toward One Death, then wrapped the energy around her body and that of Ek' Balam, and ran toward the tunnel One Death had shown her. Together, the two hurried into the darkness, and the clacking and scuttling of bones on bones echoed in Na'om's ears as she ran.

They rounded numerous corners and could see no sign of any light or hear any sounds of bats or skeletons coming after them when Na'om finally stopped to catch her breath. Ek' Balam sat on the ground and began to lick his front paw. Na'om rested beside him and realized that she could see in the darkness without touching Ek' Balam. *I must be getting used to this constant gloom,* she thought as she looked around. The tunnel was narrow and tall, but the ceiling was too far overhead to see. *I hope there aren't any more bats in here.* Even as she thought this, there was a rustling sound in the darkness, and then a river of bats whooshed down the tunnel from the direction they had just come from. Na'om flattened herself to the ground as the mass of flying mammals poured over their heads and continued past them. She saw Ek' Balam swat the air with his big paws and heard several bodies thud to the ground. She turned her head away as he crunched on the bones, sending bits of leathery wings in different directions as he ripped into the still warm bats.

"Ugh, how can you eat those?" Na'om said, and she shivered at the gruesome thought. But her stomach cramped at the idea of food, and she bent over double with the pain. Ek' Balam picked up a bat, pulled off the two wings, and plopped the lifeless, fur-covered body in front of Na'om. It was small, about the size of the mice that Tz' caught in traps for his pet tayra, Chac. Na'om swallowed several times, debating whether she should eat it or not. Ek' Balam pushed the bat toward her with his paw and stood waiting.

"All right, all right, I'll eat it, just give me a minute," she said. She closed her eyes, picked up the bat, and bit into the furry animal. Soft fuzz stuck to her tongue and she spit the bite out. Then, as the taste of warm flesh lingered in her mouth, she bit into the bat again. She chewed rapidly and swallowed, then bit again and again until the bat was gone. "That was disgusting," she said as she picked some fur out from between her teeth. She crinkled her nose and wondered if she'd vomit. But she quickly noticed the pain in her stomach was gone, and she felt stronger than she had before. Ek' Balam tossed her another bat, and she reluctantly ate that one as well.

As the energy of food pulsed through her veins, Na'om's mind grew clearer and calmer. "Itzamná!" Na'om exclaimed as a sudden thought appeared. "If the bats flew from behind us, then that means there must be an exit to the surface somewhere in front of us! Come on, boy, we have to follow those bats!"

Eager now to find her way out of the maze of tunnels, Na'om skipped along, oblivious to the darkness. It was only when she stopped to catch her breath that she grasped the air was growing colder by the minute. Fierce winds blew from every angle, which whipped her ragged shirt and skirt about her body. She felt stinging pellets hit her body, as if handfuls of tiny rocks were being thrown at her from all sides, and when she caught some in her hand, they were colder than anything she had ever touched. Her fingertips ached, and her feet stuck to the ground. Each step was strained as she yanked her foot free from the increasing bitterness that clutched at her toes and bare soles. Na'om shivered and quaked as the iciness pressed deeper and deeper into her body. It was too cold to move, too cold to think, and Na'om slowly sank down onto the ground, where a blanket of wet flakes and knobby pellets rained down and covered her.

Feebly, Na'om clasped her necklace and called to her mother, but there was no answer. She felt Ek' Balam lie down next to her, his warm body pressed tightly against her back. "Itzamná, I've never been so cold before," she cried, and the tears hardened in the corners of her eyes. Still holding the necklace, Na'om tried to picture a warm fire, mugs full of hot cacao, a bowl of Ajkun's turkey stew, but the images didn't push the iciness away. "Ati't, help me," Na'om cried. "I'm so cold, Ati't, so cold," Na'om muttered. "I can't feel my feet anymore and my legs burn with the pain. I need your help, Ati't. I'm just so cold. Help me."

Na'om thought she heard voices, but it could have been the fierce wind. She closed her eyes and drifted into blackness as the sudden storm continued to rage all around her.

AJKUN

The steady drumbeat signaling the changing of the guards woke Ajkun from a deep sleep on her mat in the corner of the hut. She looked around, unsure for a moment where she was; then she sighed as she realized she was still in Mayapán. Instantly, Na'om's death flooded her mind, as it had every day for the past few weeks, and Ajkun felt her heart cramp in grief at the loss of her granddaughter. She stuffed the corner of her shawl into her mouth to stifle her sobs and awkwardly got to her knees, then used a wooden brace in the wall of Alom's hut to pull herself up. With a deep-seated pain in her arthritic knee, she hobbled outside in the early light and wrapped her shawl tight around her body as the cool morning air blew through the small courtyard.

Ajkun shivered as snatches of dreams floated into her consciousness. *It was so dark and cold in that awful place,* she thought as she poked at the fire ring, but there were no live embers buried in the ash. "Later, Alom can light the fire again," Ajkun muttered out loud. A chill ran up and down her spine, and she crouched by the ring of rocks as if they might hold some residual heat. *It was dark, darker than night without the moon, and that stiff wind, like before a storm, and the bitter cold that surrounded me, sinking deep into my bones, sucking the energy from my very heart and soul....* Ajkun's thoughts drifted as she tried to remember more details.

Something or someone was there with me in that horrible spot . . . Na'om, yes, Na'om was there. "Na'om," Ajkun said. "And that cat of hers, too, they were both there." She needed to talk to Chiman as soon as possible and ask him what the dream might mean.

Another icy ripple went through her body, and Ajkun returned to the relative warmth of the hut and her one cotton blanket. Inside, the walls blocked the slight breeze that continued to snatch away her body heat. She shuddered as she lay down on the cool ground, but quickly drifted into a deep sleep once again.

Instantly, she was thrust back into the same dream, lost in a whirlwind of swirling wet flakes that blew about like pieces of ash and burned with a biting cold that stung her bare skin. She sensed Na'om and Ek' Balam were nearby and called out to them. "Na'om, are you there, can you hear me?" Her voice was sucked away by the wind. "Na'om?" Ajkun trembled from head to toe. She needed to find her granddaughter. "Na'om," she yelled again.

"Ati't? Is that you?" she heard a voice say.

"Yes, yes, it's me, Na'om, it's me. Where are you?" Ajkun cried as she frantically searched the darkness with her hands.

"I'm so cold, Ati't, so cold," Na'om muttered. "I can't feel my feet anymore and my legs burn with the pain. I need your help, Ati't. I'm just so cold. Help me."

"So cold, so cold," echoed Ajkun.

A hand shook her gently on the shoulder, and Ajkun opened her eyes to see Alom kneeling beside her.

"Are you all right, my friend?" Alom asked. "You were talking in your sleep. Look, I've brought you another blanket," she said as she tucked another cotton blanket around Ajkun's shoulders.

"Maltiox, Alom," Ajkun said as she looked up into the woman's lined face. "I'm sorry if I woke you." She smiled as she pulled the blankets closer around her prone body. "I'm getting old," she said. "I used to be able to adjust to the weather with no problems; now I'm chilly with the slightest shift in the wind or temperature, and my bones ache all day long."

Alom smiled and sat down next to her new friend, her back propped against the wall. "You're not alone. I feel the same way. Once the sun is up, I'll light the fire and make us something hot to drink and eat." She pulled her long skirt around her bare legs, tucking the fabric up and under her thighs. Her bare feet were still exposed, so she wriggled her toes underneath the edge of Ajkun's blankets. "Rest now; I'll wake you when it's time for breakfast."

Ajkun nodded, pulled her shawl tighter around her head, and drifted off to sleep.

She was thrust back into the swirling cold, which gripped her with icy fingers that probed deep into her core. Blind in the darkness, Ajkun struggled to stand against the fierce winds that blew from every angle. She fought to hold her shirt down, and her skirt billowed up, exposing her thighs to the bitter wind. Tears formed in the corners of her eyes and turned into crystals. She inched forward, groping with outstretched hands to feel her surroundings. The wall to her left was slick and smooth and too cold to touch. The ground underfoot was hard and burned her bare soles with its iciness. She wandered slowly, moving inch by inch toward what she didn't know. But she had to keep moving; otherwise, her limbs would freeze solid. The wind shrieked and howled, and she imagined the sounds were the voices of lost spirits, trapped in this nightmare with her.

She heard a voice in the distance, but couldn't understand what it was saying. "Na'om, is that you?" she called. More indistinguishable sounds churned all around her, but Ajkun had no strength left to say anything. All she could do was clutch her shawl more tightly around her head and shoulders and shiver in the blackness. She felt pressure on her shoulder, a gentle shaking, but was too tired to open her eyes.

Above the din of the storm, she heard footsteps receding, then sometime later, more sounds, voices, then felt a gentle rocking to and fro and suddenly, more rapid shaking, but still she couldn't open her eyes against the cold winds that blasted her from every direction. She felt her body rising into the air and clutched at the rocky ground, but grasped only air. Supported by her shoulders and feet, Ajkun felt her body sway in open space as she was lifted free of the cold dirt and then gently laid back down on soil that was warm to the touch. She curled into a tight ball to shield that heat, but the bitter cold in her bones leached into the warmth, smothering it out of existence. There came more indistinct voices and sounds, a sudden weight over the length of her entire body, then another, and yet another. And still Ajkun shivered and shook with frigidness, and she knew this must be the touch of death, for nothing in life had ever felt so desperate and lonely.

Exhausted from her battle against the storm, she sank deeper into the ground, curled on her side. Hours passed as she drifted in limbo, unafraid now of the cold and the dark. She waited for the gods to claim her body, to release her soul into the Underworld. She wasn't sad to leave for she knew she would soon be reunited with her daughter, Tu'janel, dead so many years after the birth of Na'om. *Na'om,* Ajkun thought, *soon I'll be with my sweet granddaughter, Na'om.* But the thought of Na'om brought back the thought of Satal, and she felt the harsh plant of hate inside her heart sprout new leaves as it whipped about in the fierce winds and biting cold. She yearned to face the witch in the Underworld and make her suffer, gladly sacrificing her own life for the pleasure of doing Satal harm.

She felt hard objects pressing into her spine, into her belly, and shifted to avoid them, but everywhere she moved, she felt them tucked up against the length of her body. She gave up and lay still and gradually felt an odd warmth seeping into her skin from these solid items that surrounded her from head to toe. She shivered and groaned as the heat worked its way deeper and deeper into her body, and she felt terrible pain in her fingers and feet as heated blood flowed through her veins, bringing life and passion to her core. She flexed her arms and legs, felt the rocky ground underneath her hip and shoulder, and turned onto her back under the heavy weights that covered her.

Brilliant light and intense warmth on her face forced her to clench her eyes shut tight, and the heat drove the last of the blinding cold from her mind and body. Ajkun raised an arm to shield her eyes and cautiously opened them.

She was outside, in the sun, under a pile of blankets that threatened to topple over into the roaring fire that burned brightly in the fire ring. She pushed herself up onto her elbows and shoved the blankets to one side. Large objects wrapped in deerskin lined her entire body.

"Welcome back," a familiar voice said, and Ajkun looked up to see Chiman hurrying to her side.

"What do you mean, what happened?" Ajkun said as she looked deep into Chiman's eyes. *He looks like he hasn't slept for days,* she thought as she sat up higher near the fire. It felt good to have the blast of heat on her face and bare arms, but she shivered as thoughts of that terribly cold place flooded her mind. "How long have I been out here?" She rubbed her eyes with one hand and ran the other through her matted hair. Every bone and joint in her body ached.

"Four days," Chiman said as he picked up one of the hard objects wrapped in deerskin. He unfolded the hide and removed the large rock that lay inside. "Alom couldn't wake you the other day, so she came to find me. Yakal and I moved you outside, to the fire, and I've been placing hot rocks all around your body to try and break the chill that encased you. You were so cold to the touch that we thought you might have joined the ancestors." He had a large pile of rocks in front of him by now and began to move them one by one to the edge of the courtyard.

Ajkun watched in silence as he worked and patted the blankets when he was done. Chiman sat next to her and wrapped his arm around her shoulder.

"You kept calling out for Na'om," he said. "I know you miss her deeply, as do I and all the others, but you must accept that she's gone."

Ajkun nodded her head, then looked down at the ground as she felt tears welling in her eyes. "She was there, in that same place. She called out for my help and that's when the bitter cold really crushed me. I was afraid I had met my death there." She wiped away her tears with the back of her hand. "Maltiox, Chiman, for taking care of me through all this."

"That's what old friends are for," Chiman said as he gently squeezed her in a hug before letting go. "When you feel up to it, I want to hear more about this place you were trapped in. Perhaps the shamans here in Mayapán will know what it means."

Ajkun looked around the small courtyard. "Where's Alom?"

"She's with Uskab at the market, buying some clothes for the baby."

Ajkun laughed. "When that child arrives, he'll have more clothes than all of us combined," Ajkun said as she struggled to stand. Chiman gave her a helping hand. "Ah, it feels so good to stretch and bend. In that place, I was so stiff with cold I couldn't move." Ajkun bent her knees a few times and shrugged her shoulders, loosening up her joints after being on the hard ground.

"Do you feel well enough to walk to the market for a bowl of soup?" Chiman asked. "Or should I bring you something?"

Ajkun patted his bare forearm with her hand. "I think I can make it, if you walk with me." She smiled. "I can tell you about that horrible black place on the way." She wrapped her shawl around her head, despite the sun beating down on them, and shivered as the breeze picked up, blowing bits of dust about in a tiny whirlwind. "I'm not sure I'll ever feel fully warm again," she said as a ripple of cold trailed up her spine.

Arm in arm, the two old friends made their way slowly through the city streets, Ajkun leaning on Chiman as much for emotional support as physical strength. "I don't know what I'd do without you," Ajkun said as Chiman helped her sit on a tall stool at one of the many food booths on the outer edge of the market. He patted her arm and ordered them two bowls of soup. She sipped at the hot turtle stew filled with bite-sized pieces of meat, chili peppers, and garlic. She reached for a small plate of cut limes, squeezed one into her soup, and added a pinch of salt from the ceramic bowl in front of her, which she stirred into the broth.

"Feeling better?" Chiman asked. He slurped the last drops of broth from his bowl and pushed it toward the woman behind the counter, who placed the dirty dish in a tottering stack beside a large bowl of soapy water.

"I'm not hungry anymore, if that's what you mean," Ajkun replied as she pushed her half-empty bowl toward Chiman. "Go ahead and finish it if you want. I've had enough." He nodded and started to eat. Ajkun watched him for a few seconds, but felt her gaze glaze over as images of that terrible black void filled her mind. She shook her head to clear it and concentrated on Chiman again. "If Na'om was in that place, does that mean she's still alive?"

Chiman swiped his mouth with the back of his hand. "I think it was just a terrible dream you had, and if it is real, then I have my doubts." Then he saw the anguish on Ajkun's face and tenderly wiped away the tears forming in her eyes. "I'm sorry, I shouldn't be so abrupt." He stood up and offered Ajkun his arm again. "Come; let's get you back so you can rest. And once you're settled, I'll go speak to the shamans here in the city. Maybe they'll have a better sense of what that place was and whether it's possible to live through it. But if I'm to be completely honest, I don't see how anyone could from what you've described."

Ajkun nodded and allowed Chiman to lead her back to Alom's hut. In her heart, she knew Chiman was probably right. How could anyone, even someone with special talents like Na'om, survive the bitter cold and winds of that awful place?

Na'om

As she lay under the increasing weight of the intense blanket of cold, Na'om thought she heard the voices of Chiman and Ajkun, but the shrieking winds made it impossible to understand what they were saying. Hours or maybe days passed as she huddled on the ground, shivering from head to toe. She had no idea where the sun might be in the sky, or how long she had been underground, but she did feel the presence of Ajkun nearby and quickly conjured up images of her. She pictured herself as a young girl, sitting on her grandmother's lap by the fire outside the little hut they shared in Pa nimá, and heard Ajkun's soothing voice as she quietly told Na'om one of the many stories from the *Popol Vuh*. She nestled deeper into Ajkun's chest, the smell of herbs and spices redolent on her clothes and skin, as she explained to Na'om how the Hero Twins, Hunahpu and Xbalanque, had defeated the evil lords of Xibalba. The drone of Ajkun's voice lulled Na'om toward sleep, and she closed her eyes, drifting deeper into unconsciousness.

Then, ever so slowly, tiny tendrils of warmth began to break through the dense layers of cold that had sunk deep into Na'om's bones. She shifted on the rough ground, feeling Ek' Balam's warm body still pressed against her own, and snuggled closer to him, curling deeper into his furry chest. The warmth gradually spread, awakening Na'om's desire to live. She sensed more voices and vague shapes in the black shadows, but couldn't make out who or what they were. The only thing that mattered was the flicker of heat that pressed in on her from all sides, driving the cold farther and farther away.

Eventually, Na'om could feel warmth in her fingers and toes, and she stretched again. She opened her eyes and dimly saw Ek' Balam patiently sitting by her side. He came over and sniffed her, then licked her face with his rough tongue when she sat up. The air was cool, but no more so than an early spring morning in Pa nimá when the river water was warmer than the air, creating a layer of fog that hovered above the ground.

"We survived another test," Na'om said as she rubbed Ek' Balam behind his ear. "One Death said there were several ahead of us, so I doubt we're through the worst of it." She sighed. "I should've paid more attention to Ati't when she used to tell me stories about Xibalba, then I'd know what I still have to face." Na'om sat still for quite a while, trying to remember any details from the tales she'd heard so often as a child, but her mind was blank.

Tired and hungry, she curled back up on the ground and instantly fell asleep. She dreamt of playing in the sunshine with Tz', the one friend who had always stood by her, even when the other children in the village had avoided her. Giggling and laughing, they spun around and around, arms outstretched, until they were unable to stand and fell over in a heap on the ground.

Blackness confronted Na'om when she finally opened her eyes. Realizing she was still deep underground, her heart cramped at the thought of never seeing Tz' again. And she suddenly knew she was in love with him and had been for a very long time.

Perhaps I should have let him make love to me that night when he came to me, she thought. *If I had, none of this might have happened.* But she could see that moment so clearly in her mind and how angry she had been at his attempts to push her down on her ceiba-filled mattress, without asking her if that was what she wanted. *Yes, he declared his love for me that night, but then he implied I had already had relations with the other boys in the village.* The more she thought about that moment, the angrier she grew. *I know I was right in refusing him; when we do make love, and we will, it will be on my terms, not his!* Her anger fueled her to stand and continue forward into the darkness with Ek' Balam resolutely by her side. But as quickly as her ire rose, it fell, and she once more yearned to see Tz'. *I have to get back to Pa nimá and tell Tz' that I love him; then we can move forward with our lives as one.* Determination forced Na'om forward, one slow step at a time. *It doesn't matter what those stupid skeletons have planned for me, I'll get through their tests and find my way home.*

Na'om trailed her right hand along the tunnel wall as she walked. She liked feeling the rocky surface beneath her fingertips, as it made her feel connected to something in the endless dark. At one point, she noticed the wall was wet; tiny rivulets of fluid had seeped through the porous surface and run to the tunnel floor. She stopped and held her hand under one section and managed to collect the liquid in the palm of her hand. She sniffed it, then touched it with just the tip of her tongue. It was water, sweet and refreshing water. Na'om laughed with joy.

"Drink up," she said to Ek' Balam, but he was already lapping at the puddle that had collected on the ground. She cupped both hands against the limestone and gathered small handfuls of the pure water. Nothing had ever tasted so good. When her stomach was full, Na'om washed her face in the precious droplets, wiping away layers of dried blood, dust, and dirt. *If only I could take a full bath in this,* she thought as she scrubbed at her arms a bit. But there was too much muck on her body to remove with the tiny amount of water that dribbled from the rock wall. *Perhaps I'm near another cenote,* Na'om thought. *That must be where this water is coming from, which means I may find a way out of here.*

Revived, the two set off again. Within minutes, Na'om felt the ground change underfoot. She sensed she was walking on sticks and twigs and bent down to examine the area. With her dim vision in the blackness, she was able to see the tunnel floor was scattered with white bones of all shapes and sizes. She touched Ek' Balam's back, enlarging her circle of sight, and she gasped as she saw what lay ahead. The bones grew more numerous and covered the tunnel floor in a deep layer of jagged and broken bits and pieces. Hundreds of rib cages and leg bones were tumbled among thousands of animal skulls that blanketed the tunnel as far as she could see.

"Itzamná, I've never so many skeletons in one place," she said as she held on to Ek' Balam. As they stepped forward together, she could feel

Ek' Balam's body tense up, and he stopped, his tail swishing from side to side. "What is it, boy? Do you see something?" They waited, but nothing happened. "Come on; we have to get through this," Na'om said as she started to wade through and over the jumble of bones.

Ek' Balam continued to swish his tail, and he emitted a low growl. He stopped again and sniffed at the nearest rib cage. Na'om bent down to look, trying to sense what was upsetting her companion. She tugged on a rib, and it pulled loose from the rest of them. Holding it close to her eyes, she could see deep grooves etched into the bone. She threw it aside and picked up a leg bone lying nearby. The end of it had obviously been gnawed on. It looked like many of the bones Ek' Balam left lying around the hut after one of his kills.

What could have killed and eaten this many animals, Na'om wondered. She looked back toward the direction they had come from, but despite her fears, she knew they had to keep moving forward. "Stay close, boy," she said as she touched Ek' Balam again.

With one hand on the wall to steady herself and the other on Ek' Balam, they clambered over the endless pile of bleached carcasses, which grew ever deeper as they progressed farther and farther into the tunnel. Ek' Balam continued to growl, a low rumble that echoed in the emptiness and frightened Na'om, since the last time she had seen him this upset had been the day of the attack on the village.

The going was difficult, and Na'om had to toss many bones aside so she could continue to stay connected to the limestone wall. As she paused to throw a large rib cage to one side, she caught a whiff of something odd. She stood up and inhaled deeply. *Smells like something rotten, something dead.* She gagged as the smell grew sharper the more they walked. Ripping off a strip of her skirt, she wrapped it over her nose and mouth to block the putrid scent that filled the tunnel.

Ek' Balam growled again, and Na'om felt him flatten himself close to the ground. She looked around quickly, desperate to see or hear what he sensed. Suddenly, something growled back, then there was another growl, and another, and Na'om leaned forward, straining to see. Two glowing yellow spots appeared in the gloom, then two more, and two more, until Na'om sensed an uncountable number of animals blocked their path. She let go of the wall, touched Ek' Balam with both hands, and sent a protective wall of white light out around them both. She prayed that their deep connection would keep them safe and enable her to see what kind of creatures stood in their way.

In the sudden, brighter light, Na'om saw piles of rotting animals strewn about, each one guarded by a jaguar. Each big cat was half again the size of Ek' Balam, with long yellow fangs that extended beyond its black lips. The cats' ribcages were visible beneath their mangy yellow and black-spotted pelts, and the jaguars swished their tails back and forth, snarling in unison, creating so much noise that Na'om longed to block her ears with her fingertips. But she was afraid to let go of Ek' Balam, afraid of losing what little protection the two gave each other.

She drew in a shallow breath, trying to fight the nausea created by the smell of putrid flesh and her own fear. "Itzamná, what do we do now?" she whispered. There was no answer except deeper growls from the group of jaguars ahead of her. She felt Ek' Balam shift under her touch, his back wriggling in anticipation as he prepared to leap. "No, boy, no," she said as she tightened her grip on his pelt. She rubbed her hands toward his head and grasped the thick skin directly behind his neck. Instantly, she felt him soften under her commanding touch, his head limp in her hands. "Shh, boy, relax," she said as she desperately tried to think. *We can't fight them; there are far too many of them and they're much bigger than both of us put together.* "Ajkun, Tz', if you can hear me, I need your help," Na'om whispered. But no one responded to her plea.

Gradually, she eased her grasp on Ek' Balam's neck and instantly felt him begin to quiver again. He growled and the jaguars of the Underworld growled back, a massive rumbling that forced Na'om to plunge her fingers into her ears. Her vision dimmed a bit, but she was still able to see the first twenty jaguars in front of her. Saliva dripped from their jaws, and a few began to slink forward over the half-eaten carcasses, edging closer and closer to them.

Tension knotted Na'om's stomach and cold sweat soaked into her huipil. The scent of fear brought the jaguars even closer, and one shimmied low to the ground, ready to leap.

"AHHHHHGH!" Na'om screamed, and the jaguars stopped moving. She bent down and picked up a leg bone, still covered in bits of dried skin and meat. She threw it with all her strength and hit the nearest jaguar in the shoulder. It hissed at her, but stepped back a pace. She threw another bone, and it landed near another cat. It just looked at her with its blazing yellow eyes and waited for her next move.

Na'om took a step forward, and the low growls and snarls started again. She hurled another bone, struck a cat on the head, and it yelped and backed up three feet. Encouraged, Na'om gathered more ribs and thighbones in one hand, which she heaved toward the cats. Ek' Balam kept pace with her, moving step-by-step deeper into the house of jaguars.

They slipped and slid on rotten meat that lay piled among the bones, but Na'om refused to look down. She needed to concentrate on each cat, forcing it to backtrack by striking it with a bone.

The jaguars parted before them and turned to watch them as they passed until Na'om realized they were now deep in the lair of the demon cats and surrounded on all sides. She dropped the few bones she was carrying and clutched at Ek' Balam for more sight. The cats gathered together again, creating concentric circles around them. She felt their hunger and desire pressing in on them from every direction.

Frantic, Na'om flung bones right and left, but the cats continued their advance. Ek' Balam dashed out and smacked one in the face with his big paw, but the more powerful cat slashed him with its ragged claws, opening a gash on Ek' Balam's shoulder. Ek' Balam scurried back to Na'om and bent to lick his wound. The smell of fresh blood made the larger cats slink even closer.

Na'om grabbed her necklace and cried, "Chuch, are you there? I need your help, Chuch!"

But there was no answer from the spirit of her mother.

"Tz'? Can you hear me? Anyone?" Na'om cried. She ripped another section of her skirt off and pressed it into Ek' Balam's gash. "We won't go without a fight," she said as she leaned into his side. Images flashed through her mind of the two of them out hunting in the jungle, of dancing together to the sound of Tz's bone whistle, of the days when she had first found Ek' Balam, just a small kitten without its mother. Na'om touched the scars on her face, inflicted by Ek' Balam's mother as she swayed on her paws, near death from the wound in her flank. Na'om remembered the feelings she had experienced on that hot, sunny day, the overall weariness, the pain in her side, and the tug on her child-like breasts when Ek' Balam had tried to nurse and his mother had swatted him away, creating the rip in his ear.

Bracing her feet firmly on the slippery mass of bones underfoot, Na'om took a deep breath, yanked off the fabric covering her face, opened her mouth, and let out a roar. It reverberated off the ceiling and echoed and bounced around the tunnel. She drew in another breath and roared again, louder, deeper than the one before. Again and again, she snarled and growled, and the circle of jaguars began to pull back. The cats dropped to the uneven ground and slunk backwards, their flaming eyes pinned directly on Na'om.

Encouraged, she bent down, grabbed the nearest slimy bone and threw it. It hit a jaguar in the hindquarters, and it yowled, then turned and fled down the tunnel, away from Na'om and Ek' Balam. She heaved more bones as she continued to growl, commanding respect from the pack of big cats, which continued to move away from the pair.

Gradually, as they walked backwards away from the were-jaguars, the pile of bones grew smaller underfoot, and finally, Na'om felt cool, dry dirt on her feet. She quickly turned and searched the area in front of them. There was no sign of bones or jaguars, just the limestone walls, floor, and ceiling that she had been traveling through for so long. She glanced back the way they had just come and was relieved to see darkness; no reddish-orange eyes glowed at them from any jaguars that might have dared follow them.

Exhausted from the strain of yelling, her voice hoarse, and her throat sore when she swallowed, Na'om hugged Ek' Balam gently around his head. She rubbed him behind the ear and heard a gentle purr. "Good boy," she said as she hugged him again. "Let's see if we can find some more water to drink, and I can wash that wound of yours." Grateful to be alive, Na'om plunged forward toward the next trial.

Tz'

With a small bag of cacao beans safely tucked into his leather pouch, Tz' headed back to the store where he'd seen the incense burners and knives. He hoped the small jadeite knife he'd admired would still be there and smiled as he imagined it strapped safely to his waist by its leather thong. The shop was empty of customers when Tz' arrived, but the old man was sitting on his stool at the back. *He looks like he hasn't budged in days,* Tz' thought as he headed straight for the table of knives. He scanned the surface for the one jadeite blade he'd coveted, but it was no longer there. *Naturally. I knew I'd be too late.*

"Psst," the old man hissed. He waved his hand, beckoning Tz' to come forward, and Tz' noticed he was missing one finger as he held up the small knife. The shopkeeper smiled, revealing a toothless mouth except for two upper front teeth filed into sharp points. "I put it away for you, so no one else could buy it."

Tz' took the knife. "But how did you know I'd be back?" he asked as he turned the blade over and over. It felt good to grip it in his palm.

"I know many things," the old man said. He pointed to the rows of ledgers nearby. "The one you seek is on the third shelf, the fifth one in from the left."

Puzzled, Tz' placed the knife on the counter and walked over to the books. He counted down and over and removed the ledger the man had suggested. It was old and held together with a thin, braided piece of sisal twine, which Tz' carefully untied. He gently placed the book on the counter in front of him, laying it on top of a pile of multi-colored, woven altar cloths, and stretched the first accordion page out to its full length. The limestone coating was brittle and flaking in places, but Tz' could clearly see hieroglyphs and drawings depicting what first appeared to be numerous jaguars of all shapes and sizes. Then Tz' leaned in and studied the drawings more closely, noting the almond-shaped eyes on each feline, the thick jaws and fangs on each creature, and its massive size. These were no ordinary jungle cats, and he immediately sensed a connection with them. He turned to look at the old man. "What are they?"

"Were-jaguars, part of an ancient line of people born to our ancestors, the Olmecs, who lived far to the west of here."

"How did you know I was looking for a book like this?"

"As I said before, I know many things."

Tz' carefully folded the page back in place and gave the book to the shopkeeper, who wrapped the fragile ledger in a piece of tanned deer hide. He placed the knife on top and pushed the objects toward Tz'.

"For you, only four cacao beans, and not a bean less."

Tz' would have easily spent twice that much for just the ledger, so curious was he to learn more about the were-jaguars. He paid and turned to leave when a youth about his own age entered the shop carrying a large wooden crate filled with hay.

"Hello, anyone here?" the boy shouted.

"The old man's in the back," Tz' said as he started to step outside.

"What old man? There's no one there now," the youth replied.

Tz' turned around and discovered the shopkeeper had disappeared. "But he was just here a minute ago." He looked around the store again, but there was no sign of the merchant.

"Well, I need to deliver these items and get back to work. I'll have to come back later and get paid when the owner is in," the boy said. He gently placed the crate on the floor and pulled out a ceramic censer. He blew on it, sending tiny pieces of dried grass flying, and set the incense burner on the countertop.

Tz' could see it was an image of Yum Cimil, the death god. He shivered when he looked into the skeleton's bulging eyes, which stared at him no matter where he moved in the room. He turned in time to see the boy pull another burner from the crate. It was a crouching black jaguar, its jaws open in a snarl. It instantly reminded Tz' of Ek' Balam, and he realized he hadn't thought of Na'om's cat in many, many days. Even though he knew the jaguar had leaped into the cenote after Na'om, it had never occurred to him that he was also dead.

"How much for that censer?" he asked, pointing to the jaguar.

"Sorry, that one's already sold," the boy said. "But you can order one, if you like. Just let me finish up here."

Tz' nodded. "I'll wait for you outside."

Within minutes, the young man came out of the shop, his empty crate balanced on his shoulder. He grinned. "If you order directly from the potters, you'll save some cacao beans." He tilted his head toward the store. "She adds a percentage to everything new in the store. The only bargains are the used items she sells, like that book you've got under your arm," he said, pointing to the deer hide package Tz' carried.

He held out his free hand for Tz' to shake. "The name's Box. If you follow me, I can take you to the pottery workshop run by Puk'pik, one of the best potters in the city."

Tz' smiled and hurried to follow Box through the city streets. He knew they were close when he spotted glazed clay pots of all shapes and sizes teetering in piles, waiting to be taken to the market for sale. He stopped walking and watched as several young boys each picked up a stack of black and white striped dishes tied together with sisal twine in either hand and staggered off under their heavy loads. Other youths near his own age hurried past with buckets of clay balanced on their heads. Their backs were streaked with rivulets of drying clay, making their skin look like white and gray tree bark. They disappeared into a vast inner courtyard, and Box and Tz' followed.

Tz' could see numerous potters sitting hunched over wooden benches, rolling out long strips of clay, which they quickly coiled and smoothed into plates, platters, cups, and bowls. He breathed in the wet, earthy smell that pervaded the whole area and heard the thump as another bucket of wet clay was dumped in a bin near a potter. It squeaked and squelched as it was worked by nimble fingers. Smoke drifted high overhead, and Tz' turned to look at the kilns. Multiple ovens were in use while others were being heated to fire the many rows of formed clay objects that lined the ground. Boys barely past their eighth name day carried large bundles of sticks into the courtyard, which they dropped on the ground near the ovens, while youths Tz's own age fed the wood into the earthen kilns to heat them to the proper temperature.

As he turned yet again, the sight of several wooden tables filled with small figurines drew Tz's attention. Each statue was barely taller than the length of his hand and had obviously been formed in some kind of wooden mold, since each person looked identical to his or her neighbor. But Tz' was startled to see that the faces were blank. He picked one statue up and could see small holes drilled into the back of the piece, turning the figure into a whistle. The clay was still slightly damp to the touch, and Tz' gently set it back down.

Just then, a young worker selected one of the female figures and headed toward a room off the inner courtyard. Tz' stepped closer to the doorway and could see an older potter sitting in front of a small, leather-topped table. Across from him was a woman wearing a deep blue dress highly embroidered with gold thread. The woman's hair was pulled back, extending high above her head, and was interwoven with a variety of feathers and beads. The helper set the figurine down on the table and handed the potter a round container of moist clay. The artisan quickly took a small pinch of the wet mud and began to press it onto the figurine, filling in the features of the face and hair, recreating the likeness of the woman seated in front of him in intimate detail.

"Are you here for the job?" a voice asked, and Tz' turned to find a middle-aged man with a very large belly that protruded over his loincloth standing beside him.

"Job?" Tz' asked.

"Yes, we need more young men like you to run the kilns, carry the slip to the potters, that kind of thing. I thought you were here to apply. If not, then be on your way, before you get in the way." The man stared at him, waiting for Tz' to speak.

"He's here to order a censer," Box said. He turned to Tz'. "Right?"

"Yes, yes, that's right, but the job, I want the job," Tz' stammered. "It's just, well, I don't have much experience."

The man clapped him on the back. "The name's Puk'pik, and experience isn't necessary. If you can lug buckets and haul wood, you'll do just fine. Box can teach you everything you need to know."

"Yes, great, maltiox. Oh, and my name is Tz'," he said, but Puk'pik had already hurried on to examine some new pieces being removed from a cold oven.

"Well, come on, don't just stand there," Box said. He set down the empty crate and walked toward a large pit filled with clay. He pointed to another oven, which was just being opened. "Once that cools, we'll carefully take the pieces out; meanwhile, we can bring more clay to those potters over there. All right?"

Tz' smiled. "Yes, just tell me what to do, and I'll do it." He looked around for a safe spot to put his book and hurried to follow Box.

It was early evening by the time Tz' was done for the day and able to head home where Chiman was busy tending a pot of stew on the fire. Tz' was eager to spend more time looking at the ancient book he'd purchased, but he was reluctant to let his father know he had it, so the first chance he got, he hid the packet under the blankets in his hammock.

"You're all covered with dust," Chiman remarked as he handed Tz' a bowl of thick corn, beans, and tomato stew. "Where have you been?"

"I found a job today. And I made a new friend, too. His name's Box and seems nice."

"A job, where, doing what?"

"Working with the potters in one of the many workshops."

"Wouldn't you prefer continuing your studies? I thought you'd be eager to learn more about your spirit animal. I can't see much good can come from you working so physically hard every day."

Tz' stared at his father's shadowed face. He could feel dismay and disappointment surging toward him in waves, and anger swelled inside him in response. "I'm not a child anymore, Tat. I can make my own decisions." Then as quickly as his ire rose, it fell. He hung his head. "Don't you see? It's something to do until we leave."

"In this large city, we can certainly find you some other temporary work. I'll speak to Yakal and see if he can use another person to help paint the pyramid. At least that will use some of your artistic talents."

"Tat, I don't want to work for Yakal! Please, trust me. I know what

I'm doing."

Chiman shook his head. "If we lived here, you'd have joined the apprentices studying with the shamans long ago and be around like-minded young men, not hauling clay to be made into pots and plates."

Tz' glared at his father. "I've made up my mind, Tat. Once we get back to Pa nimá, I'll resume my responsibilities to you and the village, but for now, I'll do things my way."

Chiman sighed. "Well, the rains will end soon enough. I suppose no real harm will be done in a few moons' time."

"Maltiox, Tat," Tz' said. To forestall any more conversation, Tz' faked a yawn. "I'm going to bed." He slipped into the dark hut and climbed into his hammock where the book pressed into his back, but it was too dark to read. That night, he dreamt of oversized jaguars cowering in a long tunnel, their eyes glowing reddish-orange in the dark shadows. Sniffing the air, he sensed the essence of something or someone, and he felt strangely excited. But his excitement quickly soured into frustration when the scent disappeared just before he could identify it.

Satal

Satal stretched and yawned. She had slept fitfully for the first time in weeks. The shamans of the Akab Dzib had given her a lovely hammock and soft ceiba-filled pillows to use overnight, which was a relief after so many nights spent on the hard dirt.

"My lady, are you awake?" the older shaman asked. "It's time to prepare."

"Yes, yes, of course," Satal said as she stepped onto the cool tile floor with her bare feet. This man had bathed her and rubbed her sore muscles the previous night, so she felt no shame when she dropped the soft light-blue cotton shift she'd worn overnight on the floor. *Besides, what would he want with an old thing like me?* she thought as she stared down at her sagging breasts, protruding belly, and wrinkled legs and arms.

The shaman carried a large ceramic bowl in both hands, which he set gently on a wooden table near the hammock. "I'll be right back," he said, as he hurried from the room. A few minutes later, he reappeared with a white cotton huipil and matching skirt draped over one arm, along with a cotton towel and a long gold chain looped over the other arm. He had a pair of gold earplugs in his hand as well.

"Shall we begin?" he asked, placing the objects on a small stool near the table. He reached into the green ceramic bowl with one hand and held up a rich electric-blue mixture. "Indigo blossoms mixed with clay and coconut oil," he said in answer to Satal's unspoken question. "To represent Chac and his powerful rains," he added as he began to spread the mixture on Satal's face.

She closed her eyes and willed herself to relax. The man's light touch tickled, and she wanted to laugh, but knew that might not be appropriate for such a solemn occasion. The process of spreading the blue mixture over her entire naked body took quite some time, and she twitched as he rubbed the clay into her pubic hair and nether regions. Satal's stomach grumbled as she waited for the man to finish.

"Almost done," he said as he daubed the mixture on her feet and spread it between her toes. He stood up and wiped his hand on the small cloth he'd brought with the clothes. Being careful not to smear any of the indigo paste on the clothes, he helped Satal into the shirt and skirt. They were made of finely woven linen and embroidered with a rich design of flowers and leaves in white thread on the white fabric. The shaman draped the long gold chain over Satal's head and handed her the earplugs to insert into her lobes. She pulled back her long grayish-black hair, and the man braided it for her.

He stood back to look at her sun-wrinkled face. "Beautiful," he murmured. "Fit to be a bride of Chac this gorgeous day." He motioned for Satal to precede him out of the room.

A number of other shamans had gathered in the large main hall of the Red House along with eight male sacrifices. They too were covered from head to toe in indigo paste, and each wore an embroidered white linen loincloth.

After the peace and quiet of the temple, Satal was startled to hear the roar of the crowd that had gathered in the square in front of the Red House as she stepped outside. With two shamans leading and several following behind, the group of sacrifices walked toward the sacred cenote. The crowd grew larger and louder the closer they got to the holy well. The people pressed against the edges of the sacbé, stretching out their hands in the hopes of touching one of the volunteers, but warriors lining the causeway kept the hordes back.

When Satal and the others reached the blessed cenote, the shamans lead the sacrificial group to a large wooden platform that had been erected on the edge of the well. One side extended out over the water, and as Satal stood barefoot on the warm wood, she inhaled deeply. She'd forgotten how large in diameter this sinkhole was, a hundred paces from side to side, with the water easily fifty paces below the smooth rim. The sheer limestone cliffs were pitted with cracks and crevices; some even had small ferns and bushes growing out of them.

She searched the faces of the clusters of men and women who stood a few feet away from the edge and finally spotted Kämisanel only a short distance away. He was dressed in full battle gear, with a large headdress composed of nine quetzal feathers woven into an intricate straw cap that was fastened carefully to his hair. She focused her concentration on him, and he turned and acknowledged her with a slight dip of his head, the lush greenish-blue feathers waving gently behind him as he did so.

As the shamans began their long speeches about the importance of sacrifice and the need to appease Chac to ensure a plentiful harvest, Satal closed her eyes against the glare of the sun and began to summon her own source of power.

"Camazotz," she prayed, "I'm calling on you again for help."

"Ah, Lady Satal," Camazotz said, "such a pleasure to hear from you again. But what have you gotten yourself into this time?" the bat chortled. "Not another cenote, surely?"

"It's the only way to get these men to listen to me. Do I have your word you'll assist me?"

"And what's in it for me?" Camazotz's voice boomed in Satal's head.

"More men, women, and children from the city of Mayapán. Will you help me or not?"

"Perhaps," Camazotz replied. "You can't exactly change your mind now, though, can you?"

"No," Satal agreed. She frowned, angry that the great bat was reluctant to give her any assistance. *If you won't help me, I'll just do it all myself!* she thought stubbornly.

At that point, the older shaman touched Satal gently on the arm, bringing her awareness back to the immediate moment. "My lady, do you wish to speak before we offer you to Chac?"

Satal was startled to see that she was the only sacrifice left standing on the platform. She hadn't heard the men cry out or even a splash in the water to indicate that they were gone.

"Yes, actually, I do," Satal said. She stepped forward and motioned with her hands to quiet the murmurs of the hundreds who stood waiting to watch her sink beneath the still surface of the waters below. "My name is Satal," she cried.

"Louder," someone bellowed.

Satal cleared her throat and tried again. "My name is Satal," she shouted. "I was born near this great city over five hundred moons ago and was set to marry my beloved, Ajelbal, on my fourteenth name day at the base of the pyramid. But a raiding party from Mayapán, led by a man named Q'alel, attacked the city, stole me for himself, and has kept me a prisoner all these years. It's only by the grace of Itzamná that I've managed to make my way back here." *Only a small lie or two in all of that,* she thought as she paused. Her next words needed to be chosen carefully. "I was born a Xiu and have returned to my people, the Xiu, to demand justice for the years of my life that were spent in servitude to the Cocom, our sworn enemies. I've asked Kämisanel, the leader of the warriors, to launch an attack on Mayapán to right these wrongs, but he's refused. But I demand justice and will return from the cenote to ensure that I receive it. I want you all to remember this as I give myself to Chac!" With those last words, Satal jumped off the platform and plunged downward toward the greenish-blue waters of the cenote.

She inhaled deeply just before she hit the water's surface and let herself sink down and down into the growing gloom. The water grew colder as she fell deeper, and she sank until she was up to her waist in the blue silt at the bottom. The bodies of the men who had jumped or been gently pushed just before her were stuck haphazardly in the thick blue sludge, many with their hands raised in tribute to the faint light at the surface.

Satal let loose one tiny bubble of air at a time as she slowly eased her way out of the clay and dirt before dropping the gold chain and earplugs into the muck, where they quickly disappeared. Kicking gently with her bare feet, Satal pushed toward the surface and found a tunnel in the vertical wall. She entered the opening and swam quickly along the passageway until she was able to lift her head above water and take a deep breath. The ceiling of the tunnel was just inches above her head, but as long as she could breathe, she knew she'd be fine. The waters that flowed underground were all interconnected in the region; by using an uncanny sense of direction, she swam steadily through the dark toward the cenote at the front of the Akab Dzib, the house of the shamans.

Night had fallen, with a gibbous moon high overhead by the time Satal swam into the small well at the base of the shamans' building. Wearily, she climbed the steep and pitted limestone walls until she collapsed with relief on the hard, dry ground surrounding the cenote. She felt lightheaded, giddy almost, at what she'd accomplished, as she sat up and looked around. By the light of the moon, she could see that her beautiful white clothes were stained with the indigo paste that had come off her skin. The shirt and skirt clung to her frame, molding against her body like a second skin. Behind her was the Akab Dzib, with its large stairway leading to the roof of the long, low building, where the shamans studied the movements of Venus and the stars and recorded their observations in ledgers in conjunction with their divinations.

Shivering slightly from the cool night air, her exertions, and lack of food, Satal stood up and approached the stone building. She could hear men's voices and smelled wood smoke from several cooking fires. Although wet and bedraggled, Satal walked proudly toward one of the four doorways on this side of the building.

Shouts of "Itzamná!" filled the air as the men caught their first glimpses of Satal. Then a deathly stillness overcame them, and the only sound was that of the men as they fell to their knees in supplication to her. Satal stood still, enjoying the moment of supreme power as these men, the holiest and most revered in the city, groveled on the ground in front of her.

She looked at the dozens of men and slowly walked among them, searching for the older shaman who had prepared her for the sacrificial ceremony. Eventually, she spotted him several feet away and gently tapped him on the shoulder.

"Rise, my friend," she said as she stepped back a pace.

Warily, the shaman got to his feet. He kept his head lowered, his eyes averted from Satal.

"You showed me great kindness before the ceremony, and I need someone to assist me, so I choose you. Tell me your name," Satal said.

"Tewichinel, my lady," the man said as he began to fall back down on his knees.

"No, no," Satal said, as grasping Tewichinel's arm. "No more supplication from you, please. No, right now I need food, a bath, and clean dry clothes. Can you do that for me?"

"Of course, of course," Tewichinel said; then he paused. "But surely, to have survived the cenote, only to reappear here, you must be a god and not in need of these human things."

"I assure you, I am quite human, although powerful in more ways than one." Satal looked around at the rest of the hall, where the remaining men still were on their knees. "Tell your friends and fellow shamans that I mean them no harm. No, the damage will go to those who deserve it." She yawned, despite her attempt to stop the motion. "Some food?" she hinted.

"Of course, my lady . . . Lady Satal," Tewichinel corrected. He ran to the nearest cooking fire, served up a bowl of boiled iguana and manioc root, and hurried back with it to Satal. He clapped his hands and pointed, and a stool was brought for Satal to sit on.

She slowly sat down on the hard wood and balanced the warm bowl of stew on her lap.

She took a deep breath and let it out slowly. It felt so good to finally be back in power, with people at her disposal. After a few bites, she turned to Tewichinel, who hovered nearby. "Tomorrow, you and the other shamans shall accompany me to the Hall of the Thousand Columns where we'll meet with Kämisanel and discuss plans on how and when to attack Mayapán." She took another bite of the slightly tough iguana meat and chewed it slowly. "Perhaps some of the shamans can begin to divine the most auspicious days to raid the city."

"Yes, yes, right away, my lady," Tewichinel said. He hurried to a group of his fellow shamans and whispered to them Lady Satal's orders. The group of ten men bowed their way out of the building and headed to the roof to study the motions of the stars high overhead.

The next morning was bright and clear, and Satal stood in the warm sunlight to braid her hair. After her swim and long bath of the night before, Satal felt thoroughly cleansed, inside and out. *Ha, and I managed to survive without any help from Camazotz*, she mused. *I have even more powers than I thought.* The idea filled her heart with a dark joy.

Accompanied by a group of twenty shamans, among them Tewichinel, who walked a few paces in front of Satal to clear a path through the crowds, Satal strolled slowly toward the Hall of the Thousand Columns. She grinned when she saw the populace shrink away from her, the normal shouts and conversations of a busy city dying away as she passed.

The crowd fell into step behind her until she had several thousand men, women, and children following her to the great plaza. They stopped at the edge of the green, where the warriors were once again training in the art of combat. No one stopped parrying and thrusting until Tewichinel appeared in their midst.

The ranks of men glanced at Tewichinel; then beyond him, they saw Satal. As if a great wind had swept across the flat plain, the hundreds of warriors fell flat on the ground, their bodies pressed as tightly to the dirt as possible, while they shielded their eyes with their arms. Satal laughed as she saw Kämisanel and the other leaders of the regiment turn in a group to see her standing among the fallen soldiers. They instantly fell to the smooth limestone steps that formed the temple stairs in recognition of Satal's presence.

Satal picked her way carefully through the numerous prostrate bodies and marched up the steps, where she nudged Kämisanel none too gently with the tip of her leather sandal. "Get up," she said. "You and your men have a battle to plan."

Without saying a word, Kämisanel and the other warriors rose to their knees, their heads still dropped upon their chests. "My lady," Kämisanel said, without raising his head or his eyes to look at her, "it will be an honor to serve you."

"Ha, it's about time," Satal retorted. "Tewichinel and the other shamans will deduce the perfect time to attack Mayapán, and I expect you and your men to be ready when that moment comes." She looked around at the thousands of men still lying face down on the ground. "Tell your men to rise, so they may continue their practice. I want them to be able to slaughter everyone in the Cocom city."

"As you wish, Lady Satal," Kämisanel replied. He stood up and gave an order, and just as they had fallen, the men rose as one unit, then turned and bowed to Satal.

"Now, for more immediate matters," Satal said. "I shall need a home, money, new clothes, food . . . ."

"Yes, yes, of course, my lady," Kämisanel said. "All your needs shall be met, no expense shall be spared, the city is at your command."

"Perfect," Satal said. She smiled. It felt so good to be back in charge.

AJKUN

It was just before dawn when Ajkun woke from her spot in Alom's hut. Yakal was kneeling beside her and gently rocking her shoulder to get her to wake. "Ajkun, it's time," Yakal said. He held out his hand and helped Ajkun to her feet.

"I'll be right there, just let me gather a few things. Hurry back and get the fire going and put a large pot of water on to boil," Ajkun said as she started to pack some bags of herbs into a basket.

"The water's already boiling," Yakal said. "I'll wait for you outside."

Ajkun nodded as he stepped out the door. She quickly pulled off her nightshift and dressed in her dark green huipil and skirt, then wrapped her brown shawl around her shoulders, even though the day would be hot. Ever since her strange descent into the land of bitter cold, she'd been unable to get fully warm, no matter how hard the sun beat down on them all. She pulled her scuffed leather sandals onto her bare feet and met Yakal outside.

"Alom is with Uskab, but she wanted your help with this baby. She says the child is so large that it will take both of you to catch him," Yakal said as he guided Ajkun through the still dark streets of the city.

Near the Temple of Cremations, a few torches burned low, sending smoky trails out into the still air and causing Ajkun to cough as they hurried past. A lone guard, a spear in his left hand, nodded to them from his spot at the base of the stairs, then continued his silent vigil.

Alom was filling a large turtle shell with hot water when Yakal and Ajkun arrived. The two women washed their hands, and Yakal dumped the water into the street. "I think she still has a few hours to go," Alom said to Yakal. "Best you find someplace else to rest until the baby arrives."

"I'm not leaving," Yakal said as he sat down with his back against the side of the hut. "I promise to stay out of the way, but I want to be here for Uskab if she needs me."

Suddenly Uskab shrieked, and Ajkun hurried inside with Alom right behind her.

"Shhh, child, it will be all right," Ajkun said as she quickly walked to Uskab. She was lying in the hammock, curled up on one side, grasping her belly in pain as another contraction bore down on her. Ajkun laid her hand on Uskab's stomach and asked if she could lift her shift. Uskab nodded, and Ajkun pulled up the girl's dark blue dress to see how far along she was. Ajkun nodded to Alom. "We need to get her up and out of this hammock," she said. She looked around the small room. "And we need a stool for Uskab to sit on." She poked her head out of the door and spoke to Yakal. "A stool, some blankets, and any pillows you can find, quickly now, her time is closer than we thought."

She turned back to Alom, and between the women, they managed to get Uskab on her feet. Alom unhooked one end of the hammock and bundled it on the floor, out of the way, while Ajkun helped support Uskab, who stood partially bent over, her hands resting on her knees.

Within minutes, Yakal was back with the requested items. Alom arranged them in the middle of the room and helped Uskab down onto the stool, while Ajkun pushed Yakal back outdoors.

"Is she going to be all right?" Yakal said as he touched Ajkun's arm.

"Of course, she's strong and healthy; don't worry, she'll be fine." Ajkun gave Yakal a quick hug before heading back into the hut. But she was worried, because the child was large, and Uskab was such a small girl, with narrow hips. *Please, Ixchel,* Ajkun silently prayed as she rubbed her special concoction of peccary fat and white sapote on Uskab's belly, *help Uskab deliver this child as painlessly as possible.* She wished she had her statue of the goddess of childbirth with her, but the clay figurine of Ixchel was far away in Pa nimá, and she hadn't thought to purchase another one while in Mayapán. *I promise to give you many offerings upon our return to the village,* Ajkun thought. *Just please, help Uskab with this child.*

Within minutes, Uskab cried that she needed to push, and the two older women nodded that she should. Ajkun knelt on a soft pillow in front of the young girl, ready to ease the baby into the world, while Alom supported Uskab as best she could from behind.

With concentrated effort, Uskab pushed and strained and pushed some more, and the black hair of a newborn quickly appeared. Ajkun guided one shoulder, then the other through the birth canal, and with a gush of fluids, the rest of the baby followed. "It's a boy," Ajkun said as she held the child up for Uskab to see.

Uskab smiled weakly and sank onto the pillow-strewn floor, her legs quivering from exertion. Ajkun laid the child on Uskab's chest and nodded to Alom, who hurried outside for Yakal.

"You can stay for a few minutes," Ajkun said to Yakal as he entered the hut. "But Uskab must rest, and we need to wash your son, clean the room, and burn the cord in the fire."

She stepped outside and joined Alom in washing her hands in another basin of hot, soapy water. "You arrived just in time," Alom said as she sat down near the fire. She brushed a strand of hair out of her eyes and smiled at her friend.

"You certainly could have handled that delivery," Ajkun replied as she too sat on the ground near the flames. The heat felt good on her arthritic knees.

"All the same, I'm glad you're here." Alom patted Ajkun on the shoulder. "It's good to see new life being born after so much illness in the city." She laughed. "My first grandchild; I never thought I'd see the day." She wiped away a smattering of tears with the hem of her skirt. Using her hands to push herself up from the ground, she stood and brushed the dirt from the back of her skirt. "I must go see him." As Ajkun made a motion to rise, Alom shook her head. "Rest, I'll take care of things inside."

Ajkun nodded and let her friend go. She stared into the fire ring, poking the embers with a stick to make the flames dance higher. *Second grandchild,* she thought, *Na'om was your first.* Her breath caught in her throat as she was quickly swept back in time to the day Na'om had been born, too early in the morning for the Wayeb to have fully closed, too difficult a birth for her own daughter, Tu'janel, to survive. Ajkun's pulse quickened as the emotional waves carried her far from the courtyard in Mayapán, farther back in time to when *she* had been the new mother, birthing her girl child. *Now look at me, old and gray, the days of bearing children long behind me.*

She took a deep breath and let it out quickly, trying to suppress the tears that threatened to overwhelm her. Alternating waves of joy and sorrow flowed through her, as she heard the soft cry of the infant from inside the small hut, and Uskab's gentle voice shushing the child. She wanted to hug this new life to her own chest and suckle it, despite knowing full well that her body was long past the stage of producing milk. *I'll never have another child or grandchild of my own to cuddle.* The thought stabbed her, and she bent forward with the pain as the tears spilled over onto her skirt. She sobbed, feeling the swelling emptiness that had formed the minute she'd learned Na'om was dead. *Now all I want is to go home, to be alone among my plants, roots, and herbs, surrounded by all that's familiar. This city's too full of people, there's no privacy, and no chance to hear myself think.*

Ajkun jumped when Yakal patted her arm. "You were a long ways from here," Yakal said. "Are you all right?" He threw the bundle of cord wrapped in bloody cloths into the fire where it sparked and sizzled before flaring into a bright flame.

Ajkun looked up into her son-in-law's tanned face. Pride shone through his black eyes, softening the hard lines that had formed from years of squinting against the reflective glare of the sun on limestone. She gave Yakal a half-smile as she hastily wiped her face with her sleeve. "Yes, yes, I'll be fine. Just remembering when I helped Tu'janel bring Na'om into the world." She took his proffered hand and slowly got to her feet.

Yakal nodded. "So long ago, yet it feels like it was just the other day." He stepped forward to embrace Ajkun, but she sidestepped his advance.

"Not today, Yakal," Ajkun said. "Too much has happened, much of it not good. Itzamná knows I don't blame you for the path our lives have taken, but I shan't see my daughter or granddaughter until I pass through the Underworld." She hiccupped, forcing back the tears. "I'm alone in this world now and have only death to look forward to." She rapidly brushed her hand across her eyes. "I should go. Alom can take care of things for now. I'll return later and check on the baby and Uskab. Congratulations to you both." She started to move away from the hut, then changed her mind and returned to Yakal. Grabbing his bare forearm, she said, "Promise me you'll take care of this boy."

Yakal bowed his head. "I promise. I've learned my lessons the hard way. I'll give my life to save this child."

Ajkun nodded and tapped him on the arm. "Good, then perhaps the gods will look favorably upon you now." She gave a weak smile and left the new family, lost once again in her desire to be alone.

Na'om

For hours, Na'om and Ek' Balam wandered through the darkness in search of fresh water. The tunnel floor sloped gently upward, which gave Na'om hope that they might be reaching the surface, but within minutes, the passageway slanted back down, leading deeper underground. She felt disappointment wrap itself around her like a thick blanket, and her pace slowed to match her mood. Finally, she heard the telltale dripping of liquid and searched the rock wall for the source.

A rivulet of fresh water streamed over the porous limestone, the surface of the rock worn smooth by the steady passage of water. Na'om cupped both hands against the tunnel wall and drank deeply. She heard Ek' Balam lapping at her feet and giggled when his rough tongue accidentally brushed against her toes.

"You probably don't want to lick my feet," she said as she moved a bit to the side. "After walking in all that muck left by the jaguars, who knows what's stuck between my toes." She grimaced at the thought and tried to rinse her foot by balancing one hand on the wall while splashing water on her raised foot with the other hand. She wiggled her toes as she felt the dirt and detritus slide off. "Hmm, that's better, but I wish I had a bowl of Ati't's jasmine-scented soap to use," Na'om said as she scrubbed at her other foot. She stepped away from the puddle she'd created and sat down with her back against the wall. Ek' Balam lay down beside her and began to groom his face.

She reached over and patted him on the head. "Let's rest a bit before we continue," Na'om said as she stroked him between his ears and down the back of his neck. She felt the scrap of fabric she'd pressed against the gash in his shoulder and realized it was glued to the spot with dried blood. *Guess I'll leave that alone for now. No sense reopening the wound.* She continued to pet Ek' Balam, grateful for the peace and calm the simple act brought to her. *I wish I could remember Ati't's comments about the Underworld.* Then she sat up straighter as she did recall something. "Nine levels, nine trials," she said. "Ati't said the shamans have always talked about the nine tests the gods of Xibalba forced the Hero Twins, Hunahpu and Xbalanque, to go through before they were allowed to return to the natural world." She stopped to think and began to count all the ordeals she had passed already. *The three rivers, the council chamber, the endless darkness, the deathly cold, and now the jaguars; that leaves two more tests I have to pass, and then I'll be free.*

Encouraged at the thought that most of her sufferings were behind her, Na'om laid her head down on Ek' Balam's belly and drifted into a deep sleep.

When she woke much, much later, she drank more water, and then brushed off the dirt and small pebbles that clung to her ragged skirt. "Come on, we might as well find out what lies ahead," Na'om said as the two fell into step once more. Despite the water sloshing in her belly, Na'om knew she needed to eat something again. Even the thought of another small bat or two didn't repulse her.

As if her reflections had triggered them once again, almost instantly a cloud of bats whooshed through the narrow tunnel, forcing Na'om and Ek' Balam to dive onto the rough ground. The squeaking and rustling of the thousands of mammals as they streaked past them caused shivers to run up and down Na'om's spine. She buried her head in her arms and waited for the noises to stop. Only then did she dare raise her head and look around. Ek' Balam had snatched a few of the creatures out of the air and was happily crunching on the tiny bones. He didn't bother to toss one to Na'om, but ate the last bat in two bites.

"Guess you expected me to fend for myself this time," Na'om said as she got to her feet again. She swayed a little as the blood drained from her head, and she clutched at the wall in front of her for support. She felt her stomach squeeze in on itself. "Those bats came from behind us again," Na'om said as she started to walk. "We have to be headed in the right direction."

Hunger continued to grip her, and Na'om felt queasy from the lack of any real food. She had no idea how long she'd been trapped underground, but she thought it had to have been several days. And she had no real way to know when she might face the next tests. But even as she pondered these two questions, she detected an acrid smell in the air that grew stronger and more noxious the closer she came to the source. She noticed the air was warmer than it had been in hours, too. "Uh-oh, this doesn't bode well," Na'om said as she touched Ek' Balam's back. She projected her white light around the two of them before continuing into the gloom.

Her eyes began to sting from the thick scent of urine, and she ripped off one sleeve of her shirt and pressed it to her lips and nose. Still clutching Ek' Balam, the two stepped from the tunnel into the entranceway of a huge cavern. Na'om's circle of white light penetrated the darkness, and she gasped at the sight of such a vast space, the actual ceiling lost in the black shadows high overhead. The knobby ends of stalactites jutted from the blackness like the tips of giant teeth, and some had grown so long that they'd connected with the hundreds of stalagmites that protruded from the black cave floor.

The orb of white light that surrounded them pushed the obscurity to one side, awakening the millions of bats that lived high overhead, and they began to rustle and stir with increasing frenzy. Cautiously, Na'om took a few steps deeper into the cave, and her feet sank ankle deep into the dense layers of guano that covered the cave floor. She hurried back to the tunnel, unsure of how to proceed.

"Our path lies through that cavern, but I don't know how we'll make it through that horrible slime," Na'om said as she tried to shake her feet to remove the globs that clung to her bare soles. She wound up dragging her feet on the bare dirt, scraping the muck off on the pebbles that littered the tunnel floor.

She reached for her necklace. "Chuch, are you there?" She felt a slight tingle of warmth in the black jade stone, but there was no reassuring answer.

"Looks like we've been abandoned again," Na'om said wearily. "Why is all this up to me to do on my own?" she cried. Her voice echoed in the narrow passageway and disappeared into the giant cave. That set the bats to rustling and squeaking, and Na'om shuddered at the idea of passing underneath them.

The less light we create, the better, Na'om thought just before she touched Ek' Balam. *I won't be able to see as well, but maybe they won't start flying around me, either.* She dragged her feet on the ground again, then braced herself to step back into the multiple layers of bat excrement. Ek' Balam turned his big head to look at Na'om, as if questioning her judgment in entering the cave. "I know, I know, I don't want to go, either, but what other choice do we have?" Na'om whispered.

Instead of marching directly across the center of the cave, Na'om decided to skirt the edge of it, trailing her hand on the wall as she'd done in the past. She didn't want to lose her sense of direction or miss the opening that she knew must exist on the other side of the cave that would lead the way out of the warren of passages and tunnels they'd been traveling through.

With her first step, the ammonia stench of the guano penetrated the thin fabric Na'om held against her face, and she coughed and gagged. Bats of all sizes shifted and fluttered in the ceiling, and hundreds began to flit about the huge cave. Ek' Balam's paws created little popping sounds each time he took a step, which echoed off the walls and bounced among the stalactites, causing more bats to leave their roosts and fly in looping arcs in and around the limestone columns.

As the guano rose over the tops of her feet, her skin began to blister and burn, and Na'om quickly decided to run regardless of the noise it might make. She nodded in the dim light at Ek' Balam, and she jogged as rapidly as she could through the darkness, trying to avoid the bats that darted near her head. Then suddenly, she heard a noise unlike any she had ever heard before, and an unexpected gust of wind knocked her backwards. Na'om stumbled and lurched against a stalagmite. She braced herself against the six-foot tall pillar and peered into the blackness.

"Trying to escape, eh?" she heard as she tried to comprehend what her eyes told her now blocked her path. A bat, twice as tall as any man

Na'om had ever seen, hovered just inches off the ground. Its giant wings slowly fanned the air, rhythmically lifting and lowering the mammal in a mesmerizing cycle. Na'om stepped behind the stalagmite, trying to blend in with the rough limestone.

"No sense trying to hide, Na'om," the bat said. Its red eyes pierced the darkness, honing in on Na'om and then Ek' Balam. "You two have eaten some of my distant cousins," the bat said. "You'll pay for that."

Na'om shuddered. Not only did this creature know her name, it knew everything she had done. *Itzamná, what do I do?* Na'om cried silently. She longed to touch Ek' Balam and send a beam of protection out around them, but was too afraid to move and feared the added light would only anger and arouse this giant bat and the millions of others hanging overhead.

Then, Ek' Balam nudged Na'om's thigh with his big head. Immediately, the white light appeared before Na'om could shift her weight and step away from him. The blazing orb shot out into the blackness, and at once, the air was filled with swirling, flying bats. Na'om crouched behind the stalagmite and heard the giant bat laugh. It was a high, shrill sound that pierced her ears, as if someone had driven a sharp spine into her eardrum.

She cringed and clasped her ears with both hands, dropping the cloth she'd held pressed against her face. The ammonia smell overwhelmed her, and she bent over as her empty stomach cramped in protest. Gagging, she spit in the guano. She heard the bat laugh again at her distress.

And all of a sudden, Na'om was angry, angrier than she had ever been before. She straightened her back and turned to face the giant bat who continued to float in midair. "Who are you and what do you want?" she demanded.

"I'm Camazotz, god of all the bats," the creature said as it flicked its wings a little harder. The air rippled, and the stench of moldy earth and disease drifted off his black fur-covered body. "And, a personal friend of someone you know," Camazotz added.

"Friend, what kind of person would be friends with you?" Na'om cried. Even as she spoke, she began to edge along the cavern wall again, with Ek' Balam right beside her.

"Why, Satal, of course," Camazotz said. He fluttered his leathery wings and rose a bit higher off the ground.

"Satal," Na'om said. "That explains so much. So, you must have been the one to help her from the cenote. Did you pick her up out of the water with your wings?"

"Ha, ha, ha, no, although that would have been quite the trick. No, I merely assisted the dear lady to shape-shift into her favorite form . . . ."

"The wasp," Na'om whispered.

"Yes, the black wasp. Once she reached the edge of the cenote, she was on her own and managed to escape by climbing the walls. I was actually impressed that the old woman made it," Camazotz said. "And now she owes me dearly for my help." He glided a bit closer to Na'om. "Don't think I don't see what you're trying to do," he added as he came even nearer, and another blast of fetid air filled the space between them.

"You can't keep me here," Na'om cried as she started to run into the center of the cave. She ducked behind more limestone columns, weaving in and out of the complex maze of pillars, squeezing through spots that were too tight for Camazotz to enter. She heard his giant wings beat furiously and heard him curse and cry out to his relatives to swarm and attack. Ek' Balam turned and growled, and Na'om glanced back over her shoulder to see Camazotz swooping down on her. She ran, but felt his warm breath on the back of her neck and was engulfed in the fusty smells of death and decay. Leathery wing tips brushed her shoulders, and Na'om lurched forward, dodging behind another column where she paused to swallow and gain strength. Placing both hands on Ek' Balam's head, she focused her concentration as she'd done that distant day when Satal had tied her to the wall. Na'om summoned up her internal strength, and quick as a cat, she slashed out with her arm, sending a jagged bolt of light toward Camazotz. It struck the giant bat in the middle of one wing, and Na'om could see she had damaged the thick fibrous webbing that encased the bones.

Camazotz beat the air frantically with his good wing, while trying to fold the wounded one up near his body. Na'om sent out another blast of light, hitting the bat god in the same wing. He shrieked and his millions of cousins responded, filling the cave with a sound that drove Na'om to her knees. The air churned with tiny bats the size of small avocados to giant bats larger than turkeys, all of which headed toward Na'om. Clutching her ears, Na'om struggled to her feet again. But the strident sounds penetrated her mind, plunging like knife blades into her consciousness. Mustering every ounce of strength she had left, she gripped Ek' Balam with one hand and turned in a wide circle, sending out bolts of white light in all directions. She searched the perimeter of the cave for any sign of another tunnel. "There," she whispered to Ek' Balam and nodded. The exit was behind the bat god. She aimed another flash of light at Camazotz. He squealed and lifted high off the ground, leaving a gap in the black whirlwind of flying mammals. Na'om and Ek' Balam ran through the breach, sliding and slipping in the piles of guano, and managed to enter the new tunnel before Camazotz had time to react.

Only after they had gone several hundred feet down the new tunnel, placing numerous twists and turns behind them, did Na'om finally stop to take a breath. "Itzamná, I never thought we'd get out of there alive," she said as she bent over her knees, trying to calm her breath. She looked back, but didn't see any bats following them.

Once she could breathe normally again, she rubbed her feet on the ground, scraping off the guano once again. She could see blisters forming on the tops of her feet and knew she needed to rinse them as quickly as possible to prevent further damage. "We need water, and we need it now," she said as she rubbed behind Ek' Balam's ear. He purred and started to trot down the passageway. "Hey, wait for me," Na'om cried, and she hobbled to catch up.

Tz'

In the dark before dawn, Tz' quietly rose before his father and went outside. His life had taken so many strange twists in the past few weeks that he couldn't sleep, so he gathered some food for his lunch and crept away from the house, the ancient book tucked under his arm. He hurried through the empty streets, slipped outside the gates, and headed to the young avocado orchard nearby, his mind in a whirl of thoughts. He still had a hard time believing Na'om was his sister, not the woman the gods had intended him to marry. From the day of her birth, he'd been drawn to her, but none of that mattered, for she was related by blood *and* lost at the bottom of the cenote. Even more troubling was the knowledge that he could shapeshift into some mythical creature, although if he were to be honest with himself, he'd enjoyed the sense of power he'd felt when he'd transformed into the were-jaguar, whatever that was. He hoped the ledger he carried would give him some much-needed answers.

The sun was just rising over the horizon, casting a reddish glow in the sky, but it was light enough to find a secluded spot to read. Once he was settled on the hard ground, his back against a sapling, he gently unfolded the book. He was struck once again by the size of the cats, certainly half again as big as any real jaguar, with long fangs that protruded past their upper and lower lips. He turned each page with tenderness, carefully folding and unfolding each brittle piece of bark, studying the drawings only. There were also many pages of hieroglyphs, which Tz' knew he didn't have time to read. But from the illustrations, he surmised that the Olmecs believed at some point a woman had coupled with a male jaguar, producing a line of offspring who had the ability to shape-shift into were-jaguars. Tz' wanted to try the transformation again, but he knew his father would disapprove. *I'll buy some more toad venom and tobacco and use it once we get back to Pa nimá.* He shuddered as he felt a vague echo of the were-jaguar's energy shimmer through his body, and he leaned his head back against the tree to fully engage in the sensation.

The cooing of several mourning doves brought Tz' back to the present, and he rushed to gather up his book, knowing if he didn't hurry, he'd be late for work.

As he entered the large courtyard, he waved to Box, who was already heating up one of the kilns for another firing. "You're almost late," Box said. He was getting ready to load a kiln with figurines.

"Sorry, I lost track of time." Tz' hastened to help Box. He picked up one of the statuettes and placed it in the oven. "I've wanted to ask you what these are for. I've seen some of the older men modeling them into likenesses of the people who come here, but what do they do with them once the piece has been fired?"

"They're burial pieces for the rich and elite. When a husband dies, he's buried with the likeness of his wife, and if she dies first, then his statue is placed with her. That way they stay connected through all time. You don't do that where you come from?" Box asked as he carefully placed another sculpture into the kiln.

"No. A person is buried under the floor of the hut they lived in, with a variety of tools they may have used and some food, but not with anything representing another person," Tz' said. "I guess I never thought of being joined to a person for all eternity in that way." He reached down and gently picked up a woman, which he handed to Box.

"Well, most people don't have the extra cacao beans or jadeite to afford it, which is why in a small village like yours, it's probably not done. But here, where there are so many rich shamans, politicians, artists, and musicians, it's quite common. Then when someone dies, the body, statue, and any other items a person might need in the Underworld are all buried on a small island off the coast to the west of here. The shamans who live there perform all kinds of rituals to open and close the portal to the ancestors at any time of the year." Box shuddered, despite the heat blasting from the kiln several feet from him. "Just going through the Wayeb each year is scary enough for me. I can't imagine what the shamans must see and hear on a regular basis."

Even though he kept working at a steady pace, thoughts of Na'om drifted in and out of Tz's mind for the rest of the morning. He wondered how she could travel safely through the Underworld when she hadn't received a proper burial of any kind or been given any tools or food to help her along her path. The idea gnawed at him, but he finally decided that too much time had already passed; she would be well beyond any help now.

When Tz' and the other workers stopped for lunch, he found he had very little appetite for the food he'd brought. Instead of eating, he picked up a small ball of clay and began to work it with his fingers, shaping and smoothing the damp soil absentmindedly until Puk'pik rang a small bell signaling the end of the lunch break. Eager to get moving again, Tz' left his creation on the table and didn't see Box slip it into the next kiln being loaded for a firing.

When work ended for the day, Box suggested he and Tz' get a bite to eat together. "My treat," he said as he held up several cacao beans.

"All right, but next time it's on me," Tz' said as he held up the few beans Puk'pik had given him for the week. This was not the first time Tz' had spent an evening with Box instead of with his father, but he didn't think Chiman minded. After all, he was beyond his eighteenth name day, and most men his age were married or living on their own. He liked the freedom of being with someone of a similar age, with similar interests, which was something he hadn't experienced in Pa nimá. He followed Box through the streets and stopped when he paused to look at a small table filled with hand-carved stone, shell, and obsidian ear flares in front of a home.

Box pointed to a set of plugs made from pieces of thick seashell, and the older man behind the table handed them to him. Box held them up to his earlobes in the dim light. "What do you think?"

"Too iridescent for you. Try those," Tz' said as he pointed to another, darker pair made of stone.

"Yes, I've looked at those before; they're more expensive. But I do like them." He turned to the vendor. "Will you take payments?" he asked.

The old man nodded and held up a mirror made from pyrite, but it was too dark to see any reflection. Box rubbed his hand over the carvings, which were shaped like hibiscus blossoms with a tiny green jade bead in each center. He reached into his pouch hanging at his waist and gave the man two cacao beans. "Hold these for me, and I'll bring more beans next week." He motioned to Tz', and they set off again. Three streets later, Box stopped in the middle of the alleyway and pointed up. Tz' looked to read the sign that hung overhead. "The Silowik Tukan? My uncle has mentioned this place."

"One of the best spots in the city to get a good drink; come on, I know the son of the owner. I think you'll like him." Box stepped through the open doorway.

Tz' followed right behind him, but paused once indoors. He'd never seen anything like the drinking house. Small, leather-topped tables with wooden stools arranged around them filled the room. A wooden counter ran along the wall opposite the door, and several wooden shelves filled with various gourds took up much of the space behind the counter. Crudely painted murals covered the other three walls. Even though the artwork was chipped and flaking off the walls, Tz' was surprised to see many of the paintings were of half-naked women dancing with men in loincloths. Many of the depicted men held pottery jugs above their heads, and red droplets flowed from the vessels into their open mouths. He had never seen artwork like it, and it sent a flush of blood to his face.

Box smiled at the young man behind the long counter and hurried to sit at one of the many stools. He motioned for Tz' to take a seat as well. "Nil, this is Tz'," he said. "He's working for Puk'pik."

"Good to see you, Box, it's been awhile," Nil replied. "And nice to meet you, Tz'. So, what are you drinking tonight?" He gestured to the rows of pitchers on the shelves behind him. "We have all sorts of beverages. Blackberries, raspberries, mangoes, strawberries, you name it, my dad's probably fermented it and has it in one of these pitchers."

Tz' shook his head. "I don't know; I've never really had anything alcoholic before, except for one small mug of balché when I performed the corn ceremony with my dad several moons ago."

Box grinned. "You're how old, and yet you've never had a regular drink? Don't you celebrate anything in that village of yours? Well, my friend, you're in for a treat." He motioned to Nil to pick something.

Nil grabbed a jug with a thin orange ribbon wrapped around the neck. "This is my favorite, mango and pineapple." He poured the frothy liquid into a ceramic mug and handed it to Tz'.

Tz' sniffed the cup and took a sip. The liquid was sweet and a little spicy and fizzy all at once. He swallowed and felt the fluid burn the back of his throat. He heard a noise behind him and turned to see an overweight man in a well-worn leather apron appear from a doorway in the back of the room. The man stared at the three of them, noticed the emptiness of the rest of the room, and then turned away.

"That's my father; don't worry about him," Nil said. "Drink up, it won't hurt you," he added as he glanced quickly toward the back room before pouring himself a mug. "Tat doesn't like me to drink while I'm working, but one little sip won't hurt." Nil tipped the cup back and drained it in one large swallow. "Drink; there's plenty more where this came from." He motioned to pour more of the juice into Tz's cup, but Tz' held his hand over the opening.

"That's all right, I have plenty here," he replied as he took another small taste. He wasn't sure if he liked the way the liquid bubbled and fizzed as he drank it, but the overall warmth that spread through his body was relaxing. He continued taking small sips of the fermented juice, while Box had another full mug. Tz' watched as old men with hardly any teeth and young men only a few years older than him took seats at the tables, and Nil hurried about the room, taking orders and returning with drinks for all present. Many of the customers untied leather bags hanging from their waists and dumped the contents onto the tabletops. Tz' could see bits of bones and shells, which were quickly arranged into patterns on the tables. The designs reminded him of those Chiman had taught him using seeds and beans that could be used for divination. Tz' watched as one man threw a round piece of bone, etched with markings, onto the tabletop, and then quickly scooped up several of the other pieces of bone, placing them in a pile by his mug. Another youth tossed the etched bone and grabbed two shells and a large bone in the center of the design. As the games continued around the various tables, the boys shouted, while the older men whistled through their missing teeth and stomped their feet when someone collected a large handful of bones and shells.

Nil stopped next to Tz', his hands filled with empty mugs. "You should try playing sometime," he said. "It's a lot of fun, isn't that right, Box?"

Box snorted. "You mean it's a good way to lose everything you've spent weeks earning. You know that's why I haven't been in here for so long. No, my friend, my gambling days are over." He turned to Tz'. "It's fun to play, but many of these men cheat, especially when they know you're new to the game. My advice is to enjoy the drinks and camaraderie, but stay away from the gaming tables." His stomach growled loudly, and he tossed a cacao bean on the counter. "Come on; let's get a bite to eat, all right?"

Tz' nodded and put his empty cup on the countertop. "Yes, we should go; my father will probably be looking for me." He stood up and felt a little dizzy walking toward the door. Crossing the room, he bumped into one of the crowded tables and a mug tipped over, splashing his leg and loincloth with fermented juice. "Sorry," Tz' said. He gave the man a cacao bean and motioned for Nil to bring another drink.

Nil nodded, grabbed a full mug, and a rag to wipe up the spill. "See you tomorrow?" Nil asked.

Both youths waved, but didn't say anything. When Tz' stepped outside, he was surprised to see the moon high above the pyramid. He walked quickly through the streets following Box, who wove in and out of the crowds still lingering in the area. As they neared the market, the smells of roasting turkey and fresh iguana made Tz's mouth water. *Perhaps some food will make this headache go away,* Tz' thought as he stood in line behind Box. They stood in the shadows and ate the charred turkey legs Box had purchased while watching several young couples sitting at a large table at a nearby stall. They were all laughing and smiling as they fed each other bites of food, and every now and then, one of the girls leaned over to kiss the boy beside her on the mouth.

Even after he was done eating, Tz' continued to watch, fascinated by the constant contact the couples had with each other. He ached to have that kind of relationship with a woman, and he suddenly realized that once again several hours had passed without his thinking of Na'om. He frowned, wondering how he was ever going to move beyond the pain that now filled his chest.

Box tapped him gently on the shoulder and nodded toward the couples. "Someday soon that will be us," he said.

Tz' shook his head. He knew it would be a long time before his heart was ready to accept another girl. "Maybe you, but not me." He then told Box about growing up with Na'om and what had happened to her.

"Itzamná, I had no idea," Box said. "I'm sorry the gods have laid so much trouble on you. But that must mean they have great things in store for you. My grandmother always told me that when one misfortune follows another, the gods are testing you. If they see you can handle a multitude of problems, then they heap a bounty of goodness on you later."

"Well, let's hope your ati't is right," Tz' said with a smile. "I should go. I'll see you at work in the morning."

Tz's father was still awake and sitting by the fire when he returned to the hut. "I was beginning to worry about you," Chiman said as he stood up to give Tz' a hug. "I haven't seen you for days, is everything all right?"

"Yes, Tat. I've been busy with work and my friends, that's all." Tz' realized too late that he still smelled of the fermented berries that had spilled on him. He saw his father frown, so to forestall any more conversation, Tz' faked a yawn. "I'm going to bed." He entered the dark hut and climbed into his hammock. That night, he dreamt of Na'om. They were one of many couples sitting at an outdoor table, eating and laughing with Box and several other friends. But when Na'om leaned in to kiss Tz' on the lips, he snarled at her and nipped her with his large fangs, the coppery taste of fresh blood lingering in his mind long after the dream had faded away.

When Tz' arrived at work several days later, he was startled when Box handed him a small fired sculpture. It was the piece he had created during his lunch break several days earlier.

"That's her, the girl you told me about, isn't it?" Box said.

Tz' nodded as he turned the statue in his hands. "Yes."

"I thought you might like to carry her with you, you know, like the figurines," Box said as he pointed toward the table of funerary pieces.

"Maltiox," Tz' said. He tucked the statuette into his leather pouch and went back to unloading a kiln.

That night, when he was sure Chiman was asleep, he pulled the small statue out of his pouch, kissed it on the head, and tucked it into a small hollow in his pillow. He gently placed his hand over the piece, protecting it. He was grateful to have something tangible to remember Na'om by. In the morning, after Chiman had left for the day, he ripped a soft cotton cloth in half and wrapped the piece carefully before hiding it up among the palm fronds above his hammock. He knew it would be safe there and easy to retrieve once he'd returned from work.

The days passed in a mindless blur of movement, which helped ease the grief that still tugged at his heart. Tz' lugged buckets of heavy slip and blocks of wet clay to the numerous potters, who transformed the raw materials into pots, plates, and urns to hold special spices and oils. He often went outside the city gates to collect bundles of firewood with the younger boys, toting them on his back with the use of a tumpline to help steady the heavy load. Tz' also helped Box load and unload the numerous kilns that glowed for days at a time. Sometimes the two of them stayed throughout the night to keep a kiln burning at just the right temperature to fire a special glaze the potters were using. The city was quiet then, and he and Box had plenty of time to talk about the directions their lives were taking as they fed more wood into the fires.

Tz' wasn't surprised to learn that Box would continue at the pottery workshop for as long as he was able to work. He hoped to find a woman to settle down with at some point, but so far he'd had no luck in finding the right girl.

Tz' sighed and shook his head. "I used to know exactly where my life was headed, and then everything changed when Na'om died. Now I'm not sure what to do."

"Well, you can certainly stay on here," Box said, wiping his sweaty brow with a cloth.

"Hmm, I wish it was that easy. But I promised my father I'd go back to the village and resume my training with him."

"Well, if you change your mind and return to the city, I'm sure Puk'pik will give you your job back." Box shoved some more wood into the kiln. "Based on that sculpture you made, you could probably work as one of the artists creating the funerary pieces. They make good wages doing those special pieces, far more than I'll ever earn for a living."

Tz' grinned. "I'll keep that in mind."

On days they didn't need to stay late, the two youths often went to the

Silowik Tukan for a drink where they chatted with Nil while he served the customers in the place. Tz' enjoyed the company of the two young men, and was fascinated with the ease with which they talked about the girls they liked and the general gossip they shared about various inhabitants of the city. In turn, they listened eagerly and laughed frequently when he told them stories about his childhood, of growing up in the jungle, having a pet tayra, learning to fish and hunt the wild animals that lived in the area, or spending time studying to be a shaman with Chiman.

It was only late at night that thoughts of Na'om reappeared, filling Tz's dreams, making him restless, anxious, and frustrated. As the rains pounded on the roof overhead each night, he'd cup the statuette in his palm and fall back to sleep, wondering why the gods still tormented him with images of her when she was lost to him. And when he wasn't dreaming of Na'om, he imagined being a were-jaguar, loping after a peccary or an agouti, something to quench the endless desire for fresh blood and meat. In the mornings, the various images lingered, creating a veil over everything until Tz' was sufficiently absorbed in his work to push them away.

Several days later, he heard Chiman in the courtyard preparing the morning fire. Feeling guilty that he hadn't spent much time with his father of late, he hurried to join him.

"Tz', I'm glad you're up. I need to talk to you," Chiman said as he handed Tz' a bowl of corn gruel with honey in it. "The rains are coming to an end, and we'll be leaving for Pa nimá soon. I'm wondering if you'll be coming with us. I know the village is small and doesn't hold the allure of all that you have here, but . . . it is your home."

Tz' rubbed his eyes, sweeping away the clay grit that made them ache. "I promised you I would, so I will, although it will be difficult to say good-bye to Box and Nil."

"Good, I had hoped you'd be joining us. I'm glad you've made some friends here, but it's time for you pick up your training where you left off. That's your real destiny."

"Is it? How do you know? My fate was wrapped up with Na'om, but now that she's gone, I have no idea what my future will be like." Tz' stirred his hot mush and finally ate a few bites.

"I think that's a question we all ask at one time or another, regardless of the circumstances," Chiman said. "I believe you'll find your answer back at home." He sipped at his tea and settled on the ground near Tz'. "I visited Ajkun yesterday; she's happy to know we'll be leaving soon, but saddened that Mok'onel has decided to stay here."

Tz' choked on the bit of porridge in his mouth. "She's not going back to Pa nimá?"

"No, apparently life in the city agrees with her, and she's found a young man here she likes. Why?"

"I guess I thought we'd all be returning, the whole village, that's all." He took a bite of lukewarm mush and swallowed it with difficulty. "You know Chuch wanted me to be with Mok'onel; perhaps with time, I could have learned to love her." Tz' shook his head and placed his bowl on the ground. "Nothing will be the same, will it?"

Chiman sighed. "No, I'm afraid not. Your mother and I had our difficulties, but I still miss her. And just like you, I grieve for Na'om. But that doesn't mean there aren't good things ahead for all of us."

"But Tat, I fell in love with Na'om, and she turned out to be my sister. And now any chance I might have had with Mok'onel is lost, too. Who am I destined to be with and where will I find her?"

"You'll find your way soon, I'm sure of it, and a special woman will appear who'll fill the spot you've held open for Na'om. I know you can't help having fallen in love with her, but it's time to put that aside." He put up his hand to stop Tz' from interrupting. "We can't always choose who we love. Itzamná knows I've tried to forget someone over the years . . . All I can suggest is that you come back to the village, resume your training, and wait to see what the gods have in store for you."

Tz' studied his father's face. *Tat axel is getting old, but he's still wise. Certainly, he wouldn't tell me to come home if he didn't think it was a good idea. Besides, one day he'll need me to take over as the village shaman when he's no longer able to perform the ceremonies.* He put his hand up to shield his eyes and looked at his father's weathered face. "You're right. Pa nimá is my home. I'll tell Puk'pik, Box, and Nil that I'm leaving soon."

Once he'd made his decision, Tz' realized it was the right one, and he suddenly felt happier than he had since learning of Na'om's death. Returning to the village and resuming his training would ease the sorrow he still felt, and he'd finally have the time and the privacy necessary to read the ledger he'd bought. Plus, he could practice shape-shifting again with the toad venom and tobacco already stuffed in the bottom of his pack basket. Even though the gods already had his destiny planned for him, doing a little work on his own certainly couldn't hurt.

Yakal

Yakal shifted slowly in the swinging hammock. He didn't want to crush his newborn son who was having breakfast beside him. Yakal touched the baby's head where it pressed tightly to Uskab's breast and managed a quick feel of her rounded skin under his fingertips. Uskab opened her eyes and smiled at Yakal as he drew a soft line from her bosom, up her neck, and to her cheek. "Don't get up; I'll grab a bite to eat at the market before I go to work," Yakal said as he leaned over and kissed Uskab on the lips.

"Are you sure?" Uskab asked. "He's almost done, and I'll need to change him soon, so I don't mind making you breakfast." She started to lift her head and shoulders from the netting.

"If you stay, you'll be able to go back to sleep," Yakal said as he placed his feet on the ground and stood up. "And you need the rest."

"Hmm, you're right," Uskab replied as she smiled at him again. "I am a bit tired."

Yakal grabbed his loincloth from a hook in the wall and slipped it on, then pulled a thin cotton shirt over his torso. He slid his feet into a pair of leather sandals, brushed his hands through his hair, bent to kiss Uskab one more time, and quickly left the hut as she closed her eyes. He needed her to rest, to heal, so they could make love again. It had been several weeks since they'd been together, and his body ached for her embrace. But he had promised Alom and Ajkun he would let Uskab decide when to be a couple again after giving birth. Certainly, the women knew more about the demands a newborn placed on a woman than he did, but oh, how he needed to find some relief. *At least I can find some solace in a glass of balché tonight,* Yakal thought as he hurried through the nearly deserted streets to the marketplace.

He stopped at one of the few places open at that early hour and quickly ate a bowl of iguana stew. Oftentimes, the meat was chewy, but this had simmered for a long time with chopped tomatoes, onions, and chili peppers, and the meat practically fell apart in his mouth. He wiped his mouth with the back of his hand and gave the old woman behind the cooking pot the empty pottery bowl. "Delicious, maltiox," he said as he paid her. She nodded and grinned at him, and he noticed she had only two teeth left in the front of her mouth.

No wonder she cooks her meat for so long; she has no teeth to chew with, Yakal thought as he headed toward the pyramid where he was chiseling another carving. He pulled off the cotton sheeting covering the sculpture he was working on and stood back to look at the limestone block. He had carved a likeness of a snake's head into the piece, with its mouth open wide, ready to bite anyone or anything that came near it. It was not something he would normally have considered carving, but snakes and serpents still invaded his dreams night after night. He had finally decided the gods and not Satal must be telling him to create this piece. The snake head would sit at the top of a staircase that led to a new building the shamans had requested be built. *Perhaps they've influenced me with some of their magic from the purification Chiman did,* Yakal thought as he picked up his hammer and chisel and began to chip some pieces of stone away from the inside of the snake's mouth. He needed to be careful and not remove too much at one time, just enough so that a set of fangs would appear as well as a long tongue.

The hours passed rapidly, as they always did when he was engrossed in his work, and Yakal was surprised when he finally looked up to see the sun was headed toward the western horizon. The snake's head was finished, though, and Yakal knew he could quit for the day and head home to Uskab and the baby. *Or I could go get that glass of balché,* Yakal thought as he put his tools away and washed the stone dust from his face and hands. Ever since he'd taken some of Satal's cacao beans, he'd allowed himself a drink or two in the early evenings. It helped him to relax. And visiting the bars gave him the chance to listen to the gossip that filtered through the city. He still believed Satal was alive and hoped one day someone would have news of her.

He nodded at some of the other sculptors who were busy on projects of their own before heading toward the market. *I'll grab another bowl of stew and then go to the bar. Perhaps somebody new in town might have heard or seen Satal.*

When Yakal got to the market, he was disappointed to see that the old woman who had fed him breakfast was no longer there. He wandered around a bit, looking at all the food for sale, and settled on a plate of turkey pieces cooked with chaya and manioc root. It wasn't very flavorful and definitely needed salt, but Yakal ate it anyway. He had skipped lunch and knew from experience that balché on an empty stomach was a bad combination. He headed into the poorer district of the city, pushing past the women and children who stood about in the streets until he stood outside the Silowik Tukan. Rumor had it that many of the patrons were involved in the slave trade and other unsavory deals, so there was a good chance someone might know of Satal. He made a mental note to ask the owner, Q'abarel.

Yakal stepped out of the late afternoon sun into the dark room. The numerous tables that filled the space in front of the long wooden bar were empty. Yakal nodded to Q'abarel, who stood behind the long counter wiping pottery mugs dry with an old towel. As he walked toward the back room, Yakal extended his thumb and smallest finger outward and then tipped his hand toward his mouth, indicating he wanted a drink. Q'abarel nodded, picked up a large glazed jug, and poured some frothy liquid into a clean glass. He brought it to Yakal, who had stationed himself in one of the many private seating areas in the secondary room.

"No one's here," Yakal commented as he paid Q'abarel.

"Too early, my friend. Later, they'll come to drink away their pain and gamble with their cacao beans." He raised his eyebrows as Yakal drained the glass and set the empty mug back on the table. "Another?"

"Tempting," Yakal said, "but I don't like to drink alone." He motioned to the bench on the opposite side of the table. "Have one on me and I'll take a second glass."

Q'abarel grinned and hurried back to the front room, returning within minutes with two fizzing mugs. He handed one to Yakal before sliding onto the wooden seat. "*Q'inomal*," he said, toasting him, as he raised his cup.

"Q'inomal," Yakal replied, wishing the bar owner riches and wealth in return, before he drank another long draught of the cool liquid. He set his mug down and looked around the room, which remained empty. "So, you must know a lot of the people who come here, where they work, who they work for, as well as hear any number of rumors."

Q'abarel looked at Yakal as he set his own glass on the table. "I try to mind my own business, make sure the customers are happy, that no one starts a fight, but I do hear things from time to time." He paused and looked at Yakal. "However, you don't strike me as the sort who'd be interested in any of the gossip that I might know."

Yakal nodded. The barkeeper was right; he had no real business in this place, but he needed some way to find out if Satal was still alive. In his heart, he knew she was; he just had to make sure. "If I was looking for someone, someone very particular, would you know anyone who could help me find this person?" He hesitated and then reached out and touched the older man's arm. "I could pay, only a little, but something at least."

"Who is this person?"

"I'm looking for Satal."

"Satal! Itzamná," Q'abarel said, "you must be joking. Everyone knows she fell in the cenote with that girl and her jaguar." He fell silent and looked at Yakal. "You're the girl's father, aren't you? I heard the rumors."

Yakal nodded, but remained silent.

Q'abarel shifted in his seat. "Satal used to come here, did you know that?" He wiped his forehead with the towel he had in his hand. "She was always looking for the girl and had a network of spies searching for her."

"Do you know who she talked to when she was here?"

"Of course. Ilonel, and then another man, one of the many men Ilonel employed. Let me think a moment, I'm sure I can come up with his name." Q'abarel rubbed his chin with his hand. "He has a spiral of blue dots tattooed down his left arm, Kux, that's his name, Kux."

"Does he still come in here? I'd like to meet him."

The barkeeper turned as he heard a noise from the front room. "I should get back out there." He picked up the two empty mugs and started to slide out from the table. His large belly rubbed the worn wood as he moved. "Some words of advice, my friend. Don't look for Kux; the men Satal had working for her are not good people. They'd sell their own mothers if they thought there was profit in it. Forget all about Satal, go back to your wife, live a good, quiet life. If Satal did survive that fall, then may Itzamná protect us all, for she'll be more powerful than all the shamans combined."

Yakal handed Q'abarel another two cacao beans. "Maltiox, I appreciate you telling me all this. But I believe she *is* alive and I must find her, before she has the chance to do any more harm. If you see this Kux, tell him Yakal, the stonemason, is looking for him. He can find me most days near the pyramid, working on the new sculptures for the House of Snakes."

Q'abarel slipped the beans into an inner pocket of his leather loincloth and nodded to Yakal. "If I see him, I'll pass on the information." He hurried into the front room.

Yakal could hear the murmur of voices, the scrape of a wooden table as it was moved on the tile floor, and then the clink of pottery glasses. He leaned back against the wall and closed his eyes. He didn't need to get home right away, and a few extra minutes of sleep would do him good. He had almost as much trouble getting enough rest as Uskab, since the baby often cried in the night, waking Yakal from his dreams. He had to admit, though, that he didn't mind being brought back to this realm as his dreams were often filled with snakes. They writhed and wriggled around him, trying to crawl into his body through his feet and nose. He'd even dreamt of Satal on more than one occasion. In those cases, he was a young boy again, being struck by the woman for no apparent reason, other than that he was his father's son by his servant mother, Alom. Satal had never forgiven his father for taking a lover and having children with her. Yakal yawned as he opened his eyes. Perhaps it was better not to sleep, especially in such a public place. He straightened in his seat and made a quick exit from the bar, which was rapidly filling with young and old men intent on gaming away their daily wages. He failed to notice Q'abarel standing behind the bar, pointing with one finger toward the far corner of the room, where Kux sat with a group of friends, gambling over a game of bones.

The next morning, Yakal was helping some of the apprentices

maneuver a new block of limestone into place on the steps of the House of the Snakes when he felt a tap on his back. He straightened and turned to find a man of similar age beside him. Tattooed blue dots spiraled down his left arm. "You must be Kux," Yakal said as he led the man away from the group of young boys.

"Q'abarel said you were looking for me," Kux replied.

"Yes, I need to know if you've seen or heard from someone any time recently."

"Who?"

Yakal grinned. "A man of few words, good, I like that; it makes it easier to keep things secret, eh?" he said as he laughed. Kux didn't even smile, and Yakal quickly dropped the joking. He swallowed and stared right into Kux's deep brown eyes. "Satal, I'm looking for Satal."

Now Kux did laugh, a deep roar that caused many of the apprentices to turn and look in their direction. "Oh, Q'abarel warned me you were crazy, but he didn't say how come. If you think I've had anything to do with that witch since she disappeared into the cenote, then you need more help than I can ever provide. I wanted nothing to do with her before she died and even less so now."

Yakal felt Kux's eyes boring into him. But he was determined and straightened his back. "I know she's alive, and I know you're the type of man who can be hired to find people. Name your price and help me locate her before she does any more harm."

Kux scuffed the dirt with his old leather sandals, and Yakal noticed the smooth, worn patches where he'd obviously rubbed his hands on his leather loincloth. Kux's gray cotton shirt was frayed at the hem. "Here," Yakal said as he reached into his pouch he wore around his waist and extracted a few cacao beans. "Take these, buy yourself some new clothes, and if you hear anything, any gossip, or hint of something that speaks of Satal, come find me, all right?" He pressed the beans into the man's hand.

"And if I hear nothing?"

"Then consider this your lucky day," Yakal said. He started toward the House of Snakes and then turned back to Kux. "If you do hear something, there'll be more profit in it for you." Kux nodded and hurried into the crowd nearby. Yakal watched him disappear and laughed as a sudden thought came to him. *I'll be using Satal's own beans to find her. I have more than enough stashed away to pay for this man's services.* Delighted that things were finally going in a positive direction, Yakal eagerly returned to work.

AJKUN

Ajkun glanced at the clear sky overhead and smiled briefly. *Home, we can finally go home,* she thought as she approached the group nearby. The rains had stopped several days ago, and Chiman had told her they could head back to Pa nimá. Ajkun was eager to get away from Mayapán, as the place did nothing except remind her of her loss and pain. She needed to be back in the village, surrounded by the plants and animals she knew so well. The city was too vast, too loud, and too empty for her, despite the friends she had made in Alom, Uskab, and her new baby.

"A gift, for your trip," Alom said as she held out a smooth mahogany walking stick to Ajkun.

Ajkun gripped the staff in her right hand and smiled. "Maltiox, this will definitely help on our walk to the river." She hugged Alom, and the two older women smiled through their tears as they stepped apart.

"May Xaman Ek protect you on your journey," Alom said as she wiped her face with the corner of her dark green shawl.

Uskab stood next to Alom, and Ajkun gave her a quick kiss on the cheek. The younger woman cradled her infant in her arms, and Ajkun ran her fingertips through the clump of thick black hair on the baby's head before bending and kissing him on his forehead. "*Matzaqik*, little Mayibal, may you grow up to be a fine young man." The baby smiled up at her and waved his pudgy fist before popping it back into his mouth.

Yakal stood beside his wife and son, waiting to speak to Ajkun. "Thank you for everything, for healing me and the others, for help with Mayibal's birth."

"Whether it was my herbs, Satal's death, or Chiman's ritual that cured you is hard to say, but I'm glad you're feeling better. And I really didn't need to help Uskab; she practically had the baby born by the time I arrived."

Yakal gently hugged Ajkun good-bye. "I doubt I'll see you again anytime soon," he said as he held the woman in his arms.

"No, I'll probably never come back here. But who am I to say? I never thought I'd be here in the first place. Only Itzamná knows what the future holds for any of us." She patted Yakal on the arm. "Remember your promise." He smiled in return, and Ajkun walked over to Mok'onel who stood a little way off from the rest of the group.

"Are you sure you want to stay here?" she asked the girl. "We'll miss seeing your sweet smile in Pa nimá." She glanced over at Tz', but he was looking the other way.

Mok'onel followed her gaze and then looked directly at the older woman in front of her. "Yes, I'm positive. The village holds too many memories for me, good ones and bad ones. When Chuch and the children were killed in the attack, I knew I'd never want to go back there." She nodded at Alom. "Yakal's mother has agreed to let me live with her, and I can help Uskab with the new baby." She paused and a blush appeared on her cocoa-colored skin. "I'm sure I've met someone special here, too."

"Well, I'm happy for you, my dear. I'm glad you're thinking of the future instead of dwelling on the past." She hugged the girl before joining Chiman and Tz'. They stood at the head of the group who wanted to return to Pa nimá. "I'm ready," she said as she picked up a pack basket and swung it onto her back. She nodded again to Alom, grateful to the woman for the gift of the walking stick.

Tz' set off, leading them through the main gates and onto one of the many dirt footpaths that crisscrossed the countryside. They entered a lime orchard, and Ajkun looked back just once, catching a final glimpse of the upper reaches of the city walls and the tops of the main gates through the branches of the lime trees. *Good-bye, sweet Na'om, may we meet again someday.* She stifled the sob building in her chest and hurried to catch up with the others.

* * *

It took the group almost a week to journey safely across the countryside to the river, another two days to cut mahogany trees and hollow them out into wooden canoes to carry them upstream, and several more days to reach the area near Pa nimá. As they drew closer to the village, each man and woman sat up straighter in the canoes and paddled longer and harder. *Everyone is eager to get home,* Ajkun thought as she watched the water slide past the side of the canoe. *They'll all pick up their normal lives again* . . . . She swallowed as a knot formed in her throat. *But I have no one waiting for me when I get there.*

As they rounded the last bend in the river and she saw familiar landmarks, Ajkun deliberately avoided looking at the opposite shore. She didn't want to see the well-worn path that led to Na'om's hut.

Setesik and Pempen's canoe was the first to land on the shore, and their daughter, Sijuan, nimbly hopped out and held the boat steady so her mother could get out. Pempen dropped to the ground and kissed it, thanking Xaman Ek for protecting them all on their long journey. The family gathered the few belongings they had and hurried up the path to the village.

Chiman let his canoe gently glide onto the sandy beach, and Tz' stepped off the bow. He held the canoe steady between his knees and offered Ajkun his hand to help her over the gunwale. "I'll be fine," she said, shrugging him away. She planted the walking stick firmly in the sand and stepped over the gunwale into the cool river water. She leaned on the staff and flexed her legs, as her knees ached from kneeling for so many hours on the hard wooden bottom of the canoe.

Tz' and Chiman unloaded what few supplies they had brought with them from the city, and together the three followed the other villagers up the path and into the village plaza.

Ajkun stopped at the edge of the clearing. "I thought the place would be overrun with animals and jungle vines by now," she said. She was surprised to see the square was neatly swept, and a bright fire burned under a large cooking pot in the fire pit. The rich smell of turkey and corn stew drifted to them on the light breeze.

"Hello, who's there?" Chiman called.

An older man stepped out from one of the huts, followed by a small boy of about seven. The boy ran up to Ajkun and tugged on her dark brown skirt. "Where's Na'om?" he asked.

"How do you know about Na'om?" she asked as she knelt down and looked at the little boy.

"She came to my village months ago and helped my noy with her wounded leg and told us about this place. She put me in charge of caring for the village until she returned. She promised to come back and let me play with her pet jaguar. Where is she? Is she down at the river?" the boy said as he started to run down the path.

"Wait, child, come back," Ajkun cried. She held out her arms and the boy ran to her. "What's your name?"

"Lintat."

"Lintat, that's a nice name for a boy." She held Lintat firmly by his shoulders. "Now, you must be big and brave, like your name suggests, can you do that?"

Lintat bobbed his head up and down.

"Good." Ajkun took a deep breath and glanced quickly at Chiman, who nodded his head. "Na'om isn't here; she never made it out of Mayapán. Because she was born in the Wayeb, she knew things that the rest of us didn't, and because of that, she chose to be a sacrifice to save us, her family and friends. Does this make sense to you?" The boy nodded, but Ajkun could see his bottom lip begin to quiver and the sudden tears that appeared in his big brown eyes. She felt her own eyes fill at the thought of her dear Na'om at the bottom of the cenote, and she hugged Lintat to her chest before briskly pushing him away. "Go on now, back to your noy. I must get to work."

Ajkun hurried across the plaza and down the narrow path that led to her old hut. She quickly stepped through the doorway and only then let the sob trapped in her chest escape. She sank down on the narrow bed she had shared with Na'om for so many years and cried. After a time, the sobs slowly subsided, her breathing slowed, and she wiped her face with the sleeve of her huipil. Looking around, she was pleasantly surprised to see that the hut had been swept and all her bottles, baskets of herbs, and pots of salves in the storage room had been recently dusted. But the sight of them reminded her that Na'om had been the one to collect most of the contents. She felt another wave of grief threaten to overwhelm her, so she went back outside. She smiled at her neighbors who were busy starting fires and settling back in to their own homes, and wandered back down to the river. She needed to get away from everyone, to be some place private where she could really let out her anguish.

She stepped into one of the smaller wooden canoes and quickly crossed the river. She tied the bow rope to a small bush and headed down the path to Na'om's hut, stepping over the liana vines that had grown across the dirt and stopping at the edge of the circular clearing. Other than some branches that had fallen into the middle of the space, it looked similar to how she remembered it.

The short bench she had helped Na'om build stood near the cooking ring, and an old blackened pot balanced on the rocks. The box where Na'om had stored her food was knocked askew, the pottery bowls inside licked clean by some unknown animal. Ajkun sighed and stepped into the ring of trees. She gently touched each item, but left them in place. She didn't want to change anything; it was all she had left to remember Na'om by. She entered the small hut and was amazed to see the bright flowers and vines that Na'om had painted on the walls. The gridlines drawn in charcoal had begun to fade, but if Ajkun closed her eyes, she could see the jungle flora and fauna as Na'om had imagined them. She stood still for several minutes with her eyes closed, imprinting the images into her mind.

Suddenly, she heard footsteps outside and turned just as someone filled the doorway, blocking the late afternoon sun.

"I thought I might find you here," Chiman said as he entered the room. "Itzamná, I had no idea," he added as he looked at the detailed paintings on the walls. "When did she start doing this?"

"While Tz' was away on the trading trip, before the raid on the village," Ajkun said, and a sob escaped her.

Chiman held out his arms and Ajkun stepped into his embrace. They hugged and cried together, their tears mingling on Chiman's bare chest.

Finally, Ajkun pulled away from him. "I don't know what to do now," she said.

"I do," Chiman replied as he leaned down and kissed Ajkun's full lips. She looked up at him in surprise. "We go on living; it's what Na'om would have wanted." He looked around the room. "We'll leave this place just the way it is." He scanned the room and spied Na'om's ledger that lay open on the floor. He knelt down and flipped through the pages, astonished at the colorful images. "How come she never showed me this?"

"She was going to right after the corn ceremony, but then the raiders came and took us all prisoner. It's a record of all her dreams as she saw them." Together, they looked at the images until they came to the last two pages filled with black and white drawings. They could clearly see the apex of a pyramid, the round opening of a cenote, and a girl and a jaguar falling into the water in the sketch. Then they saw the girl swimming upward, into a tunnel, pulled by the jaguar toward the light.

Ajkun looked at Chiman's lined face. "Do you think it's possible?"

"Only Itzamná knows," Chiman replied, but his wrinkled face broke into a smile, "and Na'om."

"But surely it's not possible to survive a fall like that," Ajkun exclaimed as she struggled to stand upright. The blood rushed from her head, everything began to turn black, and she clutched at Chiman who held her steady.

Chiman looked into Ajkun's eyes. "Come, let's sit outside and rest. It's been a long day, with many ups and downs." He helped Ajkun to the small bench and then sat cross-legged on the ground next to her. "I never expected to find new people living in the village," Chiman said. "They've been taking care of the place for months and say the corn, beans, and squash have been planted and are growing well. A few couples with young children have moved into the empty huts and some have built new homes, which they want me to bless once I have time. And three of the women are pregnant, so it looks like you'll be busy very soon." Chiman turned to look up at Ajkun and saw that her head was tilted back and her eyes were closed. "Ajkun? Did you hear me?"

"What, oh, yes, of course, babies to birth," Ajkun replied. She sighed and opened her eyes. "I'm sorry, my friend, I was lost, thinking about Na'om and what the drawings may mean." She frowned at him. "Not to mention that kiss; what will the villagers think if they knew you'd kissed me?"

"Let them think what they like," Chiman replied as he turned around on his knees and tried to kiss her again.

"Stop, Chiman, it's only been a few months since Chachal's death.

Why, we haven't even decided what to do with the bodies."

"Lintat and his grandfather, Mam, say there are no bodies, that Na'om burned them all in the cornfield. They scooped up the ashes and placed them in baskets so we could bury them properly when we returned." He placed his hands on the short bench on either side of Ajkun. "I don't care how long it's been since Chachal went to the Underworld. We both know we belong together and should have been together all this time. What's to stop us from doing just that now?"

"Tz'?" Ajkun replied. "How is he going to feel seeing you kissing me when he's lost his mother and the girl he wanted to marry in the space of a few weeks?" She pushed on Chiman's muscular arm, forcing him to move so she could stand up. "No, I say we wait and give everyone, including me, time to adjust to all of this." She looked at the sadness crossing Chiman's face. "You're my oldest and dearest friend, but I need time alone right now. While we were stuck in Mayapán because of the rains, the only thing I could think of was getting back to the village, getting back to work. And now that we're here, I intend to do just that. If I keep busy, then I won't have time to dwell on my loss."

"Our loss," Chiman corrected her. "She was my granddaughter, too." He stood up and smoothed his hair and loincloth. "I'll give you six moons, no longer," he said. "After that, I intend to make my intentions clear to everyone, including Tz'. He'll have to adjust, like everyone else, but I don't plan to spend the rest of my days and nights alone." He paused and looked at Ajkun, who quickly looked away. "Unless you don't want to be together?"

"Itzamná, I don't know what I want or what to think. Everything is upside down now. Please, Chiman, just give me some time, all right?" Ajkun's heart beat fast in her chest as she tried to comprehend everything that was happening to her. Part of her ached to return Chiman's kiss and to tell him she loved him. But another part feared the relationship was something neither of them was ready for. And she didn't want to hurt Tz'; the boy had suffered enough already. Seeing his father in love would only remind him of his own loss. But uppermost in her mind was what might be happening to Na'om. *If she did survive the fall and somehow managed to find a tunnel, is she trapped in the Underworld?* The thought made Ajkun shudder. No, she needed to avoid anything controversial for the moment. A clear head to think through all the ramifications of her actions and of those around her was what was needed now. And she had the new mothers to think of as well.

"In six moons' time or sooner, I'll give you my decision. In the meantime, we both have work to do. We must make friends with the new arrivals and settle back into our normal routines." She smiled at Chiman and slipped her arm through his. "Surely if you've waited this long, another few moons will do no harm."

But Chiman didn't answer as they left the clearing and headed back to the village. Ajkun quickly left Chiman's side and went in search of the new mothers-to-be. And as darkness fell over the small plaza, the old villagers and the newcomers mingled around a large bonfire, sharing stories far into the night.

Na'om

The stench of bat guano was firmly lodged in Na'om's nose, and she tried blowing it several times to remove the smell, but had no luck. It didn't help that her feet were still covered in globs of it, or that she had dragged her ragged skirt in the mess when she'd fallen to her knees from the horrible sounds Camazotz and the other bats had made.

I hope we find water soon. Even as she thought it, she felt the ground underneath her feet turn damp, and within a few hundred steps, she discovered numerous places along the walls where fresh water oozed from the porous limestone and streamed downward to form a small brook that ran from one side of the tunnel to the other. She couldn't see how wide the stream was, but she waded into the cool water and felt the burning and festering on her feet ease. Ek' Balam splashed into the water as well and finally plopped down onto his belly, letting the six inches of water wash away some of the guano stuck to his belly fur.

Na'om continued to walk and discovered the water grew deeper with each step until she was in water up to her knees. "There's enough to bathe in," she said and immediately stripped off her tattered shirt and skirt. She found a small rock sticking out from the tunnel wall and hung her clothes on it. "Just like taking a bath at home," she said as she slipped into the water. She gasped at the cold as it swirled around her shrunken stomach and small breasts, and she quickly stood up and let the water drain away. With her limited visibility, she could see she was still deeply crusted with dried blood, dirt, and guano, so she ripped off the other sleeve off her blue shirt and used the fabric to scrub her arms and legs. A small amount of the grime came off, but most of the muck was firmly embedded in her skin. *I'll need more than a quick bath in this cold water to get clean,* Na'om thought as she stood up again. She grabbed what remained of her shirt and skirt and sloshed her way through the deep water to the other side. She started to put on her filthy clothes, but realized they still smelled of guano. *I'd better try to clean these, too,* she thought as she bent and scrubbed the fabric back and forth in the water. She wrung the clothes out as best she could and decided not to put them on wet. Ek' Balam splashed through the water and stepped on to dry ground, then proceeded to shake from head to tail, splattering Na'om with droplets of cold water. "Thanks a lot," she said as she looked at her body, which was now covered in a fine layer of wet cat hair.

She threw her clothes on the ground and waded back into the water to wash again. "I really didn't want to get wet again," she said when she got back to Ek' Balam. He just regarded her with his golden eyes. "Come on, we'd better keep moving," Na'om said as she bundled her wet clothes under one arm.

But she'd only gone a few steps when she realized the air was too cold on her bare skin, so she pulled the wet clothes on again. *Maybe my body heat, what there is of it, will help dry them.* She stumbled as she tugged at the wet fabric of her skirt, landing awkwardly on something sharp under her left foot.

"Ow," she cried and stepped to the side of the tunnel. She braced herself against the wall and lifted her foot. Tiny droplets of blood appeared on the sole of her foot. "Itzamná, what did I step on?" Na'om winced as she tried to put weight on her foot. She sat down on the uneven ground and tore yet another piece of fabric from her skirt. She carefully bound the cotton around her foot and tied it on top.

"We have to find our way out of this place before anything else happens," she said to Ek' Balam as she started to hobble forward. "Otherwise we may never leave."

She cried out as she again stepped on something that poked her in her already sore sole. She hopped to one side and paused, keeping her foot elevated while she drew a deep breath. Gingerly, she placed weight on her wounded foot and continued to move forward. Just then, Ek' Balam snarled, and he lifted his left front paw, as if he'd stepped on something sharp. Na'om hobbled over to him and peered at the pad of his foot. Blood was starting to drip from a slight cut in the skin. Na'om shook her head, and let Ek' Balam lick the wound for several minutes before trying to proceed.

More sharp jabs, this time in each foot, caused Na'om to halt altogether. Cautiously, she bent down until her face was just inches from the ground. She ran her hand gently over the surface and was surprised to feel it covered with hundreds of spiky protrusions. As she stood, she felt faint and grabbed at the tunnel wall; it too was covered with jagged pinpoints that stabbed the palm of her extended hand.

Na'om didn't dare move. She knew the ground ahead of her would cut her feet to ribbons within minutes. She looked back the way they had come. *Did we miss a tunnel someplace?* she pondered. Then she realized. *This is yet another test, the house of knives, one of the last trials Ajkun talked about.* She reached out to touch Ek' Balam, eager and yet fearful to see what lay ahead. "If I've counted correctly, this might be the last test," she whispered to her friend.

The glow of light brightened the narrow passageway, and Na'om had no trouble seeing the path ahead. The whole area glittered as her beam of energy hit a thousand pointed pieces of black obsidian protruding from the floor, walls, and ceiling. From where she was standing, she could see the obsidian points grew longer and larger until it seemed the entire tunnel was blocked by the spiky, knife-like protrusions. She sank to the ground in disbelief.

We'll be cut to pieces if we try to pass through all of that. The thought brought a flood of tears. *Even if I had enough clothing to wrap around my feet, I'd never make it through without getting sliced on the rest of my body. And poor Ek' Balam wouldn't have a chance.* Na'om hiccupped through her tears.

She leaned over and placed her head on Ek' Balam, who had sprawled in the dirt beside her. The rhythmic rise and fall of his stomach was soothing, and gradually her tears dried up. Exhausted, she let her eyes close and fell into a deep sleep.

She was back in Pa nimá, watching from the safety of the jungle as the villagers gathered in the central plaza for a celebration. Staying hidden among the liana vines, she saw Chiman light the ceramic brazier outside the village temple, and thick copal smoke began to fill the air. The wind drifted the scent to her, and she coughed, causing many members of the village to turn quickly in her direction. They pointed with their fingers, their eyes like daggers, sinking into her skin, causing her to flinch, and then she saw Tikoy, her young uncle who had died in the attack on the village, wander into the square. He passed right through the villagers who stood in his way and came to stand beside Na'om. He waved his hand at the residents of Pa nimá, and they gradually faded into the thick smoke that now filled the area.

"You're not alone," he said, as he reached out to hug Na'om. "There are many who will stand beside you; you just need to ask for their help." His warm body pressed into Na'om's, and for the first time in a long time, she felt safe. Tears formed and threatened to run down her face, and she swiped at them with the back of one hand. In doing so, she brushed against the branch of a ceiba tree, and the hundreds of spines growing from the tree pricked her skin; the pain woke her from her dream, and Na'om realized she had banged her hand into the wall behind her.

With her head still braced on Ek' Balam's stomach, Na'om reached for her necklace. She held it between both her hands, caressing the shape that so resembled her dearest friend who lay beneath her. "Tikoy said he'd help us, and that there are others who will as well," Na'om said. She tried to concentrate on anyone she knew who might now be wandering the land of the ancestors. "Tikoy," she said. She waited, but nothing happened. "Tikoy, are you there?" Na'om shouted. Minutes passed, and suddenly he appeared, a shimmering shadow that floated several inches off the ground. Startled at the apparition, Na'om sat upright and scrambled to her feet, crying out in pain as she stepped on more sharp obsidian points.

"Tikoy, is it really you?" she cried as she tried to touch the shape in front of her. Her hand went right through him.

"It is," he replied. "You mustn't try to touch me though, not yet, anyway. The longer you're in contact with a spirit, the more spirit-like you'll become, and you, my dear girl, are not destined for the Underworld just yet." The shadow shifted and drifted a few feet away. "Call on the others, so we may carry you through this last trial."

"What others, who? I don't know anyone else who might help me."

"Your mother, your friends from Pa nimá who died the same day I was so badly wounded. They're here, eager to assist you."

"But why?" Na'om said. "They never wanted me in the village; they forced Chiman to send me to live across the river by myself. Why would any of them ever consider helping me now?"

"Because now that they're dead, they see things differently, just as you will once you reach the surface and can return to your life in Pa nimá. Trust me, Na'om, we want you to survive these trials and fulfill the rest of your destiny."

Na'om stood silent for a moment, thinking about what Tikoy had just said. She so wanted to see Tz' again and have a life with him. She knew in her heart that they were meant to be together, and it was obvious now that he had felt that way for some time. She had just been too stubborn and foolish to see and believe it before now. "All right, I'll give it a try," Na'om said. She touched Ek' Balam with one hand for support and clutched her necklace with the other. "Chuch," she cried. "Chuch, are you there?" Na'om waited and several minutes passed before she noticed a pale light appear, which gradually grew brighter and gained a more solid shape. She blinked her eyes a few times and was finally able to see her mother, who had died within hours of giving birth to her. The woman who hovered in front of her was almost a mirror reflection of Na'om, with the same long, black hair, high forehead, and deep brown eyes. Her breasts were small underneath her huipil, her waist thin, her hips gentle mounds that flowed smoothly under the skirt she wore to solid thighs and strong calves and wide bare feet.

Na'om took several steps forward and tried to embrace her mother, but her arms passed right through the warm air.

"As Tikoy said, we can't touch each other for very long. Hurry now, call on the villagers who died in the attack; they've promised to help you pass this test," Na'om's mother said as she stepped in line with Tikoy.

Na'om closed her eyes and instantly images of that horrible day in Pa nimá appeared in her mind. She saw the painted warriors who had rushed onto the field where the villagers were busy planting corn for the season. She noticed Tz' covered in yellow salve, sitting on a small stool after performing the corn planting ceremony. She witnessed as the men and women she'd grown up with were beaten and slashed by whips, and heard again the twang of a dozen bows as arrows were shot into the old and infirm. She saw the pile she'd made of those who had been killed and the bundles of branches and twigs she's used to burn them all so the wild animals of the jungle couldn't feast on their bones. She began to name the villagers as each body came into focus.

"Kemonel," she whispered, "and her little girl Poy, and infant son, Tze'm. Potz' and her husband, Banal Bo'j. Kon, oh Kon," she cried as she remembered his rude attention, his crude remarks, and saw again the deep slice across his young throat. Na'om opened her eyes, and they were all there, floating beside her mother and Tikoy.

"One more, Na'om, you need one more," Tikoy said. "You need nine spirits to pass safely through the house of knives."

Na'om closed her eyes again and forced herself to look at the bodies again. She saw the shimmer of iridescent feathers sewn to a deep green huipil and matching shirt and knew she was looking at the body of Chachal. *If I name her, will she come?* Na'om thought. *She never wanted me to be with Tz' and was plotting to set him up with Mok'onel.*

"Hurry, Na'om, our time here is short," Tu'janel urged her.

Na'om nodded her head and said, "Chachal."

A bright glow filled the tunnel, and Chachal appeared. Na'om gasped at the sight of her for she really hadn't believed she would appear.

"You're so bright compared to the others," Na'om cried as she quickly covered her eyes with her hand. Chachal's energy filled the small tunnel with its shimmering greenish light, blinding Na'om. She blinked several times, shielded her eyes with her hands, and tried to squint at the spirit in front of her. Her eyes, so used to the deep obscurity of the underground, continued to water, and Na'om felt increasing pressure and pain as she stared at the light.

"She has traces of her mother's power within her," Tikoy said. "We can use that to our advantage."

Ignoring the two of them, Chachal motioned to the other ghosts to gather around Na'om and Ek' Balam. "Quickly, child, we must move you through this test," Chachal said.

"Why are you doing this for me?" Na'om said as she tried to open her eyes a bit wider.

"As Tikoy said, I've learned things I didn't understand before. Your fate is wrapped around that of Tz'. He's my only son, and only you can stop the evil that is slipping inside him."

"I don't understand," Na'om cried. "What's wrong with Tz'?"

"Hush, now, there's no time to explain," Chachal said as she floated toward Na'om. "Remember that everything you do must work toward helping Tz' and returning to the village."

Na'om opened her mouth to speak again, but stopped when Chachal held up her hand. Even in death, the older woman commanded a certain amount of respect, and Na'om realized that she was still slightly afraid of her.

Tikoy, Kon, and Banal Bo'j all lay down on the ground and motioned for Na'om and Ek' Balam to lie down on top of them. Kemonel gently placed her little girl Poy onto Ek' Balam's back and handed Na'om her infant, Tze'm, to hold in her arms. Then she and Potz' lay down on top of Na'om and Ek' Balam, so that the two living creatures were carefully layered between the spirits of the dead. Chachal moved in front of the group and began to spread her energy out into an arc in front of her. The blue-green light flowed across the tunnel floor, melting the tips of the obsidian points into a solid, glassy surface. As she stepped forward, Tikoy, Kon, and Banal Bo'j crawled in unison behind her, carrying Na'om, Ek' Balam, and the other spirits safely across the glazed floor. The spirit women on top of the living also cast their energy outward, liquefying the jagged dagger points on the walls and ceiling that threatened to slash and scar them. The vicious daggers quickly solidified into ragged lumps of glossy, cold black rock as they passed.

In tiny increments, the odd group crept forward. As the tunnel narrowed and the spiky obsidian tips grew larger and longer, Na'om involuntarily hunched deeper into herself, trying to avoid any contact with the razor-sharp passageway. She turned her head to see how far they had come and cringed when she saw shreds of white energy clinging to the walls and ceiling like strips of white skin that had been peeled from an animal.

"Stop!" Na'om cried. "You're losing your souls," she shouted.

"We'll lose far more than that if we don't continue," Chachal said.

Na'om lifted her head and looked at Chachal. The woman's light had faded to a pale blue-green, and Na'om could see that the energy required to make it through this nightmare was draining Chachal of everything she had.

Na'om touched Ek' Balam and blended their spirits together. Then she sent their combined energy outward, joining forces with all of those who carried her. As soon as she did so, the group slid quickly across the slippery tunnel as if a giant hand had pushed them from behind.

"Na'om, you mustn't use your powers," Tikoy cried as he felt the extra burst of momentum. "You'll never leave the spirit world if you use your energy now."

"I can't let you do this by yourselves," Na'om said as she tried to concentrate her strength and send it out into the final jumble of sharp, serrated spikes and blades that filled the entire passageway. The spirits surrounding her were barely visible now, their energy spent. She could feel the stubby points of rock pressing in on her and pushed her white light out even farther. She lifted her head slightly and saw the spiky protrusions ahead of her begin to melt and drip molten rock onto the floor of the tunnel where it all blended into liquefied black glass. Jagged barbs tore at her hair and face, and she quickly crossed her arms over her head where she felt the sharp daggers etch lines in her bare arms. They snagged on her back, ripping the thin cotton fabric of her huipil, tracing scars into her skin that burned with a fierce and fiery heat. The melted obsidian below her began to scorch her thighs as she continued to slide across the passageway. She heard Ek' Balam growl next to her, smelled burning fur, closed her eyes, and sent a thicker wall of protective light all around him.

Together, the two of them continued to slip forward into the blackness, leaving a trail of blood and fur behind them. And then they stopped. Cautiously, Na'om opened her eyes. It was pitch black, no glimmer of any kind of light. She felt the cool rocky dirt underneath her body, breathed in the slightly damp smell of wet earth, and carefully searched the immediate area with her hands. Nothing sharp pricked them. She took a deep breath and let it out slowly before laying her head back down. She was exhausted, too tired even to try to stand. She attempted to light up the area just a tiny bit, but was too drained to conjure any kind of light.

She had no idea what had happened to Tikoy, Chuch, Chachal, and the others, and felt tears drip off the end of her nose and into the dirt at the thought of what they had sacrificed to help save her. "By all the powers that Itzamná has given me, I swear I'll not fail any of you when I reach the surface," Na'om prayed. "Maltiox, to all of you," she cried as fatigue grabbed her and dragged her into blackness.

Tz'

Tz' stared up at the thatched ceiling of his room in his parents' house. He'd been awake for hours, thinking about Na'om's journal that Ajkun and his father had found in her hut. If the drawings of her dreams did represent what could happen, then there was a chance Na'om was still alive but trapped in the Underworld. The thought sent a bolt of excitement through Tz's body. Even though they wouldn't be able to marry, Na'om was his oldest and dearest friend. He would do anything to help her return to the world of the living. But he didn't know where to begin.

Restless, he rolled over onto his side in his narrow bed. He listened to his father's snoring and remembered similar moments when he'd been awake, listening to his mother, Chachal, moving about the main room, preparing breakfast, feeding the turkeys that had always been penned nearby, or heating water for a bath. But Chachal was gone, her ashes mingled with those of the other villagers who'd been killed in the raid on Pa nimá, ashes that his father would consecrate in a ceremony to commemorate those who had died.

His mind whirled in a thousand directions. He was ready to leap into a canoe and return to Mayapán to help Na'om, even though he didn't know how, not to mention he'd just arrived in the village. He'd promised Chiman he'd continue his shamanic studies and assist him with the day-to-day issues that always cropped up for the leader of a village, and Tz' knew he should follow through on his promise, despite his desire to help Na'om. Besides, Chiman insisted the gods knew his destiny and had repeatedly told him to have some patience.

He thought back to his last days in the city, which had passed in a blur. He'd been sad to say good-bye to Box and Nil, who had made him promise that he'd come visit one day. And he'd been surprised at how difficult it was to say farewell to Mok'onel. Even though he wasn't in love with her, she'd been a part of his life for as long as he could remember; it felt strange to leave her behind. After that, he'd been eager to get away from the spot where Na'om had died and return to the village, to his home where the people and places were familiar; but now that he was back, he didn't want to be here. Every path he walked from the house to the village plaza or down to the river reminded him of his mother, and each medicinal plant he saw and every secret trail he wandered through the jungle whispered of Na'om. The memories of playing, laughing, and swimming with his childhood friend tormented him during the day and his desires for what could have been, had Na'om not been his half-sister, left him frustrated and unable to sleep.

Tz' went out into the main room of the house, removed several of Chiman's ledgers from the shelf, and returned to his room. He'd studied the books for so many years that he knew just where to look for the information he wanted. He felt ill as he turned the stiff pages, looking at the various drawings and hieroglyphs that described the numerous gods and the nine levels of tests they created for those who passed through the Underworld. They made him cringe with fear and worry for Na'om. *How can she, an innocent girl with little training in anything other than herbal medicine, survive? I can read the stars and determine the best time to plant the corn, bless the new growth, and know when to harvest, but I wouldn't know what to do under these circumstances. Meaning I can't save the one person who was so important to me. Someplace there must be another book that can tell me how to help her.* An image of the books in the shop in Mayapán leapt into his mind. *I need to get back there,* Tz' thought as he placed his father's books on the floor. Then, another thought tugged at him, one he tried to push away, but couldn't. *If we weren't meant to marry, then who is to become my wife? And how will I find her living here?*

Irritated at his own inability to move on in his life, he tossed his thin cotton blanket on the floor and stood up. *I can't remain in this house any longer. I should be living in my own hut, not staying here like some child who's afraid to become a man.* He brushed his shoulder-length black hair and tied it back with a leather thong before slipping on his clean loincloth. *As soon as he wakes up, I'll tell Tat axel that I'm moving across the river to Na'om's house. After all, I helped build it, so why shouldn't I make it mine? And If Na'om did survive the fall, then what better place to sense her presence than in that space? Plus, it'll provide the private space I need to try shape-shifting again.* The idea of transforming into a were-jaguar made Tz' shiver with excitement. He'd been waiting for weeks for an opportune time to practice; certainly, if he was ever going to master the process, now was the time.

With his reasons for moving firmly embedded in his mind, he quietly went outside, wondering what other things Na'om had dreamt about and drawn in her ledger. *Did she ever include a picture of me?* Eager to know, he headed toward the river, and once there, stepped into one of the small canoes and crossed the water to the other side. He pulled the mahogany dugout canoe up into the bushes and tied the bow rope to a tree branch before heading down the path to Na'om's hut. He paused when he reached the clearing. Jungle vines had crept across the opening, like thick green snakes crisscrossing the area, and Tz' made a mental note to bring a larger knife with him next time to hack them back. He straightened the box Na'om used to cache food and stepped into the small hut. He was startled to see the twisting vines Na'om had painted on the white walls in teals, deep emeralds, and lime greens that stretched from the floor to the ceiling, punctuated by golden-yellow and marigold-orange blossoms. *Tat never mentioned the artwork in here,* Tz' thought as he walked over to the ceiba-filled mattress on the floor and sat down. He looked all around at the line drawings still to be filled with paint and lightly touched the blossoms nearest him with his fingertips. Then he leaned over and picked up the ledger filled with Na'om's drawings, flipping through the pages, searching for some detail, some hidden vision that might tell him whether she still lived. But beyond the sketches of Na'om falling into the cenote, the pages were blank, and worse, there was no drawing of him anywhere in the book.

Disappointed, he sighed and gently placed the book back on the floor where he'd found it. It was so quiet, even the sound of the river was muted, and it felt odd to be in the hut without Na'om. As he ran his fingertips over the blankets, he remembered the evening so many moons ago when he'd tried to kiss Na'om, and she had fought him with a strength he hadn't realized she possessed. *If anyone can survive the Underworld, she will,* Tz' mused as he curled up on his side. But deep in his heart, he felt his loss for her reawaken, and he began to cry into the woolen blanket, clutching the soft fabric in both fists. Eventually, he drifted off to sleep, but he was restless, tossing and turning on the narrow bed until he fell the few inches onto the dirt floor. He sat up and looked around, unsure of his surroundings for the briefest of moments, and then everything came flooding back to him.

The whirring of two male hummingbirds just outside the door roused Tz' from his stupor, and he hurried outside. The sun was high overhead, and he knew his father would be wondering where he was, since he needed help in preparing for the day's ceremony.

Once he was back across the river, Tz' ran all the way to his father's house. Chiman was near the outside fire ring, ladling a large spoonful of corn porridge into a coconut husk bowl, when Tz' arrived.

"There you are," Chiman said as he handed the bowl to Tz'. "I was beginning to worry." He looked at his son. "Everything all right?" he asked as he sat down on the ground.

"Yes, Tat," Tz' replied. He blew on the hot mush before taking a bite. "I was across the river," he said after he had swallowed. "I fell asleep in Na'om's hut, what should have been our home." He put the bowl down on the ground. "I've decided to move in over there," he announced.

Chiman didn't say anything for a few minutes, just kept eating his own cooked cereal. "Would that be what Na'om would want?" he finally asked.

"Does it matter what she wants?" Tz' burst out. "As far as we know, she's joined the ancestors and won't be coming back. I built that hut, and rightfully, it should be mine." He picked up his bowl and headed toward the house, not bothering to look at his father.

He put the bowl, still partially full of cornmeal mush, on the table and went into his room. He didn't have much to pack, just a few loincloths, his leather pouch and whistle, his bow and arrows, two blankets, a couple of ledgers filled with notes on the special steps he needed to take before offering a blood sacrifice or performing any other ceremonies, and the small packet of toad venom he'd purchased in Mayapán. The odd feathers, bird nests, and colored rocks he'd collected over the years that filled several wooden shelves could stay; they were remnants of his childhood, reminders of foraging in the jungle with Na'om, and made his heart ache.

"Living across the river won't help you forget her," Chiman said when he appeared in the doorway to Tz's room. "It'll only make it worse."

Tz' stopped shuffling his belongings around on the shelf. He knew his father was right. If broken bird's nests could cause such sorrow, then living in Na'om's hut might be too painful. He took a deep breath and let it out slowly. "At least I'll be surrounded by her presence," Tz' said. "And if there's any chance that she is alive, maybe I'll sense that when I'm there." He turned to look at his father's lined face. "Tat," he implored, "I have to do something. I can't just continue to live here like nothing ever happened."

"Of course, I understand," Chiman said. "You've grown up right in front of me, and everything is different now. We all must make adjustments based on events in the past." He sighed. "It'll be quite lonely here, now that your chuch is gone." He waved his hand at the items Tz' had placed on the bed. "Can you wait until after the burial ceremony?"

"Yes, Tat, I can wait." Tz' set his things on the floor and watched Chiman walk slowly back outside. He knew his father was sad, especially over the loss of Chachal, Na'om, and the other villagers. People Tz' had known his whole life were dead or had remained in Mayapán after being freed from the slave market. But while they'd been away, new people had moved into Pa nimá from smaller villages up and down the river, taking up residence in the empty huts or building new ones near the village's cornfield. Most were older couples who needed to belong to a community with a leader like his father, and the few who were near his age were already married, with small children or little ones on the way. He was sure these newcomers would fill the void he was creating in his father's heart. Right now, he had to think about himself and what he needed in his own life. And that meant moving across the river where he'd have the freedom to do what he wanted, when he wanted.

AJKUN

Within a few days of returning to Pa nimá, Ajkun had settled into a rhythm that filled the hours between daybreak and dark. Each morning she walked to the river to wash while a pot of corn porridge bubbled in the fire pit, and after a bowl of the hot cereal, she visited the three new mothers-to-be, Tzalon, Witzik', and Xoral. In the afternoons, she spent time chatting with Lintat's grandmother, Noy, who had quickly turned into a close friend. They shared their knowledge of plants and herbs, gathered firewood, dug manioc roots, and ground corn together. Once their chores were done, they often went to the river to sit with their feet in the cool water and listened as the water burbled and gurgled past them. The days were busy, but the nights were not, and it was then that the memories of Na'om flooded Ajkun's heart and mind. She lay awake for hours, trying to block every sight and sound she'd encountered during the day that reminded her of her grandchild, but the reminders were everywhere. Every bush, every patch of herbs, every path and trail around the village whispered Na'om's name. *I thought coming home would help,* Ajkun muttered as she rolled onto her side one more time. *But everything reminds me of what I've lost.* Often, she fell asleep while tears still dried on her cheeks.

Only a few clouds spotted the sky as Ajkun followed the narrow path through the jungle toward the cornfield as she had done so many days before. Tzalon, Witzik', and Xoral's husbands had built their homes close to the clearing, and Ajkun swatted at a few insects as she ambled along. She took her time, giving her sore knee the chance to flex and stretch, and was grateful to have Alom's staff to help her over the roots that straddled the trail. When she stepped out from the shadow of the trees and liana vines at the edge of the corn patch, she paused, letting her eyes adjust to the sudden bright sunlight. She waved to Tzalon's husband, Ajchak, who was chopping away the many weeds that grew in between the corn stalks. But she avoided looking at the far side of the field, where a blackened ring still marked the spot where Na'om had burned the bodies of those who had died in the attack. Images of the fight flashed in her mind as she hobbled along, skirting the edge of the field, and she shook her head to clear it.

She approached the first of several huts and smiled at Xoral. The young girl was kneeling, busy planting yellow marigolds and orange nasturtiums in between bunches of red-and-white-striped spider lilies that grew around the perimeter of her oval hut. Morning glory vines filled with light-blue blossoms ran up part of the wall and across the thatched roof, while another section of the building was covered with fuchsia-colored bougainvillea vines. Ajkun offered Xoral a hand to get up. "The baby will be born with flowers in his hair," she said as she gently touched Xoral's rounded belly. She placed her ear against the girl's embroidered shift and grinned as the baby pushed outward with a foot or a hand. "Strong and healthy from everything I can see. How do you feel? Any pains yet?"

"No, nothing," Xoral replied softly. She wiped her dirty hands together and then placed them on her belly as the baby continued to kick.

Ajkun nodded. She studied the girl's unlined face, noting the one furrow of concern between her eyes. "You'll do just fine, not to worry," she said, patting the girl's strong brown forearm. "It will be any day now, though, so you mustn't work too hard." She pointed to several folded fig bark containers filled with white orchids lined up in the shade. "Such beautiful flowers, you have a real talent with them."

Xoral waddled to the orchids and picked out the largest one, which she handed to Ajkun. "For you, to brighten your home," she said as she pressed the plant into Ajkun's gnarled hands.

"Maltiox, child." Ajkun smiled as she put the plant near the path back to the village. "I'll set it here and pick it up on my way back."

Ajkun turned and saw Tzalon and Witzik' were waiting for her outside their respective homes. The two sisters smiled at her as she approached. Tzalon had planted a wide variety of gladiolas to mark the narrow path leading to the only door to the hut, and the spiky green leaves brushed Ajkun's skirt as she passed. She glanced down and saw each plant was already sending forth blossoms. "They should pop open just in time for the baby's arrival," she said, pointing to the flowers, as she followed Tzalon into the cool, shadowy hut. The interior was sparse but clean, which Ajkun was glad to note. She didn't like helping a woman birth a child if the house was dirty. She listened to Tzalon's belly. "Either you or Xoral will have your child first, but I'm unable to say which it will be."

Tzalon grimaced as a sharp pain arched up her back. Her white teeth were bright against her dark skin, and she brushed a strand of black hair out of her eyes. "I'll welcome the day," she said as she pressed her palms into her lower spine. "The pain grows worse, making it hard for me to do my work with the others."

Ajkun motioned for the girl to lie down on the small mattress in the room. She gently pushed on her rounded belly. "The baby's head is down, which is good; the birthing will go much easier. You must send word to me at once if the pains get any stronger." She held out a hand and helped the young girl sit back up. She showed herself out the door and quickly moved on to Witzik's house.

Witzik' was the older of the two sisters, with unusual deep blue eyes that startled Ajkun every time she looked at them. "Another moon cycle to go, I suspect," Ajkun said as she held a hand on Witzik's belly.

The woman nodded and sighed. "I knew Tzalon would be first."

"That's a blessing, child," Ajkun said as she sat down on the stool Witzik' offered her. "You'll get to experience holding an infant and see what life with a new baby entails long before you have your own. You'll be that better prepared because of it." She sipped the mug of cool water Witzik' gave her and placed it on the floor. "Do you and your sister have everything you need, blankets for the children, cloths to wrap them in, and the binding boards?"

Witzik' nodded and moved to a large woven basket in the corner. She pulled out a soft dark gray blanket that she'd embroidered with bright yellow dahlia flowers and several piles of white cotton cloths, spreading them on the narrow ceiba fluff mattress that was laid on the floor against the wall. "Will this be enough?"

Ajkun laughed. "For the first day or two." She stood up, handing the mug to Witzik'. "I'll ask the women in the village for any older clothing that we can turn into cloths for all of you. Three new babies in the next two moons will go through more swaddling than you can imagine."

Ajkun nodded to Xoral, who had returned to her plants, as she picked up her orchid and headed back to her hut. She placed the plant in the shade, used the bushes behind the house to relieve her bladder, and then made her way to the village plaza.

Noy was sitting on a three-legged stool outside her hut, with Lintat on the ground by her side. They were sifting through a bowl of multicolored dried beans, picking out tiny bits of dirt, rocks, and dried bean husks, which they placed in a separate bowl by their feet.

Noy nudged Lintat. "Run and fetch the other stool from inside, child, so Ajkun can rest with us."

Ajkun smiled as she sat down. She scooped a handful of beans into her skirt and began sorting through them, tossing the bits of debris into the bowl.

"How are the mothers?" Noy asked as she dumped another handful of beans into her own lap and started to pick through them.

"Doing well," Ajkun replied. "Xoral and Tzalon are near their times. Which leads me to ask if you'd be willing to assist me." Her hands went idle. "I was training Na'om to be the next midwife and healer . . . ." She swallowed and looked away. "Only Ixchel knows what will happen in the village when I'm no longer here."

Noy reached over and placed her hands on top of Ajkun's hands. "I'll be happy to help in any way that I can after the babies arrive, but I'm afraid I'd be no good at the actual delivery as the sight of blood makes me feel sick."

"Well, it's up to me, then," Ajkun said and sighed. She felt tired just thinking about the work ahead of her. "I'll need to train someone to help me, but who?"

Noy didn't reply. She brushed the bean detritus from her skirt and handed the bowl full of cleaned beans to Lintat. "Fill this with water and set it on the table. They'll need to soak before I can cook them for our meal tonight." Lintat scrambled up and disappeared into the hut.

"He's a good boy, your grandson," Ajkun said as she listened to Lintat moving around just on the other side of the wall. "You're lucky to have him with you."

"You mustn't lose hope, Ajkun," Noy said. She looked at Ajkun's lined face. "From what you've told me about Na'om, there's a good chance she's still alive."

"Does the river still speak to you of a *to'nel* with scars on her face?"

"Well, no, but that doesn't mean she's not alive."

"She'd be just a year or two younger than the new mothers," Ajkun said as she picked some bean husks off her skirt. "I should be waiting for her child to arrive . . . ." She took a deep breath and closed her eyes, leaning back against the wall of the hut.

"Shh, my friend, it will be all right," Noy said as she patted Ajkun on the knee.

The two women sat in silence for several minutes, lost in their own thoughts. Ajkun only opened her eyes when she sensed a shadow had fallen across her face.

"Chiman, saqarik, what brings you here?" she said as she sat up straighter on the stool.

"Some village business I'd like to discuss with you, if I'm not interrupting anything," Chiman said. He bent down and scooped up Lintat in his arms, who laughed when Chiman tickled him. "If you run to the river, Tz' will show you his best fishing hole," he said as he gently set the boy back down.

"May I go, Noy?" Lintat asked.

She nodded and smiled as he skipped away. "You two go on now, I have plenty to keep me busy. I mustn't spend the whole morning just sitting here in the sun." Noy smiled at Ajkun as the two women rose together. She leaned in close to hug Ajkun. "From the twinkle in his eyes, I'd say there's more than business he wants from you," she whispered and laughed.

Ajkun shook her head. "Shush, my friend," she said, but she gave Noy a quick smile as she picked up her walking stick and stepped on to the path with Chiman.

He led her toward the river, but stopped when they were beyond the eyes and ears of any of the villagers. He reached in to give Ajkun an embrace, but she backed away, almost losing her balance as she stepped on a small stick on the ground.

"What was it you wanted to talk to me about?" she asked as she pushed the stick away with her walking staff.

The boyish grin disappeared from Chiman's face. "We must do a proper burial for the villagers who died. I've studied the stars and meditated in the temple and feel we should do it in three days. Can you spread the word to the women to prepare a feast for after the ceremony? Tz' and I will take care of the rest."

"Yes, of course," Ajkun said as she studied his face. The lines around his eyes were more pronounced, and she realized just how old and tired he looked at that moment. "Noy and I will talk to the women this afternoon." She touched him on the arm. "Is there anything else?"

Chiman sighed. "No, it can wait, I can wait. Maltiox, Ajkun, I'll be seeing you then." He turned abruptly and continued toward the river, leaving Ajkun standing in the shadows.

Hmm, that certainly didn't go well, she thought as she made her way back to Noy's hut. She tapped on the doorframe with her walking stick, and Noy appeared from inside.

"Back so soon?" Noy asked as she indicated the stools by the fire.

"Chiman wants to hold a burial ceremony in three days and needs us to prepare the food."

"Is that all he wanted?" Noy said.

"He tried to hug me, but . . . I backed away." Ajkun shook her head. "I'm so confused. Aren't we too old for this type of thing?"

Noy began to laugh and couldn't stop laughing for several minutes. "I'm sorry, forgive me. I shouldn't be laughing, only, if not now, then when? Mam and I have been together for so many moons that I've forgotten what it's like to be alone, and I wouldn't change that for all the cacao beans in Mayapán." She leaned forward, placing her forearms on her knees. Her gray hair slipped forward, and Noy flipped the braid back over her shoulder. "Itzamná knows none of us is getting any younger, so if you still have feelings for him, then show him. It can do no harm as far as I can see, and certainly if two people were meant to be together, it's you and Chiman."

"It's that obvious?"

"From the first moments I saw you together, walking up the path from the river, I thought you were a couple." Noy placed her hands on top of Ajkun's and squeezed them before letting go. "After the ceremony, go to him."

Ajkun smiled. "Maltiox, Noy, you're a good friend." She stood up and smoothed her skirt. "Will you tell the women here about the feast? I must go tell the mothers."

The shadows were long by the time Ajkun made it back to her own hut, with the first few stars visible on the horizon. She bustled about, gathering wood, kindling a fire, and preparing a simple meal of boiled beans and chaya, which she ate standing up near the fire. By the time she was done, night had fallen, and she shivered despite the heat from the flames. She grabbed her shawl from its peg on the wall of the hut and wrapped it over her hair as a single bat flew by overhead. She sat for a bit, looking into the fire, trying to unravel the mixture of emotions she felt toward Chiman, but the effort soon tired her, and she hurried to bed. But she was unable to fall asleep for a long time, and when she finally did, her dreams were filled with images of Chiman and Na'om.

She was weary the next morning and moved more slowly than normal, her mind still pondering the meaning of the dreams she'd had, even as they dissipated into nothing. While she went about her daily chores over the next few days, she kept expecting to run into Chiman in the village plaza or down at the river, but they were never in the same place at the same time. *Is he avoiding me? Just because I didn't want him to be close the other day?* The more Ajkun thought about it, the more it felt as if Chiman were deliberately eluding her. She talked to Noy, who suggested that he was busy with duties of his own, which did nothing to alleviate the feelings Ajkun had. *I know there's something wrong. Never has he been so occupied that we haven't had time to speak at least once a day.* Ajkun fretted as she plumped up her pillow and settled in to sleep once again.

After checking on the mothers-to-be on the morning of the ceremony, Ajkun joined Noy, Pempen, and the other older women in preparing tamales for the feast. While they spread the cornmeal mixture onto banana leaves and filled the interior with pieces of turkey meat, chopped figs, and bits of chili peppers, they could hear Setesik and Tz' chopping out a hole in the hard-packed dirt inside the village temple. Ajkun looked up as Chiman hurried by with a digging stick, but he entered the shrine without even glancing toward Ajkun. She went back to making tamales, trying to ignore how hurt she felt. *He's busy, that's all,* she mused as she quickly folded a banana leaf into a packet and tied it with a piece of plant fiber before placing it alongside the many other tamales waiting to be steamed.

Ajkun watched as Lintat and two of his friends hurried over, each carrying a bundle of sticks on his back, which they dropped by the large fire pit set up to cook the tamales. When Witzik's husband, K'ale'n, called and motioned for them to follow, they ran off to gather more wood. Meanwhile, Xoral's husband, Tzukunel, was setting up a large spit so he could roast the large peccary and small deer he had killed the day before. After a short time, Setesik, Tz', and Chiman reappeared from inside the temple. Ajkun smiled at them, and Setesik and Tz' nodded to the women, but Chiman avoided looking in her direction. Since the men were drenched in sweat, they headed together to the river to bathe. Ajkun watched Chiman's back as he disappeared down the path. *Once again, he refused to acknowledge me.* She slapped a glob of cornmeal into a banana leaf and folded it up, not realizing she'd forgotten to add any fillings to the tamale.

For hours, the smell of cooking meat and steaming corn filled the air, and Ajkun's mouth watered. It had been a long time since she'd felt this hungry. Chiman passed her again, entered the temple, and soon the pungent scent of copal incense wafted out from the open doorway. Xoral, Tzalon, and Witzik' hurried to decorate the shrine walls with chains of nasturtiums they'd braided together, and then they inserted skull shapes cut from wild fig tree bark into the strands of orange flowers.

Once the sun had passed its zenith and the shadows of the tall mahogany trees on the outskirts of the village stretched across the plaza, the villagers put aside their work and filled the square. As Ajkun found a spot off to the side, she smiled at Noy and indicated the older woman should stand with her. Together, they turned to face the small temple. On either side of the short staircase were two dark green ceramic braziers filled with burning copal incense. The slight breeze sent the pungent smoke across the clearing and into the jungle beyond. Tz' sat cross-legged on the ground in front of the stairs. He'd spread peccary fat in his black hair, making it glisten in the sun, and attached three green and yellow tail feathers of a green jay behind his left ear. Thin, interwoven lines drawn with cinnabar and coal covered his bare upper chest and arms. He held a drum directly in front of him and began to tap out a steady beat.

After a few moments, Chiman appeared from behind the temple. He was wearing a headdress made from the long, deep-blue tail feathers of a white-throated magpie jay, a ceremonial jaguar capelet, which partially covered the jaguar spots tattooed on his shoulders and back, and a new indigo linen apron over his loincloth that extended to his mid calves. He also had a small cotton bag tied to his waist, which bumped into his leg as he walked. Ajkun was surprised at how handsome he looked in his new finery. Setesik followed directly behind Chiman, helping him carry a large brown ceramic urn, which they gently set down on the temple steps.

Chiman turned to the gathering, nodded to Tz, who stopped drumming, and held out his hands for silence.

"My friends, many of you are new to the village, and we gladly welcome you and your families to live here. But long before you arrived, others shared this space with those of us who recently returned from Mayapán. Our neighbors, men, women, and children, were killed in a fierce battle that took place many moons ago." He pointed to the urn. "Their remains are in this vessel, which I'll bury inside the temple. I ask for everyone's help in honoring the dead as I speak their names, one by one." He untied the bag from his waist and held up a handful of black, yellow, white, and red corn kernels before nodding to Tz', who began to tap lightly and slowly on the drumhead.

Chachal moved to the closest brazier and dribbled pieces of the ceremonial corn into the smoky fire as he began to recite the names of the dead. "Chachal . . . Potz'. . . " He paused between each name, allowing the corn to sizzle and pop before moving on to the next person. "Banal Bo'j . . . Kemonel . . . ."

As Chiman said each name, Ajkun could see the person's face in her mind, and she wiped away the tears that streamed down her cheeks. Noy reached out and clasped her hand, squeezing it tightly. "Such losses, such terrible losses," Ajkun muttered. *Satal is the reason for all of this,* she thought as she swiped at her cheeks again.

When Chiman reached the end of the list, she was startled to hear him say "Na'om."

"But she wasn't killed here," Ajkun mumbled under her breath. A murmur went through the group as those who had survived the attack grumbled about the girl. Ajkun thought she even heard someone say the whole thing had been Na'om's fault, but she couldn't identify who had spoken. She looked to Chiman for reassurance, but he continued to gaze everywhere except in her direction. He motioned to Setesik and the two men bent down, lifted the urn by its handles, and carried it inside. After a few minutes, they returned, empty-handed. Ajkun wondered when Chiman would paint the container with cinnabar dust, add a basket of corn to the hole, and cover everything with dirt.

Chiman raised his hands to silence the group once again. "Our people joined the ancestors many moons ago, and our time for grieving is over. Come, everyone, let's celebrate life, beginning with the delicious food we've been smelling all day long." Chiman removed his headdress and placed it inside the doorway to the temple before joining the queue of people waiting for pieces of the peccary and deer that Tzukunel was slicing with his long obsidian knife.

Ajkun hurried to catch up to Chiman, as she hoped to talk to him now that the ceremony was over, but several people stood directly behind him in the line, and she didn't want to step in front of anyone. After she had collected her food, she noticed that Chiman was circling the group, always one or two paces ahead of her.

Fine, I'll leave him be, and she sat on the temple steps to eat. But she continued to watch Chiman as he mingled with almost everyone in the square. *Perhaps he'll come over now*, she thought, as he turned in her direction. But before she could wave to Chiman, he had looked away. She sighed and picked at her food on her plate. Her appetite had disappeared.

"Is everything all right?" Witzik' asked. She set her empty dish on the step next to her and moved over so Tzalon could also sit down.

Ajkun shifted so she could see the girl beside her. "Hmm, yes, I think so," Ajkun replied. "My eyes wanted more food than my stomach, the trouble with growing old." She gave the two pregnant women a half-smile and noticed Witzik' looking at her untouched tamale. "Please, feel free to eat it," she said as she pushed the dish toward the girl.

"Maltiox," Witzik' replied. "I can't ever seem to eat enough these days."

Ajkun nodded, too absorbed in following Chiman's movements to heed much of the chatter the sisters were engaged in.

Suddenly, Tzalon groaned and clutched at her belly. She dropped her dish of food on the step, and one slice of peccary slid onto the stones.

"Tzalon, what's wrong? Witzik' asked as she turned to her sister.

Ajkun got up and placed her hand on Tzalon's belly. She could feel the baby moving under her fingertips and the girl's stomach tighten. She counted and the muscles relaxed. "Come, child, it's time," she said as she offered the girl her arm.

Tzalon leaned heavily on Ajkun's arm as the older woman scanned the crowd for Noy. She waved her over with her free hand. "The baby's on the way. Tell Lintat and the other boys to bring some dry wood from the pile near the bonfire to Tzalon's hut. Find Ajchak and let him know, then meet me at the hut. I've got to get Tzalon ready for what comes next."

Noy nodded and hurried off. Witzik' stepped beside her sister and offered her arm. Together, the three women moved through the darkening shadows to the path while everyone else continued to eat and talk. Ajkun was too busy trying to help Tzalon avoid the many roots on the trail to notice Chiman studying her as she moved away.

Tz'

It was dark by the time Tz' arrived at Na'om's hut. His few possessions were tied up in his blankets, and he plopped the load down near the door. He stepped inside the hut and looked around for a candle, but couldn't find one in the gloom. Then he decided he didn't need a light since he was too tired to stay up much longer. Physically and emotionally, the day had been more taxing than he'd anticipated.

He'd helped Setesik dig a large hole in the floor of the temple and tapped out a drumbeat for Chiman as he conducted the burial ceremony. When his father had spoken Chachal's name, Tz's heart contracted, and his stomach cramped, but he'd managed to avoid throwing up. But when he'd heard Na'om's name, he felt the same tingle of excitement and anticipation that he'd had earlier. He took it as a sign that there was a chance she was still alive and could be helped. But there had been no time to discuss his idea with Chiman, who had spent the evening talking to all the villagers at the feast.

He slipped off his clothes and settled on Na'om's old mattress. The stillness was occasionally punctured by a loud sound from the festivities still going on across the river, and Tz' sighed. *Perhaps I should have stayed and tried to make some new friends. But there aren't any single men my age in the village.* He pictured Box and Nil and wondered what they were doing at that moment. *Probably drinking a cup of one of Nil's fermented juices . . .* He shifted the blankets, reached over to his leather pouch, and pulled out the small statue he'd made of Na'om. He smiled at the figurine and kissed it on the top of the head before tucking it near his pillow, as he'd done every night since Box had given it to him.

He took a deep breath of Na'om's cinnamon-scented soap that lingered on the bedding. It brought an ache to his chest, but he bit his lower lip, forcing the pain away. He was ashamed to admit his pain, even to himself. He wanted to believe Na'om was still alive, but part of him knew there was a good chance he'd never see her again. And if that was the case, then he needed to stop the hurt before it swallowed him whole. Otherwise, he'd never be able to move on in his life and learn to love another. Slowly, Tz' drew in a deep breath, held it for several seconds, and then let it whoosh out of his pursed lips. *Tat was right; being here is not going to help me forget her.* His thoughts were still such a strange blend of longing and desire for the girl he thought he'd marry and the odd knowledge that all along she'd been his sister. He rolled around on the lumpy mattress, trying to get comfortable, but visions of Na'om kept flitting into his mind. The way she laughed as they splashed water at each other in the river, her frustration while weaving a simple huipil, her attempts to teach Ek' Balam to dance . . . Thumping his fist into another hard lump in the bed, he stared up into the darkness, afraid to close his eyes, fearful of what impressions might come next. But gradually his breathing slowed, and his eyes drifted shut.

Unexpectedly, images of the numerous funerary statues lined up on the trestle tables at Puk'pik's workshop flooded his mind. Each woman looked like Na'om, and each man looked like Tz'. Half-asleep, he reached out and stroked the figurine next to him on the bed. "I'll find a way to help you, I promise," he muttered. He closed his eyes again, but was bothered by the buzzing of some insect that flitted near his head. He swatted at the air, trying to capture the annoying creature, but had no luck and eventually fell asleep with the blanket pulled tightly over his head, with only his nose poking out for some fresh air. But in his dreams, the droning grew more intense. It filled his head with the sound of a hundred bees, and he woke up, irritated and short-tempered.

He longed for something to ease the exasperation he felt. *I promised Tat I'd stay here and continue my studies, but what more can he teach me that I don't already know? What does life in the village really mean for me now? Hours spent waiting patiently for some fish to bite my line or an animal to walk by so we can eat? Visiting all the older villagers to find out if they need help in any way, wasting my time drinking bitter cups of root tea, while they tell me stories I've heard since I was a child? Acting as Tat's aide in the various ceremonies that help govern the village while those my age raise families and enjoy life and I remain alone?*

The angry humming grew louder, bringing Tz's attention back to the room. *Did I disturb a nest in here?* he wondered. The moon was rising through the trees and cast a sliver of light across the room, and Tz' squinted, searching for the source of the noise. But he couldn't see anything. He groped around on the floor and found the handle of his jadeite knife just beside the bed. The heft of it in his hand made him feel better, even though he knew he was alone. He lay down again, but the intense buzzing in his head made it impossible to sleep. So he stared through the doorway and watched the moon glide ever higher into the sky, hidden at times by the tall trees that grew in a circle outside the hut.

Eventually, his eyes closed, and he dreamt of the small statues again, but this time, each woman's face appeared blank while the men's all looked like the same person, a man with a withered face full of wrinkles and lines, who Tz' realized was the shopkeeper in Mayapán.

In the morning, the dream of the ancient man lingered in Tz's mind, staying with him while he went about his chores throughout the day. Late that afternoon, after starting a small fire in the fire pit, he slumped against the wall of the hut, exhausted with trying to find answers. And then it dawned on him. *Maybe I'm supposed to go back to the shop; after all, the old man knew I wanted the book on were-jaguars, so he must have more information for me.* But Tz' didn't know how he could explain a sudden return to Mayapán to his father.

He stared at a small line of ants crawling across the ground in front of him, wondering what to do next. Then, images of the were-jaguars filled his mind, prompting Tz' to hurry into the hut and return with a small clay pipe, a bit of tobacco, and a dab of toad venom. Although he hadn't fasted for a few days, he felt there'd be no harm in trying to shape-shift into his spirit animal, and he immediately packed the bowl of the pipe with the tobacco. He lit the pipe with a burning stick from the fire and drew in several deep breaths. The smoke pressed tightly against his lungs and throat, forcing him to cough several times, but he continued to smoke until the tobacco was gone. He quickly tapped the hot ashes out and refilled the bowl with the toad venom. "Here goes," he said, grinning with anticipation. He inhaled a couple of times, then set the pipe down, and waited . . . and waited. Nothing happened.

Tz' stayed sitting against the outside of the hut until the fire burned out, expecting at any second to feel his skin morph and shift or at least the blaze of heat and joy that had enveloped him the first time he'd shape-shifted. But he felt the same as ever. He watched a cloud of bats fly by, grazing the treetops, headed toward the river for their nightly feast of bugs, but the only change he felt was a quick, piercing pain behind both eyes. Too tired suddenly to eat or bathe, Tz' shuffled stiffly into the hut and climbed into bed.

He fell asleep almost immediately, but woke with a start when he heard a loud whirring sound outside the hut. The moon was still low on the horizon, barely illuminating the room, but he reached out and found his knife. Clutching it tightly helped steady the pounding of his heart. Without warning, the room was plunged into pitch-blackness as something blocked the entranceway, and Tz' sat bolt upright and pointed his blade in that direction. The cloying sweet scent of death filled the room, and Tz' scrambled to his feet, crouching with his back firmly against the wall.

"Who are you? What do you want?" Tz' said.

"I'm Camazotz," the creature replied. "You summoned me, so here I am."

Tz' gasped as he heard the animal speak its name. "What are you talking about? I didn't send for you or anyone like you."

"Ha, just as I thought. You're still a child, dabbling in things you don't understand and can't control," Camazotz replied as he moved farther into the hut.

Tz' strained to comprehend what filled the doorway. *Did I conjure this god of the Underworld instead of shape-shifting?* He could see two red eyes in the darkness and the outlines of two papery wings on either side of a fur-covered body. The stale, musty smell of wet rot overwhelmed the small space, and Tz' gagged. He quickly covered his nose and mouth with one hand, while willing himself not to throw up. "Get out of here," he shouted as he lunged forward. His knife blade slipped through air, and he lurched and fell on his knees.

Camazotz laughed. "Ah, poor boy, you're so confused. I can feel the anxiety and dismay rippling off you in waves. You were so eager to transform into a were-jaguar, and here I am instead!" He laughed again and shifted his shoulders. His wingtips brushed the walls, leaving smears of black gunk on the painted murals.

"How did you know that's what I was trying to do?" Tz' said. He backed up against the wall, carefully watching the bat's face.

"You're the grandson of one of the greatest witches of all time. Do you honestly think we haven't been keeping an eye on you? Now that you've finally shown some true talent, I've come to assist you in your endeavors."

Tz' slumped to the floor. He couldn't believe what he was hearing, yet the urge to reconnect with his spirit animal was so strong that he was willing to imagine the bat god was there to aid him. "Wait, what do you mean I've *finally* shown some abilities?"

Camazotz chortled again. "You've been hiding behind that stupid girl, letting her develop her skills while your own have been languishing deep inside. But now that she's gone, you're free to work on your own talents." He turned and swept Na'om's careful array of pots, gourds, and baskets of herbs on the floor into a jumble, and Tz' watched as the bat stomped them under his hind feet.

The mention of Na'om sent a bolt of hatred through Tz', and he lunged at the bat again, but missed. He scurried beneath one wing, came up behind Camazotz, and thrust headlong at the bat, but only managed to slash into the mattress lying on the floor. He swirled and jabbed at the massive creature looming over his head, but each time he shoved forward, his knife blade swished through emptiness rather than connecting to fur, muscles, and bones.

Camazotz snickered at Tz's ineffective strikes. "You're so weak, still a child instead of a man . . . or a were-jaguar," he taunted.

Tz' rushed at the bat. He bounced off the opposite wall, as if the giant mammal had disappeared, dropping his knife in the process. But Camazotz was still hovering in the air, his head nearly touching the thatched ceiling, when Tz' turned around.

"No wonder your sweet Na'om, your true beloved, rejected you . . ."

The bat cackled.

"Don't you dare speak of Na'om!" Tz' demanded as he plunged toward the giant bat, who easily outmaneuvered him.

"Ah, poor girl, she's still lost in the Underworld and hopefully will never see the light of day again," Camazotz said. "But if she does, Satal and I will be waiting for her." The bat edged closer to Tz', trapping him in the corner.

Tz' coughed as the fetid smell of the bat filled his nostrils. "Satal! She died in the cenote," Tz' said as he gagged and sank to the floor, his back against the wall.

"Ha, wrong! Thanks to me, your grandmother is alive and plotting her revenge on those who accused her of treason," Camazotz said as he stepped closer and curled his wings forward, wrapping Tz' in his embrace. "Satal's blood runs through your veins, but I'm beginning to think you're like your mother, unworthy of being her successor. Pity; I had hoped we could spend more time together, but it's best I get this over with quickly."

Tz' pushed against the bat with all his strength, but the creature continued to press him into the wall. "Get off me," he cried, as he struggled to breathe. The matted fur of the large bat compressed against his face, chest, and arms, and he felt a thousand tiny mites crawling on his skin. He thrashed and scratched at the bat god, but Camazotz didn't move. Smothered by the creature, Tz' grew dizzy from lack of air and quickly blacked out.

Daylight was streaming through the doorway when Tz' woke up. He was curled up in the corner of the hut, pressed tightly against the wall. As he slowly sat up, his head ringing with an incessant buzzing, he looked around the hut. It was a mess, and he shivered as he recalled the giant bat that he had battled in the night. He looked at his arms and legs, searching for bites or marks from the insects that had swarmed over his skin, but there was nothing there. A faint, fetid scent lingered in the air, and three distinct black smears marred the wall farthest from the doorway, but the bat god was gone.

He struggled to his feet and stepped out into the warm sunlight, blinking at the brightness. Still fearing the god of the Underworld's tainted touch, Tz' hurried to the river, where he stripped off his loincloth and plunged into the cold water. Imagining bugs still scuttled about under his skin, he squatted in the shallows and rubbed his body with sand until it ached, and then he sat down, letting the river flow around his muscular body. After a few minutes, he realized the buzzing in his head had stopped. He could hear the river as it gurgled over the rocks, the wind as it sighed through the mahogany trees high overhead, and the faint sounds of laughter from the village. The silence was refreshing, invigorating, and Tz' felt energized for the first time in weeks. He left the river and headed back to the hut, determined to clean up the mess he had created. But the minute he stepped into the clearing, the droning returned, driving into his ears with an intensity that made him wince. He looked at the hut, but he couldn't bring himself to go back inside.

He shook his head and jumped up and down on one foot in an attempt to get rid of the noise as he paced around the small clearing, trying to figure out what to do next. *Camazotz said Satal was still alive. If that's true, then I must warn Yakal and the others in Mayapán. And more importantly, the bat god knew Na'om is still alive, too, which means there must be a way I can help her.* Tz' grabbed his bundle of items and headed back to the river, but he paused on the path. *Will Tat believe me when I tell him what I saw and heard? Other than the marks on the wall, I have no proof that that thing even exists. And Tat will know I was experimenting on my own with the toad venom . . .* Tz' shook his head, confusion and frustration mingling in his mind. *I'll tell Tat I've changed my mind about living here for now, that I'm going back to Mayapán to study with the shamans, so I'll be better prepared to take over his duties someday. But I won't mention my idea of helping Na'om or say anything about Camazotz and what happened here last night. The less he knows, the better.* He dropped his blankets into the canoe and pushed off from shore. Satisfied with his decision, Tz' left his possessions in the bottom of the canoe. There was no need to unload them, as he would leave right after he'd said good-bye to his father and Ajkun.

SATAL

Satal looked around her new accommodations and grimaced. She hated the blood-red walls and vibrant yellow doors that opened into small bedchambers off the main room. The air in the house was stale, tainted with the scent of sweaty flesh, fermented berries, and sour balché. Considering the number of bedrooms, she suspected the place had been used as a house of pleasure, emptied in haste to provide her with a home. Barefoot, she padded past the numerous wooden chairs with worn leather seats and the long wooden table that filled one area of the main room and sat down on one of the many ceiba-filled mattresses that filled reclining bamboo frames. At the end of each reclining couch stood a small leather-topped table with a copper candlestick and a beeswax candle. Bits and dribbles of wax were stuck to the tables, and Satal picked impatiently at the spots while she waited for Tewichinel and eight other shamans to return from the market.

"You're sure you can trust these men?" Sachoj's voice echoed in Satal's head.

"Of course I'm not sure, but what other choice do I have? Tewichinel promised me that he's picked the most stalwart men from all the shamans and that they will do my bidding without question. We need a bigger army than the one Kämisanel can muster if we're going to conquer the people of Mayapán. By calling forth Camazotz and the gods of Xibalba, we'll be invincible, but I can't summon them all myself. No, I need these men to learn the dark arts and become intimate with the lords of the Underworld. Then, when the day of the battle arrives, each shaman will march at the head of a battalion of men who serve under that particular god. " She plucked a large glob of beeswax off the table and hastily stuffed it in her pocket when she heard someone knock on the thick wooden door. As it swung inward, she could see Tewichinel and the other shamans in the front courtyard. They were laden with parcels, which they placed on the floor as they entered the great room.

"Your army grows stronger every day, my lady," Tewichinel said as he bowed low before Satal. He placed yet another basket of supplies near her feet. The other shamans hovered near the entrance to the large room, surrounded by bags and baskets.

"I ordered you to go to the market and come straight back," Satal said as she sat up on the edge of the recliner she was in. "Do you think I want to sit around here idly waiting for you? We have work to do."

"Yes, yes, of course, Lady Satal. I meant no disrespect. Some of your provisions, the rarer ones, took a bit of time to procure, so I sent a few of the men to check on Kämisanel and the others while I waited. They report that the army has swollen in size with young and middle-age men conscripted from the villages as far south and east as Tulum."

"Excellent. The more warriors, the better. I'll check in on them myself later today." Satal stood up and motioned to all the supplies. "Unpack all these goods straight away on the empty shelves at the end of the room and then come sit. We have a lot to do if we're to be ready when the day of the battle arrives."

"My lady, we'll work here?" Tewichinel asked. He glanced nervously behind him to the other shamans, who only shook their heads or shrugged their shoulders.

"From now on, you'll be staying here with me, so I can train you in the dark arts."

Tewichinel gasped, and the shamans behind him muttered to each other. One thin, older man began to back out the door.

"Stop! You, you're Yuxba', are you not?"

"Yes, Lady Satal," Yuxba' replied as he bowed ever lower to the floor.

"None of you shall be leaving, do you hear me? You've all sworn allegiance to me, and Tewichinel has assured me that you are the most fearless of the whole bunch of you. Surely, Yuxba', you're not afraid of the gods?"

"I am, my lady, and rightfully so. We serve the gods as best we can, but to wander into the darkness . . . ." Yuxba' stopped as Tewichinel interrupted him.

"To openly call forth the lords of the Underworld is most dangerous, Lady Satal, and I might add, against the wishes of the council. We'll all be sacrificed instantly if we're caught." He dropped to his hands and knees, placing his forehead on the floor, and the other shamans followed suit. "Do not ask this of us, I beg you, my lady."

"You and the council and everyone else in this city follow my orders now, is that understood?" Satal tapped Tewichinel on the shoulder with her foot. "Get up, all of you, and take a seat." She picked up one of the many bags on the floor and untied it as the group of men made their way to the numerous chairs in the room. She breathed in the musty smell of dried leaves before dropping the bag back on the floor. "Perhaps a simple demonstration is in order to show you what's possible."

She pointed to Yuxba'. "Did you get the jequirity beans?"

"Yes, my lady, they are in that gray leather bag closest to the door," Yuxba' replied.

"Ah, yes, good," Satal said as she poured several of the red and black beans out on to her open palm. They looked like small legless bugs with black heads and red bodies. Satal held one up to her nose and sniffed it. "Good, they're fresh, so I won't need to use much." She set one bean on a nearby table. "Someone fetch me some water."

Koyopa, a short fat man with a streak of white through his black hair, quickly hurried to do her bidding. He placed a green ceramic mug and matching pitcher next to the jequirity bean. Satal poked in another bag and extracted a large chunk of charcoal, which she also set on the table.

Then she reached into the pouch she carried at her side and pulled out a small obsidian blade. She picked up the jequirity bean and nicked the end of it before carefully setting the knife on the table.

"My lady, wait," Tewichinel said as Satal moved to place the cut bean in her mouth. "You'll come to great harm if you taste that."

"Have faith, Tewichinel, now watch and learn." Satal touched the tip of the bean to her tongue and instantly felt it go numb. She quickly dropped it as the rest of her mouth burned and tingled. She picked up the mug of water, drank deeply, and felt the toxin shiver through her body, turning it hot, then cold, then hot again. A harsh buzzing filled her ears, and she knew she was shape-shifting. Her skin twisted and turned as her skeleton stretched and thinned. Her clothing ripped and split as first her arms and then her legs turned black and segmented. Then the fingers on each hand turned into claws covered in fine black hairs. Her back split open, and she unfolded iridescent greenish-black wings that she fanned, lifting herself up. She hovered, a six-foot black wasp, several feet off the floor. She looked down at the shamans, who had fallen onto their knees, and laughed.

"Come now, don't be afraid," Satal said, her voice insect-like and raspy even to her own ears. "If *I* frighten you, how will you ever join forces with Camazotz, Yum Cimil, and the other gods of the Underworld?"

One by one, the shamans slowly raised their heads to stare in awe at Satal, who continued to fan her wings ever so gently.

Finally, Tewichinel broke the silence. "You'll teach us to become like you?"

"I shall train you to use the jequirity beans and make a variety of concoctions that will enable you to shape-shift as I have, but what form you'll become depends on you." Satal slowly lowered herself until she could rest her insect legs on the floor. "Hand me the charcoal," she demanded.

Yuxba' picked up the piece and gave it to the wasp woman. She nibbled on the gritty substance for a few minutes and dropped the rest on the floor. "Stay here, all of you," Satal commanded as she flew out of the room and into the small bedroom she had claimed as her own. She didn't want to reappear naked in front of these men. The charcoal quickly forced the toxins out of her blood stream, and she rapidly shifted back into her human form on the cool tile floor. Weak from her exertions, she managed to sit upright and reach the edge of the gray wool blanket that hung from her hammock. She tugged on the fabric and wrapped it around her body before slowly getting to her feet. She could hear the men muttering among themselves as she shuffled back to the main room, but they quickly went silent when she reappeared.

She sank into the nearest sofa and was grateful for the softness of the ceiba-filled mattress underneath her. "As you can see, it takes a bit of effort to perform this feat. You must all stay strong during the battle, which is why you must begin your training today." Satal noticed Yuxba' was staring at her left arm. It still sprouted several long black hairs, which she plucked out rapidly.

"My lady, may I make a suggestion?" Tewichinel said. He pointed to the bits of charcoal and her torn clothes on the floor. "We'll need someone to provide us with the remedy and clothing after the battle is over. Perhaps it would be wise if we chose one or two from among us to perform these services?"

"Hmm, not a bad idea," Satal said. She looked at the group of men in front of her. "Who among you wants to shape-shift and who would prefer to be an assistant?" She waited for several minutes for an answer, but none of the men said a word. "Fine, I shall make the decision. Yuxba' and Pataninel, it will be your job to aid us. The rest of you will learn to transform and commune with the gods." She slowly stood up, but quickly grabbed Tewichinel's arm before she lost her balance. "Go now and gather your things from the Red House. Tell none of the other shamans what you've witnessed here today; they'll learn in due time. I must rest a bit, but I expect you back before sun fall." She leaned on Tewichinel's arm, and the shaman helped her to her room where she eased into her hammock.

"I shall be just outside your room, my lady, if you should need me," Tewichinel said as he backed toward the door.

"What about your things?"

"Yuxba' and the others will bring me what I need. My desire is only to serve you."

As the days passed, the group of shamans grew more comfortable in the presence of Lady Satal and dropped much of their formalities with her. She was glad. Their constant bowing and subservience had quickly become tiresome, and it impeded their training, which she insisted on practicing each day. Because Yuxba' and Pataninel were not among those who were learning to shape-shift, she'd given them the tasks of taking care of the meals, the cleaning of the house, the shopping in the market, and other daily chores that couldn't be ignored. She knew they felt both relief and envy as they watched their fellow shamans begin the arduous process of transformation. It was a painful art, one that had taken her many years and many mistakes to learn, but despite the men's protests, she pushed them to try. Her band of shape-shifters had only a few moons to learn the technique, if they were going to lead the army against the people of Mayapán.

Na'om

Na'om came to when Ek' Balam licked her hand yet again. His rough tongue tickled the back of it, and she wearily opened her eyes. She was still lying on the cool ground, but had curled into a ball on her side. The tops of her thighs were sore to the touch, as if she'd spent too many hours out in the sun, and she could trace scratches left in the skin on her forearms and shoulders. She stretched, sat upright, and Ek' Balam nudged her shoulder with his big head.

"Just give me a minute," she said as she gently pushed him away. Her head hurt, her body hurt, her stomach was empty, and she desperately needed water to quench her thirst. She slowly stood, pausing midway to stop her head from spinning. She steadied herself against the tunnel wall and tried to project some light into the darkness. She could see only a few feet in front of her, but it was enough to find out that there were no more obsidian daggers anywhere in sight.

Na'om grinned and rubbed Ek' Balam's ear. "We did it, we passed the last test," she said, and she smiled again. She was certain that all they had to do now was find water, then make their way to the surface, and they'd be free at last.

With slow but steady steps, Na'om started off, Ek' Balam pacing by her side. Every now and then, she paused to listen for the telltale drips that would indicate water, but heard nothing. She touched Ek' Balam, and despite the piercing pain it produced in her head, she pushed their energy outward. She hoped the extra light would show them what she could not hear. But even though the walls of the tunnel were damp and tiny bits of moss grew here and there among the rocks, there was no spot where enough water had collected for her to get a drink. Her throat was so dry that swallowing was difficult, and Na'om panicked. To have come so far only to die of thirst now was not possible. She tried licking moisture from the stony wall in front of her. It was coarse, sandy, and tasted of salt, and she spat it out with what little saliva she was able to produce. She tried plucking a piece of moss and sucking on it, but it filled her mouth with a strange, bitter taste, and she quickly spat it out as well.

"Come on, maybe there's water someplace up ahead," Na'om said as she patted Ek' Balam on the back. The two trudged forward, their pace growing slower and slower as each hour passed. Na'om was too weak to use her energy to see by and stumbled along in the dark, but gradually noticed that the passageway was starting to brighten. The blackness steadily retreated until the light in the tunnel was like that of a late summer evening, muted, soft, and bluish-yellow. Eager to find the source, Na'om quickened her pace.

Finally, they rounded a curve in the passageway, and the area opened into another large cave. In the center was a deep pool of turquoise-blue water. A shaft of bright light shone on the water, and Na'om shielded her eyes from the harsh beam with her hands. Peeking through her laced fingers, she hurried to the water's edge, and with her eyes closed tight against the glare, she scooped up great handfuls of the sweet liquid. It soothed the abrasive dryness in her throat, and when she felt satiated, she gradually opened her eyes. The brightness made her eyes tear, and she hurried to cover them again, but Na'om realized she could see down through the clear water to the sandy bottom several feet below. She glanced to her right and saw Ek' Balam slip gracefully into the water and begin to swim, paddling swiftly to the spotlight of sunlight. He circled around and around in that patch of brightness, and Na'om tilted her head to stare up at its source.

At least fifty feet overhead, there was a ten-foot hole in the ceiling of the cavern, and through it, Na'om could see a small block of azure-blue sky. She gasped at the beauty of it; she had forgotten how blue the sky could be. She longed to touch it, as it belonged to the world above, the world of the living, the world of her people, not the gruesome and cruel black world of the gods of death. A rush of joy flooded her heart, and she trembled as she thought of Tz', Ajkun, and Chiman. *I might see them soon, I will see them soon*, Na'om thought as tears quickly formed and fell in tiny droplets to the water below.

She looked toward the center of the pool where Ek' Balam was still paddling in the bright sunlight. Although weak from hunger, she knew she needed to join him and soak in the cleansing heat from that one sunbeam, so she quickly slipped into the refreshing water and swam out to the circle of daylight. She floated on her back, letting the light sink into her skin, rocked by the wavelets caused by the constant paddling of her loyal feline friend. She felt the tension of the past drain away from her in that focused beam, and as it moved, she moved with it, until the light slowly began to fade as the sky far overhead covered with dark clouds, blocking out the sun. She watched Ek' Balam swim back to the pool's edge and climb out, where he stood and shook from head to tail before lying down in the sandy dirt to groom.

Reluctant to lose sight of that patch of the world above, Na'om remained floating in the pool until heavy droplets of water began to bounce on the surface all around her. They jarred her sense of peace, reminding her that she still had to find a way out if she was ever to view the sky in its entirety again.

Weary from her efforts to stay in the water, she awkwardly climbed out and lay down in the sandy soil next to Ek' Balam. Shivering suddenly with cold, she edged closer to the jaguar and curled into a ball against his stomach. He tilted his head and licked her once, along the side of her face, then put his head down, and closed his eyes.

Na'om closed her eyes and listened to the patter of raindrops hitting the water nearby. She thought she'd never heard a more beautiful sound, even more pleasing than the sound of rain on the roof of her own hut, and she fell asleep dreaming of the walls she had half-painted with bright green vines and yellow and orange flowers in her home.

She held a paintbrush in one hand and slowly dabbed more orange into the center of a nasturtium blossom. She had painted the flowers so they grew in clusters toward the ceiling of the hut, which was cast in shadows from the late afternoon sun. Then Na'om gasped as she saw the flowers begin to wilt and fade, their brilliant colors shifting and running together until they formed a river of deep brown mud that flowed down the walls and threatened to cover her.

Startled, Na'om jerked awake. The light overhead was gone. In its place was a patch of black sky almost indistinguishable from the rest of the gloom of the large cavern. Na'om felt tears forming. She was so close to returning to the world of the living, yet still had no idea how far she needed to travel before she actually got out of the endless maze of tunnels and passageways. *If only there was a way to climb through the roof of the cavern,* she thought. But she wasn't a spider, able to hang upside down. With no rope to aid her, she was stuck on the ground. The tears dropped silently to the sand pressed against her cheek, and she hastily brushed them away. She placed her hand on Ek' Balam's chest and felt his steady breathing, which calmed her. *If he's not afraid, then I shouldn't be either. We'll wait until daylight so we can search this cave for another passageway and then head on our way.* She closed her eyes again, but after several minutes of fidgeting, she realized she wouldn't be able to go back to sleep. Instead, she twisted on her back, her head positioned so she could see the first rays of light when they started to shine through the opening in the cave.

She clung to Ek' Balam's chest, soothed by his presence, and despite her best intentions, she drifted back to sleep.

This time, cold water woke her. She was lying in several inches of it, despite being several feet from the edge of the pool, and she hurried to stand up. Water dripped off her ragged clothes and flowed into the flooded pond. Looking skyward, she saw from the angle of the sun that it must be late afternoon again. The crystal-clear water in the pool was murky and dirty, the sandy bottom obscured by stirred-up sand. Na'om glanced around the cave and saw Ek' Balam on the far side. He was sitting patiently in front of a tunnel opening.

Na'om double-checked her directions, making sure the passageway through which they had entered the cave was behind her before skirting the edge of the pond to join Ek' Balam. With one last glance at the darkening sky, Na'om took a deep breath and plunged back into this next section of tunnel. "Itzamná, I hope this is the last time we enter the dark," Na'om said as she touched Ek' Balam's head and sent their beam of light out to illuminate the way.

The passageway curved right and left, went up and down, but gradually began to head steadily downward. Na'om stopped walking, worried that she might have overlooked a different passageway that they should have taken back in the cave. "We don't want to go deeper underground," she cried. She started to turn around and head back the way they had come, but Ek' Balam continued to walk forward, and Na'om turned and scurried to catch up to him. "You must know the right way," she said as she petted him behind the ear. His purring filled the tunnel and forced the fear from Na'om's heart.

Together, they continued forward, and once again, the darkness was gradually replaced with a distant glow of light. Certain that they were going to find yet another cave with an opening to the sky, Na'om hurried toward the brightness, her devoted jaguar by her side.

They half-ran, half-stumbled through the sandy soil, and Na'om had to shut her eyes against the radiance in front of them. Heat pushed out at them, making it hard to breathe. With her eyes tightly shut, Na'om ran blindly forward. "It must be the way out, we've found the surface," she cried. "The heat and the light have to be the brilliance of the sun." She stumbled, caught herself, and continued running, ignoring the pressure on her lungs as the heat continued to press down on her.

Within an instant, she felt like she was fully encircled by the light. She pressed her hands to her eyes to protect them from the sudden glare, and peeked through her interlaced fingers, expecting to see bushes or trees, the bright blue sky high overhead. Instead, blinding orange and red flames surrounded her on all sides, and she caught just a glimpse of Ek' Balam illuminated by fire before she sank to her knees, overcome with exhaustion and smoke.

A deep roaring filled her ears, but Na'om was too numb to take notice. The searing heat of the conflagration sucked all the air from her lungs, and she felt dizzy from the lack of oxygen. Then, without warning, a wave of cold, muddy water hit her in the side, causing her to lose her balance. She groped in the swirling maelstrom for something to hold on to and felt Ek' Balam's soft tail sliding between her hands. She grasped onto his fur, holding on for life itself as she felt the two of them whirled around in a vortex of rainwater. Tossed and tumbled, she had no sense of up or down, and only the briefest of seconds to snatch a quick breath before being pummeled by the wave of water that carried them on its back through the increasingly narrow tunnel.

She scraped her hands and knees on rocky protrusions while scrabbling to catch a foothold on the soft sand underneath her feet as the water continued to push inward on all sides, its force growing more powerful as the tunnel constricted its passage. Suddenly, Na'om lost her grip on Ek' Balam as she tried to avoid a huge rock that protruded from the roof of the tunnel, and had just a quick glimpse of the jaguar being sucked away by an extra gush of water before she struck her head and one arm and blacked out.

YAKAL

Several weeks passed before Yakal saw Kux again. The tattooed man was hovering near the stonemasons' tent when Yakal arrived to drop off his tools one morning. He was late for a council meeting, and he quickly motioned for the man to follow him. He didn't want the other workers to overhear anything Kux had to say, and they could talk while they headed to the Temple of the Warriors.

When they were a safe distance from the other masons, Yakal stopped walking. "Well, have you discovered anything?"

Kux nodded his head and then stuck out his hand. "Pay me first, then I'll tell you what I've learned."

Yakal frowned, but did as the man asked. He shoved three cacao beans into his grimy fist. "That should be sufficient. Go on now, tell me."

Kux looked all around the area and then stepped even closer to Yakal. "You were right, she's alive," he whispered. He scanned the space around them again, as if looking for someone.

"Ha, I knew it. Where is she? Tell me what you know."

"She's raising an army in Chichén Itzá, made of men and other things," Kux said.

Yakal studied the man's face. It was covered in numerous scars and his nose had been broken at some point in the past. "You're terrified of her, aren't you? What are these 'others?' Come on, man, speak up, she can't hear you here." He gripped Kux's forearm and squeezed it tightly. "She's using black magic again, isn't she?"

Kux nodded. "My sources don't have any details, but she's got a group of shamans living with her in one of the large pleasure houses, and they say the people of the city hear strange sounds and see odd lights at all hours of the day and night. She's also forced any able-bodied man from far and wide around the city to join her army of warriors. Everyone's being made to work for her, crafting weapons and armor, enough for hundreds upon hundreds of men."

"And do they know when she'll attack?"

Kux shook his head again. "No, but when they do, may the gods protect us."

Yakal pulled out three more cacao beans and pressed them into Kux's hand. "Tell your informants to keep up the good work and have them send word as soon as they hear of a possible date for the battle to come."

Kux nodded and hurried away into the crowd, headed toward the market and the main gates of the city. Yakal watched him disappear and then ran up the steps and into the temple.

"Sorry I'm late," he said as he slid into one of the wooden chairs at the long table and nodded to the others who were already there.

Kubal Joron and Matz' both smiled. "It's perfectly understandable with a baby in the house," Kubal Joron said. He turned to Nimal, who was seated at the far end of the long table. "Shall we begin? I can start off with the amounts of corn that have been harvested of late . . . ."

Yakal coughed loudly, interrupting the older man. "If you don't mind, I have something rather more important to discuss, something that won't wait."

He shook his head and grimaced as he stared at the empty chair at the head of the table. It was the wooden chair Satal had always used whenever the council had convened. No one had removed it, and no one dared sit in it, so it just sat there, empty, but at that moment, Yakal could swear he felt her presence in the room. He abruptly got up, grabbed the chair by one arm, and dragged it out of the room before sitting back down. Nimal, Bitol, Kubal Joron, and Matz' all looked at Yakal, surprise written all over their faces.

"Well, that was a bit different," Kubal Joron said as he patted his lips with his ever-present cloth. "Do tell us what's gotten into you, Yakal."

Yakal placed his hands on the table in front of him. "You all know I think I saw Satal after she fell into the cenote, but what you don't know is that I've had a man searching for her. I just spoke with him, and he's informed me that she's alive and well and raising an army in Chichén Itzá, an army comprised of both men and whatever she and her shamans are summoning with black magic."

Kubal Joron turned pale and clutched Matz's hand. "Utzil, whatever shall we do?"

Nimal stared intently at Yakal. "You're positive about this? Can you trust the man who gave you this information?"

"Yes, who is this mystery man?" Bitol said. "I'd like to meet him and question him myself."

"His name is Kux, and I don't trust him at all, but from the look on his face, the man is scared, and I believe him." Yakal swiped a hand across his chin and mouth. "We must get ready for a battle the likes of which we've never seen."

"My men are always training," Nimal said, "but we'll need more armor and weapons if what you say is true. How will we pay for them?"

Yakal laughed. "I've already thought of that. We'll use the cacao beans Satal left behind to cover the expenses."

"That seems only fair," Matz' said with a laugh.

Yakal turned to him and smiled. It was a rare moment when Matz' spoke, as he always left any conversation to Kubal Joron, who was the more vocal of the two. "I'm glad to see that makes you smile, Matz'. But in case our defenses aren't enough, we should tell anyone in the city who can go live with relatives outside the walls that they should do so. The fewer people here, the better. Only those with no place to go should remain."

"Yes, excellent idea," Kubal Joron said. "Of course, we'll stay put, won't we, Matz'? I'll hire extra guards to protect us. That old witch won't force me from our lovely palace."

"Will anyone in the city believe us? I mean, Satal was proclaimed dead many moons ago," Nimal said. "We can't force anyone to leave, and without proof, I'm not sure the people will have confidence in us and go."

Yakal shook his head. "You're right, of course, but we must try to persuade them. I also think we should increase our defenses along the walls."

"What do you suggest?" Bitol asked.

"If we dig trenches outside the wall and line them with tiles so they can hold oil, then when Satal does attack, we can light the pits with flaming arrows shot from the top of the wall and hold back any army."

"Hmm, not a bad idea," Nimal said. "It will cost us more beans, though." He laughed. "Fortunately, there are plenty of those to go around. For now, I think we start preparations, but withhold any information from the general population. And when we have a better idea of when the attack might occur, then we can let people decide if they want to stay or go."

"Excellent idea, Nimal," Kubal Joron said. "Now, if there's nothing else, can we resume our normal business? I do so want to take a nap before lunch. Am I right, Matz'?"

The younger man nodded.

"Yakal, let us know when you hear any more news from this man, Kux," Nimal said. "All right, Kubal Joron, tell us about the corn harvest."

Yakal sat and only half-listened to Kubal Joron's discussion on the number of corn fields that had already been harvested. He couldn't concentrate on the details of running the city when he knew there was a good chance Mayapán could fall when Satal and her army attacked. Images of Uskab and Mayibal filled his mind. *May the gods protect us,* he prayed as Kubal Joron's voice droned on.

AJKUN

Within days of Tzalon giving birth to a little girl, Xoral's waters broke, and after a two-day labor, she delivered a healthy baby boy in the early hours of the morning. Ajkun was exhausted, having spent much of her time by Xoral's side, snatching only moments of sleep on a mat on the floor. She needed a day's rest and a full night's sleep, but had promised to look in on Tzalon before she went home.

She looked up when there was a knock on the doorway to Xoral's hut and was glad to see Noy.

"I thought I'd come spell you for a bit, but I see I'm too late," Noy said as she approached the bed where Xoral lay, the baby wrapped in a blanket by her side. "Boy or girl?"

"Boy," Xoral said proudly as she lifted him up for Noy to see.

"We'll need another set of binding boards since Tzalon is still using the other ones," Ajkun said. She could hear the weariness in her own voice as she packed up her herbs and ointments. "I'll speak to Setesik when I return to the village proper and have Lintat run out here with them once they're made." She patted Xoral on the arm. "Rest now, and I'll be back later this afternoon to check on you."

She motioned to Noy and the woman followed her outside, out of earshot of Xoral. "Watch her carefully for the next few hours. The birthing

222 Rise of the Jaguar Woman

was long and difficult; she'll need plenty of tea to help regain her strength."

Noy hugged Ajkun. "Don't worry; this part I can do. It's catching the baby that frightens me." She laughed as she heard the infant cry and then the reassuring tones of Xoral's voice as she put the baby to suckle. "I do love babies; they bring such joy to the world." She patted Ajkun on the back. "Go, my friend, get some much needed rest. And don't worry about Tzalon; I'll check in on her as well."

Ajkun yawned, picked up her walking stick, and readjusted her leather satchel on her shoulder. "Maltiox; I'll see you later." She walked slowly along the trail and was glad to meet Pempen near the river.

"How are the mothers?" Pempen asked as she waited for Ajkun to catch up to her.

"Doing well, considering the long labor Xoral had. She needs a set of binding boards for her son. Do you think Setesik can make them quickly?"

Pempen nodded. "Of course, I'll tell him as soon as I return from the river." She held up three water gourds. "It won't take me long."

"Have Lintat take them to Noy; she'll know how to wrap them securely around the baby's head."

"Go and rest, Ajkun, you look exhausted." Pempen gave Ajkun a quick embrace and gently pushed her in the direction of her hut.

"Maltiox. Itzamná knows I can use some sleep." Ajkun hurried to her hut and sat down on her mattress. She removed her sandals and stretched, but was unable to relax. Her thoughts kept returning to Chiman. She hadn't seen him in days and missed the comfort of his voice and the strength behind his embraces. She swiped at a tear as it ran down her cheek. *Oh, go to sleep, you old fool,* she said to herself as she twisted onto her other side. She fluffed her pillow and was asleep within seconds.

A thin sliver of light was shining through the open doorway when Ajkun finally woke up. She sat up, disoriented by the direction of the sun, and when she looked outside, she realized she'd slept until the early hours of the next morning. Groggy, she shook her head to clear it, but knew the best thing would be a bath in the river. She grabbed a towel, her coconut shell full of soft soap, and a clean shirt and skirt. The dew was thick on the leaves as she ambled down the trail, and she breathed in the fresh air. When she reached the stream, a layer of fog hung over the river, blocking Ajkun's view of the opposite shore, for which she was grateful.

Even now, after so many moons, she still expected to see Na'om appear on the far side of the river and always felt such sadness when she didn't.

The warm water was soothing to Ajkun, but she shivered when she stepped back onto the riverbank. She dressed rapidly and found a patch of sunlight to stand in, welcoming the heat of the day on her face and wet hair. The fog slowly dissipated, and Ajkun was surprised to see a canoe on the opposite shore. *Whoever is over there?* she wondered.

Back at her hut, she had no embers in her fire pit to kindle into flames, so she meandered toward Noy and Mam's hut, hoping the elderly couple was awake despite the early hour. She took her time, as much of the trail was still in shadows, obscuring the roots and rocks that threatened to trip her. As she rounded a bend in the path, she spied a large pile of still steaming scat. Cautiously, she approached, searching the nearby trees and liana vines for signs of movement, but she only saw a column of leaf cutter ants making a path in the duff and a blue-crowned motmot as it flashed from tree to tree, searching for insects in the overturned leaves.

She was glad to step into the clearing in the village center and see Noy and Mam seated by their fire, a pot of corn porridge bubbling off to one side. "Saqarik," she called out as she approached. "Maltiox," she said as she accepted the stool Mam offered her. The older man squatted next to the fire and ate the last of his gruel while Noy hurried to dish out some porridge for Ajkun.

She handed Ajkun a bowl of honey, which Ajkun drizzled into her cereal. "Why didn't you wake me?" she asked as she blew on the hot porridge.

"You were so tired; we all thought it best if we just let you rest," Noy replied. "You look better."

"Yes, thanks. How are Xoral and the baby? And Tzalon and her child? I need to go out and see them again."

"Doing well, so you mustn't fret. I spoke to Witzik', too and all appears fine. Oh, Sijuan brought out the binding boards and spent most of the day with the mothers. She's a natural with young children."

Ajkun relaxed. "Well, good, I'm glad Ixchel has favored the girls with healthy babies." She took several bites of her porridge. "Hmm, I wonder, perhaps I can train Sijuan to be my assistant. I must speak to Pempen and Setesik about it."

"Good idea," Noy replied as she took Mam's empty bowl and placed it with hers. She pecked Mam on the cheek and waved as he headed off down the path to wash at the river. She turned to Ajkun. "The mothers want to talk to Chiman about setting a naming day for the babies. Perhaps you can tell him?"

"Hmmm, I'm not sure about that. I haven't spoken to him in days, not since before the burial ceremony." Ajkun placed her half-empty bowl on the ground, leaned forward on her forearms, and held her hands out to the fire. She didn't want to talk about Chiman as it only made her heart ache. "I should go, chores to do, you know. I'll need a few embers to take with me," she said as she stood up. "Maltiox for breakfast."

Noy nodded, scooped out some small coals into an earthenware dish, and handed it to Ajkun. "Bring the bowl back any time."

Cupping the warm dish in her hands, Ajkun headed back home. She was thinking about whether to sweep the courtyard, gather firewood, or go find Pempen when she heard a set of feet running from behind. She turned and narrowly missed being knocked over by Chiman.

"Utzil, you startled me. Where ever are you going in such a hurry?"

"To come see you," Chiman replied as he stepped back.

Even in the early morning light, Ajkun could see Chiman was flustered. "What's wrong?" She placed the too warm bowl of embers on the ground.

"It's Tz', he's leaving. He's going back to Mayapán. He's wanted to leave for days, but I wouldn't let him go until he could say good-bye to you."

"But why? I don't understand. I thought he wanted to be here."

"He wants to return to Mayapán and continue his training with the elders there who have more experience than I do. But I suspect there's more to his decision than that. I'm sure his memories of Na'om and Chachal are affecting him, as they are all of us." Chiman took a deep breath and let it out slowly. "And he told me that perhaps there's a chance he'll meet someone to share his life with."

"But you told him about Na'om's ledger, about the drawings that show she might be still alive. He can't give up hope."

"Yes, but as we all know, he could never have married her since they're related by blood."

"Except I don't think they are . . . did you tell Tz' that we think Chachal was already pregnant by another man when she met you?"

"No, how could I? We have no proof; as far as Tz' or anyone else is concerned, he's my son." Chiman paced back and forth on the path. "He's been sleeping across the river in Na'om's hut for the past several nights, hoping to sense her presence, but says he's felt nothing." Chiman hung his head. "I don't know what to do other than let him go with my blessing."

"Oh, Chiman, the pain never stops, does it?" Ajkun said as she stepped over to him and wrapped her arms around his waist. For the briefest of seconds, he was stiff, his arms by his side, and then he embraced her as well. She leaned into his chest and breathed deeply of the earthy, spicy, incense-filled scent that was Chiman. "I'm so sorry this is happening." She felt Chiman's back tense and looked up into his lined face. "No, not this," she said as she squeezed her arms a bit tighter. "This whole thing with Tz' . . . isn't there any way to convince him to stay? What about Sijuan? She's a nice girl . . . oh, what am I saying? She's no replacement for Na'om." She put her head back against his chest. "We'll get through this, together, all right?"

Chiman nodded as he stepped away from Ajkun. "I must go back and help Tz' pack the things he'll need for his journey. He wants to leave before the sun is too high overhead. Meet us at the river?"

"Of course. I'll bring a few things for his trip." Ajkun stood on her tiptoes and pecked Chiman on the cheek. "I've missed you," she called out to Chiman as he headed back to his own home, but he didn't stop. *Hmm, I don't think he heard me,* she thought as she stooped to pick up her bowl of embers. She sighed. The coals had gone out.

Word traveled quickly through Pa nimá and most of the villagers were at the river to see Tz' leave. Ajkun pushed through the group and found Tz' standing by his canoe. "For Uskab to use with the baby," she said as she gave him a small basket full of herbal salves. Tz' nodded and tucked it in among his other gear.

"Remember, when you get to the city, go directly to Yakal's house," Chiman reminded Tz' as he gave him a hug. "He'll be able to help you find lodging and work."

"Yes, Tat axel, I know, we've been over this before."

Chiman nodded. "Did you give an offering to Xaman Ek?"

"Yesss, Father, the traveler god has been well fed," Tz' said. He held up his hand to stop Chiman from saying anything else. "With blood *and* corn. Now, I really must leave."

Ajkun studied Tz's face as he hugged Chiman. She'd never heard such exasperation in the young man's voice. *Something's not right with him,* she mused. *Perhaps it's only his frustration from waiting for days to leave.* "Safe travels, Tz'. May the gods watch over you," she said as she wrapped him in her arms.

"Maltiox, Ati't. I'll send word once I reach the city to let you know I've arrived." Tz' stepped into the stern of the dugout canoe and pushed off the sandy bank with his paddle. He dipped the blade into the water and quickly steered into the current, turning only once to wave good-bye to all those who had gathered on the river to wish him well.

Ajkun and Chiman continued to stand by the water, long after the other villagers had returned to their chores. They watched as Tz's canoe disappeared around the first bend in the river. Only then did Ajkun let the sob she'd been holding inside escape. She turned to Chiman, pressing her face into his chest. "Oh, what will happen now that our children are gone?" She felt something drip into her hair and looked up to see Chiman was crying as well. She tugged on his arm, forcing him to sit down with her on the edge of the water.

Chiman wrapped his arm around Ajkun's shoulder and wiped his face with his other hand. "We wait and see. Perhaps Tz' will find a nice young girl and bring her back here." He smiled through his tears. "Meanwhile, we keep on living, helping those who need us here."

Ajkun sighed. "I know; you're right. But we're growing old, you and I; we must find people willing to take our places someday. I had set my hopes on Na'om becoming the new midwife, and you, I'm sure, thought Tz' would one day be the new shaman . . . ." Abruptly, she stopped chattering, as Chiman remained silent. She knew Tz's departure was too fresh and painful, just like the loss of Na'om, to contemplate finding others to take their places. She listened to the rippling of the water as it swept past the many rocks and boulders in the stream, hoping to hear it speak to her as it did to Noy, but there was nothing.

Long moments passed with neither of them saying anything. Ajkun's mind drifted back to the days they'd spent in Mayapán, searching for some clue that would indicate why Tz' felt so compelled to go back. There had to be more to it than wanting more training. She wanted to ask Chiman, to find out more of what Tz' had said before he left, but was afraid to interrupt Chiman's silence. *Focus on the moment, only this, the river, the sunlight, being close to your oldest friend,* Ajkun admonished herself. Eventually, she inched closer to Chiman, nestled her head against his shoulder, and closed her eyes. "Hmm, this is nice."

"Yes," Chiman replied. He reached up and stroked her hair.

The heat of the sun made Ajkun drowsy, so she lay down on the warm sand and short grass and felt Chiman stretch out beside her.

"Remember when we used to do this as children? We had nothing to do all day except lie in the sun . . . ." Chiman said. He moved his hand until he found Ajkun's and squeezed it.

"Yes, until one of our mothers called and we had to run or be late for a meal," Ajkun laughed. She thought of rolling over to give Chiman a quick kiss, but before she could move, she heard feet pounding down the path.

She sat up, brushing the hair out of her eyes, and watched as Chiman sprang to his feet and stepped several paces away.

Lintat came running around the bend in the trail and slid to a stop in front of Ajkun. "Sijuan says . . . the other mother . . . ." he coughed heavily and bent over to catch his breath.

"Witzik'? Her time has come?" Ajkun asked as she struggled to stand. Lintat nodded and squatted down to snatch a handful of water from the river. Chiman hurried over and offered Ajkun his arm, which she clasped, allowing him to pull her to her feet.

"Utzil, the girl's not due for many more days. I must get my supplies and head right out there." She turned to Lintat. "Maltiox, Lintat, for coming to tell me. Are you all right?"

"Yes," he replied as he wiped the water from his mouth.

Together, the three walked quickly back to Ajkun's hut. Ajkun gave Lintat a piece of honeycomb and sent him off to Noy while Chiman waited for her to pack more birthing supplies in her satchel.

Together, the couple hurried along the trail to Witzik's home. Just before they stepped out into the clearing, Chiman stopped Ajkun in mid-stride with a hand on her forearm. He leaned down and kissed her on the cheek. "Come see me later, when this is all over?"

Ajkun smiled. "Of course. We have much to discuss, old friend." She patted his hand gently and hurried to Witzik's hut.

She was pleased to see there was already a large pot of water bubbling in the fire pit, which Tzalon was tending. She had her baby girl wrapped tightly to her back with a dark green shawl and turned to smile at Ajkun as she approached. "Sijuan is inside with Witzik'," she said. She pointed to a turtle shell full of warm water. "For you, to wash your hands."

"Maltiox, Tzalon. And how is your little girl doing?" she asked as she peeked in at the sleeping infant.

"Very well. She eats and sleeps and eats some more." Tzalon laughed.

Sijuan appeared in the doorway to the hut and beckoned to Ajkun. "Her pains are close together, very close," she said as she held the leather door covering aside so Ajkun could enter the small room.

Ajkun set down her satchel and removed her bowl of sapote salve. She lifted Witzik's shift and instructed Sijuan to rub the liniment into the woman's belly while she checked the progress of the baby.

"Ixchel, I can already see the baby's head," she exclaimed. She motioned for Sijuan to help Witzik' sit up and then to squat on the floor. "Kneel and hold her from behind, using your forearms to support her weight." Sijuan nodded and helped Witzik' into position.

"All right, Witzik', time to push," Ajkun said and within a minute, she held the new baby in her arms. "A little boy," she said as she placed the infant on Witzik's chest. She turned to Sijuan. "Grab those cloths and bring them here, we must wrap the baby up so he doesn't catch a chill. And in a few moments, you can help me wash him in a basin of warm water."

Suddenly, Witzik' groaned. "There's more, I can feel it." She leaned forward, straining to push.

Ajkun bent and snatched the new baby out of the way as Witzik' curled forward. The infant wailed, and Ajkun rocked him back and forth as she shouted to Sijuan, "Quickly, child, take a look."

Sijuan knelt in front of Witzik'. "There's another baby coming," she cried. She looked up at Ajkun. "What do I do?"

"Wait until Witzik' pushes again, then ease the baby's head out, and the rest will follow. Utzil, I never expected this," Ajkun said as she tried to shush the screaming child in her arms. "Soon, little one, soon your chuch will feed you."

With a shout of her own, Witzik' pushed and Sijuan caught the baby.

"It's a girl," she said as she held the infant up before handing it to Witzik'.

Witzik' lay back on the mattress, tucked the infant girl under one arm, and took the boy from Ajkun. "Ixchel has blessed me with twins. K'ale'n will be so proud." Both babies found nipples and began to nurse. Witzik' closed her eyes, exhausted from the labor.

"Come, Sijuan, we'll let them eat for a bit before we wash them." She motioned for the girl to follow her outside where Tzalon was sitting by the fire, nursing her own child.

"Is everything all right?" she asked as she put the baby on her shoulder to burp her.

Ajkun laughed. "Two healthy babies, a boy and a girl. She's feeding them right now." She poured more water into the basin and washed, then motioned for Sijuan to do the same. "You did a wonderful job in there, Sijuan. I'd love to teach you more, if you care to learn."

Sijuan blushed and smiled. "Yes, please, I'd like that very much. But I must check with Chuch and Tat axel first."

"I'm sure Pempen and Setesik would be happy for you to learn the ways of the midwife and healer." She watched as Sijuan took Tzalon's infant in her arms. "You were born to be around children, that much is obvious."

It was only after the newborns had been bathed in warm water infused with perícon blossoms that Ajkun realized they needed two more sets of binding boards. She turned to Sijuan, who was helping Witzik' clean herself after the birthing. "Run and tell your father we need more boards for these two."

But Sijuan hadn't reached the doorway when there was a knock on the doorframe. Chiman poked his head inside and smiled at the group of women. "I've brought a set of boards, and an extra set, just in case."

"There'll be no extras, as Witzik' has produced two healthy children, a boy and a girl."

"Itzamná, twins, we *are* blessed. I must consult the stars and determine a good naming day for all our new villagers." Chiman stepped aside to let Ajkun out. "Is there anything else you need?"

"Plenty of rags from everyone in the area," Ajkun laughed. "With four infants, they'll go through many more than we have now."

"I think we'll have to call this area the 'nursery' from now on!" Chiman smiled as one infant and then another began to cry. "They all sound strong and healthy. But perhaps that's my signal to leave. I'll leave you women to it, then." He gave Ajkun a quick hug and hurried off.

Witzik' soon discovered that feeding two infants at once was no easy task, and Ajkun spent the next several days living with the newest mother, helping her switch children from breast to breast and changing their rags for clean ones as needed. Sijuan also stayed as much as she could, helping Tzalon and Xoral with their infants, and learning as much as Ajkun had time to teach her in any spare moments. Noy came by frequently, but more often than not, she was needed in the village proper to help Mam and to take care of Lintat. But she assured Ajkun that they were keeping an eye on her hut, making sure no animals moved in during her absence and that the flowers she had planted in her courtyard were well watered.

Finally, several days after Witzik' had given birth, Ajkun felt she could go back home. The three mothers were seated around a central fire, one of many concessions Ajkun had suggested to make their lives easier. After all, she had reasoned, it was far easier to tend one flame than three. They had also agreed to reorganize their living quarters so that their husbands could get some much-needed sleep at night. Since Xoral and Tzukunel's hut was the largest of the three in the area, the women and children had shifted into the one space. Tzukanel had moved in with Ajchak, sharing his hut closest to the cornfield, while K'ale'n remained alone in the middle house.

The three men joined the women at the fire and graciously accepted the bowls of corn porridge that Ajkun scooped out for them.

As the oldest of the three young men, K'ale'n was the first to speak. "Ajkun, I think I can say that I speak for all of us in saying maltiox for all your help over the past few weeks. It's certainly been a busy time for you, and we appreciate that you've shared so much of your expertise with our wives and our children. From now on, there will always be firewood at your hearth and fresh meat for your supper, small gestures to repay you for all your kindnesses."

Ajchak and Tzukunel smiled and nodded in agreement as K'ale'n spoke. Ajkun looked around the circle of young couples with their new children nestled in their mothers' arms and felt a surge of love for all of them. "Maltiox, all of you, it's good to have you here, to have you a part of the village." She felt tears welling in her eyes and quickly wiped them away, momentarily embarrassed that everyone would see her crying. She swallowed hard, forcing the lump in her throat to go away. "I know you've all heard the stories, so I'll admit that it's been difficult these past several moons, losing my granddaughter and now Tz' as well." She paused, at a sudden loss for words, wondering if she would ever see either of her favorite people again. "I miss them terribly and pray the gods will return them to me, to all of us here in Pa nimá . . . . In the meantime, I'm honored to be a part of this small gathering of such loving families."

Ajchak helped Ajkun to her feet and handed her her mahogany walking stick, which had been leaning against the hut wall. "Would you like help back to the village?" he asked as he continued to brace her while Ajkun caught her balance.

"No, no, I can find my own way, maltiox." She bent and kissed each of the children on the forehead. "I'll come back once I've spoken to Chiman and found out when he wants to conduct the naming ceremony."

Only after Ajkun had gotten new embers for her fire from Noy, done several chores around her house, and bathed in the river did she feel ready to find Chiman. Once again, several days had passed since she'd seen him, and the thought made her heart flutter as she walked the familiar path to his house. The two-room hut was visible through the trees, and Ajkun realized she had not been to the spot since before the attack on the village. The place looked different, and it took Ajkun several minutes to put her finger on what had changed. *The turkeys in their pen are gone, there's no laundry on the line, and somehow, everything looks more . . . .* Ajkun groped for the word . . . *relaxed, if that's possible . . . .* She laughed. *Without Chachal's stern voice harping on every little thing, even the trees in the yard have let down their guard.* Ajkun chortled again, and the sound echoed through the little courtyard.

"Hello, Chiman? Are you here?" Ajkun called. She waited for a response, but the wind in the old avocado tree in the yard was the only answer. She walked to the edge of the river, waiting several minutes while watching the rush of water flow by. She looked up and downstream, but the numerous grasses and bushes growing along the riverbanks blocked her view. Turning back toward the house, she thought of leaving Chiman a note, but realized she didn't have any writing utensils with her. Even though it was peaceful in the area, Ajkun could still hear Chachal's strident voice echoing in her head, and it felt wrong to enter the house uninvited to look for paper and a quill. She turned to leave, but was surprised at the disappointment she felt. *Oh, you old fool,* she whispered as she headed across the clearing, *you'll see him tomorrow, and that's soon enough.*

But she hadn't gone more than ten paces down the path when she heard footsteps behind her. "Ajkun, wait," Chiman called out as he ran up beside her.

"Utzil, you startled me! Where were you?" Ajkun demanded as she planted the tip of her walking stick into the ground just inches from Chiman's bare foot.

"Fishing, downstream from the house . . . . I didn't hear or see anything until the last minute. I had a large eel on my line, which took me quite some time to reel in." He grinned. "Want to stay for dinner?" he said as he offered his arm to Ajkun.

"You know fresh eel is one of my favorites," Ajkun replied as she placed her free hand on his strong forearm. "If you clean it, I'll cook it."

It only took a short while for Chiman to strip the eel of its skin, gut it, and wash it. He cut several thick slices of the fish and laid them on a thick banana leaf before handing them over to Ajkun. "I'll need coconut oil, cornmeal, salt, and a pan," she instructed Chiman as she struck two flint rocks together to make sparks for a fire.

Chiman hurried inside the hut and returned with the items she'd requested. As he placed them on the ground, he nodded toward the house. "If you need anything else, just go in and find it. I must wash the smell of the eel off before we eat." He went back indoors, returning quickly with a thick towel and a bowl of soap. "I'll be back soon," he said as he waved to Ajkun.

The stars were appearing in the sky overhead as Ajkun dredged the eel in cornmeal and set it to fry in the open flat pan. A single bat flew by, low enough to cause Ajkun to duck her head, and she shivered, despite the heat from the fire. *Every time one of them flies by, I feel so cold,* she mused as she poked at the eel. It was sticking in the pan, and she realized she'd forgotten to tell Chiman she needed a utensil to flip the pieces. She hastily moved the pot off the direct heat and entered the house.

It was dark inside, and it took Ajkun several minutes to adjust to the dim light. She found a candle, went back outside, lit it from the fire, and reentered the hut. *Itzamná, I haven't been here since before Chachal died.* The thought sent a shiver up her spine. But everything that might have reminded her of the woman was gone. There was no sign of her tools, her embroidery or weaving, or her clothing, nothing to reflect that a woman had ever lived in the house. *Hmm, Chiman must have removed everything without saying a word to anyone. I suspect he did it right after Tz' left; otherwise, he might have mentioned it to me.* Then she shrugged. She had done the same thing when her much older husband, Tajinel, had died so many years ago. It had taken her only a few days to get over her grief and to rid herself of any reminders that they had been a couple. After all, the marriage had been one of convenience only, to hide her pregnancy by Chiman; Ajkun had never really felt any love for the older farmer she'd been forced to marry.

She found a small, flat, wooden paddle that would suffice to flip the slices of eel and hurried back outside. Night had fully fallen, as it did so quickly in the jungle, and she was grateful for the cheery blaze in front of her.

"Ah, that feels good," Chiman said as he appeared from the direction of the river. He turned around and around in front of the flames. "The water was colder than I expected!" He squatted next to the hearth and placed another stick on the fire before going into the hut. He returned carrying two stools in his hands, which he placed at a comfortable distance from the flames. He went back inside for plates, mugs, and a jug of mango juice that Noy had given him just that morning.

Ajkun slid several pieces of the hot fried eel onto his plate before helping herself. They ate in silence, the burbling of the nearby river and the crackling of the fire ample conversation for the two old friends. They both finished eating at almost the same time and placed their plates on the ground. Chiman leaned back and looked at the stars overhead.

"Such vastness between the stars; I wonder how the gods travel such distances."

"In ways we can only imagine," Ajkun said. She glanced to her right and ducked as two bats flew by. She shuddered and rubbed her arms. She wished she had her shawl to wrap over her bare skin.

"Are you cold?" Chiman asked. He hurried to throw more wood on the fire. The sparks leapt into the air, pushing away the blackness that surrounded them on all sides. "I can get you a blanket . . . ."

"No, no, I'm fine, really, it's just the night breeze and . . . ." Ajkun hesitated. She suddenly realized that recently the sight of bats made her feel the same depth of cold that she'd experienced while in Mayapán. "You'll laugh, but the bats, they bring back memories of that awful cold place I was stuck in for so long."

Chiman held out his hand. "We'll go inside, where you'll be warm."

Ajkun wavered. She knew it was late and she should go to her own hut, but a tiny spark of heat flared up inside her, and she let Chiman guide her to the house.

Once inside, the lone candle tossed their shadows on the stucco walls, making it appear as if several people filled the room. Having left the stools outside, Chiman ushered Ajkun to the end of the bed. "I can go get the chairs, if you prefer," he said as Ajkun delayed sitting down.

"No, no, this is fine," Ajkun replied. She felt hot and cold all at once, as she perched on the foot of the bed. Chiman balanced carefully on the narrow mattress next to her, his bare thigh just a few inches from her skirt. She could feel the heat of his body through the thin fabric and felt a fluttering inside that she'd long given up on ever feeling again. "We need to have the naming ceremony, for the new babies," she heard herself say as if from a distance. *What is wrong with me?* she wondered as her heart beat faster.

Chiman's response was to lean in and give her a kiss on the lips.

"Oh, goodness, I wasn't expecting that," Ajkun said as she licked her lips. She could taste cornmeal and eel and salt, and smell the sweetness of the jasmine-scented soap Chiman had washed with. Her heart skipped a beat, and she put her hand out to steady herself, brushing Chiman's thigh in the process.

He grinned, his teeth white against his shadow-filled face. He placed his own hand over Ajkun's and held it there before leaning in to kiss her again. This time, Ajkun was prepared and closed her eyes, sighing as she felt the tip of his tongue ever so gently probe her lips. His hand stroked her shoulder and moved toward the top of her breast.

And then she heard Chachal's voice in her ear, as if she were standing right next to them, and Ajkun jerked away from Chiman.

"What's wrong? Did I hurt you?" Chiman said. He sat back, looking at Ajkun in the wavering candlelight.

"No, no, you did nothing . . . it's me, it's this place . . . I should go home," Ajkun said as she stood up. She wobbled, her knees weak.

"Don't go, please," Chiman said as he held out a hand to steady Ajkun. He shook his head, looking around the small room. "She's still here, isn't she? Even though I got rid of all her things, Chachal still lives in this space." He stood up and paced the floor, blocking Ajkun from reaching the doorway. Then he turned and grinned at her. He grabbed the two blankets off the bed and took her by the hand. "Come; I know where we'll go."

There was a tiny slice of moon overhead, barely enough to see by, but the instant Chiman stepped off the path and into the jungle, Ajkun knew where he was taking her. She smiled in the darkness and squeezed his hand. As young children, they had wandered through the nearby woods, exploring all its secrets, and had discovered a small opening among the numerous ceiba and mahogany trees. They had spent many afternoons playing house in the dappled sunlight in their private spot, and when they'd become lovers, they'd used the space as their private, open-air bedroom.

"I'm surprised you still know the way," Ajkun said as she twisted around a large tree in her path.

"You'd be shocked if I told you the number of times I've returned here over the years," Chiman said as he stepped into the clearing.

The moon's faint rays of light shone on the spot, and Ajkun gasped. A tiny hut, barely six paces across, but big enough to stand up in, was tucked in under the first branches of the large mahogany trees. "Whenever did you build this?" Ajkun said.

"Years ago, not long after we broke up. I used it when I needed to get away from Chachal." Chiman smiled as he pushed open the miniature door. "Watch your head when you enter," he said as he ducked down and disappeared inside.

Ajkun quickly followed. Except for the indistinct light from the doorway, the room was black, and Ajkun hesitated, unable to discern anything, including Chiman.

"I'm right here," Chiman said as he reached up and touched Ajkun's hand. He pulled and Ajkun knelt. She could feel the softness of the blankets under her and shifted her body so she could sit beside Chiman.

"Now, where were we?" Chiman softly asked as he touched her chin and brought his lips to hers.

Now that they were finally together, neither one of them was in a hurry, as their two bodies already knew each other intimately. Slow and sensual, their lovemaking lasted until the first *krrrrs* of several fork-tailed flycatchers filled the air outside. And then they slept, wrapped in each other's arms.

Bright sun shone directly down into the little clearing when Ajkun finally woke. She looked over at Chiman, who lay sprawled on his back, both arms above his head, fast asleep. She leaned in and kissed his chest before lifting his right foot to retrieve her skirt and shirt. They were wrinkled and needed washing, but Ajkun tugged them on anyway. She didn't want Chiman to see her old body in the light of day. She hurried outside to relieve her full bladder and listened to her empty stomach grumble. Her mouth was dry, and she wished she had thought to bring a water gourd with them. *Utzil, who was thinking at all last night?* she mused as she tipped a few bananas leaves toward her mouth, drinking in the minute drops of dew that still clung to the innermost parts. She wandered around the jungle for a few minutes and found a bunch of bananas that were close to ripe. She picked several, ate two, and brought the rest back to the hut.

She peeked inside and saw Chiman was still asleep. Her stomach grumbled again. *Itzamná, I need to get back to the village and check on the mothers.* She poked Chiman with her foot, and he rolled over onto his side, opened his eyes, and smiled.

"Up already?" he said as he yawned and stretched.

The blankets slipped off, exposing his bare body, and Ajkun was startled to feel desire ignite in her once again. She shook her head, attempting to ward off her feelings. "Huh, the sun is already on its way down again," Ajkun said. She turned away, hoping that by doing so she could gain some control over her emotions. She listened as Chiman stretched again, but was surprised when he didn't get up.

"Aren't you hungry?" she asked over her shoulder. "I know I am, and I have to check on things in the village." She waited, but there was no answer. She turned around. Chiman was still lying on his side, propped up on one elbow, staring at her.

"Aren't you getting up?"

"Hmm, yes, I think so," he replied. He held out his hand and laughed. "The villagers are fine. You told me yourself that Sijuan and Noy are able to take care of the mothers from now on. No one needs you right now except me." He tugged on the edge of her skirt. "Please?"

Ajkun took a deep breath and then smiled. "All right, but hand me one of those blankets. I'll be right back. It's been a long time since any man has seen this old body in any bright light, and I'm afraid it hasn't fared as well as yours over the years." She stepped into the clearing, quickly removed her clothes, and wrapped the soft cotton blanket firmly under her arms, tucking the ends in so it couldn't come undone.

"Ah, a package for me to unwrap," Chiman said as he helped Ajkun lie down beside him.

"Oh, no, you just close your eyes this minute," Ajkun replied as she tried to place her hand over Chiman's face, shielding his view. The two tussled for a moment, and then Ajkun relaxed as Chiman nibbled on her ear before leaving little kisses all over her face. "Butterfly wings," she said as she sighed. "I'd forgotten those."

The shadows had crossed the clearing by the time the couple finally emerged from their secret spot. Hand in hand, they hurried back to Chiman's house where they kissed and embraced before Ajkun insisted on leaving.

"I must go home," Ajkun said as she tugged on her hand that Chiman refused to let go.

"When will I see you again?"

"Goodness, we just spent several hours together . . . ." She looked at Chiman's lined face and could see the young boy in him even after all the years that had passed. He had always been the earnest one, fearless in pursuing that which he most desired. She leaned in and gave him a quick peck on the cheek. "Soon, I promise, but I need some time alone now." She squeezed his hand and pulled free, hurrying down the path to her own house before she changed her mind.

A large bundle of sticks and branches lay next to her fire pit, and when she poked the blackened coals, she was pleased to see that someone had banked the last fire just so, and that embers still showed signs of life. She quickly got the fire going and put a pot of water on to boil. It was only when the flames leapt high that she realized something had been moving around the courtyard. Large, familiar tracks crisscrossed the dirt and circled the hut. She bent down to inspect them and realized that they were jaguar prints. *Itzamná, why would a jaguar come here, so close to the village?* For a brief instant, she wondered if it was Ek' Balam and almost called out his name, but knew that would be impossible. He and Na'om were long gone. As she thought of her granddaughter, the old ache returned with a jolt to Ajkun's heart, and she suddenly realized that being with Chiman had driven that pain away. *I must ask him about these tracks next time I see him.* Her heart skipped a beat at the possibility.

A cup of tea to calm my nerves is what I need first, she thought as she moved about her small house, preparing an herbal mixture from the many baskets and bags of dried plants that filled the shelves of her storeroom. But she kept stopping to reflect on the previous hours with Chiman, wondering if it had all been a fantastical dream. Then she smiled as she felt the soreness of her body and the places that hadn't been pleasured for years and knew it had been real. She was so wrapped up in her thoughts that she didn't hear Noy enter the hut and jumped when the woman placed a hand on her shoulder.

"Ixchel, I didn't hear you come in," Ajkun said as she spun around, spilling some of her dried tea mixture on the ground.

"I knocked, but you were a thousand paces away," Noy said as she helped Ajkun sweep up the herbs on the floor. "I heard noises and came to see if everything's all right. When you didn't return last night, I was worried." She picked up two mugs off the shelf and followed Ajkun outside. She handed the two cups to Ajkun and then leaned in to pluck a few sticks out of the older woman's hair, which she threw into the fire.

Ajkun nodded, poured the hot water, and handed Noy a cup before settling on the hard ground. She sipped at her tea, trying to hide the smile that persisted in forming on her face.

Noy studied Ajkun for a few moments in the deepening twilight. She squinted and tilted her head to one side. "Your whole body is outlined in a purplish-white light . . . . You were with Chiman last night, weren't you?"

Embarrassed to say anything, Ajkun tried to hide her grin behind her mug of tea.

Noy laughed. "Oh, I'm so happy for you. Itzamná knows it's about time." She put down her empty mug as she stood up. "You're welcome to come for dinner; there's plenty of turkey stew. Unless you'd rather be alone . . . ."

"No, a meal together would be nice. I'd like to see Mam and Lintat as well. I just need to wash and change my clothes, all right?"

"Yes, of course, take your time."

It didn't take long for Ajkun to bathe and change at the river. She smiled, thinking about Chiman, as she hurried along the well-worn path to the village center, but she also kept watching the shadows in case the jaguar was still about.

She was startled to see Chiman already seated on a woven banana leaf mat when she arrived at Noy and Mam's house. He stood up and helped her settle on the available stool near the fire. They both kept smiling at each other, and Mam exchanged a quick wink with Noy. Ajkun nodded hello to Mam and hugged Lintat when he came running over.

"Mam was just telling me that he's seen jaguar scat near the river," Chiman said as he sat down again. "We must warn all the villagers, especially the new mothers."

"It was at my hut last night," Ajkun said. "There are tracks all around the place."

"Really, Ati't, did you see it?" Lintat asked as he tugged on her arm. "I'd like to see a jaguar." He hopped up and down. "Maybe it was Ek' Balam."

"No, sweet child, it wasn't Ek' Balam," Ajkun said as she pulled Lintat onto her lap. "Another jaguar, not one so nice and tame as our old Ek' Balam, so you must be very careful as you run about the jungle, all right?"

The boy nodded and leaned his head against Ajkun's shoulder.

She turned to Chiman. "Why would a jaguar come to my house?"

Chiman shrugged and then he grinned. "Perhaps one of Ek' Balam's lady friends misses him and came to see where he was. They leave their scent everywhere, so it wouldn't be difficult for a female to find out where he'd been living. I'll have Tzukunel set a live trap for this one; we don't want to hurt her if she's friendly to Ek' Balam."

The evening passed quickly, with the four friends sharing stories long after Lintat had been sent to bed. Finally, Ajkun yawned, picked up her walking stick, and thanked everyone for a nice night.

"I'll walk you home," Chiman said as he stood up. "With that jaguar still on the loose, I want no harm to come to you."

Noy hugged Ajkun and whispered in her ear. "Remember, life is short, so enjoy every minute of it."

Ajkun and Chiman stepped onto the path and quickly held hands once they were out of sight of the others. They walked in silence back to Ajkun's house.

"Still want to be alone?" Chiman asked as he kissed Ajkun gently on the top of her head.

"With a jaguar coming to my door? I don't think so," Ajkun replied as she pulled him inside and let the deer hide covering fall over the doorway.

Tz'

Even from outside the city gates, Tz' could see the pyramid of Kukulcan rising high above the rest of the surrounding buildings. Its white limestone sides reflected the sun, sending beams of light out like a beacon into the scrubby brush and fields around Mayapán. After he passed through the main double gates, Tz' used the pyramid to get his bearings and headed directly to Yakal's house. Although it was mid-afternoon, he hoped his uncle would be home, so he could warn him that Satal was still alive. As he entered the neighborhood where Yakal lived, Tz' threaded his way through a group of young mothers who stood gossiping together while their toddlers played near their feet. Nearby, four old men were in an animated discussion right in the middle of the street. He shook his head, amazed at the number of people.

Tz' hesitated before stepping into Yakal's small courtyard. There was no sign of his uncle, but he could hear singing coming from the hut. He tapped lightly on the fencing, then opened the gate and entered the yard. "Yakal? Uskab?" He set his basket of belongings on the ground and waited. The singing stopped, and Uskab appeared in the doorway, her baby boy in her arms.

"Tz'," Uskab said as she rushed forward to give the young man a hug. "It's so good to see you again, but what are you doing here?" Uskab shifted the infant to the other arm. "I was just singing to little Mayibal before he takes his nap."

Tz' looked at the infant who smiled up at him. "He's getting so big so quickly. Before you know it, he'll be running all over the place." He turned to his things and found the container of salves Ajkun had sent with him. "From Ati't, for the baby," he said.

"Maltiox," Uskab replied as she hitched Mayibal up on her hip. "Yes, this one's eager to be on his feet. That's why Yakal built the fence around the yard. Come, sit, you must be tired after your long trip." Uskab bustled about the little open space, fussing with the fire pit while balancing Mayibal in her arms. "Let me get you something to eat."

"No, no, I'm not hungry," Tz' said as he lightly touched Uskab on the arm. "I'll eat later, when Yakal is here. Is he at work?"

Uskab nodded. "He's just finishing a new coat of plaster on the far side of the pyramid. The council plans to paint the entire surface, if they can find enough artisans to do it." She looked at Tz' and grinned. "If you're staying in the city, Yakal can put you to work right away!"

Tz' smiled. He knew Uskab meant well, but he already knew what he planned to do. However, he needed to speak to Yakal before he could put his ideas into motion. He tickled Mayibal under the chin and made the baby laugh. "I'm going to go find Yakal. I'll see you later this afternoon." Then he pointed to his blankets and bundle of clothes. "It's all right to leave my things?"

"Yes, yes, of course," Uskab said. "You're family and can stay as long as you like." Mayibal began to squirm in her arms and let out a little cry. "He's hungry again and then needs his nap."

Tz' nodded and headed back into the street. He wound his way through the steady flow of people and finally found the base of the pyramid. Scaffolding had been erected on two of the four stepped sides, and several men were busy drawing designs in black charcoal on the white plaster, blocking out intricate geometric patterns, animal shapes, and silhouettes of the gods. He tried to picture what the structure would look like when it was finished, but was interrupted when he felt a hand thump him on the back.

"Tz'!" Yakal said. "What in the name of Itzamná are you doing here? Did something happen, is everyone all right?"

Tz' turned and hugged his uncle. "Everyone's fine, Tat and Ajkun send their greetings." He gestured toward the pyramid. "This has turned into quite the project," he said.

"Yes, isn't it? See where those men are drawing? We've decided to build the plaster out into three-dimensional figures and then paint them. We won't do that everywhere, of course, but it should add to the beauty of the whole building." Yakal hugged Tz' again. "I never expected to see you back here, especially not so soon. Are you hungry? I was just about to eat, and Uskab always packs plenty for my lunch." He walked toward a small pole shed, open on all sides and covered with a thatched roof to provide some shade. He pointed to a wooden stool and sat on one himself. "Sit, rest, tell me why you're here."

Tz' took the gourd Yakal offered him and drank several swallows of the watermelon juice before speaking. He leaned in closer to Yakal. "I came to warn you. Satal is alive."

Yakal choked and coughed on the piece of turkey he was eating. When he could breathe again, he grabbed Tz' by the arm. "Say no more for now; we'll go find someplace private to discuss this." He hurriedly repacked his lunch into his leather satchel and motioned to one of the stonemasons working nearby. "Keep working with the plasterers, and I'll be back in the morning."

The mason nodded and turned back to the stepped wall in front of him.

"Come on," Yakal said. He motioned for Tz' to follow him. "Let's go outside the city where there are fewer ears to hear this information."

Once they'd found a private spot in a gully several minutes beyond the walls, Yakal sat down in the shade of a ceiba tree and motioned for Tz' to sit as well. "All right, now start from the beginning. How in the name of all the gods do *you* know Satal is alive?"

Tz' quickly told his uncle about his battle with Camazotz and what the bat god had said about Satal plotting revenge on those who had accused her of treason. "I came back to warn you about her."

Yakal nodded. "I have the same news. For weeks, I've been going to the Silowik Tukan to listen to the gossip in case any of the men who go there to drink and gamble has heard anything about Satal. And then I met Kux, a man from Chichén Itzá, who confirmed she's alive and taken over control of the city. She's amassing a huge army and plans to attack, but we don't know when." Yakal took a sip of watermelon juice. "No one except members of the council knows this information, so you can't tell a soul. We don't want Satal to learn that we know some of her plans."

Tz' nodded. "Don't worry, I won't say a word." Anger surged through his body as he thought about what his grandmother had done and was still planning to do to those he loved.

"Oh, how I wish the old witch had died when she fell! I'd give all the cacao beans I own to the gods if they'd bring Na'om back instead," Yakal said.

"The gods may ask you to pay that debt." Tz' grinned at Yakal, who looked confused. "You don't know about Na'om's ledger. Tat and Ati't found it in her house, filled with drawings of her dreams. The last ones she did showed her swimming with Ek' Balam into a tunnel in the side of the cenote. Tat and Ati't believe she might be alive, and even Camazotz said she was wending her way through the trials in the Underworld. Not that it would do me much good even if she did return." He sighed.

"Why, what do you mean? I thought you wanted to marry her?" Yakal said.

Tz' shook his head. "I can't marry my half-sister."

It was Yakal's turn to grin. "I'm glad you're sitting down, Tz', for I have news for *you*. Growing up, your mother, Chachal, and I were never very close, even though she was my half-sister. But I did keep an eye on her and long suspected something that Kux verified for me. Shortly before Chachal met Chiman, she was seeing a man named Alaxel, a member of one of the elite families in Chichén Itzá. He swept Chachal off her feet, taking her to parties and dances, but when they began to talk of marriage, my father, Q'alel, insisted she marry Chiman instead. Q'alel refused to let her marry someone with Xiu blood in his veins. He was a full blood Cocom, you see, and realized he'd already diluted the family bloodline by marrying Satal, a Xiu. He was determined to bring more Cocom blood back into the family lineage, even though Chiman was so much older than your mother. I remember how she cried and cried at Q'alel's decision, knowing she'd be leaving Alaxel and all the fun here in the city to go live in Pa nimá. But shortly before we left for the village, Chachal and Alaxel became lovers, which means, Tz', there's a good chance Chiman's not your real father."

Tz' stared at his uncle. He couldn't speak for several minutes as the idea worked its way through his mind. Finally, he said, "So, if he's not, then this man Alaxel is?"

Yakal nodded.

"Where do I find him?"

"Kux told me Alaxel returned to Chichén Itzá shortly after losing Chachal. But he didn't know where Alaxel lives in the city or even if he's still alive."

"And does Tat axel know about this? Did you send him a message?"

"No, of course not. How would I explain in a letter that you're not his son? It's only hearsay anyway, and with Chachal dead, how could I prove it?"

"But if it is true, then that means Na'om and I aren't related . . ." Tz' fell silent as the idea whirled around in his head. He felt a pressure deep inside his chest build and build until it erupted in loud bubbles of pure, joyous laughter. He laughed until his sides ached, and the tears flowed down his cheeks in salty streams. He smiled through his tears at Yakal who sat staring at him. "Don't you see? This means Na'om is *not* my half-sister! Which means I can marry her once I find her." The sense of urgency that Tz' had felt ever since leaving Pa nimá intensified, and he jumped to his feet. "Now it's even more important that I find a shaman who can teach me more about the Underworld. I can use the knowledge to find Na'om and to help defeat Satal." He held out his hand and pulled Yakal to his feet. "Are there any cacao beans left from the fortune Satal had?"

Yakal nodded. "Yes, why do you ask?"

"I'll need currency to pay for information, supplies, that sort of thing, and don't have the time to earn it."

"Come on, we'll go get Nimal. It takes two members of the council to remove any of the cacao beans from the Temple of Warriors."

The two men quickly made their way back into the city, found Nimal, and Tz' tucked a small bag of beans into the leather pouch tied around his waist.

"Shall we go see what Uskab's made for supper?" Yakal asked. He shaded his eyes against the late afternoon sun so he could see Tz'.

Tz' gave his uncle a hug. "You go ahead. I'm going to surprise Box and Nil and have a couple of drinks with them."

"Well, remember not to say anything to either of them about Satal."

Tz' nodded before quickly making his way through the warren of alleyways to the pottery shops. He hoped Box was still at work, but ready to quit for the evening.

Sure enough, his friend was just taking off his leather apron when Tz' arrived. He tapped Box on the shoulder, and the youth turned around in a hurry.

"Tz'! What are you doing here? Have you come to get your old job back? I hope so; it'd be great to have you work here again."

"Actually, I have other plans. But let's not talk about that right now. I'd rather go get a mug of something at the Silowik Tukan, my treat," Tz' said with a smile. "Maybe we can persuade Nil to have a mug, too."

Box laughed. "I've never known Nil to say no, even when he's supposedly working. Come on, I can't wait to hear all your news."

The two friends made their way to the drinking house, which was empty at that hour. Nil was behind the counter, arranging all the ceramic cups in neat rows, when they walked through the door.

"Tz'! What are you doing back here?" Nil exclaimed. He hurried to give Tz' a hug. "Acan! When you left, I thought I'd never see you again. Sit down, you too, Box, and let me pour you both something."

Tz' grinned as he looked about the room. The sound of snoring came from the back room, and he sucked in the stale smells of spilled juices and the faint scent of vomit that always lingered no matter how many times Nil mopped the tile floor. "It's good to be back," he said as he picked up the ceramic mug in front of him and took a long drink. He wiped the froth from his upper lip as he set the cup back down. "Now that's good, really good. What is it?"

"A new recipe I've been playing around with, pineapple, lime, and mango juices. After you left, Tat decided I should start learning how to make all the drinks, and when he discovered I could make them as well or better than he could, well, he turned the whole process over to me." Nil leaned down and grabbed a small wooden keg from under the counter. He poured a small amount into two tiny cups and handed one to Tz' and one to Box. "Try that, but take it slowly."

Tz' looked at the youth and then sniffed the cup. It burned his nostrils a bit, and he grinned. "It smells potent," he said, taking a sip. A blaze of heat went down his throat as he swallowed. "Itzamná! What is this stuff?" he said as he almost dropped the cup on the countertop.

Box quickly tossed back his cupful and drew in a sharp breath. "Wow."

Nil laughed. "It's another experiment I'm working on made out of cactus juice. It's a bit harsh, but I think with some more time spent in the barrel, it will be as smooth as the finest cotton and still kick like a caiman." He put the small barrel back under the counter. "But enough of me, what are you doing here?" He thumped Tz' on the arm. "It's so good to see you."

"Yes, come on now, tell us what's brought you back, since we know it wasn't that you missed us," Box said and laughed.

Tz' looked around to make sure the room was still empty. "Remember my telling you about Na'om? Well, I have reason to believe she's still alive, so I've come to find a shaman who can help me find her in the Underworld."

Box whistled through his teeth. "Itzamná, that sounds dangerous!"

Nil gulped down another glass of fermented juice. "Entering the Underworld is more than dangerous; it borders on black magic. The city council was going to sacrifice Satal for her witchcraft. Are you sure you want to go down that path?"

Tz' thumped his fist on the counter. "I know it's risky, but there's a good chance Na'om's not my sister, which means I could one day marry her . . . She's the one I'm destined to be with, I know it. Don't you see I have no choice but to help her?" Tz' stared at his friends, hoping they could understand the deep desperation he felt. He knew if he didn't find a way to help Na'om, he'd never be able to live with himself. "The trouble is, I'm not sure where to find someone who can help me, which is why I need your help." He turned to Box. "You said the funerary pieces that are made at Puk'pik's workshop are sent to an island off the coast and that the shamans there live in close proximity to the Underworld. Do you know how to get there?"

"Not really, but I'm sure Puk'pik would know."

"Why go so far away?" Nil asked as he acknowledged some customers who had seated themselves at a table. "Someone here in the city must know a bit about all that stuff." He leaned in close to Tz' so only he could hear.

"What about finding the shaman or shamans who taught Satal? She had to have learned at least some of her witchcraft from someone."

Tz' smacked the palm of his hand on the table. "Of course; why didn't I think of that? But where would I even start searching for him?"

"Well, if it was me, I'd poke around some of the shops where they sell all those dried plants and animal parts and odd paraphernalia. I mean, that is the type of thing you use for spells and stuff? So someone there has to know what to do with it all . . ."

"Nil, you're smarter than you look," Tz' said and laughed. He knew just the shopkeeper to talk to. He drained the last drops from his cup and stood up.

"Remember, you didn't hear anything from me, all right?" Nil said as he took Tz's empty cup.

Tz' nodded, but before he could move to the door, Box put his hand on his arm and stopped him.

"Hold on, not so fast. All the stores will be closed by now, so you might as well sit back down and relax. You can get your answers tomorrow, but for now, we need to celebrate that you're back in town."

Tz' sighed. He knew Box was right. Everything had to wait yet another day, even though the delays were making him sick with frustration. He forced a smile on his face and sat back down. "Another round, Nil, for all of us," he said.

Although it was late by the time he got back to Yakal's hut, Tz' was up with the first rays of the sun. After a quick wash and breakfast with Yakal, Uskab, and Mayibal, Tz' hurried toward the shop where he'd purchased his book and toad venom. *The old man will bound to have more answers for me*, Tz' thought as he walked rapidly past the marketplace, entered the street, and found the correct store.

A middle-aged woman dressed all in black sat hunched on the high stool at the back of the store. She was busy running her fingers up and down a list in a ledger and didn't look up until Tz' rapped impatiently on the wooden countertop with his knuckles.

"Well, what is it?" the woman asked as she looked at the empty counter in front of Tz'. "If you're not buying anything, then be on your way."

"I'm looking for someone," Tz' said. "The old man who worked here several moons ago, is he around?" He peered behind the woman, hoping the storekeeper was in a back room someplace.

"Old man, what old man, I'm the owner of this shop and have been for years," the woman replied. She squinted her eyes and moved her head closer to Tz' to see him better. "Who are you?"

"Just a customer," Tz' replied. "I bought a knife and a book back during the rainy season from the old man who sat where you're sitting now."

"This man, were his front teeth filed into sharp points, and did he have one missing finger on his left hand?" The woman glared at Tz'.

He tried to remember the details of the storekeeper, but the image of the man was hazy in his mind. When pressed like this, he realized he didn't really know what the man had looked like other than being older than anyone Tz' knew. "I think so, yes."

"Hmmm," the woman said, and she slid off the stool. She remained hunched over, her head barely visible above the countertop. "That was my father, who used to run this store, but he died many years ago. I don't know who you are or why you claim to have seen him, but the man you truly seek is not here, and I don't know where to find him." She hobbled around the front of the counter to stand in front of Tz' and beckoned him to bend down so he could hear her. "Be careful; the dark arts can be deadly in the wrong hands," she whispered. Then she straightened her hunched back as best she could and pushed Tz' in the stomach. "Go on with you now; seek your answers elsewhere."

Confused and disappointed, Tz' stumbled back into the busy street where the moving crowd jostled him about, carrying him along like a leaf in a brook. As he pushed through a small knot of people haggling over bright colored bundles of feathers, he felt a hand tug the back of his loincloth. He spun around and discovered the knife he carried on his hip was missing. A small boy, barefoot and dressed in a ragged cotton loincloth, was hurrying away from him.

"Hey, you, stop. Give me back my knife!" Tz' yelled and elbowed his way through the thicket of people. He saw the boy glance over his shoulder before disappearing into one of the many shops.

Tz' dashed into the shadowy interior, but there was no sign of the boy. Only a swaying tattered curtain in the back of the store indicated he had ever been there. Tz' quickly pushed the ratty fabric aside and found himself in a narrow corridor barely wider than his shoulders formed by the outer walls of the many houses and shops. There was no sign of the boy, just the constricted space that snaked its way through the jumble of buildings. Tz' took one last look back into the store before heading into the gloom.

Tiny patches of daylight broke through in places where the roof of one building ended and another began, but Tz' didn't see any place where another doorway opened onto the corridor. He hurried along, meandering right and left, wondering where he'd meet the boy again. At one point, he had to shimmy sideways to ease past the tight space, and then suddenly, he came to a dead end. A solid section of stone wall faced him, and Tz' realized it was part of the wall that surrounded the city. He pushed against the stones, thinking there might be a hidden doorway, but none of the rocks budged. Dejected and frustrated, he turned to head back the way he had come and stumbled as the ground rose up just slightly under his feet.

"Itzamná, now what?" Tz' said as he moved several feet away. A solid block of ground pushed upward, and he could see the little boy's face as he peeked through the opening. He hurried to grab the edge of the hidden door and pulled it out of the way. Peering into the hole that appeared, he could see the boy was standing on the top rung of a small ladder.

"Come on, follow me," the boy said. "Put the door back once you can," he added, as he scrambled quickly down the rungs.

Tz' almost lost sight of the boy as he disappeared into the dark. He dropped to his knees, scrabbling to find his footing on the short bamboo ladder. It ended in a tunnel so low Tz' had to stoop over or risk banging his head. The boy returned his knife, then grasped his hand and walked with ease in the blackness while Tz' shuffled along behind him as best he could. His shoulders and neck ached by the time the tunnel opened up into a large cavern, and he was able to stand upright again. He looked around in the dim light, wondering where he was and how in the name of all the gods he was going to find his way back to the surface. He shivered as he thought of Na'om being trapped in some similar space, but without a guide to help her.

The boy quickly moved to another tunnel on the opposite side of the cave and pointed toward a distant gleam of light. "He's waiting for you down there," he said.

"Who's waiting?" Tz' questioned, but the boy just smiled and vanished

into the shadows. Eager to meet the person who had summoned him, Tz'
hurried ahead, but stumbled on the rough ground. Mustering his courage,
Tz' strode forward into the small cave and raised his hand to shield his
eyes from the sudden light. A fire burned in the center of the cave, and a
multitude of candles flickered in various niches and crevices where they'd
been placed in the rock walls.

"Come in, come in," a voice croaked.

Tz' peered past his hand, searching the area for the source of the
voice. He finally spied the oldest man he'd ever seen perched on a short,
three-legged, leather-topped stool on the far side of the cave. The man's
long hair was whiter than cotton, and his face was lined with a thousand
wrinkles. He wore a thick black woolen cloak that fell to below his knees,
covering his scrawny arms and torso, and heavy black stockings and
sandals on his feet. Tz's mind flowed with a hundred questions, but before
he could say anything, the man spoke again.

"Yes, yes, all in due time, the hows and the whys and the where am
I's. Right now, the only thing you need to know is that you're in the right
spot to learn what you need to help your friends defeat Satal." The ancient
man pointed to a blanket spread on the ground in front of him. "Have a
seat, Tz'. We have little time to waste."

Biting his tongue to hold back even more questions, Tz' obediently
sat down.

"My name is Najtir, and yes, I was the shaman who taught Satal the
basics of the dark arts when she was a young woman. But she quickly
moved on into even deeper and darker methods than I knew, and when
she realized I was going to expose her, she had me sentenced for sacrifice.
Fortunately, the few friends I had at the time managed to smuggle me
away, and I've remained hidden all these years, living like a bat in these
caves under the city." He paused and took a sip of water from a cup. "The
boy who brought you here is just one of many who cater to my needs."

"But how did you know I was looking for you?" Tz' finally asked.

"Ah, dear boy, just because I was ignorant years ago doesn't mean I
didn't continue to experiment and learn things. After all, what else was
I to do with my time? Accessing a person's thoughts is an easy task, if
you know how."

"So I'm to remain here with you, in this cave? My uncle and my friends will wonder where I am if I don't appear soon."

"No, no, now that Satal has fled the city, it's safe for me to return to the land of the living. You'll go back and move into her palace, where we'll have plenty of space and privacy to conduct the training you truly seek." Najtir drank some more water. "I rather cherish the idea of seeing the sky again. Is it still as blue as I remember?"

"Yes, as blue as a crowned motmot's feathers."

"Oh, the birds, there are so many I've forgotten, what they look and sound like. So much of my life has been spent down here, wandering the passageways, learning the ways of the creatures that live underground; it'll be good to return to the surface and be among other people again." The man waved his hand, and Tz' turned in time to see another young boy appear from the shadows. "Take him back to the city." The boy nodded and stood waiting.

Reluctantly, Tz' got to his feet. There were so many things he wanted to know, but he didn't dare press the old man for answers.

"I'll arrive in three days," Najtir said. "That gives you time to get the palace cleaned and have my room made ready for me." He closed his eyes and sat very still, causing a shift in the energy of the cave.

Tz' shivered as the emptiness pervaded the area, and he wondered for a moment if the man had died.

"No, I haven't; now go with this boy," Najtir said without opening his eyes.

Tz' grasped the young boy's hand and allowed him to lead him through a series of winding passageways, which ended in a small opening that led above ground. Tz' crawled after the child and was surprised to see it was almost dark. He turned around, spotted the torches burning on the walls of Mayapán, and hurried after the young boy, who was headed toward the nearest gate. Tz' joined a group of farmers, slipped inside without being stopped by the guards, and quickly made his way to his uncle's home.

Yakal and Uskab were playing with Mayibal by the fire when he arrived. "Utzil, you look like you've had a rough day," Yakal said when he saw Tz'.

Tz' glanced down at his shirt and loincloth and realized he was covered in dirt. "I didn't realize I'd gotten so dirty," he said, but he didn't explain his condition.

Uskab pointed to the large pot on the fire. "I was going to bathe Mayibal, but you need the water more than he does. Help yourself."

Once he had washed and eaten a plate of fresh tamales, Tz' sat down near Yakal. "I need to go live in Satal's old house," he said. He held up his hand to stop his uncle. "Best not to ask why; let's just say it's in our best interest if I do."

"All right," Yakal replied. "I'll try to find someone to clean the place and do a few repairs on the roof where it leaks. You should be able to move in in a few days."

"Maltiox," Tz' replied, but didn't say anything else.

He lingered by the fire long after Yakal had retired with Uskab and Mayibal. The bright flames danced and flickered, then began to die out, but Tz' made no move toward bed. Now that he was alone, he wondered how Najtir had known he was looking for him and why he'd been able to see the spirit of the shopkeeper. Then he heard Chiman's voice in his head, reminding him the gods had his destiny already planned for him. *Of course, the gods are behind all this.* Then the thought that Chiman was not really his father crowded into Tz's mind. He could scarcely believe that Chachal had had a secret lover; the image certainly didn't match the picture he held in his head of his mother. *If Alaxel is really my father, is there a way to find him? But what would I say to him? He probably doesn't even know I exist.* Tz' shook his head. *Best to let that mystery remain one, at least for now.* He thought about Na'om, wondering where she was in the Underworld and how she was able to find enough food and water to survive. He pictured her trying to cross the river of blood or get through the house of jaguars with only Ek' Balam's help, and hoped she was able to find the inner strength to make it through the trials.

A piece of burnt wood collapsed, sending a spray of sparks into the dark night, and suddenly, two images collided in his mind—one of the Underworld's house of jaguars from one of Chiman's ledgers, the other of the were-jaguars in the ancient book he'd purchased. In that moment, he realized his spirit animal was one of the creatures from the land of the Underworld, and he felt a rush of elation and energy speed through his body. At that moment, he craved more than anything the power and ability that came with being a were-jaguar. *I have to figure out how to shape-shift again. I must have done something wrong when I conjured up*

Camazotz instead of transforming. Tz' looked down at his hand in the last bit of firelight, imagining it shaped like a giant paw, with a long claw on each digit, and smiled. *Of course, Najtir will teach me. That's why the gods have sent him to me. And I'll use my powers to help Na'om and defeat Satal.*

Satal

Satal motioned for all but two of the shamans to sit down. "Chiwekox and Ch'o, you're the last two to shape-shift. Take a slice of the jequirity bean and do as you've been instructed. The rest of us will be here to help you if you should run into any trouble," Satal said. She sat down in one of the many comfortable chairs to watch the transformation.

Chiwekox and Ch'o nodded and picked up the tiny slivers of bean. At the same time, they nodded and touched the cut edges to their tongues. Each instantly began to transform into his particular shape. Chiwekox was the first to complete the alteration, shifting into a boa constrictor many paces long. He slithered across the floor, his scales scratching on the tiles as he moved. Satal was particularly pleased to see him reappear as a snake as it reminded her of her great-grandmother, Sachoj. She had been so powerful that many of the buildings in Chichén Itzá, including the sacred pyramid, were adorned with serpents, had columns in the shape of snakes, or had geometric patterns reminiscent of snakeskins incorporated into the tiles and facades in her honor.

Satal waited impatiently for Ch'o to finish his transformation and smiled when he finally emerged as a large rat with blood-red eyes. But her grin quickly faded. When Chiwekox saw Ch'o, his natural instincts took over, and the giant boa constrictor slithered after Ch'o, who squealed and squeaked in terror as he scurried about the large room. The two creatures knocked over tables and chairs in the continuous pursuit before Satal finally managed to grab the giant snake's tail. Chiwekox coiled himself around and around her body, while Pataninel helped Ch'o eat a piece of charcoal and resume his human shape.

Just as Satal was finding it a bit difficult to breathe, Yuxba' managed to toss a chunk of charcoal in the snake's mouth, causing Chiwekox to reappear.

Both naked men huddled on the floor, shaking from their experience.

"My deepest apologies, Lady Satal," Chiwekox said as he knelt before her. "I had no intention of harming you or Ch'o."

"Of course you didn't, you only did what came naturally," Satal replied as she sank onto a nearby chair. "But we mustn't have that happen again. Yuxba', from now on, you'll work with Ch'o in one of the bedrooms, while Pataninel will work with Chiwekox here with the others. And on the day of the battle, we must make sure neither sees the other during the attack or Itzamná only knows what will happen."

The shamans all nodded in agreement.

"All right, now that we know what image each of you will assume, you must continue to practice so you can transform quickly and easily at will and still maintain enough strength after you assume your human shapes to be useful." She nodded to Koyopa, the heavyset shaman with the white streak in his hair. "I think it best if you practice at night, while the others sleep. We don't need anyone getting zapped by your lightning bolts."

"As you wish, Lady Satal," Koyopa replied.

She smiled at Yuxba' who had appeared with a tray piled high with tamales, which he set on the table near her.

"After we eat, we'll move on to the next phase of our work, which will be to summon some of the lords of the Underworld who will work with us during the battle. As you know, I'll manifest into a black wasp, and my personal ally is Camazotz, but we must find out who each of you will be joined by." She turned to find Pataninel, who was helping Ch'o to his feet. One ankle was swollen where the man had whacked it against the wall while trying to escape Chiwekox, and he hobbled to a nearby chair. "Did you prepare the tincture as I requested, Pataninel?"

"Yes, it's in the kitchen. I'll fetch it right away." The thin man hurried out of the room and returned a few moments later with a large pitcher of water and several mugs on a tray along with a small bottle stoppered with a piece of cork. He set the tray on the table, and Satal picked up the bottle. She removed the cork and smelled the contents.

"Perfect, this should work quite nicely." She poured six drops into each mug, then filled them with water. "Finish eating now, we've no time to waste."

The shamans set aside the uneaten portions of their food and hastened to retrieve a cup.

"Shall we proceed one at a time or all at once, my lady?" Tewichinel asked.

"All at once, of course. I must know who my allies will be so I can plan the battle accordingly." Satal drained her cup and watched as the shamans did the same.

The men looked at each other and then around the room, but nothing happened. "Utzil, don't any of you know anything?" Satal said. "Sit down, and in your mind, call to the gods of the Underworld. One of them will eventually hear you and manifest in the room. But it will take time and concentration." She shook her head. "And you call yourselves shamans!"

Within the hour, Satal felt the first stirrings of something arriving from the Underworld and was not surprised when Camazotz made his appearance in the room.

"Lady Satal, you summoned me?" the giant bat asked. He floated several feet off the floor, filling the large room quickly with the fetid smell that always wafted around his body.

"Yes, yes, we need you and your friends to join us, so we can prepare for the battle, side by side. Who else is coming, do you know?"

Camazotz laughed. "You speak of this as if it were a party we'll be attending!" He waved his wings and drifted up toward the ceiling. "Ah-Cun-Can, I believe, which is why I'll remain up here. We still don't like each other, even after all these millennia."

Satal laughed. "The serpent god, wonderful, we'll pair him with Chiwekox."

As she spoke, the god of snakes materialized. He was covered with a hundred serpents in a vast array of colors that writhed and twisted around the god's wasted shoulders and torso. One small green snake flicked its tongue at Satal, and she grinned.

A loud crack filled the room as Koyopa's ally, Ah-Pekku, the god of thunder appeared. Roiling black clouds streaked with a sickly tinge of green hovered just above his head, and the scent of ozone rapidly replaced the foul smell emanating from Camazotz's body. Next to arrive was Hun-Batz, the howler monkey god, who went to stand next to K'oy, who had shape-shifted into a spider monkey just the day before.

"Wonderful to see we can call on the monkeys to join us," Satal said. She grinned as Yum Cimil appeared, but the skeletal figure with the bulging eyes barely looked at her as he went to stand next to Sina'j.

"Still upset with me for not bringing your statue when I fled Mayapán, I see," Satal said as she shook her head. "Well, death in the guise of scorpions is a wonderful addition to the army, and you'll soon have plenty of bodies to satisfy you."

Buluc-Chabtan, Tlacolotl, and Poxlom were the last gods to appear. Tewichinel bowed to Poxlom, god of diseases, as he came to stand next to the shaman. Open sores and pustules covered the god's entire body, and when he opened his toothless mouth, he emitted a foul odor that forced Tewichinel to pinch his nose closed. Ixtzol, who could shape-shift into a centipede, fell to his knees in supplication to Tlacolotl, who was enveloped in a thick cloud of evil and darkness. He placed it like a cloak on Ixtzol's shoulders, and the man almost vanished from sight.

Ch'o grinned at Buluc-Chabtan. "We'll do well together, my lord," he said as he bowed to the god who enjoyed killing people and roasting them on skewers. Buluc-Chabtan carried a bundle of long, barbed spears in one hand and had an immense obsidian blade hanging from the leather belt around his waist.

Satal looked around the room. She was pleased so many different gods had appeared. *Under the cover of darkness provided by Tlacolotl, and thunder and lightning given by Ah-Pekku and Koyopa, we can advance on Mayapán with Kämisanel's army of trained militia, as well as wasps, rats, snakes, scorpions, centipedes, and monkeys, followed by a good dose of disease. If that doesn't kill everyone in the city, then my name isn't Satal.* Satal grinned as the plan continued to unfold in her mind. *It's a pity Chac didn't show up as well, but he can be so fickle, providing beneficial rain or torrential downpours.* She shrugged. *Ah well, perhaps he'll be persuaded to make an appearance on the night of the attack.*

Yum Cimil cleared his throat, bringing Satal's attention back to those in front of her. "When is this battle to take place? If it's many moons from now, then I could use some sustenance long before then." He looked at the other gods, who nodded their heads in agreement with him. "We need some sacrifices if we're to continue to help you."

Satal sighed. "All right, all right. Tewichinel, have the guards round up any infants born in the last moon cycle and have them beheaded. Drain their blood and leave it as an offering in the fourteen stone *chac mools* found throughout the city, then skewer the heads on stakes at the tzompantli. Any mother or father who protests can be beheaded as well."

Tewichinel nodded and left the room to carry out Satal's orders.

"Satisfied?" she asked Yum Cimil.

"Yes, Lady Satal, maltiox," the death god replied. His bare bones clacked together as he settled into his seat.

"Now that that's settled, let's prepare our plan." She nodded to Yuxba'. "Bring paper and ink so you can write all this down." The shaman hurried out of the room and returned quickly with the implements.

It was quite late at night before Satal was satisfied with the details of the attack, but as she eased into her hammock that night, she knew it was a good plan.

The next day, after she had instructed the group of shamans to continue with their practices, she pulled Tewichinel aside so she could make a visit to the warriors' training ground to check on Kämisanel's progress with the troops.

The head of the regiment bowed deeply when Satal arrived on the parade grounds. She looked over the open plain at the hundreds of men moving in block formation. "They've improved quite considerably since the last time I was here," Satal said. She smiled as the men moved in unison forward and back across the open plaza, much like a spider weaving its web.

"I've been making them train day and night, in all kinds of weather, as you requested, my lady," Kämisanel said. "Those who complain of the blazing sun or the ankle-deep mud after a period of rain are quickly sacrificed so they can't taint the others who have sworn their allegiance to you."

"How are the tanners doing on making the armor we'll need?"

"Hunters have brought in every deer and peccary for many, many days' travel around the city, my lady, and the tanners are working night and day to process the thousands of hides. The extra meat has flooded the market, and even the poorest of the citizens are eating like the elite, with plenty for everyone these days." He pointed to flocks of crested caracaras high overhead. "Even the birds are gorging on the guts and innards."

"And the weapon makers, how is their progress?"

"Obsidian spears and knives are being chiseled by the hundreds, the bow makers are carving wood until their hands bleed, and the fletchers are making as many arrows as possible. But they're quickly running out of feathers to fletch them."

"Send a portion of your men north to the coast and another group south to the jungle and tell them to shoot down and trap any birds they see. Meanwhile, tell the elite in the city that they must give up their feather headdresses and hats for use by the military."

"As you wish, Lady Satal." Kämisanel snapped his fingers, and one of his trusted guards ran over. He left quickly after receiving Kämisanel's orders. "Those not occupied with producing gear or weapons have been put in the fields to tend the corn, manioc root, beans, and other provisions we'll need on the march to Mayapán." He paused and Satal motioned for him to continue.

"Go on, what else is there?" The late afternoon sun beat down on Satal's head, and she wanted nothing more than to return home and have Tewichinel massage her sore feet.

"Some of the members of the city council raised complaints about the amount of cacao beans being spent on all the preparations. They claimed the city coffers were almost empty. But I quickly silenced them by confiscating everything in their possession, which has been more than enough to continue with all the tasks at hand."

"Excellent, excellent work, Kämisanel. You're to be commended for all of this, and when Mayapán falls, you'll be properly rewarded for your efforts." She nodded to Tewichinel that she was ready to return to her home.

"Always a pleasure to serve you, Lady Satal," Kämisanel said as he bowed low to the ground.

If Satal had been a younger, more agile woman, she might have skipped or danced on the way back to the palace she shared with the shamans. But she satisfied her desire to celebrate by nodding to the crowds of people who lined the sacbé and watched her pass. Their adoration filled her heart with a richness she hadn't felt in years. It felt so good to be feared and respected.

But once one hundred infants, twenty-seven mothers, and fifteen fathers had been sacrificed to appease the gods, the general populace of Chichén Itzá had more fear than respect for Satal. They joined the thousands in the outlying villages who resented her ability to take whatever and whomever she wanted at a moment's notice. But Satal was used to having enemies and didn't care as long as people did as she demanded.

Then, a few days later, while Satal was walking through the crowded marketplace in search of herbs for a new tincture she wanted to make, a grieving father forced his way through her entourage of shamans and almost stabbed her with his knife. At that moment, Satal felt a tiny bit nervous. She realized she was just one against thousands who might wish her harm. She shrugged off her worries, though, as Tewichinel and the other shamans hustled her out of the area and back to the safety of her palace. Satal ordered Kämisanel and his troops to remove the people living in the houses near her and had a perimeter of sentries posted all around the area. Not only did it provide a peaceful place for her to walk, it gave the shamans more privacy and space to practice their shape-shifting. And Satal was able to have her house to herself again, although Tewichinel insisted on living with her instead of with the other shamans.

The sentries acted as a barrier to anyone wishing to see Satal, allowing her to regulate the amount of time she had to spend interacting with the city council and members of the elite families in the city. And the normal population couldn't reach her at all.

AJKUN

Ajkun woke up to the sounds of growling. In the early morning light, she hurried outside with her walking staff, shuffled down the path, and into the thicket of avocado and mango trees near her hut. She could barely see the wooden cage that Tzukunel had baited with fresh meat, but there was definitely a jaguar trapped inside. It had taken over a week for Tzukunel to entice the cat to enter the enclosure. He had set the cage in numerous places near the village, but finally had settled on this spot behind Ajkun's hut since that's where there were the most tracks.

Ajkun breathed a sigh of relief. *At least it will be safe to walk the paths at night,* she thought as she returned to her house. She had not enjoyed being out after dark, coming home to her own house after hours spent with Chiman, and she'd also worried about Lintat, who liked to visit the nursery after his chores were done for the day. She dressed quickly and headed to Chiman's house. The sooner the cat was relocated, the better. She hated to see any animal penned up when it was used to total freedom.

Chiman was making a mug of hot cacao when Ajkun arrived. "What brings you here so early?" he asked as he poured a second cup full and handed it to Ajkun.

"There's a jaguar in the cage, a young female, I think," she said as she sat down on the nearest stool. She blew on the mug and sipped the frothy, bitter liquid. "And here I thought you didn't know how to cook."

Chiman laughed. "I've had to learn a thing or two over the past several moons." He put a pan on to heat, went to the hut, and returned with several turkey eggs. "Breakfast?" he asked as he cracked the eggs into the pan.

Ajkun smiled and nodded. "Where will you take the cat?"

"Downstream, where it will hopefully find a new place to live. Tzukunel and I will be gone a few days," he said as he slid the cooked eggs on to a plate. "Will you be all right while I'm away?"

Ajkun laughed. "Of course. We've only been together a short while. Before that, I was alone all the time . . . well, I did have Na'om to keep me company." At the thought of her granddaughter, Ajkun fell silent. It had been so many moons since she'd disappeared into the cenote that Ajkun had almost given up hope of ever seeing her again. Chiman didn't speak either, both lost in their own thoughts.

"You should be hearing from Tz' soon," Ajkun finally said.

"Once again, you've read my mind," Chiman replied as he leaned in and gave Ajkun a quick kiss. He stacked the plates and pan together and placed them inside the house to wash later. He held out his hand to Ajkun. "Let's go see this cat of yours."

"Mine? Oh no, I wish nothing to do with it. It was troublesome enough to have Ek' Balam around, but I knew he'd been tamed since he was a kitten. This one's a wild one, through and through."

The couple could hear the jaguar long before they reached Ajkun's house, and many of the villagers were standing several paces from the cage, staring at the cat, when they approached. The jaguar lay low in the wooden enclosure, her tail swishing from side to side, growling and hissing at the bystanders. Chiman pushed through the group, motioning for them to move back even farther. "I wouldn't want any of you to get hurt if she should somehow manage to escape."

Ajkun could see the jaguar through a gap in the crowd and felt sorry for the beautiful animal since it had no room to move around in the cage. She stepped forward, entranced by the black markings on the tawny yellow fur. "Ek' Balam's spots were never so visible," she murmured as she came even closer.

The movement caught the feline's eye, and she turned her head, staring directly at Ajkun. The jaguar stopped hissing and spitting, sank onto its stomach, and lay quietly, just watching her.

Chiman turned, saw Ajkun, and shook his head. "I see where Na'om got her abilities," he said as he touched Ajkun on the arm.

"She needs food and water," Ajkun said, moving back in the direction of her house. She returned a few minutes later with a large pottery dish, a water gourd, and a cotton bag. She put the platter on the ground and filled it with water, then used her walking stick to push the dish toward the cage. The jaguar could just lick the edge of the bowl with her tongue, slurping up droplets of water. Ajkun untied the cloth bag and extracted a dried fish, which she tossed into the cage. The cat pounced on the herring and ate it in one bite. Ajkun pitched in four more fish, which the cat quickly ate before returning to the bowl of water. Satisfied, the jaguar lay down, put her head on her front paws, and closed her eyes.

"All right, everyone, the show is over," Chiman said. The villagers grumbled, but left the area to start their fires and do their morning's work.

Tzukunel arrived as the others were leaving, followed by Lintat, who skipped beside Noy. Mam leaned heavily on Noy's right arm, shuffling through the brush as Noy helped him navigate the rocky ground.

But when Lintat saw the jaguar, he ran ahead of the others, headed toward the cage. He stopped only when Chiman grabbed him by the arm. "No, Lintat, you mustn't get too close." He pushed the boy behind him, and Ajkun held out her arms to him as he began to cry.

"Come, now, a big boy like you mustn't be upset," she said as she picked Lintat up and balanced him on her hip. "Chiman doesn't want you to get hurt, that's all." She stepped toward the jaguar. "You can see the big cat from right here, but no closer," she said as she let Lintat slip to the ground. She handed Lintat a salted herring, which he threw toward the cage, but the fish bounced off the bars and landed on the ground a few feet away. Lintat started to run for the herring, but Ajkun grabbed him. "No, Lintat, let me get it." She forced the boy to stand still, then turned, took several steps, picked up the fish, and gently tossed it to the jaguar. The cat raised her head and caught the herring as it sailed through the bars of her cage.

"You may have to come with us when we take her down river," Chiman remarked to Ajkun as the cat put her head back down. The jaguar closed her eyes, intent on ignoring everyone around her.

"Oh no, that's a job I'll leave for you men. I'm sure she'll be fine; just don't leave her confined for too long."

Tzukunel nodded. "I'll tell Xoral, gather my things, and ready the canoe. We can leave before the sun is high overhead."

Ajkun watched the young man run back the way he had come. She handed the bag of dried herring to Chiman. "You'll need these." She waited in the shade with Lintat, Noy, and Mam while Chiman went to get his own things for the trip.

Tzukunel returned quickly with Ajchak and K'ale'n. With Chiman helping, the four men carried the caged jaguar down to the river. She hissed a few times, but as long as Ajkun stayed within sight, the cat was docile. The bow of the large dugout canoe sank deep into the water when they placed the cage in it, and the jaguar arched her back and swished her tail, thumping it on the sturdy wooden bars.

"She doesn't want to go for a boat ride," Lintat said as he crouched on the riverbank. "Can't you just take her across the river and let her go over there?"

"She'd just swim back," Chiman replied as he patted the boy on the head. The cat snarled and hissed as the canoe rocked in the water. "I'm not sure we'll get very far with her acting this way, though."

"Lintat's right; you should let her loose on the other side. Maybe all she needs is a push in a different direction to find a new place to call home," Ajkun said.

Tzukunel shrugged. "I'm willing to give it a try if you are." Chiman nodded. Both men left their gear on the sand, stepped into the canoe behind the cage, and quickly began pushing the boat off the beach. As the water lifted the canoe, it tipped to one side, and the jaguar let out a growl and swiped at the bars with her large front paw.

"Quickly now or she'll swamp us," Chiman said as he paddled with all his strength.

Once they reached the opposite shore and rammed the bow of the canoe into the soft sand and mud, Chiman motioned for Tzukunel to hop into the water behind the canoe. "Keep your paddle at the ready, in case she turns and attacks," he instructed the younger man as he popped open the door to the enclosure.

As soon as she sensed freedom, the cat bolted out of the cage, took a flying leap over the gunwales, landed in the shallows, and bolted into the underbrush. Tzukunel jumped back into the dugout and back paddled with Chiman until they were several paces from shore.

"Well, that was easy enough," Chiman said as he stepped back on the bank by Ajkun and Lintat. "Let's hope she stays over there."

Later that afternoon, Ajkun and Chiman were enjoying cool mugs of mango juice with Noy and Mam in Ajkun's courtyard when Lintat came running from the direction of the river.

"Noy, Ati't," he cried. He stopped to catch his breath.

"Utzil, child, whatever is the matter?" Ajkun said as she refilled her mug and handed it to Lintat. The boy took a sip, swallowed, and held up his hand. "Did you see the jaguar again?"

Lintat shook his head. "No, two men, in a canoe, paddling upstream, toward the beach.

Chiman and Ajkun exchanged glances. "Itzamná, what can they want?"

Chiman gave his empty cup to Ajkun. "Perhaps they carry some word from Tz'. In the meantime, we must offer them a place to rest and some food."

Noy nodded. "We'll take care of it. Go now, and find out what they want."

Chiman returned to Ajkun's house a short time later, alone. He carried a small scroll in his hand. "Where are the men?" Ajkun asked. She continued smearing cornmeal onto banana leaves to make into tamales.

"Gone already. They said they'd rather camp back downstream. I'm glad; they weren't very friendly." He held up the piece of paper. "It's a message from Tz'. He says he's doing well." Chiman paused.

Ajkun stopped folding the edges of the banana leaf over a packet of cornmeal and looked at Chiman. He was frowning. "What's wrong? What else does he write?"

"He's moving into Satal's old house. Before he left, I told him not to go near that place." Chiman crushed the scroll in his hand and almost threw it into the fire, but Ajkun stopped him.

"Here, let me see," she said as she pried his fingers open. She left traces of sticky cornmeal on his hand, but Chiman didn't seem to notice. He started to pace in the small courtyard while Ajkun unrolled the paper and read the glyphs quickly. She shook her head, wiped her hands on a towel, and sat down. "Well, there's probably no harm in it. It's just an empty house now. Perhaps Yakal suggested he live there."

Chiman stopped walking and kicked at a small pebble with his sandaled foot. The rock whizzed into the underbrush on the other side of the path and clattered against a tree trunk. "I don't know; I have a bad feeling about it. I should go to the city and talk to Tz'." Frustration was written all over his face.

"You'll do no such thing; the boy needs to grow and learn a bit on his own." Ajkun indicated the empty stool next to her. "Come sit down; fretting won't make it any better." She patted Chiman on the knee. "I know you're worried, but he'll be fine." She pointed at the stack of tamales she had made to feed the strangers who had brought the note. "I hope you're hungry!"

Chiman gave Ajkun a half-smile. "I'm sure you're right about Tz'. I haven't forgotten that I was young and impulsive at that age, too." He brushed the dried cornmeal from the back of his hand and stood up. "I'll go invite Setesik, Pempen, and Sijuan to join us for supper."

The days continued to spiral by in a flurry of tasks for Ajkun. She visited the nursery every morning to play with the infants and often stayed to share the midday meal with the three families. Holding the infants brought her such joy, helping her forget the loss of Na'om, as if she'd rubbed a soothing salve on that bubble of pain. Breathing in the smell of milky babies, having them suck on her fingers or knuckles while they waited for their mothers to feed them, even wiping away their spit-up made Ajkun smile, more than she had in years. A few hours each day were spent with Sijuan, teaching the young girl the many uses of the herbs and plants that grew in the area. And during the remaining hours of the late afternoon, she visited Noy. Mam frequently joined the women when he tired of working. After a cup of tea, he'd slip into the hammock hanging between two mango trees and drift off to sleep while the women chatted and worked on their weaving or embroidery. And Ajkun always spent her evenings with Chiman, which brought her a different type of happiness. Sometimes they stayed in their private hidden hut in the jungle, but most often, they curled up together on the narrow mattress in her home. A few times, Chiman had suggested they spend the night at his house, but Ajkun still felt Chachal's presence lingering in the premises and always said no.

Many times, the couple joined Noy, Mam, and Lintat for an evening meal, or they visited Setesik, Pempen, and Sijuan to share food and stories until long after dark. When the cries of any of the newborns wafted through the trees, the couples would laugh and remark on the differences between their lives now and back when their own children had been young.

Chiman performed the naming ceremony for the new babies on a bright sunny day when the sky overhead was the rich blue color of cotinga feathers. The whole village came to watch as he sprinkled river water on each child's head and smeared a dot of cinnabar paste on each forehead. Ajchak and Tzalon named their little girl Tuney; Xoral and Tzukunel chose Kab for their son's name; and Witzik' and K'ale'n named the twins Ali and Ala. Shortly after the naming day, the binding boards were removed, making it much easier for the mothers to nurse the children.

Ajkun tried to explain to Noy the bliss she felt when she was with the infants, but the older woman only nodded and smiled. "You don't have to tell me; I still remember when Lintat was an infant. I'd spend most of my day with him and only gave him to his mother so she could feed him." She sighed. "I'd come with you to see the children more often, but Mam needs me more each day. Do you know we've been together for over five hundred moons? I don't know what I'll do when the ancestors call him home."

Ajkun patted Noy's hand. "Let me know if I can help in any way."

Several nights later, as Ajkun was drifting off to sleep beside Chiman, she heard rustling in the bushes outside the hut. She sat up, trying to figure out what might be moving around in the dark. She nudged Chiman, but he didn't wake. There were more sounds of movement and then they abruptly stopped. *Whatever's out there is still there*, Ajkun thought as she lay back down. She had trouble sleeping the rest of the night, knowing something was resting on the other side of the wall.

At first light, she slipped out of bed, picked up her heavy walking stick, and went to investigate. The female jaguar lay curled up on the ground, her nose tucked between her front paws. "Itzamná, what are you doing here?"

The cat lifted her head and stared at Ajkun with her amber-colored eyes.

"Who are you talking to?" Chiman asked as he came around the corner of the hut. "Oh ho, your friend is back!" he said as he backed up several feet. "I guess she didn't like it on the other side of the river. . . . We can take her farther downstream, but if that doesn't work, we may need to kill her."

Ajkun turned around and glared at Chiman. "You'll do no such thing! Don't you see, she's a good omen. This jaguar knows Ek' Balam is still alive and coming home someday, which means Na'om is still alive as well." She pushed past Chiman, headed toward the hut.

"Where are you going?" Chiman said. He tried to grab Ajkun's arm, but she moved too quickly.

"To get her some food and water, of course. If she's decided to stay with me, the least I can do is feed her."

"Utzil, first Na'om and now you . . . ." Chiman shook his head. Keeping his eyes focused on the feline, Chiman backed away. "I must visit the temple and ask for guidance."

"Do what you must; I intend to keep her," Ajkun said. She felt a new blossom of hope sprout in her heart as she thought of her beloved Na'om. *Surely, this jaguar is a sign that you're still alive. Stay strong, wherever you are, so that you may return to us someday.*

Tz'

The sky was clear and the sun already hot when Tz' walked rapidly to Satal's palace. *My palace*, he thought, and smiled. *Everything is falling into place so easily. Later today, Najtir will arrive, and my real training can begin. Not only will I be able to aid Na'om, but I'll have the ability to overthrow Satal, too.*

Once he was past the guard on duty, Tz' paused to look around at his new home. The workers were gone after repairing the damage to the roof, and the place exuded a sense of peace and quiet. Bougainvillea vines filled with magenta-colored blossoms climbed the limestone block walls that formed the inner courtyard. Three steps led up from the inner square to a wide covered patio and the large wooden and intricately carved front door. Tz' paused at the bottom of the steps, looking to the left of the door. During the night, some animal had obviously rooted through the outdoor kitchen area, tipping over many of the baskets and containers, and piles of scat lay here and there among the jumble. *One more thing for me to clean,* Tz' thought and sighed. Yakal had told him that no one had dared entered the house to clean it, meaning it was bound to be dusty after so many moons lying vacant.

But Tz' was unprepared for the stench that assaulted him when he stepped inside. *Rotten, like an animal has died in a corner of the room.*

Tz' pinched his nose with his thumb and forefinger and looked around. He spotted a black patch high up on the opposite wall that blotted out part of the mural underneath and trotted over to look at it. *Camazotz was here! These marks are just like those he left on the wall of Na'om's hut the night I battled with him.*

Tz' stepped to the open door and drew in a deep breath of fresher air. *It's just more proof that I'm on the right track.* The thought that Satal had communicated with the horrid creature in this house both repelled and excited him.

Tz' stopped just short of the entranceway to survey the house. The main room was almost bare of furniture; only a few leather and bamboo chairs and a worn, leather-topped table sat in the far corner. *It's no wonder Satal had so many cacao beans. She certainly didn't spend much on creating a comfortable home.* He glanced upward and noticed where a patch of plaster was missing. Brownish water stains spread like vines across the ceiling from the spot, and he made a mental note to find someone to replaster and paint the area. *I hope the workers managed to fix the leak from the outside.*

He headed down the long hallway and stopped in the first doorway. Yakal had told him it had been his mother's room when she had lived in Mayapán, long before he was born. Faded and yellowed white huipils and skirts covered in elaborate embroidery hung from pegs driven into the walls. Bits of plaster crunched under his leather sandals, and Tz' looked up to see where another large piece of the ceiling had fallen to the floor. Not only were his mother's old clothes still hanging on the walls, there were also several shelves on one wall filled with dusty odds and ends. He slowly touched the items that had been left undisturbed for so many years, covering his fingertips with grit. He blew on one shelf, exposing a candle stub stuck in a pottery saucer, several clay figurines that were chipped in spots, and a large scallop shell, its inside a smooth layer of iridescent mother of pearl. Various rocks and smaller shells, short lengths of ribbons tangled together, balls of embroidery thread in a rich assortment of colors, and several stingray spines carved into needles filled another. He laughed silently. *Chuch saved every little thing, just like I do,* he mused. Seeing these objects made him wonder what his mother had been like as a girl and as a young woman in love. *She certainly wasn't the unhappy person who lived with Tat. But if she was sent away from the man she truly loved, then it's no wonder she was so bitter and resentful of Chiman.* He felt a strange connection to his mother at that moment, knowing what it was like to be separated from the one person who made his heart soar.

He moved across the room and brushed his fingertips along the top of a wooden trunk, leaving a streak in the dust. When he lifted the lid, he saw a few carefully folded undergarments and a pair of worn leather sandals, which he placed on the floor. Underneath there were several corn husk dolls on top of a thick, woolen, deep-gray blanket. The dried corn-leaf doll limbs cracked and flaked as he lifted the blanket and discovered a stack of fig bark ledgers on the bottom of the trunk.

Tz' picked up the top book and unfolded the accordion-style pages. Filled with glyphs, it contained a list of everything his mother had purchased at the market one day. The next page and the next had the same type of information, accounts of purchases made and cacao beans spent. Tz' quickly opened the rest of the books, but they were all the same. He sat on the floor, remembering how his mother had kept careful track of the number of baskets of corn, beans, squash, and manioc root harvested each year from the village gardens, and a host of other details of daily life. He'd always thought she'd written it all down because Chiman had asked her to, but from the looks of these ledgers, his mother had always kept track of the minute details of her life. *What about the bigger things, Chuch? What about this man, Alaxel, who Yakal claims is my real father?* He was irritated that there was no mention of his mother's secret lover in any of her books. As he placed the items one by one back in the trunk, a small wedge of paper slipped out from between the fine cotton undergarments and fluttered to the floor. Tiny glyphs covered the sheet on both sides, and Tz' realized it had to have been written by someone other than his mother because the handwriting was unfamiliar.

He read:

My dearest one,
I lie awake each night thinking only of you, of your sweet smile, and the way dimples form in the corners of your cheeks when I make you laugh. Your voice is a soothing balm to my troubled soul, and I look forward to our meeting tonight. I thank you for granting me my wish before we share the news of our union with our families. My whole body aches for you, for you are the

*one I wish to share my life with until the ancestors call us both
home. Until I see you later, sweetest one, know that my head
and heart are filled only with thoughts of you. A.*

He read the letter three times before he stuffed it into his leather pouch
around his waist. Here at last was proof that his mother had been in love
with someone before Chiman, but the note only added to Tz's curiosity.
Then, it suddenly felt odd, even wrong, to look at these personal items
from his mother's childhood, and Tz' quickly dropped the trunk lid,
sending a cloud of dust into the air. The girl who had lived in this room
was a stranger to him, someone who had betrayed his father. *Better to
remember Chuch the way I knew her and not as this person.*

He stood up and dusted himself off. Looking around the room again,
he nodded. *There's no need to keep any of this any longer. This can be
Najtir's room.*

He continued down the hallway, his feet leaving small tracks in the
dust on the tile floor, and entered the larger bedroom. He was surprised
to see a large cage in one corner, its door ajar, and several ropes hanging
slack on the closest wall. Anger flushed through him as he realized Satal
must have kept Ek' Balam in the cage and probably had tied Na'om to
the wall. He ran his hand over the scratches in the wooden bars, trying
to guess what had transpired that last morning so many moons ago, but
everything he imagined just fueled his frustration and anger. He turned
abruptly and walked past the one hammock hanging from two hooks in
the wall, noticed the netting was old and slightly torn in places, and knew
he needed to replace it. Then he headed to a large wooden cupboard, its
door slightly ajar, against the far wall. The copper hinges creaked as he
swung the door wide, and he saw several old cloth bags, three candle
stubs, a pile of faded flower blossoms, and a dusty, black monkey skin full
of holes tossed over an object. Several carrion beetles fell out of the fur as
he pulled out a stained ceramic censer shaped like Yum Cimil. He almost
dropped the ugly skeleton statue with the bulging eyes in his haste to set
it back onto the shelf. He turned around and surveyed the room again.
*Hard to believe this is everything Satal owned. No wonder there are bags
and bags of cacao beans. But that's all right; I still like the place. There's
certainly plenty of space for two of us, and I'll be too busy with my studies
to need much else.*

He spread his arms wide, trying to gauge the size of the room, and realized with a start that he could put his father's whole house inside the space. A deep niche in the nearest wall caught his eye, and he walked over to it, wondering why there were no soot marks on the plaster from a candle. *What did Satal use this for?* he pondered as he ran his fingers over the smooth shelf. A long gray hair clung to his hand along with a dusty cobweb, and he shook them off onto the floor. Then he reached into his leather pouch and pulled out the small statuette of Na'om, which he'd been carrying ever since leaving Pa nimá. He set the figurine on the shelf and smiled. It fit perfectly, as if it had been made to go there.

Motes of dust drifted in a sunbeam coming in from the window high in the far wall, and Tz' realized with a start that the day was rapidly advancing and he had much to do. He spent the next few hours cleaning out the rooms of all the old, unwanted stuff, making a huge pile in the courtyard to have taken away later in the day. Hungry from all his hard work, he dashed to the market for a bite to eat. He didn't know when Najtir was arriving, and he didn't want to miss greeting the old shaman, but when he returned, the ancient man was already seated in one of the worn leather chairs in the main room.

He was leaning forward, his forehead pressed into his hands, which were cupped over the end of a long wooden cane, and he appeared to be sleeping.

Tz' approached quietly and sat down next to the man. He didn't know what to do. He kept glancing over, but the shaman didn't move. In fact, Tz' had a hard time distinguishing if he was even breathing. He fidgeted in his chair, moving closer to the edge of it and was just about to rise, when the old man spoke.

With his head still lowered, Najtir said, "You need to learn to relax. Otherwise, you'll never be able to concentrate on shape-shifting."

Tz' opened his mouth to say something, then shut it quickly. *He's right. I have no patience. But how can I? Na'om is lost in the Underworld, and Satal is building an army and could launch an attack at any moment. There's no time to sit and meditate with so much at stake.* He opened his mouth again, but Najtir placed his arthritic hand on Tz's knee and compelled him to stop.

"Take several deep breaths and loosen your grip on everything in this world," Najtir instructed. He lifted his head, looked at Tz', and waited for him to comply. "Now, close your eyes and imagine your spirit animal. Conjure it in your mind, every limb, every muscle, every tuft of fur. Feel yourself becoming that animal."

Tz' pushed back in his seat, closed his eyes, and envisioned the were-jaguar. At first, images of the creatures illustrated in his book flitted past in his mind, but as he forced himself to concentrate, the picture shifted, and from a distant spot high in the air, he could see himself as he had been months before in the temple when Chiman had helped him. His hands clenched the rounded arms of the chair as his body pushed and pulled against itself. But no matter how hard he focused, the imagery remained elusive. He could see the animal, but he couldn't become one. Frustrated, he opened his eyes and looked at Najtir.

The old man laughed. "You give up too easily, Tz'. These things take time, and you only worked at it for a few moments." He suddenly stood up, using his cane for support, and reached one hand into a pocket in his long black cloak. He pulled out a small drawstring bag, loosened the twine holding it shut, and extracted a small red and black bean. "Bring me a piece of charcoal from the fire pit, a pitcher of water, and two mugs," he instructed. "And a candle or two; it's getting dark."

Tz' ran to get the items and set them down on the table in front of them.

Najtir held up the bean. "Do you know what this is?"

Tz' shook his head no.

"A jequirity bean; it's the quickest method to shape-shift into a spirit animal. But one must be very careful to use it only when another person is around who can provide the antidote." He pointed to the charcoal and water. "Without the charcoal to flush the toxins from your system, a person can remain trapped in his animal form for too long, often with dire results." He drew back the long sleeve on his cloak and revealed his forearm.

Tz' gasped. Instead of skin, the shaman's arm was covered in thick, greenish-brown scales that shimmered in the flickering candlelight.

"I was fortunate that my hands and face returned to normal after ingesting the charcoal, but I can't say I had such good fortune with the rest of my body."

Tz' looked at the tiny bean again and shuddered. Although he longed to become a were-jaguar again and feel the incredible sense of power he had experienced before, he didn't want to be stuck in that shape forever.

"Which is why I'm here to force you to eat the charcoal," Najtir said. He smiled. "Your thoughts are written on the air between us. All I have to do is read them. Which means I must teach you to shield them; otherwise, Satal will know your intentions long before you act on them." He handed Tz' a mug of water. "Drink; your blood is too much like sludge right now."

When the shaman was satisfied that Tz' had ingested enough water, he scraped the edge of the jequirity bean with his thumbnail and held it out to Tz'. "Just touch the bean to the tip of your tongue and let the toxin flow through you."

With a shaky hand, Tz' pinched the jequirity bean between his thumb and forefinger and brought it to his mouth. He stuck out his tongue and licked the bean, then quickly dropped it on the table, as if it had bitten him. Instantly, his tongue went numb, and he felt a rush of nervous energy surge through his body. He leaned back in the chair, waiting for more to happen, then remembered how large his body had grown when it morphed, so he dropped to the floor to give himself room to shape-shift. His mouth prickled and burned, his teeth ached, and his throat grew so dry he could barely swallow. And then the sensations stopped. Tz' looked up at the shaman, wondering if he should say something, then thought better of it. *He knows what I'm thinking practically before I do,* he mused, *and will tell me I'm being impatient again.*

Several more minutes passed, and finally Tz' could wait no longer. "It didn't work," he complained as he sat back down in the vacant chair.

"So I see," Najtir replied. "It's most unusual; the jequirity is the strongest of all the shape-shifting toxins. It really makes no sense why it didn't work." He leaned forward to look more closely at Tz'. "Somehow, I think your grandmother has a hand in this." He looked around the room. "Her energy remains strong in this house; perhaps that's what's blocking your attempts. We'll conduct a thorough cleansing of the place and try again tomorrow." The old man put an arthritic hand to his mouth and yawned. "I must rest now."

Disappointment exuded from Tz' in waves, and Najtir held up his hand to shield himself. "Don't despair; you'll find your strength one way or another."

Tz' nodded and showed Najtir to his room.

The next morning, Tz' helped Najtir smudge the entire residence with copal smoke. They even opened the door to the washroom at the far end of the hallway, letting the smoke filter through a spider web stretched across the squat hole in the floor and the basket of dried corncobs in the corner of the small room.

Once Najtir was satisfied the energy in the house had been cleansed, they returned to the main room where Tz' again tried to shape-shift using the jequirity bean. But beyond the tingling sensation on his tongue and mouth, Tz' felt nothing out of the ordinary. He lashed out with his foot, knocking the chair in front of him over on its side. "Itzamná, what's wrong with me? Why doesn't this work?"

Najtir shook his head. His long white hair fell over his face, and he quickly brushed it aside. "I don't know. But you mustn't grow discouraged, Tz'. There are still plenty of things to learn that will be useful in your quest to help Na'om." He held out his hand. "Come, help an old man to his feet. Perhaps some food is in order, and I know just the place." The two headed toward the market.

Clutching Tz's forearm, the old man led him down numerous narrow lanes, past stalls filled with tanned deer hides, reed and cornhusk baskets, pottery urns and bowls, wooden furniture, and bins of salt, and into the heart of the market where he finally stopped at a small booth. Only a few stools were set out in front of the long wooden counter, and no one appeared to be around. But they could hear noises coming from the behind the curtain that divided the booth into halves.

"T'ot, are you here? It's me, dear, Najtir. I hope you still have some of your delicious salted crab cakes." The shaman motioned for Tz' to sit down at the counter as he went behind it. "She's an old, old friend, but almost deaf, poor woman. I'll just peek behind the curtain and see if she's here."

Tz' nodded. He was too preoccupied with wondering why he couldn't shape-shift to worry about food, although the tantalizing smells of roasted turkey and haunches of venison wafting toward him from many of the other food stalls made his stomach cramp. *Maybe Najtir's magic isn't as effective as I thought. He claims to have continued his studies after he went underground, but maybe Satal is the only one with the necessary skills to shape-shift.* For a distraction, he looked at the canvas banner stretched above the countertop and studied the pictures of crabs, crayfish, eels, sharks, and other sea creatures he couldn't identify while he waited for Najtir to return. Just as he was beginning to wonder if he needed to go in search of the shaman, the man reappeared, followed by a woman as ancient as Najtir. Her wispy white hair was pulled back in a tight bun on the back of her head, exposing her high forehead. Deep wrinkles near her eyes and mouth told of a lifetime of laughter, and when she grinned, the few white bottom teeth she still had stood out in sharp contrast to her heavily tanned skin. She carried a large round platter piled high with crab cakes in one hand and a bowl of octopus ceviche in the other.

With some effort, Najtir hoisted himself onto the stool next to Tz' and patted him on the arm. "You're in for a treat."

T'ot placed the food in front of the pair, then reached under the counter and pulled out two black and white striped plates, which she gave to Najtir and Tz'. She hobbled across the empty booth and reappeared with a bowl of thin, toasted corn wafers and several small bowls of dark red and green sauces on a tray, which she set on the counter, before motioning for the men to begin.

Najtir plopped a crab cake on Tz's plate and took two for himself. He smeared some green sauce on top of them and bit into the first one. "Ah, delicious," he said, "just as I remember them." He nodded at Tz'. "Well, go on, try it."

Tz' picked up the crab cake without adding any sauce and took a big bite. Salt, crab, corn, and spices he couldn't identify filled his mouth, and he ate the whole thing in three large bites.

"Utzil, you were hungry!" Najtir said as he placed four more crab cakes on his plate. He waved to T'ot to come over. "YOU'VE GOT ANOTHER CUSTOMER, DEAR," he shouted as he pointed to Tz', who had almost finished the entire stack on his plate. "WHEN WILL YOU HAVE SOME MORE?"

The old woman smiled and held up one finger.

"TOMORROW?" Najtir shouted.

The old woman nodded and grinned before heading back behind the curtain.

"Excellent; we can return tomorrow for lunch," Najtir said as he tossed a few cacao beans on the counter. "Shall we resume your training?"

Tz' nodded. Now that his hunger had been sated, he was eager to attempt shape-shifting again, but Najtir forced him to practice blocking his thoughts for the rest of the afternoon. It was tiring work and a skill Tz' had terrible trouble grasping.

That night he lay awake long after Najtir's snoring echoed through the hallway, wondering why all his efforts were being thwarted. *I've never had this much trouble with any of the shamanic rituals Tat axel has asked me to perform. We've cleansed the house of any negative energy, and Najtir trained Satal, so he must be a powerful shaman in his own right. I just don't understand.*

Every day for almost two weeks, Tz' concentrated on shape-shifting in the mornings, only to find his efforts obstructed by some unseen force. And with each passing day, his impatience grew. Without the power to shift into a were-jaguar, he had no way to offer Na'om support or to crush Satal. He avoided seeing Box and Nil and abstained from any drinking in case the alcohol was blocking his ability, but it didn't help. He thought of talking to Yakal about his dilemma, but quickly realized his uncle knew far less about shape-shifting than he did since he had never trained to be a shaman. *Satal is the only person I know of other than Najtir who's explored the dark magic of the Underworld.* Tz' wondered what his grandmother would think of his weakness and inability to transform. *But some of her blood still runs in my veins,* so *perhaps she'd help me, if I asked.* Shocked by his own thought, Tz' buried it deeply in the back of his mind, praying to Itzamná that Najtir wouldn't find it the next time they worked together.

The following afternoon, Tz' threw the latest jequirity bean against the nearest wall. *Na'om could die before I ever figure this out. And Satal might attack the city any day now. How can I stand up to her and her magic if I can't do the simplest little things?*

"Like block your thoughts?" Najtir chided. He shuffled toward the front door. "Come; let's get a bite to eat."

Tz' groaned. Each day, they returned to T'ot's booth to eat salted crab cakes. Najtir relished them, savoring each bite as if he was eating them for the very first time, but by now just the thought of all the salt and crab mixed together made Tz' ill. But he didn't wish to offend his instructor, so he followed him to the marketplace once again. However, as soon as

Tz' put the first piece in his mouth, his throat constricted, and he spit the food back on the plate. "I'm sorry; I guess I'm not hungry," he said as he pushed the crab cakes away. The salt, crab, and corn lingered in his mouth, burning his tongue and the insides of his cheeks, and Tz' hurried to drain the last bit of water from the mug in front of him.

He waited patiently while Najtir ate his fill of the salty food, then helped the old shaman back to the house. The sun was still high in the sky, casting only a few shadows on the tiles in the inner courtyard.

"I think I'll sit here for a bit and rest," Najtir said, pointing to a corner. He leaned his back against the limestone wall and tilted his face to the sun, watching the sky. "Just as you said, as blue as a crowned motmot's feathers. I don't think I'll ever see anything quite so beautiful."

Tz' looked up, but the splendor of the brilliant blue sky was lost on him. His throat and mouth were still raw from the taste of the salty crabmeat, making his stomach roil in protest. Exasperation and weariness battled in him. "I think I might be getting sick. I'm going to lie down for a little bit." He walked to his hammock, where he fell into a deep, dreamless sleep.

A thin shaft of moonlight illuminated the room when Tz' woke up. Disoriented at first, he quickly realized how many hours had passed. *Utzil, what will Najtir think of me?* He ran with bare feet down the long hallway and into the main room where he looked around for the shaman, but there was no sign of him. He backtracked and poked his head in his mother's childhood room, but the old man wasn't there, either. *Maybe he's in the kitchen.* He tugged on the heavy wooden door, but with one quick glance, he could see the area was empty. Then he focused on the corner of the courtyard where Najtir had been sitting hours earlier. A dark shape still filled the space, and Tz' felt his stomach lurch in dismay.

He ran to Najtir and almost touched him, then quickly withdrew his hand. Too many times over the past couple of weeks he had started to engage the old shaman, only to be told to be silent and have more patience or that he was meditating and not dead as Tz' had presumed. *He's meditating, that's all,* Tz' thought. But the longer he looked at the dark shape in the shadows, the more convinced he became that the shaman was dead. And yet, he couldn't bring himself to touch him or even to lean in close and feel for the slightest puff of breath to be absolutely sure.

He's dead; I know it. There's no other reason for him still to be seated here. How will I explain this to anyone? And what do I do with the body? When the council finds out that he's died, they'll ask why he was here and what I've been trying to learn. Then they'll accuse me of witchcraft and sentence me to be sacrificed.

Panic set in, and Tz' ran back into the house. He hurried down the empty corridor to the main bedroom, grabbed his few clothes, and shoved them into his pack basket. He added his thick blanket from the hammock, quickly scanned the room in the dark for anything else of value, and satisfied that he had everything he needed, he ran back outside. Swinging his basket onto his shoulders, he crept past Najtir, who remained silent in the corner. "Sorry, old man, but I can't afford to get caught. Now there's only one place I can go and one person who can teach me what I need to know in order to save Na'om," he whispered. *And hopefully, I can block my deeper thoughts from her.* Tz' slipped into the empty street and headed directly to one of the smaller gates. He didn't dare risk going to Yakal to tell him he was leaving or that there was a body in Satal's old house. *Better to let him find out like everyone else and then the city council can't implicate him in any way.* He strode past the sleeping guard, slipped into the shadows outside the city, and started the long march to Chichén Itzá and his grandmother, Satal. It was only as the sky began to lighten on the horizon and he was forced to hide for the day in a thicket of small copal trees far away from the sacbé that Tz' realized he'd left his statuette of Na'om tucked into the niche in the main bedroom.

SATAL

Tewichinel and Satal were conversing at the large wooden table in the main room of the house, going over the final details of the battle as they looked at rough sketches of Mayapán, when there was a knock on the door. She motioned to Tewichinel and sat watching from the security of her chair as he opened it.

Two of the many sentries who guarded the house stood on the tiled patio. Between them was a young, muscular man. "Yes, what is it?" Tewichinel asked. He stared at the youth in front of him, who was dressed like the thousands who worked for a living in a simple cotton shirt, loincloth, and scuffed leather sandals.

"This boy claims he's related to Lady Satal," one of the guards said. "He insisted he be brought to her house. We told him she wasn't to be disturbed, but he said she would see him once she knew his name."

Intrigued by the conversation, Satal walked over and joined the group. Both guards bowed deeply, but the youth did not. "Well, what is it?" Satal demanded.

At that point, the young man did bow and then stood upright. Satal noticed he didn't show any signs of fear. "I'm Tz'ajonel, Lady Satal. I'm your grandson, born to your daughter, Chachal."

There was a long pause as Satal stared at the boy. "How do I know you are who you say you are?"

Tz' motioned to the guards. "If these men were allowed to return to their duties, I'd be more than happy to answer any questions about my identity."

Satal nodded and waved to the sentries. "Well, you heard the boy, get back to your posts." The two guards backed away from the door and only turned around when they were safely in the street. Satal pointed to the open door and ushered Tz' inside, but didn't offer him a chair at the large table. Once she was seated, she asked, "Where have you been living?"

"I grew up in the small village of Pa nimá, but moved to Mayapán several moons ago. I've taken up residence in your old palace, actually."

"Describe the interior of the house."

"One large bedroom in the back, a smaller one near the main room, an outside kitchen, and a large courtyard which was overgrown with bougainvillea vines when I moved in."

Satal was still suspicious. "Hmm, that proves nothing; you could be describing any number of houses in that city." She leaned in to get a closer look at Tz's face. "If your mother was Chachal, then who was your father?"

Tz' laughed. "Ah, Yakal warned me that you were tricky. I believe my real father is Alaxel, a member of the elite of this city and lover to my mother, before she married Chiman, the man who raised me."

"So, you're my grandson," Satal muttered as she stood up, grasped Tz' firmly by the arm, and pulled him toward the more comfortable chairs in the other side of the room. She pushed him gently in the back. "Please, sit down, and make yourself at home." She turned her head toward Tewichinel. "Get rid of everything on the table," she whispered before turning back to smile at Tz'. The shaman nodded, bundled together the pieces of fig bark paper, and took them away.

"You must be tired after your long journey," Satal said as she sat down in a padded leather chair opposite Tz'. "I'll have my servant bring you some food and drink, and then you must tell me about yourself." She clapped her hands together and Tewichinel reappeared. "Bring my grandson a plate of roasted iguana and fresh manioc root and a pitcher of mango juice."

"At once, my lady," Tewichinel said as he bowed and left the room.

Tz' smiled. "Maltiox, that sounds delicious." He shook his head. "I'm

284 RISE OF THE JAGUAR WOMAN

afraid there's not much to tell about my life that would interest someone of your stature, Lady Satal."

She leaned forward in her chair and stared intently at Tz's face. "You look like your mother around the eyes, but that jaw says you're definitely Alaxel's son. Would you like to meet him? I could have my men see if the man is still alive and have him brought here."

"Maltiox, Lady Satal. Finally meeting my true father is one of many reasons why I've come to the city."

"And the others are?"

But Tz' had no time to respond before Tewichinel returned with a loaded tray. "Eat, and then we'll talk," Satal said as she pointed to the plate of dark iguana meat and boiled cubes of manioc root covered in a spicy tomato salsa. She poured a mug of juice for herself and another for Tz', which she placed on the small low table set in between their chairs.

They sat in silence except for the chewing sounds Tz' made as he quickly ate the manioc and somewhat tough iguana. He washed a large piece of the chewy meat down with a swallow of juice and handed his empty plate to Tewichinel, who had hovered beside the youth the whole time he ate. "Maltiox, that was delicious," Tz' said as he drank some more juice.

After Tewichinel left the room again, Tz' said, "I traveled all this way to study the dark arts with you, Lady Satal."

"My, my, you're a bold one," Satal laughed. "I like that, I do. Not many would dare speak of such magic. Surely you must know that even the suggestion of studying it is reason enough for the council to sacrifice you to the gods."

It was Tz's turn to laugh. "Maybe that was the case in Mayapán, but not here in Chichén Itzá. From the rumors I've heard around the city, black magic is being used on a regular basis by you and many of your shamans."

"Oh, is that so?" She shook her head and sneered at Tz'. "And you think you have the ability to learn this black magic, eh?"

"Why wouldn't I? We're related by blood, Lady Satal, which must be an indication that I have some abilities. I just need to learn how to use them."

"And to what end? You must have a reason or purpose behind what many would consider complete madness."

Tz' fidgeted in his chair under Satal's scrutiny.

"Ha, it's the girl, of course, it's written all over your face!" Satal laughed. "You want to bring Na'om back from the Underworld, don't you, boy?" She shook her head and chortled again. "You're as stupid as everyone else. *If* Na'om has survived the tests put in front of her, she *might* return to the world of the living. But I frankly don't think she has the strength to make it through them. But I'm glad you're here, truly I am. It will make it so much easier, if she does return to the world of the living, to entice her to the city, where I'll finally be able to sacrifice her properly and absorb all her powers."

Satal smiled as Tz' tried to lunge at her, but found he couldn't move his legs. "Dear boy, you must take me for an old fool, to think that I'd let you march in here and demand training in ways that are far beyond your comprehension and for a purpose that would be detrimental to my own plans." She laughed as Tz' twisted his upper body, but couldn't move his arms. "My blood may run in your veins, but you're as ignorant as your mother was when it comes to magic." She grinned. "You want to learn the dark arts? Well, let me provide you with your first lesson. So many plants can be good for the body if properly prepared and harmful when they're not. In your case, that manioc root you just devoured wasn't soaked in water for a sufficient amount of time to draw the toxins out of it. The poison is filtering through your body, causing paralysis."

"Argh!" Tz' shouted as he tried to move.

"It will wear off over time, don't worry." Satal clapped her hands, and Tewichinel hurried into the room, followed by four guards, who quickly surrounded Tz' in his chair.

"Remove this boy and lock him away under heavy guard. Assign a slave to tend to his needs, food, water, and whatever else he may request, but he must remain guarded at all times. Is that understood?"

"Of course, Lady Satal," Tewichinel said. He nodded at the sentries, who picked Tz' up by his arms and feet and carried him away.

"What shall we do with him when we leave for Mayapán?" Tewichinel asked.

"He'll remain here, under guard, and I'll take care of him when we return." Satal smiled. "After slaughtering a whole city, one young man won't be difficult at all."

Daylight had barely crossed the threshold of Satal's room when she slipped out of her hammock. Many full moons had come and gone since she'd first arrived in Chichén Itzá, but the day the shamans had deemed favorable for traveling to Mayapán had finally arrived. She was eager to lead her personal army of shamans and gods into battle alongside Kämisanel and the hundreds of warriors he commanded, and she hummed and smiled as she picked out her outfit. She opened her wooden wardrobe and dressed in her best black huipil and skirt, tossed a dark gray woolen shawl around her shoulders, and slipped on a pair of leather sandals before drawing a turtle shell comb through her long, graying hair, which she quickly tied into a braid. Then she reached into the cupboard and removed three small, stoppered vials, which she tucked into the pocket of her skirt. She looked around the small room she'd called home for the past several moons and wondered if she needed to bring anything with her. Then she shook her head. Her entourage of shamans would carry anything and everything she might require on the long journey. And once Mayapán had been ransacked, she could take anything she wanted from that city and have it brought back to Chichén Itzá.

"Before you leave, I thought you might like to know about Na'om," Sachoj hissed in Satal's mind.

"Utzil, woman, have you no sense of timing? Don't you see I'm leaving to start the march on Mayapán?"

"Humph, well, obviously her whereabouts aren't important . . . ." Sachoj said. "I'll leave you alone."

"No, wait, tell me, quickly now," Satal replied.

"She's passed more tests than I thought possible and is heading toward her final trials; I wouldn't be surprised if she survives!" Sachoj said.

Satal could hear the admiration in her great-grandmother's voice and shook her head. "Don't worry; if she does, we'll be ready for her," Satal said.

As always, Tewichinel was waiting for her in the main room of the palace. *Does this man never sleep, eat, or need to take a shit?* Satal wondered as she gazed at the older man's face.

"Is everything all right, Lady Satal?" Tewichinel asked as he bowed. "I heard voices."

"Yes, yes, it was just me, talking to myself," Satal said as she brushed away a fly that buzzed around her face. "Today's the day; lead the way to the Hall of the Thousand Columns," she commanded as she pulled her shawl more tightly around her body against the cool morning air. "It's time to tell Kämisanel that we're all going with him."

"As you wish, my lady," Tewichinel replied. He clapped his hands and the other shamans appeared from the shadows in the courtyard. They were dressed in loincloths, jaguar skin capes, and sandals, just like Tewichinel. Several of the men picked up pack baskets and swung them onto their backs before placing leather tumplines around their heads to help ease their loads. They quickly formed a group around Satal and ushered her through the silent streets of Chichén Itzá toward the warriors' practice grounds.

The sounds of hundreds of men moving in unison reached Satal's ears long before she caught sight of the groups of warriors prepared for battle. Formed into units of ten men abreast by ten men deep, each section was led by a group of youths too young to fight. Several of the boys carried drums that hung from thick leather cords slung around their necks, while others held conch shells and trumpets fashioned from dried deer hide. They would beat and blow the rhythm to which the army would march, keeping every warrior in step with his neighbor.

Cotton banners painted with the images of her shape-shifting shamans and the gods of Xibalba hung from long poles, which were carried by the strongest of the young boys, a fact determined by numerous wrestling matches that had been held throughout the past several moons.

Each warrior was dressed in gear provided by the city—leather loincloths, leather vests stuffed with crushed salt or ceiba fluff, and strips of leather wrappings on each forearm and shin. Some units of warriors held long spears tipped with obsidian in their hands, while others had wooden bows and quivers of arrows on their backs, and each man carried a wooden shield, painted to match the banner in front of his particular unit.

Satal smiled as she surveyed the hundreds of illustrated rats, monkeys, snakes, scorpions, spiders, and centipedes that faced her. She knew that sight alone would cause panic in Mayapán.

She strode up to Kämisanel and the other leaders who stood on the steps of the temple. They were also dressed for war in full leather battle gear, but she noticed their shields were covered with a fine layer of opalescent shells, and each man wore a feather headdress over his black hair. The tips of the quetzal feathers in their headgear brushed the ground as the men bowed to Satal.

"Lady Satal, you honor us with your presence this morning," Kämisanel said as he stood up again. "The men are ready to march; we leave in just a few minutes."

"Good; I'm ready to go whenever you are," Satal replied.

"My lady?" Kämisanel said. He shook his head, and a set of tiny bells braided into his hair jingled at the motion. "The world of war is for men, my lady," he said as he bowed deeply.

"Ha," Satal laughed. "I will not sit here while you lead these men into battle. No, this is my army, my revenge. I will go to Mayapán to extract every ounce of pleasure from this battle that I possibly can."

"But Lady Satal, it is a hard march, with little time to rest, and the battle itself will present many dangers."

"I made the trip here all by myself with no difficulties." She turned and pointed to the group of shamans clustered just behind her. "Now I have these men to assist me, so I won't delay your progress. Some of the many slaves can carry me as quickly as you'll be able to move. In regards to the battle itself, I shall lead the first attack with my shamans, and you and your men will follow." She held up her hand to silence the warrior in front of her. "I was in charge of the entire city before I left; so who knows the movements of Nimal, the head warrior in Mayapán, and his men better than me? No, I travel with you. Once we've done our tasks, your job will be to break down the city walls and to kill or capture as many of the inhabitants as possible."

"As you wish, my lady," Kämisanel said again as he bowed even lower.

Before the sun had reached the tops of the nearby ceiba trees, the entire battalion of men was headed out of the city proper. The old, the women, and their children lined the sides of the sacbé to watch the procession pass. Many of the younger women silently wept, unsure whether they would see their husbands return in a moon's time or be told they had passed on to the land of the ancestors.

Satal strode as quickly as her arthritic knees allowed her to the outskirts of the city, but then she had to let the tens upon tens of warriors pass in front of her so as not to delay their progress. She climbed on to a wooden litter carried by four slaves, and with her group of shamans, they walked just ahead of the hundreds of slaves forced to carry the food necessary to feed such a large group. The army would demand water from every cenote they passed, but they couldn't expect to find food for so many from any one village.

Long before the sun rose over the countryside and long after it had set, Kämisanel pressed the troops to march. Satal knew they needed to make haste, as word would quickly spread that a vast army was on the march toward Mayapán. Each day that passed gave the people of the city more time to prepare, and Satal wanted to attack while they were still vulnerable.

Not that they'll ever be ready for what we're about to launch at them, she mused as she shifted her weight on the jostling litter.

Throughout the long hike, Kämisanel and the other generals remained at the head of the army, far in front of their troops, the slaves, and Satal and her shamans, arriving at a resting spot long before Satal. But they were quick to appear busy when word rippled through the crowds that she had finally come into camp. With Tewichinel and two other shamans guarding her front, and the other elders on each side and behind her, Satal and her group flowed through the men squatting near small cooking fires until she could claim her spot under the cloth shelter Kämisanel erected each night.

On the last day, Satal was pleased to see the men were busy consulting various drawings of Mayapán when she arrived. They were still a short distance from the city, but Satal knew the local villagers, loyal to those who lived inside the walls, had already warned Nimal and the others of their advance. Every minute they delayed the attack gave the men of the walled city more time to prepare, and she hurried to talk to Kämisanel.

Kämisanel looked up from the drawings spread on a blanket on the ground and bowed. "Lady Satal, how may we be of service?" He motioned for one of his young assistants to bring a stool for the woman to sit on.

She pointed at the younger generals in the area. "All of you, leave us." Kämisanel nodded, and the men quickly left the tent.

"We will attack the city tonight," Satal said. "If we delay until the morning, Nimal will have his guards positioned in every strategic spot on the walls, and the rest of the warriors will be ready for any hand-to-hand combat that comes their way."

"But my lady, the men are weary from the long march. Surely it would be better to wait until they've rested a bit before launching the assault. And it's almost impossible to fight in the dark."

"I thought you'd be reluctant," Satal said. "Which is why I've brought along something that might change your mind. What you're about to see shall be spoken of to no one, is that understood?"

"Of course, Lady Satal," Kämisanel replied.

Satal nodded to Tewichinel and the other shamans who stood off to one side. The elderly healer stepped forward and placed a ledger on the table in front of Kämisanel. He unfolded the accordion-style pages, spreading the paper the length of the blanket in front of the warrior, displaying a vivid scene of men fighting men with knives and spears while high overhead the night sky was filled with a thousand, thousand stars.

"The shamans have been reading the heavens for longer than you or I have been alive," Satal said. "They know the best time to plant the corn, to harvest it, and pound it into flour, along with hundreds of other details of daily life." She pointed to the drawing, poking her finger at the brilliant reds, yellows, blacks, and whites. "They have foreseen this battle and it takes place at night." She stepped back and folded her arms across her chest, waiting for Kämisanel to reply.

He leaned in to study the drawing more closely. "You're positive that this illustration depicts *this* battle?"

"Ha, you doubt the shamans and me?" Satal laughed. "I suspected you were simple, but surely even you must have some faith in the reading of the skies." Satal watched as Kämisanel's face flushed with red.

The warrior bowed low to Satal. "My lady, I don't presume to know anything in your presence," he said, as he slowly stood upright again. "I will tell the generals to have the men ready. We'll attack at the darkest part of the night, when the citizens of Mayapán are fast asleep."

Satal nodded. "Good. My shamans and I will be ready as well."

"My lady?" Kämisanel questioned.

Satal grinned as she flipped the entire book over, exposing the back of the painted pages. Another image unfolded in front of the head warrior, depicting an army only the lords of the Underworld could imagine.

"Itzamná," Kämisanel exclaimed as he bent down to examine the drawing more closely. "Is this why you've traveled with us?"

Satal nodded. "Once we've had our fun, then your men can come in and clean up the rest of the city. The whole battle should only take a few hours; by daybreak, Mayapán should be ours."

Kämisanel had turned quite pale. "How do I know my men will survive all of this?" he asked as he gestured with one hand toward the illustrations.

"Whether they do or not is of little consequence to me," Satal replied as she refolded the book and handed it to Tewichinel. "The objective is to destroy Mayapán, and I think, with what we have available to use, that we should have little problem in doing so." She nodded to the shamans, who clustered around her. "We'll lead our attack in a few hours' time; have your men ready to follow shortly after that. There will be quite some noise in our preparations, so tell your men not to be alarmed."

"As you wish, my lady," Kämisanel replied. He bowed, but Satal had already swept out of the shelter and into the advancing night.

The group of shamans, with Satal in the center, quickly moved out beyond the perimeter of the army's camp. Satal nodded to Yuxba' and Pataninel. "You'll gather our clothes and make your way to the city walls. Once Kämisanel's men have breached the gates, you can enter and come find us." The men nodded, but didn't speak. "You've got the charcoal, I presume?" Satal added, and both men smiled.

"In our pouches, Lady Satal. We are well prepared to help each of you when the time comes," Yuxba' said as he bowed low to the ground. "And we have the jequirity beans, as well," he added as he held pulled out several of the red and black beans from his bag around his waist.

"Excellent," Satal said, reaching for one of the shaman's water gourds. She took the three vials from her skirt pocket that she'd brought from Chichén Itzá and poured the tincture into the water gourd. She shook it rapidly and took a long draught before handing it to Ch'o. The group of shamans passed the gourd until it was empty, and then they sat down to wait. Although they had practiced on numerous occasions, it still took time before the gods of the Underworld answered their summons.

As usual, Camazotz was the first to arrive, and he immediately let loose a high-pitched shriek to rouse all the bats in the surrounding area. A vast cloud of them appeared and flitted high overhead, their wings rustling like dry leaves in a high wind. Buluc-Chabtan, Ah-Cun-Can, and Hun Batz materialized soon after. The dry scrub brush and ground filled with a thousand snakes and howler monkeys, but the shamans and

Satal quickly lost sight of them when Tlacolotl arrived and spread a deeper cloak of darkness across the sky.

With a loud crack and the pungent smell of ozone, Ah-Pekku made his entrance.

Satal shook her head. "Always has to make sure we know he's here," she muttered at the god.

Yum Cimil and Poxlom were the last two gods to arrive, and once they'd settled in with the others, Satal nodded to the shamans. Each man removed his clothing and bundled it together for Pataninel, while Yuxba' handed out slices of jequirity beans to each naked man.

Satal was glad the night was so dark as she was not comfortable undressing in front of so many, but she had little choice in the matter and hurried to step out of her clothes. She took her slice of bean and rapidly shifted into her black wasp form, preferring to spend more time as a wasp than a naked old woman with the many lumps and bulges that made up her aged body.

The shamans quickly followed Satal's example, touching the jequirity to their tongues. Soon, the air was filled with squeals and howls as monkeys and rats congregated on the scene, followed by the slithering of thousands of snakes, centipedes, spiders, and scorpions. Satal summoned her own special friends, and a swarm of wasps appeared in the black sky, hovering near the cloud of bats.

The army of gods and animals divided into four separate groups and headed toward Mayapán. They would surround the city on all four sides and attack when they saw Satal dive with her mass of wasps over the main entrance gates.

YAKAL

Yakal's mind churned with a thousand worries as he slipped out of the hut, leaving Uskab and Mayibal to sleep in the hammock. Although the night air was warm on his bare chest, he shivered while he relieved his full bladder. His head ached, and his muscles were tense, as they often were before a major thunderstorm, even though the rainy season had long since ended. Daybreak was hours away, and when it arrived, he knew the vast number of soldiers from Chichén Itzá, who had made camp a short distance from the city walls, would attack. He hoped that Nimal and his men were ready for them and wished they'd had more time to prepare. Only two of the four trenches he's suggested be built around the city were complete and filled with oil. He sighed. It would have to be enough. Then he went over the plan he had made with Uskab once again just to make sure he wasn't forgetting any detail. As soon as the first birds began to sing, Uskab and Mayibal would go to his mother's house and awaken Alom, and his sister, Masat, then the group would head to Kubal Joron and Matz's house. The male couple had volunteered their home as a safe refuge once the battle began, and Yakal had gladly accepted their invitation for his family. Kubal Joron had hired several private guards to surround the house and protect all who sheltered inside. Yakal had insisted that Uskab and the baby go directly to the one inner room that had no windows and only one doorway. He wanted them as far removed from any fighting as possible.

He looked up into the night sky, marveling at the beauty of the crescent moon hanging like a cradle of light in the darkness and the sheer abundance of stars, and he silently prayed that he would live long enough to see the stars shine once again. Just as he was about to return to the hut and try to get a few hours' sleep, he noticed a blackness fly swiftly across the face of the moon. He blinked rapidly and swiped his eyes, but the image was gone. He shook his head and watched the sky for more signs of movement. Another large black shape flew by, followed by a cloud of darkness, and Yakal shivered again. *Something's wrong, very wrong*, he thought as he hurried inside to wake Uskab.

"Get up, hurry," he said as he prodded Uskab. Mayibal began to cry, filling the air with his high-pitched sobs.

"Yakal, what's wrong?" Uskab said as she tried to shush the baby.

"Go and wake Chuch and Masat, then run to Kubal Joron's palace. I'm not sure what's happening, but I believe Satal has started the attack. I have to go warn Nimal." Yakal could barely see in the hut, but he thrust his obsidian knife into Uskab's hand.

"Won't you need this?" Uskab said as she tried to give the blade back to Yakal.

"I'll get another from Nimal. Go now, before it's too late." Yakal kissed Uskab and Mayibal. "I love you," he cried as he turned and ran out of the house.

Itzamná, protect my family tonight, I beg you, he prayed as he ran through the silent, dark streets toward the main gates of the city. As he ran past the marketplace, he could see sentries moving about in the torchlight at the top of the Temple of Cremations. Beyond the temple, on the wall that faced the enemies who were camped nearby, large copper braziers burned brightly every fifty paces, and Yakal could see the silhouettes of the guards who patrolled back and forth. He was glad Nimal had his men ready even though sunrise was hours away. When he arrived at the gates, he was relieved to see Nimal standing outside on duty, illuminated by several torches stuck in brackets on the guardhouse walls.

"What's wrong?" Nimal asked as soon as he saw Yakal running toward him.

"Did you see the shapes that flew past the moon just moments ago?"

Nimal nodded. "I thought I was imagining things. I've alerted everyone posted on the walls, but so far, it's been quiet." He patted Yakal's arm. "Don't worry; we're ready to fight." He looked at Yakal, dressed only in his loincloth and sandals. "Wait here," he said as he disappeared into the guardhouse. He returned minutes later with an old vest made of a single thick sheet of leather with two armholes cut in it. A loop of leather went around the neck and two thongs tied in the back to keep the sides tucked under the arms. "It's one of our practice vests; not much, I'm afraid, but at least you'll have a bit of protection." He also had a short obsidian knife with no sheath, which he gave to Yakal. He put on his own ceiba-stuffed vest stamped with the image of Kukulcan's pyramid inside a large circle, tugging it over his ample belly. Yakal thanked him and slipped on the training vest. It was tight underneath his armpits, and he knew it would chafe his skin, but he kept it on anyway.

Suddenly, a shriek echoed from the far side of the city, followed by another, and another. Yakal looked at Nimal. "What was that?"

But the man didn't have time to answer as howls, squeals, squeaks, shouts, and screams of terror filled the air.

"Sound the alarm!" Nimal shouted at the nearest sentry. The man nodded and stumbled over his own feet as he rushed to thwack the large drum standing nearby. The booming sound bounced off the walls, blending with shrill screeches, harsh buzzing, and high-pitched shrieks. A flash of light streaked across the sky followed by an instant crash of thunder, and Yakal's heart thudded rapidly in his chest. Another flash of lightning came, then another, followed by roiling rumbles that Yakal felt in his feet and legs as they shook the ground. He waited for the rain, but it never appeared.

In the next burst of light, he looked up and saw a massive cloud of bats swooping down on top of them. "Get down," he shouted and tugged on Nimal's arm, pulling him to the ground. The bats shrieked as they flew by, attacking the sentry pounding the drum.

"Itzamná protect us!" Nimal cried as he got to his feet again. "Light the fires," he shouted to the guards cowering on the top of the wall. The men grabbed arrows from the quivers on their backs, lit them in the nearby braziers, and stood to shoot, but had to duck and swerve as the swarm of bats streaked past them. Many dropped their burning arrows, where they sizzled out on the stones under foot, and one man lost his balance and fell with a thud to the ground. Yakal hurried to his side, but the warrior was dead, his neck twisted at an odd angle.

The archers stood again, grabbed new arrows, pulled back their bows, and let loose, sending the flaming arrows directly into the trenches dug on two sides of the city. A blaze of light flared high in the sky as the oil ignited in the ditches.

Sudden, explosive popping sounds merged with a thousand hisses and squeals, and shouts of 'Itzamná' rang out from the warriors. Yakal scrambled up the side of the wall to stand next to one of the sentries. From the light of the burning oil, he could see thousands of rats, snakes, and scorpions scampering and slithering away from the flames, and beyond them a field of creatures that stretched far into the darkness. The serpents and scorpions caught in the trench bubbled and popped, sending clouds of acrid smoke in the air that mingled with the rank scent of scorched fur and roasted meat from the burning rats. The men near him started to stomp and jump about, and Yakal watched as a wave of scorpions poured over the top of the stones, waving their tails and clicking their pincer claws. He grabbed a torch and swept it across the rocks, igniting the insects in a circle around him. He stopped to catch his breath, and several dozen pairs of red eyes peered at him in the dark. Tens of rats had made it across the trenches, their fur sleeked down with oil. He swung the torch back and forth, running along the rough stones, touching the flames to the animals nearest him. They were bunched so close together that they quickly ignited their neighbors, and ear-piercing squeals made Yakal cringe as the rats fell to their deaths below. Jagged bolts of lightning and the boom of thunder pierced the sky, and Yakal stooped down low as more bats flew past him.

Screams and shouts for help came from behind the men on the wall, and Yakal turned and looked back into the city, but everything was blanketed in black. Even the torches on the top of the nearby temple had vanished. He slipped back down to the ground and found Nimal. "I'm going to find Bitol and see how he and his men are doing beyond the pyramid."

Nimal nodded and grabbed one of the many torches off the

guardhouse. "Take this with you and good luck."

Yakal held the lit torch in front of him to illuminate the way as he jogged toward the sounds of screaming women and children. He thought of Uskab and Mayibal and ran even faster, straight into a crowd of people heading the other way. He grabbed one older man by the arm, forcing him to stop. "Why are you running?" he said as he held the torch near the man.

The man's arms and legs were covered in welts and one eye was almost swollen shut. "Wasps and centipedes, thousands of them, like a river coming over the tops of the walls." The man shivered as the toxins continued to work their way through his body. "Itzamná, we'll all be in Xibalba before dawn." He pulled his arm loose from Yakal's grip and hobbled away.

More screams and howls penetrated the air, and from Yakal's right, another charge of citizens appeared from the blackness. "Run," one woman shouted as she reached out for Yakal. He looked beyond the crowd that flowed past him. A horde of spider and howler monkeys was racing toward him, careening, bouncing, and leaping off the sides of the huts and buildings on each side of the narrow alleyway, their teeth bared and their claws outstretched to grasp and claw anyone in sight. Yakal turned and ran on into the night, crunching centipedes underfoot as he went. He stooped low when he heard an incessant droning and winced when several wasps stung bare spots on his arms.

The area he was in was so dark, despite the torch he carried, that he almost missed Bitol and his men as they ran toward him in the street. "You can't go any farther in that direction, my friend," Bitol said when he grabbed Yakal. He shivered. "Centipedes cover all the huts; only the gods know how many they've killed so far."

Yakal was the only one with a light, and he quickly surveyed the large group of warriors in front of him. Many were in obvious pain from the multiple stings, nips, and puncture wounds that covered any bare skin. "It's just as bad near the main gates, only there it's rats, scorpions, and snakes. But the trenches filled with oil are holding them off for now."

They could hear the clicking of a million legs as the mass of centipedes moved closer, and Bitol shook his head. "What do we do?"

"We must gather everyone that we can in the center of the city, near the Temple of Warriors and the larger palaces, and then set fire to each street in this area and hope the blaze burns them."

"But that will destroy much of Mayapán," Bitol said. "We must discuss this with Nimal."

"Nimal has his own problems. Trust me; I saw what's waiting for us once the oil in the trenches burns down. We must act now or we'll all perish."

Bitol nodded and motioned for his men to group together. "All right, gather as many torches from the marketplace as you can find, and working in pairs, fan out across this part of the city. If you hear anyone calling for help, try to reach them, but if all you see are those horrible insects, then set them on fire. We'll meet back at the Temple of Warriors and then go help Nimal."

The men grimaced, but did as they were told. Bitol reached out and hugged Yakal. "In case we don't see each other again in this world," he said as he ran to catch up to his warriors.

Yakal spun around and ran toward Kubal Joron's house. He had to know that Uskab and Mayibal were safe. But he had only gone a few hundred paces down one of the many alleyways when he heard a raspy laugh high over his head. He held the torch out to one side, looked straight up, and gasped as he saw a giant black wasp hovering over his head. "Satal!" he shouted as he ducked into a crouch and began to dash down the street.

"Run all you like, Yakal, you won't make it," Satal snarled as she zipped toward him, her long stinger poised to strike.

Yakal dove toward the ground and rolled, but dropped his torch on the ground where it began to splutter. Satal stabbed again, narrowly missing his left leg. He rolled, scrambled toward the torch, and grabbed it just before it went out. Rolling again, he held the torch up to catch a bit of wind, which reignited the oils, and he shouted as the wasp's stinger struck him in the chest, knocking the wind out of him. He swung the torch back and forth in front of his body, keeping Satal away so he could get into a crouch and scrabble to the nearest wall. With something solid behind him, he slowly stood and faced the wasp, which still hovered nearby.

"You won't win, Satal," he cried as he swung the torch back and forth in front of her. He lunged forward and almost caught her in the midsection with the tip of his flame. He breathed in the stench of burnt skin and smiled. He swung the torch around and around his head as he moved rapidly down the street. Ducking and dodging Satal's stinger, he made it to the nearest corner, where he met two of Bitol's men. They each carried a lit torch and a bundle of wood, which they piled against the walls and on the ground between the buildings. Yakal nodded, and the men applied their torches to the dry wood, setting it afire.

Satal screeched as the flames arced high into the air. "This is just the beginning, Yakal," she warned as she flew off.

Yakal smiled at the men, who were backing away from the flames. "Keep the fire moving away from here; we don't want to burn ourselves up!" He hurried down more deserted streets, grateful to see that the thousands of insects Satal had let loose on the city had yet to reach the area. On street after street, he met Bitol's men setting the place on fire. Many of the buildings in this part of the city were old, and the dried palm fronds used to thatch the roofs quickly burst into flames, igniting the wooden beams and poles inside each structure. The stucco walls blistered and cracked in the heat, and soon a thick haze of smoke hovered just a few feet above Yakal's head. He coughed and coughed as the harsh air filled his lungs, making his eyes water and his head pound. But he quickly noticed that the constant buzzing overhead had stopped as thousands of sleepy wasps drifted to the ground. He stomped on as many as he could and motioned to the men nearby to do the same.

Tens of bats also fell to the dirt, and the warriors took pleasure in pitching their bodies into the flames where they snapped and crackled, disappearing in a flash of light. He could hear indistinct voices shouting above his head and then an ear-piercing wail that forced him to his knees as yet more bats burst into flames, and he wondered who or what was hovering just above the smoke.

Hundreds of older men, women, and children were huddled in groups against the base of the thick walls of the Temple of the Warriors and on the wide patio when Yakal arrived and many more people were crammed indoors. Sentries stood at each of the round columns that supported the tiled roof high overhead, and troops were stationed every five paces in a semi-circle on the open parade grounds in front of the large building. Each man held a torch, and fires were burning in a perimeter around the whole section. In the light, Yakal could see Bitol standing next to Nimal, and he ran over to the men.

"In all my days, I've never seen or heard of anything like this," Nimal said. "The gates of Xibalba were opened tonight . . . ." He paused at the sound of distant shrieks, followed by the growls and roars of monkeys.

"Satal's behind all this," Yakal said. "She, or the thing she's become, spoke to me and warned me that we wouldn't win." He grinned. "But then the smoke from the fires caused the swarms of wasps she was leading to fall to the ground, along with hundreds of bats. We have to keep the fires burning until daylight, when hopefully the gods of the Underworld and their kind will disappear."

He looked around, surveying those who had survived the attack. "These people should be safe here for now. But I must go check on Uskab, Mayibal, and the others hiding at Kubal Joron's house." Nimal and Bitol nodded and Yakal took off on a run. The air was less smoky in the wider streets away from the temple, and he felt the sweat that had beaded up under his leather vest begin to cool. His chest ached where Satal's stinger had punched him, and he was glad Nimal had given him the vest to wear.

He rounded the corner and almost shouted with joy. The house looked unscathed, and the men Kubal Joron had hired had lit fires near the entrance to the large courtyard, keeping everything at bay. He paused as he approached the entranceway, though and looked down at the ground. A wide band of something reddish stretched out on either side of the doorway and continued down the street. He bent to look more closely and was surprised to see it was salt.

He jumped over the wide trail and strode to the front door. Three guards blocked the entranceway, but quickly moved to one side when Yakal nodded at them. He hurried into the main room, which was full of people; some he knew, others he didn't. He looked for Uskab and his son, but they were nowhere to be seen.

Kubal Joron spotted Yakal immediately and rushed over to him. "What's going on out there? It sounds absolutely horrendous, and there's so much smoke, will we be all right here?"

Yakal smiled wearily. "You're safe for now, but Satal has attacked with our worst nightmares, and the gods of the Underworld are helping her. The smoke is from fires we've set on the north side of the city to try to stem the tide of centipedes and wasps flowing over the walls."

Kubal Joron gasped and hurried to dab his lips with a scented cloth.

"It gets worse; snakes, scorpions, bats, even a horde of monkeys are all out there, terrorizing everyone. It looks like Satal has summoned all the gods of the Underworld to create havoc on the city." Kubal Joron turned pale, and Yakal put out his hand to steady the older man.

"Are the trenches working?" Kubal Joron asked as he patted his forehead.

"For now, but once it burns down, I'm not sure how we'll stem the flood of evil ready to crawl and slither over the walls."

"Oh, I do hope the salt we placed all around the house holds them off."

"I don't understand," Yakal said, frowning.

"It's been blessed by the shamans, dear boy, who promised us it would ward off any evil. Utzil, it had better for the price we paid for it," Kubal Joron replied.

Yakal looked around the room, searching for his family.

"Don't worry, they're all safely tucked in the room as we discussed," Kubal Joron said after he'd taken a deep breath. "Come; I'll show you." He pushed through the crowd and the incessant murmur slowed and finally stopped as people realized Yakal was in the room.

"What's happening?" someone shouted.

"What's making all the noise out there?" a man yelled.

"When can we go home?" another called.

Yakal turned and held up his hand. "I'll speak to you all in just a moment." Then he ducked through a doorway guarded by a sentry and followed Kubal Joron down a long hallway to a door set in the stucco wall. He opened it and saw Uskab, the baby, and Alom squashed on the floor below shelves of folded clothes and piles of leather shoes. Memetik pulled aside a few shirts hanging from hooks on the wall and grinned.

"Yakal!" Uskab shouted as she leapt to her feet to hug him.

He embraced everyone, and tears ran down his face as he held his loved ones in his arms. Uskab started to gather her things together, but Yakal placed his hand on her shoulder. "I'm afraid the battle's only just begun," he said as he smiled at Mayibal, who grinned and drooled down his chin. He wiped the spittle from his son's mouth. "You have to stay here until it's safe to come out, and only the gods know when that will be."

Uskab began to cry silently as she nodded and settled back down on the floor. She put Mayibal to nurse to quiet his whimpering and smiled weakly at Yakal. "Be safe, my love," she said as he closed the door on the group.

Yakal returned to the main room where he quickly gave the others a brief description of what was happening. Several of the women fainted, and many of the men looked ill.

"I must get back out there and help the others," Yakal said as he headed toward the main door. "Don't come out, for any reason, not until I return and tell you it's safe."

Kubal Joron nodded and shut the door rapidly as soon as Yakal had stepped through.

He ran back through the streets under the cloud of smoke that hovered just above his head. It was only when he neared the Temple of the Warriors that he realized the sky was growing lighter. *Daybreak at last*, he thought as he spotted Nimal and ran toward him. *Perhaps we'll have a reprieve now.*

But his optimism was short-lived as he heard the distant rumble of a hundred different drums beating out a rhythm matched by the blowing of trumpets and conch shells. The steady pounding of an army on the move caused the air to vibrate and the ground to shimmy, and Yakal rushed to join Nimal and his large group of soldiers. The old warrior was giving his last orders to his men, and Yakal waited for him to finish before addressing him.

Nimal shook his head as he watched the regiment run to defend the walls against the newest invaders. Only a select few of his sentries remained to tend the fires around the perimeter of the safety zone, and they obviously needed more help. "Pray to Itzamná, Yakal, for I don't know if we'll survive another battle. So many of my men are dead or dying from poisonous stings and bites that I'm not sure we'll last out the day."

Yakal pointed to the older men, women, and children huddled against the walls of the temple. Many had fallen asleep despite the din of the previous night, and they were just beginning to stir as rays of sunshine broke through the hazy smoke drifting overhead. "We'll get them to help. The women and children can tend the fires, while the men must join the battle along the walls. Although they may be old, they've seen many skirmishes in their time and still know how to fight. And there are those inside who know the healing arts, who can help any who are sick."

Nimal clapped Yakal on the back, making him wince with the force of the blow, but he still gave the older man a brief smile. "Kubal Joron's given me an idea, too. I'll take several volunteers to the marketplace, to the salt seller's section, and bring back whatever we can find. If we ring these streets with salt, it should help hold anything back if the fires die down."

"I'm putting you in charge here, Yakal," Nimal said as the two walked over to the nearest sentry standing by one of the bonfires. "Anything this man tells you to do, you do it, is that understood?" The guard nodded to Nimal. "Good; tell the others." The young warrior sprinted away.

Nimal headed back toward the citizens near the temple with Yakal beside him. When the old men saw Nimal, they stood and formed a group. "We know why you're here," one man said. "But we have nothing to fight with other than our bare hands."

"That may have to suffice," Nimal said. He turned to Yakal. "I've got to go see if the gates are holding, but if I can get away, I'll come back to check on you. Good luck, my friend," Nimal said as he crushed Yakal in a tight hug. He led all the older men away.

As soon as Nimal was gone, Yakal rounded up the women and children and explained the need to keep the fires going and about getting the salt in the market. They quickly decided among themselves who would go and who would stay. And then another group of women and girls who had been hiding in a nearby house arrived. "We'd like to help," one woman said as she pointed to the cluster of older women and young girls near her. "We can bring back as much oil as we can find, for the fires and for more torches."

Yakal smiled. "Good idea. And we'll need cloth for bandages, salves for the wounded, and food." Then he looked at several young boys, too young to fight, but old enough to be of help. "The cenote is only a few blocks away. If I send you with armed guards, do you think you can fill the water buckets and bring them back?" The boys nodded, and Yakal could see they were happy to have something to do other than sit and wait.

Just as he was about to leave, he noticed Kubal Joron, Matz', and the many rich men who had been safely ensconced in the well-guarded palace approaching, followed by the women and children who had been hiding there as well. He hurried to hug Uskab and Alom and gave Mayibal a quick kiss on the cheek. "What are you doing here? I told you to stay indoors until it was safe to come out."

"We couldn't just sit and wait," Kubal Joron said. "Not when we knew how bad the situation was out here. There must be something we can do to help even though we're not trained to fight."

"Yes, all right," Yakal said. He was pleased to see the elite were willing to risk their lives, since so many less fortunate were doing the same for them. "Take these boys for water, so the sentries can remain on guard here." Kubal Joron nodded, grabbed a torch, and moved away, with Matz' close beside him.

"Uskab, perhaps you can help settle the mothers with young children, and Alom, can you see who might be ill and set up a separate place for them, away from everyone else?" He leaned in close to his mother. "We don't want any diseases to spread through the crowd."

The women set about their tasks, and Yakal nodded to the women and girls who had volunteered to go with him to the market. "All right, let's go," Yakal said.

As the group he led moved away from the protection zone, Yakal could see the damage was far worse than he had imagined. Bodies lay strewn about on the streets and in the doorways, many covered with so many bites, stings, and welts that they were unrecognizable. Yakal grimaced as he wondered how many more lay dead inside the homes they were passing, and he made a mental note to tell Nimal they would need to bury the bodies before the heat of the day caused them to swell and bloat. He entered yet another street, only to stop in horror. Several small fires burned in the alleyway. Numerous bodies, many missing limbs and body parts, hung over the dying flames from long spears stuck into the ground, and Yakal suspected the god of war, Buluc-Chabtan, was responsible for the atrocities. He quickly turned around, forcing the women behind him to stop. "Whatever you do, don't look down there," he shouted as he ushered the women to go past him.

As they approached the market, they could hear the battle raging on the outside of the city. Shouts and screams blended with the thwack of wooden staves and the clash of obsidian knives as the Mayapán soldiers pushed to keep the Chichén Itzá warriors away from the gates and walls. *As long as our human enemies can't scale the stones,* Yakal thought, *we might have a chance.* A loud whirring overhead forced him to look up, and he saw a wave of arrows plummeting to the ground only a few hundred feet away. "Hurry; we haven't got much time," he shouted. "Search for things you know we'll need, then meet me at the salt booths."

The women scattered in all directions while Yakal headed straight for the salt stalls. Baskets and baskets of white, pink, and red salt filled the vendors' booths, and he stacked three containers on top of each other to carry back to the safety zone. Within minutes, the women had returned, loaded down with pack baskets stuffed with items. Each woman grabbed a basket of salt as well, cradling it in her arms as the group hurried away.

Only when everyone was back inside the safe area did Yakal breathe a sigh of relief. While the sounds of the humans battling for possession of the city ebbed and flowed all around them, Yakal instructed the women to pour the salt in a thin line around the whole section, but they quickly ran out before they had completed a full circle.

They wound up making four more trips to the market for salt and other items they deemed necessary including blankets, pots, more food, empty water gourds, herbs for the wounded, and digging sticks.

Everyone who was able took turns scraping out a massive, shallow pit in the middle of the practice grounds in front of the Temple of Warriors, and Yakal sent the sentries out to retrieve the closest bodies, which were piled like sticks inside the long trench. As each body was added, dirt was shoveled over it to ward off the stench, and when it was full, Yakal called a halt to the process. "We'll have to burn the rest if and when we find them," Yakal said.

In between tasks, he hurried to check on Uskab, who had set up a small area inside the large main room of the temple for the children. Giggles and laughter echoed off the ceiling high overhead as the children played, and Yakal had to smile even though he knew men were dying only a short distance away.

Alom had taken over four of the smaller chambers and set them up as makeshift sick wards. Improvising with what she could find in the temple, she had laid mats on the ground for the wounded to lie on, and the men, women, and children were packed together with only inches of space between them. The air reeked of fear-infused sweat, blood, and vomit, and Yakal stifled his instinct to turn away. *If Chuch can stand this, then so can I.* Several older women and four younger girls were tending to the injured with the few supplies they'd been able to collect from the market. Alom strode over to the doorway when she saw Yakal.

"How are they?" he asked.

"Some have monkey bites, which we've cleaned with fresh water and wrapped with rags, others have multiple stings and burns from the wasps and centipedes, and we've applied what little salves we have to ease the pain," Alom pointed to the far corner of the room. "Those over there are covered in scorpion stings and may not make it through the night, I'm afraid."

Yakal nodded. "Give them whatever you have to help them, and if any of them die, send one of the girls to the sentries outside the main door and have them collect the body." He hugged his mother. "I must get back outside, but send for me if you need me."

As late afternoon shadows began to creep across the region, the noise of the battle beyond the walls finally ceased, and Nimal appeared a short time later. He was covered in dirt and blood and a large gash covered in a dirty rag ran down his left forearm. When he saw Yakal, he clapped him on the back.

"They've given up, the whole lot of them, well, those who can still move, that is," Nimal said. He took the mug of water Yakal offered him and drained in one long gulp. "Maltiox," he said as Yakal refilled it. He looked about the rough encampment and nodded his approval at everything that he saw.

"We should be able to let these people head back home, don't you think?" Nimal said.

Yakal laughed bitterly. "Not if I know Satal. Those men have fled the walls because she's launching another attack tonight, and they don't want to be anywhere near here when her army of evil marches again."

Nimal turned pale. "May the gods protect us then, for we've just about used up all our supplies, and I know my men are worn out from fighting in the hot sun."

"Tell your men to gather here; this is the only place we can properly defend against Satal. We've collected food, water, and fuel for the fires, which will thwart her progress just as it did last night. If we can hold out long enough, she'll soon grow weary of all of this and return to Chichén Itzá."

Bitol arrived with his group of soldiers a short while later and agreed with Yakal, so Nimal pulled what remained of his troops inside the protective circle of salt and fire. They built up some of the bonfires so they blazed fiercely, providing plenty of light, and smothered others to create clouds of smoke that quickly filled the whole parade grounds. And then they waited as night slowly descended.

Nimal made sure all the women and children were safely inside the temple, and despite the horrors they had witnessed, many of them fell asleep as the night progressed, curled up in blankets on the tiled floors. That left all the men outside on the wide patio that ran the length of the building. A few of the elite grumbled at this, until Nimal pointed out they were free to return to their own homes at any time. Yakal laughed silently when he saw their faces turn pale at the thought. Nimal turned and joined his soldiers, pacing the perimeter and watching for signs of movement or sounds of an invasion.

With no one on the walls to fight them and no fires in the trenches to stop them, Yakal knew it wouldn't take long for Satal and her thousands of insects and animals to fill the streets of the city, searching out anyone who might still linger in the numerous homes and buildings. And when they found no one, they'd strike the city center.

He sensed Satal's presence long before he heard the buzzing and whirring of thousands of wings above his head. "Get ready," he yelled to Nimal. But the layer of smoke kept the swarms of wasps and bats from flying in for an attack. Lightning flashed, thunder roared, and through the haze, Yakal saw Satal sweep by overhead, followed by the giant bat god, Camazotz. Close on their heels was a massive cloud of bats and wasps that quickly disappeared as the light faded. But Yakal could feel the breeze the thousands of wings created as the mass circled the area again and again.

Nimal ran along the perimeter they'd built. "Keep the fires burning regardless of what you see on the other side of the flames," he warned his men. But shouts and screams rang out as a wave of rats and centipedes rushed directly at the guards while scorpions and snakes slithered and scuttled in from the sides.

"Stand at your posts," Nimal shouted as he hurried up and down the fire line. "Steady," he cried as some of his men fell back several steps to avoid the crush of rats pushing through the open spots between the various bonfires.

Yakal and several other men rushed forward with torches and set the animals afire. "Bring some oil," Yakal shouted. He grabbed a digging stick and quickly scratched a narrow, shallow ditch directly behind and between two of the bonfires. He snatched the container of coconut oil from one of the older men and dumped it along the line he'd made, and flames from one fire raced along the track, linking it to the next. The soldiers nearby hurried to follow his example, which slowed the crush of centipedes advancing on them.

Yakal glanced overhead as he felt the wind stir his hair and realized Satal and Camazotz's steady sweep around the area was forcing the smoke to lift and dissipate. If their smoke cover disappeared, nothing would stop them from attacking. He grabbed Nimal's arm and pointed upward. "We need more smoke, now!"

Men scrabbled to throw handfuls of dirt on the flames, which tamped down the fires, creating thick smoke, but as soon as the blazes died down, the onslaught of rats increased. Then one man screamed as a large howler monkey leapt over the fire line and landed on his chest, ripping and biting him as they both fell to the ground. Yakal grabbed a digging stick and stabbed the monkey in the back, lifted it high, and held it in the fire where it screeched and screamed while its fur caught fire. He swung the burning monkey behind him and then flung it forward with all his might and watched as the flaming body landed a short distance on the other side of the fires into a cluster of monkeys who screeched, shrieked, and stomped about as they watched their cousin die.

"Get more wood on those fires!" Bitol cried as he hurried to join Nimal and Yakal. "We'll never survive the night at this rate," he said. The three men ducked as they felt the swish of wings overhead.

"We have to get Satal," Yakal said. "If she dies, the others will stop their attack." He looked around, trying to think of something, anything, that might draw her out and away from the rest of the group. He grabbed Nimal's arm. "Give me four of your bravest men; I've got an idea." He ran to the food area and grabbed a large bowl, poured in some salt, and added water to create a thick paste, which he smeared all over his body. Then he took the remaining salt and added it to several water gourds, shaking them to mix the salt and water as he hurried back to Nimal. "Give me your vest," he said and Nimal quickly removed the thick, padded garment and handed it to him. Yakal took the older man's torch and knife as well.

Yakal held on to two of the water gourds full of salty water and gave the rest to the men Nimal had chosen, each of whom carried a lit torch. "Ready?" he asked.

"Wait, what are you going to do?" Nimal cried.

"There's no time to explain," Yakal shouted as he nodded to the men and leaped over the fires and into the street beyond. He swung his torch in front of him, clearing the area of insects, the foot soldiers following just behind, and they too swept their torches about, keeping the hundreds of bugs at bay. Running low to the ground, Yakal only went as far as the nearest corner. He knew if they moved too far away from any protection, his idea had no chance of working. He pitched his torch into the street, which pushed the scorpions back several feet and he leapt into the space. "Satal," he shouted as he poured a ring of salt water all around him. "Satal, I'm here, let's finish our battle once and for all." He nodded to one of the guards who tossed him a water gourd, and he poured a bit of the water on the torch, making it go out.

Illuminated by the guards' torches several feet away, Yakal waited in the semi-darkness. A giant shadow flickered across the nearest wall, and he spun around to face Satal, who buzzed his head as she flew past. Yakal pulled the corks from the water gourds he held and motioned for the men to do the same.

Satal's wings fanned the air about Yakal, and he could hear the clicking of pincers as the scorpions on the ground nearby grew bolder and advanced on him. *Itzamná, give me strength*, Yakal prayed. He bent his knees, bracing himself.

"Ha, so it's come down to just the two of us, eh?" Satal rasped as she floated several feet above the ground in front of him. "I'm been wanting to kill you for years; pity it'll be over so quickly," she added as she darted in to stab Yakal with her giant stinger.

The impact of her blow into his chest shoved Yakal backward several feet, and he gasped, but he managed to throw the contents of the gourds into the air, hitting Satal on one wing and the side of her wasp-like face, blinding her in one eye. She screamed as the salty water made contact with her exoskeleton, and she stabbed again and again at the air, the walls, and things at random as the pain coursed through her body.

Swerving and bending, dodging her stinger, Yakal scuttled away from Satal. The men with him threw their salt water on the ground and walls behind him, creating a barrier that Satal couldn't pass. Her angry buzzing filled the air, and the men flinched as the harshness penetrated their ears, but then Satal quickly sped away.

"Come on, back to the others, before she has time to retaliate," Yakal barked. Bent over with pain, he ran with the guards back through the street to the safety of the fires. But once he was inside the perimeter, he collapsed.

Nimal and Bitol hurried to remove his vest. It had been pressed so tightly into his chest that he couldn't breathe. As soon as the leather was removed, Yakal sucked in a deep breath of air and grimaced as he felt his broken ribs move inside him.

"Quickly, take him to Alom," Nimal instructed.

Yakal cried out as the men picked him up under his arms and feet and lugged him the short distance to the temple, but he passed out before Alom could examine him.

Satal

Excruciating pain coursed through Satal's body where the salt water had hit her, as she flew haphazardly through the dark streets of Mayapán. She was blind in one eye, and her left wing no longer functioned properly. She kept bumping into the walls of the nearby buildings and finally collapsed a few streets away from her encounter with Yakal. Wet and hurt, she screamed until she felt something tear in her throat.

In the darkness, she could sense the insects she had summoned advancing on her, eager to take her to Xibalba, and she hung her head, ready to join the ancestors if it stopped the pain in her body. And when torch light bounced off the walls, growing brighter as it approached, she was ready to admit defeat to Yakal.

So she looked up in surprise when Tewichinel, Yuxba', and Pataninel knelt beside her and gently wrapped her with a warm blanket. Yuxba' produced a lump of charcoal, which Satal rapidly chewed. She instantly shifted back into her human form.

Tewichinel pointed to a small litter nearby. "Come, Lady Satal, let us take you to safety."

She nodded, unable to speak. The men lifted her carefully and placed her gently on the wooden litter, and she watched as the walls of the city she had meant to conquer drifted past as they ran through the streets.

Daylight was fast approaching, and she knew the gods of Xibalba would not return for a third night, not now, not knowing what their enemies were capable of doing. She caught one glimpse of the marketplace and an area cordoned off by ropes as they passed. A cotton banner dragged on the ground, hanging from one cord still tied to an upper beam, and she strained with her one good eye to read what it said. "Meals for the needy, provided by Na'om," she whispered as she read the glyphs, and then she blacked out.

She woke to find herself on a soft ceiba-stuffed pad, dressed in a long-sleeved black shirt that had the left sleeve torn away. Her damaged arm was wrapped in bandages from the shoulder to the palm of her hand, and she could smell an odd mixture of spices and herbs emanating from the wrappings. Bandages swaddled her head, covering her left eye and part of her cheek, and she winced when she touched the corner of her mouth. She was lying under a hemp tarp that blew and flapped in the light breeze, and beyond the tent, she could see white clouds scudding across the blue sky. She twisted her head when she sensed movement behind her and smiled weakly when Tewichinel's weathered face appeared in front of her.

"My lady," he said as he bowed. "How may I serve you?"

Satal lifted her arms weakly. "Help me to sit up," she whispered. Her throat still throbbed from screaming. She smiled as Tewichinel held a mug to her lips, and she sipped the lukewarm tea. It soothed the soreness, and she smiled again. "Maltiox, my friend," she said. "Where are the others?"

"Recuperating, my lady," Tewichinel said as he knelt on the ground beside Satal's mattress. "They have some minor injuries and will recover quickly."

"And Camazotz and the other gods?"

"They returned to the Underworld as soon as they saw you were hurt, I'm afraid." Tewichinel bowed his head. "They took their servants with them, as well, leaving the city empty except for the creatures that were died or dying."

"And Kämisanel and his warriors, I suppose they've given up, too," Satal whispered. She motioned for the cup of tea and managed to bring it to her lips with her one good arm.

The shaman nodded. "I'm sorry, Lady Satal, that the battle didn't go as well as we had hoped. But given sufficient time, we can attack again."

Satal shook her head. "No, there'll be no more battles here. Yakal and the other men in Mayapán, they know what they're facing now and how to beat us." She paused and let her eyes drift shut for a moment. But all she sensed was darkness and pain. Even Sachoj was silent. She opened her good eye and stared at Tewichinel. And then she smiled, "No, we'll return to Chichén Itzá as quickly as possible and wait for the people of Mayapán to counterattack. They'll want revenge for the damage we've caused. And Yakal and the others will want to make sure I'm dead once and for all." She sipped some more tea.

"Then we must make sure you're always safe, my lady," Tewichinel said.

Satal smiled. "Don't worry, my friend. My grandson, Tz', is the key to my safety. We'll let these fools think we have him under house arrest, which will temper their attempts to kill me. But when we return, we'll take him to the cenote in front of the Akab Dzib and throw him in. If he wants to help Na'om, then let him join her in the Underworld. Maybe there he can learn some of the dark magic he's so eager to master! And if Na'om should reappear from the Underworld, her first thoughts will be to come and get him back, but she'll do nothing to protect herself if she senses he's in any danger. When she's at her most vulnerable, we'll attack and crush them all." She lay back down and closed her good eye. She was exhausted, wounded beyond repair, but the pain only added fuel to her already burning desire to consume Na'om, body and soul. Once the girl's blood had mingled with her own, she knew she'd be invincible. Despite the agony, the thought brought a smile to her face.

YAKAL

When Yakal opened his eyes, Uskab was sitting a few inches away. She leaned in and gave him a long kiss on the lips, and he smiled. "Hmmm, I liked that," he said. He tried to sit up and cried out with pain as his broken ribs shifted ever so slightly despite the heavy layer of bandages wrapped around his torso.

"Good to see you're awake, my friend," a voice said, and Yakal looked up to see Nimal. Behind him were Bitol and Kubal Joron. Uskab smiled at the men and moved out of the way so they could prop Yakal up against the wall. He thanked his wife as she tucked a small pillow behind his head.

"You'll be pleased to know the battle is truly over, thanks to you," Nimal said as he crouched down to be eye level with Yakal. "As soon as Satal disappeared, so did all the creatures from the Underworld."

"What about the troops outside the walls? Have they returned?"

"Gone as well," Bitol replied. "They're many hours from here at this point; all that's left are the dead and dying. My men are burning the bodies to stop the spread of disease."

"We wouldn't have survived without your heroics," Kubal Joron said as he bowed ever so slightly to Yakal. "The entire city is in your debt. When you're well enough, we propose to honor you properly, but for now, consider this a small token of our gratitude." Kubal Joron clapped his hands, and two young boys appeared, carrying covered baskets in their hands, which they set down on the floor near Yakal.

"What's all this?" Yakal said as he pointed to the containers. He moved to lift one of the lids, but the effort caused him too much pain.

"Matz' and I collected some tribute from our friends. If not for you, we wouldn't be here."

Yakal shook his head and pushed at the closest basket with his foot. "Maltiox, but I don't want it. Use it to repair the city and to repay those who lost everything in the attack. I'm just glad to be alive, thanks to that vest you loaned me," he said as he smiled at Nimal.

Nimal grinned. "Thank the gods it was sufficient to ward off Satal. I'll have a new one made as soon as the tanners are back to work. We'll leave you to rest, then."

The group moved away, and Yakal spent the rest of the day and evening resting with Uskab and Mayibal by his side.

By morning, he felt well enough to walk, and with Uskab's help, he hobbled outside and breathed in some fresher air. But the winds still smelled of burnt fur and flesh, and the acrid smoke of charred plaster, rocks, and wood. He looked about the parade grounds, at the blackened circles where the bonfires had raged just a short time before, and shook his head as the images of the past few days flashed past his eyes. He knew it would take the city quite a while to recover, but already there was energy in the space that whispered of momentum forward. He could see women tending to children in the bright daylight and stirring pots of food for those who were hungry. The wounded and those well enough to move were sitting in the sunshine, soaking up the vitality the sun provided. Down the street, groups of warriors searched each structure that remained standing, removing human bodies that had been trapped inside, which they placed on litters to be carried away for burning outside the walls. Others used flat scoops hastily carved from planks of wood to scrape up the hundreds of dead insects, rats, bats, snakes, and monkeys that littered the ground everywhere Yakal looked. These were tossed into fires burning on almost every street corner. More soldiers came behind, marking the buildings deemed beyond repair with a red spot so they could be torn down later.

Yakal wrapped his arm around Uskab's shoulder and smiled down at Mayibal who was nestled against her chest. It felt good to hold them,

316 RISE OF THE JAGUAR WOMAN

to know that they had survived. But despite the pleasure it brought him, he knew none of them was truly safe as long as Satal was still alive, and deep in his heart, he knew she was. *She might be badly wounded, but she won't rest until one of us is dead.* Which meant, when he was able, he needed to go to Chichén Itzá and finish what he'd started.

Tz'

Tz' was curled into a ball on a thin mattress when he heard footsteps echoing down the long passageway leading to his darkened cell. *Who is it?* he wondered. He'd spent days and days locked away, his only visitor a young boy who brought him fresh food and water to bathe with once a day. To pass the endless hours, he'd replayed the moments with Satal over and over again, looking for any place where he could have acted differently, and realized he should have been more subservient to her. *If I'd begged her to teach me, rather than been so arrogant, perhaps I wouldn't be stuck in here.* Flickering candlelight cast several shadows on the stucco walls, and three armed guards appeared outside the metal bars of his small enclosure, but they quickly stepped to one side to let Satal open the door.

Tz' hurried to stand up. "Lady Satal," he said as he bowed. He glanced upward, noticing the bandages that wrapped the old woman's face and arm. "Grandmother, you're hurt," he said as he grabbed his one stool and placed it near her. "Please, let me help you."

"Ha, you think you can win me over with a tiny bit of sympathy? I'm too old for games, boy. No, I've come to grant you your wish; you do still want to learn the dark arts, don't you?"

Tz' tried to hide the surprise on his face with no avail. "Yes, yes, very much so. Tell me what I must do to make you proud of me."

Satal laughed and then turned to the guards. "Seize him!"

Tz' tried to run, but the men quickly moved into the cell and grabbed him by his arms, which they bound behind his back with a piece of sisal rope. One of the men took a short length of rope and twined it around Tz's legs, hobbling him.

"I don't understand," Tz' cried as the guards pushed him into the passageway. "Where are they taking me?"

Satal laughed again. "You'll see soon enough."

The group made their way outside and hurried down the empty streets of Chichén Itzá to the Akab Dzib. A sliver of moon was reflected in the black surface of the cenote in front of the temple, and Tz' gasped when the guards forced him to stop on the edge of the limestone well.

"You want to learn the dark arts? What better place to master them than in the Underworld! Give my regards to Na'om if you should chance to see her," Satal said. She nodded her head, and the men shoved Tz' in the back.

He screamed, thrashing and kicking as he fell, but the ropes around his feet and hands were too tight. He hit the black water chest first and instantly sank, headed toward the deep gloom of the bottom. He landed on his side in the soft mud, his arms stretched out in front of him. He clawed at the silt, but the more he moved, the deeper he sank, and he quickly lost his ability to see in the murky water. He let a few bubbles escape from his mouth, then continued to thrash about, hoping the ropes so tightly bound about his hands would suddenly loosen.

"Na'om, can you hear me?" Tz' prayed. "I need your help!" But there was no answer. Tz's last thoughts just before he blacked out were how he'd never learn to shape-shift, and worse, he'd never see Na'om again.

Na'om

Something kept pecking at Na'om's foot. She kicked out and the jabbing stopped, only to start again a few minutes later. She jerked her foot away, heard a strange *sqwoak*, and felt a slight rush of wind on her lower bare leg. A heaviness pressed down on her upper thighs and belly, and when she moved, some of the weight slid off her to one side. She took a deep breath of air; it smelled fresh and salty. Bright light danced on her closed eyelids, and for a moment, Na'om couldn't open her eyes. They were glued shut with a thick layer of scratchy sand that rolled between her fingers as she rubbed it away. Cautiously, she opened her eyes a tiny slit and blinked multiple times against the brilliant light.

In the sudden glare, everything looked white, too white, with no defining outlines. It was all just vague and blurry shapes, and she quickly squeezed her eyes shut again. The last things she remembered were being swept along inside the narrow tunnel in a flood of dirty rainwater, losing touch and sight of Ek' Balam, and then banging her head and arm on a big rock. She reached up to her forehead and winced as she felt a lump above her temple. Covering her left eye with one hand, she squinted with her right, which rapidly watered from the painfully intense light. Na'om sneezed several times in quick succession, and her head instantly pounded with pain at the sudden movement. She groaned, shifted her weight, and finally grasped that her body was half-buried in sand, which she tried to push away. Throbbing raced up her right arm. A large gash stretched from the back of her hand almost to her elbow. A dense covering of sand had stemmed the blood, but Na'om knew she'd need to clean the wound before any infection set in.

She lay back down, overcome with pain and exhaustion, shutting her eyes against the sheen of light. Shadows and shapes instantly filled her mind as she drifted in and out of consciousness. They came at her from all directions, moving in and out of her vision so quickly that she was unable to decipher who or what they were. Then one image popped into clear view; Satal was being carried in a litter surrounded by a dozen shamans dressed in their ceremonial jaguar skin robes and quetzal feather headdresses. Na'om gasped at the sight of her one true enemy and woke up. Several hours had passed; the light was no longer directly overhead, but her head still pounded as she squinted to see her surroundings.

Several feet away, small waves swished in and out along a shoreline, and beyond them was a stretch of blue water longer and wider than she could have ever imagined. Brushing away clumps of damp sand that clung to her tattered skirt, she struggled and sat up to get a better look. The motion caused a flock of large black-headed birds with red beaks and gray and white feathers to take flight. They skimmed away along the water's edge, just inches above the crest of waves. Through her interlocked fingers, which blocked some of the sheen off the bright blue waves, Na'om watched the endless cycle of the water as it moved back and forth on the shore. The action was mesmerizing and soothing, and Na'om took in deep breaths with each incoming wave and exhaled with each outgoing one, as she waited for her headache to subside. Eventually, it faded to a dull ache, and as her eyes adjusted to the constant light, she looked even more closely at her surroundings.

She was sitting in a smooth pile of damp sand and dirt. Her entire body and what remained of her huipil and skirt were covered with a thick layer of it, turning her dirt-encrusted skin a strange shade of pale white. Clumps of sand clung to the strands of her snarled and knotted long black hair. Small bird tracks crisscrossed the area near her feet, and she suddenly knew what had been pecking at her. She lifted her one foot and could see random small marks in the layer of sand and grime that encased it. Twisting her upper body, Na'om peered over her shoulder and saw an oval black opening in the sand dune several feet behind her. She shivered at the sight of it and quickly turned again to look at the pure white sand and the line of waves and blue water in front of her that curved out of sight to the left and right. *That must be the ocean that Tikoy talked about when he was in the village,* Na'om thought as she continued to look at the water. *Nothing else could be so big.* Thoughts of Tikoy sent Na'om's mind racing back to the moment when he and the other spirits had helped her pass through the house of obsidian knives. *I wish I knew what happened to them all,* Na'om thought, and then she quickly pushed those memories away. That trial was behind her, there was no sense dwelling on the past. Then it finally struck her. *If that's the ocean, then we survived!*

Elated, Na'om tried to jump to her feet, but was too weak even to stand. She knelt in the sand, her hands out in front to steady herself. Her body swayed in the slight breeze, and she felt close to fainting. Any sudden movement caused a rush of pain in her head. She took deep breaths to calm her queasy stomach and half-crawled to a broken tree branch lying nearby. Planting the end of it firmly in the dirt, she used the stick to support her weight as she pushed herself slowly upward until she was standing. She swayed on her feet while sunlight bounced off every particle of sand, causing instant pain to her head and eyes. Clutching the branch firmly with one hand, she used the other to shield her eyes from the glare and looked in the immediate area for any sign of Ek' Balam. *His black fur should be quite visible against all this white,* Na'om thought as she started to limp and hobble slowly down the beach. Every few steps, she had to stop and take deep breaths to ease the pounding in her head. After twenty feet, with still no sight of Ek' Balam, she dropped to the ground, too tired to continue. She needed food and water and a place to get out of the overly bright sun. She knelt for several minutes in the hot sand, her head lowered toward her chest, mustering enough energy to get up again.

Worried that she had gone the wrong direction, Na'om shuffled back to where she had been. She limped past the entrance to the tunnel, turning her head to avoid looking at the area. She staggered two dozen paces farther, but still saw no sign of Ek' Balam. Panic began to build, and Na'om could feel her heartbeat drumming rapidly in her chest. *Where is he? Itzamná, what happened to him?*

Tucking the stick under one arm, she wrapped her hands around her eyes, creating a tiny tunnel through which to look. She scanned the whole beach, looking for anything that might remotely indicate Ek' Balam was nearby. But there was nothing. *Maybe he didn't make it out of the tunnel.* With dread, Na'om wobbled back to the dark hole in the sand dune and cautiously approached the entranceway. Her skin prickled with sudden cold the closer she got to it, but she could see there was nothing inside. Then she looked down at the damp sand and noticed large paw prints leading away from the passageway and into the dunes behind the tunnel opening.

On her hands and knees, Na'om scrabbled up through the soft sand, following the tracks, but quickly lost sight of any more in the sandbanks behind the cave. The area was covered with small creosote bushes, tufts of thick grass, and thorny, scrubby ceiba trees similar to the ones she had wandered through when she had first approached the city of Mayapán. The ground sloped downhill from where she knelt, and she could see pools of dark blue water in among the bushes and shrubs. Balancing on her knees, she panned the surrounding area for signs of movement, but there was no sign of the jaguar. "Ek' Balam!" she shouted, but her throat was dry, muting her voice, which was swiftly carried away by the light breeze. She swallowed several times, trying to bring some moisture to her mouth. "Ek' Balam!" she cried. She cupped her hands around her mouth and tried yelling again. There was no sign of him in the tangle of brush and bushes that grew all over the dunes. Exhausted, she sank to the sand and almost gave in to the wash of exhaustion that flowed through her.

Dejected, Na'om hobbled down to the water's edge, but one taste of it told her it was far too salty to drink. Spent, she sank into the damp sand. She dropped her walking stick and curled into a ball, floating on the edge of consciousness. Her mind swirled around and around, circling an image that grew brighter as she concentrated on it. It was Tz', sitting cross-legged on the ground under a lime tree, reading an old book. Waves of intense longing flooded Na'om, and she ached to join Tz' and tell him how she felt, but something poked her in the foot, and she came to, instead.

"Argh, go away you stupid bird," she sputtered as she wearily waved her hand in the direction of her foot. Something poked her again, and Na'om opened one eye. The sight in front of her caused her to jerk upright.

An older woman dressed in a pale green shirt and skirt with a long stick in her hand stood a few feet away.

Startled, Na'om tried to stand, and the woman backed away from her. "Wait," Na'om croaked. Her throat burned from all the screaming she had done. "Water, do you have any water?" Na'om whispered, as she scrawled forward. "You must help me," she begged the woman.

"Who are you? Where did you come from?" the woman asked.

Too weak to answer, Na'om pointed back toward the cave entrance in the sand. She heard the woman gasp and saw her move several more steps away as she began to mutter to herself.

"I don't mean you any harm; I thought you were another bird pecking at my foot." Na'om stopped as a wave of dizziness hit her. She took a deep breath, dropped her hands in the sand, and begged the woman to help her. Several minutes passed, and Na'om was just about to raise her head when she felt a tap on her shoulder. The woman had touched her with the long stick.

"You say you came from there?" she asked as she pointed with her hand toward the cave.

"Yes, I don't know how long I was underground, but yes, I woke up to find myself a few feet from the mouth of the tunnel," Na'om said. "How did you find me?"

"I heard someone yelling and came to investigate. Was someone else with you in there?" the woman said as she pointed again at the cave entrance.

"Yes, well, my friend, but he's a jaguar, a black jaguar . . . ." Na'om stopped talking when she saw the woman move several steps backward and then glance quickly all around her. "Please, don't go." She held out her sand-encrusted hands. "I swear by Itzamná that I mean you no harm, I just need water and food; it's been so long since I've eaten."

With a final look at the dark passageway, the woman motioned for Na'om to stand. "You must go into the water and stay there until I return," she said. "I'll bring you food and water, but you must do as I say; otherwise the gods of the Underworld will follow you out here into the light." She shuddered and pointed with the stick to the ocean. "Quickly now, into the water with you." She brandished the stick as if she might hit Na'om with it, so Na'om staggered into the waves up to her knees.

The instant her body came in contact with the salt water, froth and foam began to boil all around her. Startled, Na'om turned to go back to shore.

"No, no," the older woman cried as she motioned for Na'om to stop walking. "Hurry, you must get all the way in; the salt in the water is drawing out all the poisons in your body." She flicked her hand, and Na'om let an incoming wave break on her. The water bubbled and fizzed all around her, and she stood up sputtering as foam continued to form on her face even as the water drained away.

"Stay there, don't move, I'll be back as quickly as I can," the woman cried as she began to hurry down the beach.

"Wait, where are you going?" Na'om cried. She was terrified the woman was an apparition and that she'd never see her again. She began to wade toward shore, but something in her mind made her stop and obey the woman's orders. She watched the woman grow smaller and smaller and eventually disappear around a bend in the beach. Minutes passed, and there was no sign of anything or anyone except a group of bright pink-feathered birds that flew by. Na'om stared at them in wonder as she had never seen such a glorious color in a bird.

She continued to splash and swim about in the warm water, but was dismayed to see that once the foam settled, all the water around her had turned a murky black. She moved away from the area, and right away, the clear water began to boil and bubble.

"Good, good, it's working," a voice cried, and Na'om turned to see that the woman had returned. She had a large pack basket on her back and carried a water gourd in her hand.

Na'om splashed toward shore, but stopped in ankle-deep waves when the woman held up her hand. "Remove what's left of your clothes and let them float out to sea. I've brought you something to wear once you're clean. Then take a shell and scrape off as much of the mud and dirt as you can." She paused as she rummaged around in the pack basket and held up a smaller basket. Reddish liquid dripped from the bottom of it. "I'm going to hand you this container of fresh salt and a piece of cloth," the woman said. "Once you've scraped your skin, rub the salt paste all over your body and through your hair, then take the cloth and scrub yourself as hard as you can. With the help of all that is good in the world, you might be able to rid yourself of the taint that stains your skin." She stretched out her hand, and Na'om awkwardly grabbed the basket before it fell into the water.

She placed the container of deep pink salt crystals on the wet sand in between her feet, stripped off the once-beautiful blue embroidered outfit that Ajkun had so carefully made for her, and flung the torn and jagged pieces of cloth out into the ocean. One large wave caught them and seemed to swallow them whole. She picked up an empty clamshell and worked the rough edge of the shell up and down her body, scraping off the layers and layers of blood, guano, entrails, and dirt that had accumulated while she was underground. The globs of grime dropped into the water where they hissed and bubbled before disappearing. She was dismayed to see how thin she was; her ribs were clearly visible underneath her skin, and her hipbones jutted out too far. *Itzamná, how long have I been gone?* she wondered as she began to rub the salty blood-red paste all over her skin. Using her left hand, she worked the mixture into her tangled hair. Lumps of the wet paste fell off as she bent and moved and the water roiled around her feet. When the basket was empty, Na'om took the soft cotton cloth in one hand, and beginning with her hair, she scrubbed and rubbed it. Droplets of sand and dirt fell into the ocean and changed the water to a bubbling, frothy black. She slowly worked her way down her body, balancing on one foot to scour the opposite leg and foot, then switching to the other side when she was done. She carefully scrubbed around the cut on her arm and was relieved to see that it wasn't as serious as she had first feared. When she had worked the reddish paste deep into her skin, she waded out until the water was chest high and dunked under the incoming waves, letting the surf rinse through her hair time and time again. She scrubbed her whole body again with the cloth, washing away the thick salt paste. When she finally felt clean, she realized she felt lighter, happier, and her headache had disappeared. Using what little energy she had left, she pushed through the waves toward shore.

As she emerged from the water, the late afternoon sun glinted off her wet bare skin, and Na'om stopped moving as she caught sight of her arms. They were covered with an intricate pattern of dark brown spots outlined in irregularly shaped brownish squares. She rubbed at the skin, but the delicate lines remained. Then she looked down at her small breasts and thin waist; they were also covered with the design. She raised each leg and was shocked to see the same shapes. She touched her face, but though she could only feel the four scars that ran from her eye to the corner of her mouth, she knew she must have the same pattern there as well. *What's happened to me?* She looked again at her brown arms and the arrangement of the pattern; the brown ragged-edged rosettes looked like ink on her skin. *Or like Ek' Balam's spots when he lies in the sun,* Na'om thought. Anxiety filled her as she realized she had yet to find him. She sloshed toward shore, eager to continue the search for the jaguar.

The woman had kept pace with Na'om as she'd moved through the water and was waiting for her with a large, slightly torn, white towel at the water's edge. She gasped when she saw Na'om's naked body and almost dropped the cloth in her haste to give it to her. As Na'om quickly wrapped it around her etched body, she watched the woman glance back and forth between her and the entranceway to the tunnel. Then as Na'om stepped onto dry sand, the woman fell to her knees in front of Na'om and placed her head on her outstretched hands.

"No, no, don't do that," Na'om cried as she bent down next to the woman. She gently touched the woman's shoulder. "Please, please, get up," she cried as she tried to lift the woman under her elbow. But she had no strength in her limbs and sank to the wet sand. "I want to thank you for helping me," she said, looking up at the woman as she got to her feet by herself.

"You carry the marks of the most powerful spirit. Who are you?" the woman asked as she shifted her weight and then stepped backward.

"My name's Na'om, and I live in a village far to the south of here. I promise to tell you my story, but first, I need water and food." Na'om eagerly took the gourd that the woman held out to her and drank some of the juice. She had forgotten how sweet mangoes tasted, and she licked her lips to savor the drops that clung to the corner of her mouth. She tilted the gourd to drink some more.

"Easy, child, don't drink too much at once or your stomach will protest," the woman said.

Reluctantly, Na'om stopped before she gulped any more of the sugary juice. She knew the woman was right and instead took several small sips. "Maltiox," Na'om said as she handed the gourd back to the woman.

"Come," the woman said. "I live just around that bend," she said as she pointed down the beach.

Na'om followed the line of her outstretched hand, squinting against the late afternoon sun that reflected off the water and sand. Several hundred feet away, she saw a group of birds pecking at the sand near the water's edge. Suddenly, a black shape darted across her line of sight, coming from the sand dunes and headed right toward the birds. "Ek' Balam," she shouted and hobbled toward the jaguar. The flock took flight, and Ek' Balam stopped and looked in Na'om's direction.

"Sorry, boy," Na'om said as she stumbled up to the cat and hugged him. "I thought I'd lost you," she cried as she rubbed him behind the ear. She glanced behind her and saw the older woman standing at a safe distance, her pack basket on her back, her gourd on its string hanging off one shoulder.

"This is your friend who came out of the tunnel?" the woman shouted.

"Yes, he won't harm you," Na'om said. She motioned with her hand for the woman to come closer.

"You must take him into the water with you," the woman said while still standing at a safe distance. "He needs to be cleansed, too."

Na'om sighed and dropped the towel on the damp sand. "Come on, you heard what she said," Na'om said as she pushed Ek' Balam with her hands. He turned his big head and looked at her with his yellowish-green eyes. Na'om nudged him, and together the two entered the water. It frothed a bit around Ek' Balam, but didn't turn black or roil about as it had when Na'om had been in the ocean.

"Nothing's happening," Na'om shouted above the noise of the surf.

"He's a spirit animal, it's to be expected, but one must always be sure," the woman said. She held out the towel. "Come, it's getting late, and I need to check my drying fish." She handed the towel to Na'om, who quickly wrapped it around her chilled body.

"My name's Kärinik," the woman said. She handed Na'om the gourd. "Drink, the juice will give you strength."

Na'om nodded and took a swig of the liquid. Then, leaning on her stick, she fell into step beside Kärinik. The two walked slowly without talking, Ek' Balam pacing beside Na'om. Every few minutes they paused so Na'om could catch her breath. She kept looking all around her as they walked; she couldn't believe how beautiful the world looked. The slowly setting sun had turned the clouds alternating shades of pink, purple, and gold against the sapphire-blue sky, and the ocean reflected the colors in the crest of the waves. The breeze was still warm, the towel was soft against her bare skin, and she could feel the energy of the mango juice beginning to flow throughout her body. Overwhelmed with gratitude for being alive, Na'om felt tears well up, and tried to wipe them away before Kärinik could see them.

Kärinik stopped walking and tentatively placed her hand on Na'om's arm. "Go ahead and cry, child," she said. "With the help of Itzamná and all the gods, you've just been reborn. If that doesn't warrant a few tears, I don't know what does." She held out her arms as Na'om sobbed.

Na'om stepped into the older woman's embrace and felt her wrap her strong arms around her. She wept again at the warmth of another person's touch. "You, you remind me of my ati't," Na'om said as she snuffled and tried to control the steady stream of tears that ran down her face. Suddenly embarrassed at her outburst, Na'om stepped awkwardly away from Kärinik.

Kärinik smiled at Na'om. "My grandchildren are younger than you, but you're welcome to call me 'Ati't,' if you like." She shifted the basket on her back and looked at the darkening sky. Rainclouds were rapidly building on the horizon.

"I have to hurry and collect my drying fish before the rains come," she said and started to jog.

Weak as she was, Na'om half-ran next to her. Ek' Balam loped beside the two women, down the beach, and around the corner. Then Kärinik headed inland, following a narrow path worn into the sand. As they crested a sand dune, Na'om saw Kärinik's hut tucked underneath several coconut trees several hundred yards from the ocean with the open doorway facing the sea. Fresh palm fronds covered the roof, and the walls gleamed with a new coat of whitewash that glowed peach-yellow in the setting sun. Yellow and orange nasturtiums grew in ceramic planter boxes placed along the length of the one-room hut, and a pile of coconuts in their greenish husks lay off to one side. In the neatly swept courtyard in front of the house, Na'om could see several tall, pyramid-shaped racks full of drying fish. They hung from pieces of twine tied to wooden crosspieces and were all shapes and sizes. Just the sight of all that food made her stomach cramp with hunger, and she swallowed several times to ease the pain.

Suddenly, the wind shifted, bringing with it the smell of the drying fish. Without hesitation, Ek' Balam pushed past Na'om and streaked down the path. He jumped on the nearest rack, knocking it over.

Kärinik screamed and ran toward Ek' Balam. "Get away from there," she shouted as she swung her walking stick at the jaguar.

His mouth full of semi-dried fish, Ek' Balam uttered a low growl, but slowly backed away from Kärinik, dragging the remains of a two-foot barracuda with him.

"Wait, stop," Na'om shouted as she saw Kärinik swing the stick again. "He doesn't mean any harm; it's just been days since we've eaten anything." Na'om stopped talking when she saw Kärinik had dropped the stick and was trying to pick up the rack. "Let me help," she said as she strained to lift one side of the wooden structure. It was too heavy with all the dogfish, barracuda, and killifish on it.

Na'om sat back on her heels and watched Kärinik sort through everything on the ground. Those that were covered with sand she tossed toward Ek' Balam, who warily grabbed another of the barracudas and dragged it several feet before lying down to eat it.

Without saying a word, Kärinik went into the hut and returned with a large basket. She swiftly untied the fish still attached to the structure and placed them into the basket. When the wooden frame was empty, she righted it and then began the slow task of rehanging each piece on a wooden crosspiece.

"I'm so sorry," Na'om said as she handed a fish to Kärinik. The woman didn't say a word, just took the piece of twine, and wrapped it securely around the frame so the fish hung down between the wooden supports.

Finally, when they'd all been rehung, Kärinik motioned to a pile of older palm fronds. "Help me lash those on top of all these racks, just in case it should rain tonight, although I doubt now that it will." She looked up at the sky and Na'om followed her gaze. The dark clouds on the horizon had disappeared, and Na'om could see the sun beginning to set in the ocean.

"It's so beautiful," Na'om said as she handed Kärinik a frond. "Living in the jungle, surrounded by tall mahogany trees, we don't see the sun go down like this."

Together, the two women battened down the remaining racks of fish, and Kärinik motioned for Na'om to enter the hut. She stopped in the doorway. "Your jaguar, what do you call him, Ek' Balam, he must stay outside."

Na'om nodded and went back outdoors. She shuffled slowly over to Ek' Balam, but as soon as she approached, she could see he was fast asleep, a half-eaten dogfish lying right beside him.

"I don't think you have to worry," she said and smiled at the older woman as she entered the hut.

While Kärinik rummaged in a small wooden trunk, Na'om looked around the large room. A hammock was strung across one corner; in another were two small stools and a table made of pieces of wood lashed together with twine. Wooden shelves were fastened to the back wall and held a variety of baskets, gourds, cotton sacks, and leather bags. Intermingled with this were all kinds of seashells in a rainbow of colors. Na'om wandered over to look at them more closely, as she had never seen such an assortment of shells before. She turned around when the lid of the trunk dropped back into place.

Kärinik held a white huipil and skirt out to her. "It's my daughter's old outfit that she wears sometimes when she comes to help me with the fish," she said. "Put it on while I make us some supper."

"Maltiox," Na'om replied. She draped the old towel on one of the stools and pulled on the skirt. It started to slide off her thin body, so she held the extra fabric in one hand and tied it into a knot. She slipped the soft cotton shirt over her chest where it hung down below her waist, and she quickly tucked the shirt into the skirt to help hold it up.

"Itzamná, you are thin," Kärinik said when she turned and saw Na'om. "Sit child, rest, while I heat up this shark stew."

Na'om was glad to sit down at the table, and she watched as the woman hurried outside with a large earthenware pot. She returned a few minutes later and placed a gourd on the table and two ceramic mugs. "Have some more juice while we wait for that to warm." She handed Na'om a mug and sipped at her own cup.

"So, how long were you underground?"

"I don't really know," Na'om said. "I fell into the cenote on the first day of the Wayeb."

Kärinik choked on her mango juice and started to cough. When she could breathe again, she said, "On the first day of the Wayeb? But that was many, many moons ago . . . ."

"What?" Na'om cried. "How can that be? I thought we'd been gone a few days, that's all. Isn't this the beginning of the rainy season?" Tears welled in her eyes, and she brushed at them with one hand.

"No child, that ended some time ago; we're only a few moons away from a new Wayeb cycle." She patted Na'om on the hand. "Where was this cenote?"

"In Mayapán," Na'om whispered.

"Itzamná, then you don't know what's happened," Kärinik said.

"What? You must tell me."

Kärinik touched Na'om on the shoulder as she stood up. "Tomorrow, after you've rested. Shh, don't cry; some food and some sleep will do you wonders." Kärinik fetched the stew and set the pot on the floor near the table. She filled a large coconut bowl with the steaming hot fish mixture and set it on the table in front of Na'om.

"Eat now and then you must sleep. I'll tell you what little I know in the morning."

Na'om nodded, but didn't say a word. Her mind was racing with the idea that she'd been gone for so long. *What has happened to Ati't and Chiman and Tz'? Are they still in Mayapán or did they return to Pa nimá? I have to find them so they know I'm still alive. It doesn't matter what this woman thinks; I must go to them.* She started to rise from the table.

"Where are you going?" Kärinik asked as she hurried to Na'om's side. She grabbed Na'om's left arm and forced her to sit back down.

Na'om struggled against her. "Stop, let me go. I need to get to Mayapán and then back to my village. My grandmother and friends will think I died long ago; I have to find them."

"You need to eat before you fall over," Kärinik said as she pushed Na'om into her seat. "After you've had a few weeks' rest and food, then we can talk about traveling to Mayapán. By then, it might be safer to travel there. But you won't survive the trip if you don't get some food on those bones." She pushed the bowl of shark stew toward Na'om.

"You're right, I do need food," Na'om replied as she picked up a spoon carved from coconut shell. She took a bite of the thick soup; it was salty from the shark and filled with chunks of manioc root and other vegetables she didn't recognize. Eagerly, she ate another couple of bites, but then had to stop as her stomach, empty for so long, began to complain. She sipped the broth and then pushed the bowl away. "It's delicious; I just can't eat any more."

Kärinik nodded. "Let me clean that wound on your arm and then you should rest. You've been through so much."

Worn out and on the verge of tears, Na'om climbed into the hammock, and Kärinik covered her with a thin cotton blanket. She gently pushed the hammock, and it rocked slightly. Na'om felt her eyes begin to close, despite all the questions she still had. She heard Kärinik move back toward the table. "Wait, please don't go," Na'om cried as she struggled to sit up in the still moving hammock.

Kärinik hurried over to Na'om. "I'm right here, and I'm not going anywhere," she said as she tucked the blanket back up around Na'om. "Now, close your eyes, and in a little bit, I'll join you in that hammock. But first, I need to finish eating and clean up the dishes." She pushed the hammock again, setting it swaying, and Na'om drifted off into a deep, deep sleep.

In the middle of the night, Na'om woke in the pitch darkness, crying out in fear. Visions had swarmed through her mind, coming at her from all directions. She'd seen Tz' in a small temple on top of a pyramid, and his skin was stretching and cracking all over his body. Then, Ajkun and Chiman were locked in an embrace on one of the many paths connecting the village to the river. Suddenly, she was outside the gates of Mayapán, watching as soldiers dressed in leather battle gear marched in rows of ten men abreast on the top of the sacbé. Then she'd been battling Camazotz again, only this time Satal was standing next to the giant bat god. She'd grown in size and shape until she towered over Na'om. Regardless of what energy Na'om sent in their direction, they were able to dodge her missiles. Slowly, Camazotz and Satal stepped away from each other. They carried a large net in their hands, which they threw over Na'om, who was immediately trapped by the heavy webbing. Although she clawed at the tough sisal cords, she only managed to get her fingers tightly entwined in the netting. Frantic, she strained against the rough ropes, writhing around and around, which caused her to become more entangled. She screamed, waking herself up, and discovered her fingers were stuck in the netting of the hammock, which swayed in the dark room.

There was a quick flash of light in the far corner, and Na'om shrieked again as the huge shadow of an older woman appeared on the whitewashed wall. Her heart pounding, Na'om struggled to get up, knowing her only chance of battling Satal was outside where she wouldn't be trapped.

"Shh, child," Kärinik said as she quickly placed the single candle she had lit on the small table and hurried to Na'om's side. "There's no need to scream, I'm right here." She climbed into the hammock and wrapped Na'om in her arms. "It was just a bad dream, just a bad dream. Nothing can harm you now." Kärinik gently pushed Na'om back down into the hammock. "I'm going to make you some tea, to calm you and help you sleep. Just lie here and be still. Dawn is several hours away, and you need your rest."

Na'om just nodded her head and allowed the woman to tuck the thin blanket up around her chin. She stared at the ceiling, unable to close her eyes for fear she'd be thrown back into the same nightmare. *Satal is still alive. I have to get well enough so I can find her before she causes any more harm to my family.* Pictures of Ajkun and Chiman flooded Na'om's mind. Even though her eyes were open, she no longer saw the thatched roof of the hut overhead, but saw once again Pa nimá and the people she loved tucked safely in their beds. She felt tears slip down her cheeks and wiped at them with the blanket.

While she waited for Kärinik to bring the tea, Na'om quickly projected a protective white shield around her body and then sent her mind to search the huts for evidence of Tz'. But she couldn't find him anywhere in the village. *Where is he? Why isn't he living with Chiman?* She sent her mind out farther, into the jungle surrounding the village, but there was no sense of her childhood friend anywhere in the vicinity. Then she decided to visit her old house, knowing the sight of her own home would help calm her and give her strength. Na'om quickly pushed her spirit across the river and down the well-worn path to the magical circle of mahogany trees where she and Tz' had built her home. She paused on the edge of the clearing; the moon was bright overhead, casting few shadows, and she could plainly see her fire ring, the small bench she had built, even the spot where she had kept a wooden box to store her extra food. But the box was missing, as were several of her pots and water gourds. She stepped into the circle and instantly felt an electric tingling move up and down her spine. It filled her head with the deep buzzing she had experienced before travelling to Mayapán; it was the sound she associated with Satal. Her pulse quickened at the thought of the evil woman, and Na'om pushed her spirit rapidly toward the hut. Inside its protective walls, she would be safe from Satal's powers.

As she stepped through the doorway, her eyes quickly adjusted to the dimmer light, a result of living for so long underground. She gasped at what she saw. All her belongings that she had so carefully and lovingly placed just so in the small space had been tossed here and there. Broken bits of pots and gourds lay scattered on the floor, and her baskets of dried herbs had been stomped on and flattened into the pounded dirt floor. Her ceiba mattress was flung against one wall, its fluffy insides spilling out from several gashes in the thick cotton fabric. And then she saw the worst of the damage. The brilliant teal, deep emerald, and lime-green vines and bright golden-yellow and marigold-orange blossoms that she had so painstakingly painted on the walls had been smeared with some kind of black substance, obliterating the beautiful designs underneath. Cautiously, Na'om stepped forward and gingerly sniffed the wall. It smelled of must and decay, of wet and rot, and she knew that somehow Camazotz had been there and smeared his essence on her walls. She touched her finger to the dark goop and instantly felt a jolt of pain race up her arms.

The sensation jerked Na'om back into her body. She took a deep breath and let it out, forcing the lingering smell of that awful mess from her nose and mind. Just then, Kärinik approached with a ceramic mug full of warm tea. Na'om sat up in the gently swaying hammock and took the cup from the woman. "Maltiox," she said as she breathed in the vapors rising from the cup. The sweet smell of honey was mixed with that of chamomile and passionflower blossoms, and Na'om smiled. These were the herbs Ajkun had always served her as a child. She took several sips of the fragrant tea before handing the cup back to Kärinik. She let the woman tuck her in again and closed her eyes with a sigh. *Time enough in the morning to figure out what that vision means*, she thought as she felt the herbs begin to work their magic on her tired body.

Bright light was streaming through the open doorway when Na'om finally sat up and looked around. The wind brought the scent of the ocean and the cawing of a few birds, but otherwise, there was no sound. "Kärinik?" she called. "Are you there?" Na'om stood up and held onto the still moving hammock when she became a bit giddy. There was no answer. Na'om quickly hurried to the door and stepped out into the bright light. She winced as the sunlight hurt her eyes.

I must make some kind of hat to wear until my eyes readjust to this brightness, she thought as she hurried to the nearby bushes to relieve her bladder. As she stepped back onto the neatly swept courtyard, she noticed that the racks of drying fish had been uncovered, the palm fronds stacked against the hut. She searched the area for any signs of movement. "Kärinik?" she called again. She was answered with a wet nose pressed against the palm of her hand.

Startled, she looked down to see Ek' Balam standing next to her. She bent down and hugged him around his neck, then placed a kiss on the top of his head. "Isn't it beautiful?" she said as she stood up again. The sand dunes stretched in front of her, sloping gently down to the ocean, which lay like a blue band as far and as wide as she could see. She closed her eyes and lifted her face to the sun. "Maltiox, Itzamná, maltiox for sparing my life." Ek' Balam nuzzled her hand again. "And for saving my friend's life, too," she added. She opened her eyes and petted Ek' Balam. "Have you seen the old woman?" she asked.

As if in response, Ek' Balam turned around and headed back the way he had come. Na'om noticed a small path in the bushes that grew in the dunes and turned to follow him. But she had only walked a few feet when she saw Kärinik approaching her. The woman carried a pack basket on her back and waved to Na'om, who stopped and waited for the older woman to arrive.

"You're awake at last," Kärinik said as she patted Na'om's arm. "I was afraid I had brewed too strong a tea for you when you continued to sleep right through breakfast." She edged warily around Ek' Balam and motioned for Na'om to return to the hut. "I was just out checking my fishing nets and your friend here insisted on coming with me. I gave him a few of the smaller fish, so he's had something to eat, but we must get something in you. You are far too thin!"

Na'om was grateful to sit down at the table while Kärinik bustled about the fire ring outside. Just standing outside for that brief amount of time had worn her out.

"I hope you don't mind fresh fish," Kärinik said when she placed a plate full of small fried herring on the table in front of Na'om. She put a bowl of chopped papaya and avocado down next to it. "That's the last avocado, I'm afraid. A bit mushy, but better than nothing." She sighed as she picked up a piece of the soft fruit. "One of my favorite foods," she said as she swallowed the piece and reached for another.

"After all this time without any food, anything looks wonderful," Na'om said as she picked up the crispy fish and bit into it. The luscious taste of grease and salt mingled in her mouth, and she sighed with delight. "They're delicious," she said between bites. She ate three more before pushing the plate away. Suddenly, her stomach was full, too full. "Last night, you promised to tell me what happened in Mayapán."

Kärinik nodded. "I wasn't there to witness it, so much of what I'm about to tell you has traveled from person to person until it reached Xiat, the village where my daughter, Alixel, lives. She's the one who told me of the great battle that took place many days ago."

Na'om drew in a deep breath and held it. She was afraid to hear what Kärinik had to say.

"Breathe child, the past is in the past, and nothing can change that." Kärinik popped a piece of papaya in her mouth and chewed slowly. "They say a great army of evil creatures—rats, snakes, scorpions and the like, led by the gods of the Underworld—attacked the city during the darkest part of the night. And when daybreak came, the warriors from Chichén Itzá followed. For two nights, the men, women, and children of Mayapán held off the gods of Xibalba, and for a full day, they did the same with the men who followed Kämisanel, the head warrior of the Xiu. But hundreds were killed and hundreds more were severely wounded."

Na'om felt the greasy fish twisting in her stomach, and she hurried outside to be sick. She took several deep breaths of the salt air before standing upright again, and she wiped the corner of her mouth with her sleeve. "Satal, she's behind all of it," Na'om said as Ek' Balam came and stood beside her. She patted the big cat on the head, grateful for his faithful presence. "We must find her and make her pay for what's she done." Na'om turned at the sight of Kärinik beside her and sipped the mug of water Kärinik handed her. "I have to get to Mayapán," she said.

"There's sickness throughout the region," Kärinik said. "Healers have been called in from many areas south and east of the city to help stem the diseases. As weak as you are, you're in no condition to travel anywhere, especially into an area filled with illness."

"But my family, my friends, I must know if they are all right," Na'om said. "And more importantly, I must find the woman who's behind it all and destroy her. Only with her death will the people be healed." Na'om turned her back on the vast ocean and pointed into the scrubby dunes behind the hut. "Show me the path to this village where your daughter lives. Once I'm there, I'll find someone to guide me the rest of the way." She patted Ek' Balam again.

"You'd get lost among the warren of lagoons before you got halfway there," Kärinik said. "And your family is probably safe in the village you came from. I'm sure they must have returned to it as soon as the rivers were passable." She wrapped Na'om in her arms, cradling the girl against her chest. "Shh, it'll be all right. If you need to leave, then I'll go with you."

Na'om looked up and smiled wearily at the older woman. "You're sure you want to get involved?"

"I made that choice when I found you on the beach; I'm not turning my back on you now. Besides, I can visit Alixel and her family along the way. Come and sit, child, and tell me of this woman you spoke of. If I'm to help, I must know who my enemy is." She led Na'om to the nearby coconut trees. Na'om's legs trembled as she half collapsed onto the sand.

Kärinik noted her lack of strength. "You must give yourself a day or two to recuperate before you talk of seeking revenge. Do you feel comfortable telling me what happened to you?" she asked Na'om.

Na'om nodded, but still didn't speak. *Where do I start?* she pondered. *So much has happened, back in Pa nimá and while I was underground, my whole life has been one trial after another.*

"You can tell me as much or as little as you want," Kärinik said as she picked up the pack basket full of fish that she'd left in the shade.

As she watched Kärinik clean the fish, string them with twine, cover them with salt, and hang them to dry on the empty wooden racks, Na'om slowly began to tell her story. She started with meeting the jaguar in the jungle so many years in the past, receiving the scars on her face, and of raising Ek' Balam from a kitten to an adult cat. Then she rushed to tell Kärinik how she'd been shunned from the village because of her prophetic dreams, then the attack on the village, and finally her battle with Satal, which ended with them both in the cenote of Mayapán.

"Satal is this woman you spoke of earlier, who you think is responsible for the attack on the city?" Kärinik said as she washed her hands in a bowl of clean water. She threw the contents into the bushes.

Na'om nodded, suddenly too weary to speak.

Kärinik waved her hands over the turtle shell full of fish guts and a cloud of flies flew upward. "I must go bury these," she said as she headed to the hut for a digging stick. "But I want to hear the rest of your story when I return."

Na'om watched the older woman balance the large shell on one hip and use the stick as a cane to walk through the soft sand dunes. She stopped a hundred paces from the hut, scratched out a hollow with the fire-hardened point on the stick, dumped the fish guts in it, and rapidly covered it with sand. Using more fresh water, Kärinik rinsed the turtle shell and left it in the sun to dry before sitting next to Na'om.

"You believe Satal has the ability to summon the gods of the Underworld?"

Na'om nodded. "When I was underground, I spoke to One Death and some of the other gods who guard the sacred fire. . . ." Na'om shuddered at the thought of the talking skeletons and how their bones clicked as they moved about the vast underground chamber. "They told me Satal is alive, which means she's more powerful than I suspected. But to survive the fall into the cenote, she had to have help. If the visions I've had are as true as all the others, then one of her allies is Camazotz."

"The bat god." Kärinik shook her head. "It will take more than an army of wounded men to conquer her, I'm afraid."

"Which is why Ek' Balam and I must get to the city. Hopefully our combined powers are enough to destroy the evil that Satal has pressed down upon the land." Na'om sighed. Suddenly, she didn't know if she had the strength to fight Satal again.

Kärinik turned and knelt in front of her, lifting her chin with her fingertips. She looked deep into Na'om dark brown eyes. "Don't despair; she may have gained strength these many moons, but you have as well. I doubt even the highest shamans have ever heard of a person who could pass the many tests of the Underworld and live to tell the story. The shamans talk about the Hero Twins and claim they were able to perform that feat, but they are only stories, as far as I know. Yet, here you are, living proof that it's possible, which makes you extremely strong. Your battle is between good and evil, and good always prevails, always. Promise me that whatever happens, you'll remember that." She stopped and waited for Na'om to speak.

Overwhelmed by the woman's confidence, Na'om felt tears leak from the corners of her eyes. "I promise," she said as she brushed away the droplets that ran down her cheeks. "Maltiox for believing in me." She placed her hand gently on the older woman's arm. "If you're willing to lead the way, I'll do everything I can to repay you someday."

Kärinik nodded. "Of course." She bustled about the fire ring and set a pot of water on to boil. "And who is Tz'?" she asked.

Startled, Na'om turned to look at the woman. She had deliberately not mentioned his name in her storytelling. "How did you learn that name?"

"You kept saying it over and over again in your sleep this morning. I suspect he's someone important to you."

Na'om nodded. "He's my childhood friend, he's the one who rescued me when I got these," she added as she touched the scars on her face. "I didn't realize how much I cared for him until I was lost in the Underworld. I need to find him; I think he's in real danger." Na'om took a deep breath, debating whether she should tell the woman that she could spirit walk. Finally, she decided she had to trust her; after all, Kärinik knew she had survived months in the Underworld, so the fact that she could spirit travel shouldn't alarm her. "I tried to find him in my village this morning, when I sent my spirit out on a quest, but there was no sign of him. I have the feeling something awful might have occurred." Even as she spoke the words, she knew she was right. In her head, she began to sense increasing pressure, and then suddenly, the awful buzzing she linked to Satal filled her mind. She gasped and clutched her ears.

"Na'om, what is it? Are you all right?" Kärinik hurried over to the girl and wrapped her in her arms. Gently, she helped Na'om stand. "Come, you've overdone it. It was foolish of me to press you for some many answers."

Na'om let the woman lead her into the hut and gratefully sank down into the hammock.

"You rest for a bit; I'll wake you when it's time for supper."

Na'om nodded and offered a weak smile. "I'll be better soon, just a short nap is all I need."

Kärinik tucked the blanket in around her. As the woman left, Na'om muttered to herself, "I have to get stronger. Tz' needs me. I mustn't let Satal destroy him," and she closed her eyes. She instantly began to dream. One vision after another engulfed her mind in such a rush that she had no chance to tell where one image ended and the next one started. She saw Yakal, covered in open sores, trembling on the floor, with Chiman by his side, Tz' fighting against Camazotz in her hut, and groups of foreign warriors who marched and fought in mock battles. Superimposed over them all was an image of Satal, a large smile plastered to her wrinkled face. As each scene was replaced with another, Satal's smile turned into a grin that stretched her mouth wide, showing her worn and yellowed teeth, teeth that threatened to snap and tear at Na'om like a mad dog ripping apart a small-eared shrew. Na'om jerked awake, listening for any sounds of danger. But all she could hear was the soft distant swoosh of the ocean as it gently swept in and out along the shoreline and the occasional clink of a mug or plate as Kärinik washed the dishes outside.

Na'om knew she needed to rest, but she was fearful of returning to the dreams. She tried closing her eyes, but instantly sensed Satal's presence again, so she pushed herself out of the hammock and tottered outside.

"Is everything all right?" Kärinik asked as she dried her hands on a towel and hurried over to Na'om. "You look so pale."

"Bad dreams," Na'om replied as she took in a few deep breaths. "I'd rather not talk about them." She wrapped herself in the blanket Kärinik handed her and sat down with her back against the hut. The afternoon sun had warmed the stucco walls, and the heat felt soothing against her skin. "How did you know about the salt water, that it would cleanse me?"

"Around here it's common practice to use salt to purify things. We eat it, use it to preserve our food, bathe with it, even burn it to cleanse the air. My grandmother taught my mother, who then taught me. I've passed the knowledge on to Alixel, but she's not as interested in learning about the herbs and plants like I was as a child. I'm afraid the old ways will be lost at some point."

"We don't have these methods where I come from. If I ever see my ati't again, I'll share it with her." Na'om was silent for a moment. *I do hope Ajkun is well.* She shook her head. *She is well; she has to be.* "Don't you get lonely, living so far away from everyone?"

"I used to, but not anymore," Kärinik replied as she dried her hands on a towel and began to cover the fish on the drying racks with palm fronds. "My husband, Chapal Kär, built this hut many, many years ago, and we loved being here together." She paused and wiped her salty fingers on the hem of her skirt. "When he disappeared, I couldn't stand to be here, so I moved back into the village, with my daughter and her children. She only had one at the time, but the house was small, and there were far too many people around, always knocking on the door to visit. I longed for the quietude of the ocean and this place, so I moved back out here several years ago and have been here ever since."

"What happened to your husband?"

Kärinik didn't answer right away, and Na'om wasn't sure the woman had heard her. "I'm sorry; that's none of my business." Na'om patted the sand next to her, and Ek' Balam came and curled up beside her. She rubbed him behind the ear, and his gentle purring mingled with the incessant swishing of the waves on the sand only a few hundred paces away. The sound was soothing, and Na'om almost closed her eyes. But she was afraid of what she might see and forced herself to stare into the horizon where the sun was slowly setting. "Why were you so afraid of the cave out on the beach?"

Finally, the woman turned from her fish and squatted down near Na'om. Her hands were covered in salt, and she brushed them together, letting clumps of the reddish salt fall to the ground. "Chapal Kär told me about that cave, many, many years ago, when we first moved out here together. He always warned me to stay away from it since caves are the known entrances and exits to and from the Underworld. I never went near it because just the thought of it terrified me. But I noticed that Chapal, despite his warnings, seemed drawn to the place. He said he was fishing beyond that area as the fish were bigger and more plentiful in that direction, and every time he returned, he did have a full basket. More and more often, though, he disappeared for longer and longer periods of time. When I questioned him as to where he'd been, he always had some excuse, but I suspected he was going to the cave. One day, Chapal said he was going to check some fish traps he had set quite a distance from here, so he packed a small basket with some food and said he'd be back late in the afternoon. I watched him walk up over that dune," Kärinik pointed with her salt-covered hand, and Na'om turned to see the path they had come in on from the beach the previous day. "He paused at the top and turned back to wave. I wanted to run after him, to tell him not to go, but of course, he would have laughed at me, so I just waved back. Then he turned and continued walking. I waited for quite some time and then snuck out on the beach and wandered down to the cave. I dreaded going near the place, but I could see my husband's footprints in the sand led to the entrance. I sat down twenty feet from the spot and waited until dark, but he never came out. He's never come out in all the years I've been here." Kärinik sighed and stood back up. She poured fresh water over her hands, rinsing them into the nearby bushes.

"I'm so sorry," Na'om said as she stood up and gave Kärinik a hug.

"When I heard your voice calling in the wind, I thought you might be him. Then when you said you had been with someone, I thought perhaps you had found him inside." Kärinik gave a small smile. "I pray to Itzamná to return Chapal to me, even after all these years." She swiped at her eyes, which were filling with tears.

"If I ever find a way, I'll bring him back to you," Na'om promised, although she wasn't sure anyone could survive for years and years in that labyrinth of tunnels or handle the ordeals she had been through. If she hadn't had the help of Ek' Balam and the ability to shield herself with protective light, she doubted she would have survived, either.

By now, the shadows had lengthened, and the early evening wind was cool on Na'om's bare legs. She looked at the dark waters lapping the even darker sand. Another day had gone by without her helping anyone, and that thought made Na'om angry. "I need to leave as soon as possible," she said as she picked up a small stick and broke it into tiny pieces. "I have to find out what's happened to my family."

Suddenly, two bats flew by overhead, and Na'om cringed at the sight of them. Ek' Balam let out a soft growl and smacked the air, bringing one of the furry mammals to the ground. She listened as he quickly crunched on the tiny bones and shivered as she remembered eating them. The other bat flittered just out of reach, swooping back and forth above their heads, and Na'om felt another shiver run up her spine.

"We'll leave as soon as you feel strong enough to travel," Kärinik said as she blew on the embers in the fire ring. She added a bundle of twigs and the blaze flared up, pushing away the gathering darkness. "But I would suggest giving yourself at least a few days to recuperate. If Satal is anything like you've described to me, she'll be stronger than before, whereas you've expended a great deal of energy just making it back to the land of the living. I wish my grandmother, Kunaj, were here now; she'd have many ideas on how to quickly strengthen you, physically and spiritually."

"You sound like you were very close," Na'om said. She watched the one bat continue to swing back and forth in the air above their heads.

"Yes, I loved spending my days with her; she was a kind person who always helped those less fortunate, even when she had little to spare herself."

Na'om nodded. She felt the same way about Ajkun. Then she had an idea. "What if I try to reach your grandmother in the Underworld? Perhaps if I call to her, she'll hear me and provide some answers."

Kärinik shook her head. "You're still too weak; a task such as that might drain away any energy you've gained in the past day." She patted Na'om's hand. "Don't worry; I haven't forgotten everything she taught me. Tomorrow, while you rest, I'll go in search of a few herbs and plants that I think might help." She carefully balanced a large ceramic pot on the three hot stones in the fire pit. "I'm afraid it's more fish soup for supper," she said as she stirred the pot with a wooden spoon. "And more tea to help you sleep."

"Anything is fine, really," Na'om replied. She continued to watch the bat as it circled about and suddenly wondered if Satal had sent it to spy on her. She didn't dare share her suspicions with Kärinik, though. "I'm a bit chilly, despite the fire," she said as she stood up and headed toward the hut. "I'll set the table while you finish heating the stew."

She took a burning stick from the fire and used it to light the beeswax candle on the table. It was only indoors, away from the prying eyes of the bat, that Na'om felt any better. As she placed two coconut bowls on the table, she smiled as she heard Ek' Balam leap into the air and smack the bat to the ground. She smiled again. *At least Satal won't get any help from that one.*

AJKUN

The moon had waxed and waned multiple times in its endless cycle since their return to the village when Ajkun and Chiman were startled awake by a loud knocking on the wall of Ajkun's hut. In the dim light of the early morning, Chiman slipped on his loincloth and hurried to lift the deerskin covering over the doorway. Lintat stepped back, lifting his tear-stained face to speak, but no words came out.

"Ajkun, dress quickly, there must be something wrong with Mam," Chiman said as he lifted Lintat into his arms. The little boy pushed his head into Chiman's shoulder, hiding his eyes.

Ajkun hurried as fast as she could through the dawning shadows to Noy's house. She found her friend rocking back and forth by the fire, her arms wrapped around her body, tears streaming down her face. Noy lifted her head and gave a wan smile to Ajkun. "Is it Mam?" Ajkun asked, but she didn't need an answer. She hugged Noy tightly and felt tears forming in her own eyes. "I'm so sorry. He was a good man." She left Noy and went into the hut. Mam's body was laid out on the bed, wrapped in a bright red cotton blanket.

"Chiman will have Tzalon and K'ale'n dig the hole for the burial," she said as she hugged Noy again. "Let me make you a cup of tea, all right?"

Noy only nodded as the sun slowly rose over the plaza.

The village gathered to say their good-byes to the older man, who was laid in a deep hole dug in the floor of Noy's hut. Chiman placed a bowl of corn kernels, Mam's obsidian knife, and his favorite pottery mug in beside the body before signaling to Tzalon and K'ale'n to cover it. Ajkun spent the afternoon with Noy and Lintat, trying to console them, but as she well knew, only time would take away their pain.

That night, Ajkun lay awake long after Chiman had drifted off to sleep. Wrapped in his arms, Ajkun listened to his deep, steady breathing. "Maltiox, Itzamná, for giving me these last few moons full of bliss. I've been so happy that my anger toward Satal has finally disappeared. I only pray that someday you'll send my Na'om back to me before I'm called to join the ancestors." She wiped away the tears that threatened to fall on Chiman's chest, kissed him lightly, and snuggled even closer.

Ajkun spent the next week with Noy and Lintat, helping them adjust to the empty space that filled their lives. She longed to visit the nursery and see the children, but knew Noy needed her more than the babies did.

But one morning, Noy surprised her by suggesting they go see the children. "I think seeing new life will help us both remember that death is part of the whole cycle," she said as she touched Lintat on his shoulder. "You'd like to see the babies, wouldn't you, Lintat?"

The young boy nodded and smiled at the two older women. "May I go ahead?" he asked.

Noy had barely given her consent when Lintat took off running down the path that led to the cornfield. "He needs to be around other children now, even little ones," Noy said as she linked her arm through Ajkun's arm. Together, the two women made their own way to the nursery.

Just once, Ajkun glanced behind her. "Stay, Sia'," she said. The female jaguar stopped in her tracks and lay down near the path, watching as Ajkun continued to walk away.

"Will she stay there until we come back?" Noy asked as she twisted her head to look at the cat.

"Probably; she keeps an eye on me unless I tell her otherwise. She won't let me touch her, but she stays close by." Ajkun shook her head. "I'm still not used to it."

The two women waved to Ajchak and Tzukunel, who were hoeing out weeds from between the tall cornstalks. The bright yellow tassels blew in the wind, sending out a sweet scent, and Ajkun smiled. "It will be a good harvest this year," she said as she paused and took a deep breath. The burned spot on the far side of the corn patch was hidden from view, and Ajkun could almost forget the tragic day that had happened, so many moons ago. "Itzamná, it's been too long," she muttered.

They continued to the row of huts and were welcomed by Sijuan, who was holding Xoral's little boy, Kab, in her arms so Lintat could see him. When the women arrived, Sijuan put Kab on the ground, and Lintat squatted next to him. He laughed when the boy crammed his fist into his mouth.

"Utzil, they've all grown so much bigger than when I saw them last," Ajkun exclaimed. She chuckled as she hurried after Lintat, who was trying to catch Kab. The chubby boy was the first of the four infants to crawl, and he was headed toward the basin Xoral had left on the ground. She scooped him up in her arms, lifting him with a bit of difficulty, but Kab gurgled and smiled as she swung him onto her hip. "Oh, you're getting to be so big," Ajkun said as she tickled him under the arm.

Noy appeared from inside the hut, with little Ali in her arms, followed by Witzik' who held Ala. The boy continued suckling as she sat down on one of the many stools near the fire pit. "All this one wants to do is eat," she said as she placed Ala on the other breast.

Tzalon quickly joined the others. Tuney, Tzalon's infant girl, was sound asleep, safely wrapped in a shawl on her mother's back. "At least my little flower here still takes her morning nap," Tzalon said.

Ajkun walked over and gave Kab to Sijuan before bending down to pick up Ali. "Come child, sit with me, and I'll give you something to play with." With a sigh, Ajkun sat on an empty stool, placing the little girl on her lap. "Utzil, I'm tired already, and the day has just begun." She pulled a smooth block of mahogany out of her skirt pocket and gave it to Ali to suck on.

The young mothers laughed. "You work too hard, Ajkun," Witzik' said as she burped Ala on her shoulder.

"I don't mind, really, I don't." Ajkun said. She smiled at the group and felt her heart swell with love for all of them. *If only Na'om were here as part of this group; she and Tz' would have a child this age by now.* She reached out and took Ala from Witzik', who needed to feed Ali. Lintat came and stood next to Ajkun, peering into Ala's deep brown eyes.

"When will he be able to go fishing with me?" he asked as he shook Ala's pudgy hand.

"Oh, not for many, many moons, I'm afraid," Noy replied.

Lintat wandered around the group, going from one mother to another to look at the children, but Ajkun could see he was growing bored. She called him over to her. "I could use a mug of cold water; do you think you can fetch some from the river for me?"

Lintat stood up straight and took the water gourd that Tzalon offered. "I'll be back faster than lightning," he said and grinned as he ran down the path to the river.

"He's well past his eighth name day," Noy said as she watched Lintat disappear from view. "Mam was beginning to teach him the things a man needs to know, but now, I don't know what will happen."

"Chiman will train him, I'm sure of it. I'll speak to him later this afternoon," Ajkun replied. She patted Noy fondly on the knee. "Don't fret, it will all work out."

All the women were engrossed in the children and failed to hear the sounds of someone rapidly approaching the cluster of homes. It wasn't until Sijuan looked up and saw her father hurrying towards the group that they realized he was near.

"Tat axel, what brings you here?" Sijuan said as she moved to give Setesik a hug.

Ajkun looked up from tickling little Tuney. "What's wrong?" she asked as she handed the girl to Tzalon and stood up.

"It's Chiman, you must come quickly," Setesik said. "He's received some bad news, I'm afraid."

Noy looked at Ajkun. "Go, I'll wait here for Lintat to come back from the river, and then we'll come find you."

Ajkun nodded and took Setesik's arm. She clutched her walking stick in the other hand, and together the two friends made their way rapidly back to the village plaza. Chiman was sitting on the temple steps, a piece of rolled fig bark paper in his hand.

He looked up when Ajkun approached. "A messenger arrived this morning with this," he said as he held up the scroll. "It's from Yakal. There's been a horrible attack on Mayapán. Many were killed and others are dying from disease and their wounds."

"What about Tz'? Does Yakal have word of him, is he all right?" Ajkun could see Yakal's broken seal on the back of the paper as she reached for it.

"He says Tz' left the city before the attack, but doesn't say where he might have gone." Chiman paused and rubbed his eyes. "The battle was led by Satal. I don't know how she survived the fall into the cenote, but from what Yakal has written, she was at the head of an army supplied by the gods of the Underworld."

"Itzamná!" Ajkun's face paled, and Setesik helped her sit down on the step next to Chiman before her legs gave out. She unrolled the parchment and read the glyphs. "Thank the gods Uskab and the baby are safe, Alom and the rest of the family, too." She continued scanning the page. "They need any medicines we can send to fight the illnesses that plague the city and the surrounding villages." She placed the scroll on the step next to her and leaned into Chiman's strong body. "Yakal's not telling us the whole story. Tz' wouldn't just leave without saying where he was going." She shook her head. "Satal is behind his disappearance, I'm sure of it." Hatred for the old woman flared in her chest.

Chiman patted Ajkun on the knee. "We don't know that for certain. He might have learned I'm not his father and gone in search of the man. Regardless, I've already sent a reply with the messenger telling Yakal I'm on my way. I'm leaving as soon as I can pack my things. I'm going to find Tz', wherever he is, and bring him home!" He turned to Setesik, who had picked up the paper and was reading it for himself, and placed his hand on Setesik's shoulder. "You'll be in charge of the village while I'm gone."

"And Pempen must look after the women and children. Noy and Sijuan can help." Ajkun said. She stared at the two men. "I'm not letting you go by yourself, Chiman!"

Just then, Noy and Lintat arrived. "What's happened, where are you going?" Noy asked.

"Mayapán was attacked by warriors from Chichén Itzá, and Satal led the way with her own army of evil spirits from the Underworld." A surge of renewed hatred poured into Ajkun's heart, causing her face to flush. "We're leaving for the city right away."

"Well, Lintat and I are going with you," Noy said. The young boy nodded in agreement.

The older woman held up her hand to stop Chiman and Ajkun from protesting. "You need all the help you can get to fight that evil woman. She took members of my village and family from me over a year ago when she sent raiders up and down the river looking for Na'om. I'll not sit here and wait while she does more harm." She patted Ajkun on the arm. "Besides, you're the closest to family that we have now, and I don't want to lose you, too."

Chiman looked at the two women and sighed. "I can see there's no sense in arguing with either one of you. Pack lightly, so we can make good speed on the river, and meet me at the water's edge as quickly as possible." He nodded to Setesik, and the two men hurried away toward Chiman's hut.

Ajkun walked to her own house and nodded to Sia', who was lying in the shade of the large avocado tree. "Itzamná, I'd forgotten about you," she said. She cocked her head to one side, wondering what to do. "You can't come with us and you can't stay here," she finally said. "Argh, I have no time for this!" She rushed inside and began sorting through all her herbal tinctures and salves in the small storeroom. She packed as many vessels as she could in her large basket, which she set by the open doorway. Then she rolled an extra set of clothes into a bundle and stuffed them into another basket, along with several bags of dried corn, beans, and fish. Ajkun took two of her water gourds, slung them over her shoulder, and headed outside with her small pack basket on her back.

Lintat and Noy were standing near the courtyard, watching as Sia' slowly rose and stretched from the tip of her tail to her shoulders. "What shall you do about her?" Noy asked.

"I don't know," Ajkun replied. She motioned toward the large basket full of her medicines. "It's heavy, but do you think you can carry it?" she said to Lintat.

The young boy nodded, bent down, and with Ajkun and Noy's help, managed to get the basket on his back. He strained under the load, but smiled. "I can do it," he said and started to walk slowly to the river.

Ajkun picked up her walking staff, linked arms with Noy, and headed toward the river as well. Sia' followed the women, and once at the water, she gave one last glance at Ajkun before slipping into the river and swimming to the other side. She shook from head to tail and disappeared into the brush.

"Well, at least that problem's solved," Ajkun said as she arranged her baskets in the bottom of the large canoe. She hugged Pempen and Sijuan, who had come with Setesik to see them off. "Oh, the children, I didn't get a chance to say good-bye!" She looked at Chiman.

"There's no time, Ajkun. The attack was many days ago, and we have many days' worth of travel ahead of us before we even reach Mayapán. Itzamná only knows what's happened to Tz' during all this time." He motioned for her to get into the dugout.

"Yes, of course, you're right," Ajkun said. But she turned back to Sijuan. "Kiss them and hug them every day for me, all right?" She felt her eyes watering at the possibility that she might never see the children again, and her throat constricted, making it difficult to breathe. She blinked several times and swiped the tears from the corners of her eyes.

"I'll tell them Ati't will be back as soon as she can," Sijuan said as she helped Ajkun get settled in the canoe. "Chuch and I will take good care of all of them."

Lintat knelt in the bow to look out for rocks, while Ajkun and Noy sat in the middle with the gear stashed between them. Chiman took the stern, and with Setesik's help, pushed the loaded dugout into the water. The three set to paddling and quickly were out of sight of those they'd left behind.

***

Ajkun sighed as the upper parts of the walls of Mayapán appeared over the treetops. They had made it. She was tired, more tired than she ever remembered being. Her arms and shoulders ached, and blisters had formed on the palms of her hands. Anxious to make the journey as quickly as possible, Chiman had them paddle far into the night, until the dark rocks were invisible in the blackness of the surrounding water, and he'd started each morning just as the sky turned pink. They'd kindled only a few fires on the entire trip, just long enough to cook a pot of beans or fry the fish Lintat had caught while traveling the river.

"Utzil, I never expected to see this place again, and certainly not this soon," Ajkun said as they stepped out from between several lime trees and headed toward the main gates of the city. Thoughts of Na'om rushed at her the closer she got to the walls, and she stopped to shake her head. She couldn't dwell on what had been when there was so much they needed to know and do. She looked around and was startled by the lack of activity on the wide sacbé in front of the gates. "Where is everyone?"

"Sick or dead," Chiman said. A frown was etched on his face, and Ajkun wondered if he'd ever smile again. He led the group to the gates and nodded to the sentry on duty. "Come on, let's find Yakal. He's been put in charge of repairing the walls, but said he goes home for lunch every afternoon."

Noy glanced around her and quickly grabbed Lintat's hand. Small groups of men hurried past them, carrying buckets of sand and stones on their shoulders or balanced on their heads. Worry and fear had carved deep lines into their faces. "You stay close to me, do you hear?" Noy said. Lintat nodded and moved to stand between Noy and Ajkun. "If this is quiet, I can't imagine what it looked like before. I've never seen so many people in one place."

Ajkun scanned the area, remembering what it had been like for her to see the thousands of people moving about on their daily tasks for the first time. But now, no children played in the shadows cast by the wall, no women carried baskets of goods to sell, and the tantalizing smells of a thousand different meals were gone. She shook her head. "It's different, but still overwhelming," she said as she linked arms with Noy.

The four hurried along the side of the marketplace, which was almost empty of vendors and buyers. An older man with no teeth offered to sell them bundles of cloth bandages, but Ajkun shook her head no, as she walked past. *There's always someone trying to make a profit on another person's misery,* she thought as she slowed and looked about. Broken poles leaned precariously into one another while ripped pieces of woven sisal tarps and coverings flapped in the light breeze. No one shouted at them to purchase a new basket, skirt, or stool for their home. Nobody offered them a bite of turkey stew or a piece of roasted manta ray. The stacks of caged birds that had filled the air with trills, whistles, and cheeps were long gone, only a pile of tiny feathers marking where they had once stood. Of the stalls that remained undamaged, many had been converted into makeshift resting places for the sick and injured. Men, women, and children lay about on remnants of woven mats or directly on the bare ground, covered by thin blankets and frayed pieces of fabric. Several women wandered up and down the rows of the injured and sick, offering them water or stopping to change a bandage. The stench of vomit and old blood filled the air, and Ajkun swallowed multiple times to keep from retching. She knew the scent of decay, and it pervaded the entire area. She shook her head and hurried after Chiman, Noy, and Lintat.

"I must find out who is in charge of helping those poor people," she said as she caught up to Chiman. "But my small basket of herbs will barely make a dent in the amount of need I see."

"Every little bit will help," Chiman said as he stepped into a side street. He waited for two men to cross in front of them. They carried a body wrapped in a dirty cotton sheet.

Ajkun watched as they turned the corner and felt a shiver go up and down her spine. "I had no idea it would be this bad," she whispered to Chiman. She glanced at Lintat whose eyes were big with fear. "I worry about the boy, seeing all this."

"He's had to grow up quickly in a very short time, first with Mam and now this. But he seems all right with everything." Chiman picked up the pace as they neared Yakal's house.

Alom was the first to spot the group as they turned yet another corner and entered the narrow alleyway by her house. She ran to embrace Ajkun, and two women smiled through their tears.

"When Yakal told me Chiman was coming, I had no idea you'd come, too," Alom said.

"I couldn't let him come by himself." Ajkun quickly introduced Noy and Lintat and could tell Alom was pleased to meet another woman of a similar age. Lintat slipped the heavy basket full of herbal medicines onto the ground and rubbed his bare shoulders. The leather straps had marked his skin, and Ajkun made a mental note to rub some salve into the sore spots.

"Come, come, you must be so tired after your trip," Alom said as she beckoned the foursome to follow her into the courtyard. She motioned to the stools near the fire pit. "Sit, please, while I get you some food and drinks." She nodded to her youngest daughter, Masat, who had appeared in the doorway to the small hut.

"Masat, it's so good to see you," Ajkun said as she gave the girl a hug.

Masat blushed, which showed off the two dimples in her cheeks. "Chuch, let me get the food, while you visit," Masat said. Alom nodded and sat down with the others.

"She's been a great help to me these past few weeks," Alom said as she followed Masat with her eyes. "She's kept the house and cooked all the food, giving me time to work with the sick and injured." She turned to Ajkun. "I don't suppose you brought any of your wonderful salves and tinctures with you?"

Ajkun smiled. "A whole basket of them, but from what we saw as we passed the marketplace, I'm not sure it will do much good."

Just then, Yakal arrived, followed by Uskab, who carried little Mayibal in a sling on her back.

"Thank the gods everyone is all right," Ajkun said as she hurried to hug the adults. She peered at Mayibal who studied her with his brown eyes. "He's gotten so big."

Uskab smiled. "We were very lucky as he managed to avoid any sickness. Many children didn't survive after the attack so I give thanks to Ixchel every day for our good fortune." She lifted the boy off her back and set him on the ground. Mayibal wobbled for a moment and then toddled on sturdy fat legs to Ajkun.

"Ati't," he said as he held out his arms.

"Utzil, how does he remember me? He was only an infant when we left!" Ajkun scooped up the sturdy boy in her arms and planted a kiss on his cheek.

"He could never forget you," Uskab said and smiled.

Chiman turned to Yakal. "I, we, want to hear the details of what happened here, and I want to know when the city is planning to counterattack. But first, I need to know what happened to Tz'."

Yakal sighed. "It's complicated. He was training with a very old shaman, a man named Najtir. Tz' was trying to learn to shape-shift, but not having any success with it, and he grew more impatient as each day passed. Najtir suspects Tz' went to Chichén Itzá to study with Satal since she is an accomplished shape-shifter, a fact we all know now. Najtir is still living in Satal's palace, so you can question him yourself." Yakal motioned for everyone to begin eating.

"There was no sign of Tz' during the attack?"

Yakal shook his head. "To be honest, I don't know. Any of those creatures could have been him, but in my heart, I don't think they were. No, I'm afraid Satal did something to him long before she came here, but I don't know what."

Chiman started to rise from his seat, his food untouched, but sat back down when Ajkun tugged on his loincloth. "Let Yakal finish telling us what happened," she said. "When will the city counterattack?" Ajkun asked.

"So far, no one has made a plan. Too many are sick or injured to think of retaliation." He held up his hand to stop Chiman before he could speak. "That doesn't mean some of us aren't thinking about it. I've already asked the shamans to study the stars to find the most auspicious time . . . ." He paused and rubbed his eyes. "But Nimal and I already know it will be several moons before any one of us is ready to confront the army Satal attacked us with."

Chiman set his bowl on the ground, and Ajkun laid a hand on his shoulder. She gave him a half-smile. "I know you want to go find Tz'. We all want to bring him home, but you can't do it alone."

Chiman sighed. "This woman has learned to read my mind." He patted Ajkun's hand. "You're right, of course, I must be patient. But I can't just sit here!" He stood up and began pacing the small area. "I want to speak to this shaman as soon as possible. He must know more than he's saying."

Mayibal waddled to Uskab and climbed up into his mother's lap. "Shh, little one, he means you no harm," Uskab whispered as she wrapped her arms around the boy.

"I'll take you there once we're done eating. And until we can muster an army, there's plenty of repair work inside and outside the city walls, plus Nimal can use help training the new recruits who arrive on a daily basis," Yakal said. "Disease has spread into the cenotes across the countryside, and almost all trade has stopped now that the city has shut down, so the people in all the small villages around here are hurting as well. They're sending any able-bodied men to build a new army. But it will all take time."

Chiman took a deep breath and let it out slowly. "Of course. I'll speak to Nimal later today, after I've met with Najtir."

Ajkun turned to Alom. "Noy and I want to help you with the sick and injured, but it's no place for Lintat."

Yakal spoke up. "He can fletch arrows with Memetik and the other boys who are too young to train as soldiers. Bitol has a whole group of young men working with Xik', the master fletcher in the city. I'm sure they could use an extra pair of steady hands."

Lintat grinned. "Mam was teaching me to carve arrows and attach the feathers before . . . well, before . . . ." His smile disappeared, and he looked down at the ground.

"Mam was my husband, Lintat's grandfather," Noy said. "He joined the ancestors a short while ago, and we still miss him dearly." She wrapped her arm around Lintat's bony shoulders and hugged him. "We mustn't focus on that now, though," she said as she stood up and dusted a few crumbs of tamale off her skirt. "There's plenty of work to do to keep us all busy, and I'm ready to begin." She looked around the group.

Ajkun was surprised to see her friend still had so much energy after the long trip. After all, she was older than Ajkun by several moons. With a grunt, she stood up and nodded to Noy. "Let's start, shall we?"

Yakal and Chiman, with Lintat by his side, left the women to work out sleeping arrangements and a host of other issues. Ajkun watched as Chiman walked away without a glance in her direction. Noy noticed as well and patted her arm in comfort. "He'll be by your side tonight, never fear."

Ajkun nodded. She knew Noy was right. That night was not the issue. She knew, once the army was ready to march, Chiman would be in the lead while she and the other women were left in Mayapán, waiting for their return. She wanted to march with him and make Satal pay for everything the witch had stolen from her. She wanted to see Tz' and know that he was all right. And she wanted to see Chiman smile again and return with him to Pa nimá. The thoughts churned in her stomach, fueling her anger toward Satal. Tension tightened her jaw and shoulders and formed a hollow pit in her belly. Then Mayibal giggled as Uskab tickled his foot, and the sweet sound of his laughter released Ajkun from her anger. Images of the children she'd left in Pa nimá flitted across her mind's eye, superimposed on the scene of Uskab with her son right before her. *We fight for the safety of the children,* she thought as she followed Noy and Alom back to the marketplace and the people who needed her immediate help.

Na'om

Na'om woke in the hut, and although she was alone, this time she didn't panic. She knew Kärinik was out checking her fish traps. *And probably collecting those herbs she mentioned yesterday,* Na'om thought. But the older woman was laying out a variety of baskets near a blanket spread on the packed sand when Na'om stepped outside.

"You're up, good," Kärinik said as she turned toward Na'om. "Any more dreams?"

"A few, but nothing I really remember; the tea helped," Na'om said. She pointed to the blanket. "For me?"

"Yes, I remembered an old ritual my grandmother taught me, a way to rid the body of any ill winds that might be lingering near it. I think it's best if we perform the ceremony now, while your stomach's still empty. We want as little as possible in your system, so the spirits that might still be hovering nearby have less to hold onto." She helped Na'om lie down on the blanket with her arms at her sides. She sprinkled white mullein and orange marigold flowers around Na'om from her head to her bare toes and then placed a ring of reddish salt crystals outside of them. Then she picked up a coconut bowl and smeared a paste of crushed lobelia blossoms and lime prickly-ash juice on Na'om's forehead. "This will help draw out any bad winds and protect you during the long journey ahead," Kärinik said as she spread a thin line of the flower paste down Na'om's arms. Then she removed several grayish, lime prickly-ash branches covered in narrow dark green leaves from a large basket nearby. She took several of the spiny branches in each hand and began to wave them back and forth in the air a few feet above Na'om's body.

"Just lie still and try to think of things that brought you pleasure back before you fell in the cenote," Kärinik said as she swept the branches from side to side and up and down Na'om's prone form. "Good thoughts will displace any malingering spirits that still cling to you."

Nodding her head, Na'om closed her eyes. She felt the gentle swish of air as Kärinik moved the branches back and forth and almost giggled as they tickled her bare skin. Concentrating, she pictured dancing with Ek' Balam while Tz' played his bone flute and of splashing water at Tz' while they played along the riverbank. These visions quickly morphed into the excitement she'd felt while building her very own hut with Tz's help, and then the calm and peace she'd experienced while drawing and painting the murals on the hut's walls. These pictures swirled about, shifting into an image of the ocean as she'd seen it when she'd first awakened on the beach. The wide expanse of blue water stretching as far as she could see and the pink and peach-streaked sky above it was a sight she would never tire of seeing. She understood now why Kärinik had returned to her hut in the sand dunes despite the lack of companionship. Even though she loved the area around Pa nimá, there was something incredibly freeing about seeing the ocean and the way it extended beyond her ability to see.

She sensed Kärinik dipping the branches lower and lower, waving them faster and faster over her body. The leaves swept her skin, brushing away any evil that had traveled with her from the Underworld. With two solid thwacks against the soles of her feet, any remnants of malevolence were driven from her body, and she opened her eyes.

Kärinik was squatting by her ankles, drinking from a gourd. "How do you feel?" she asked as she handed the juice to Na'om.

"I'm not sure; better, I think," Na'om replied as she sat up and looked around. She took a deep breath and let it out. "Definitely stronger. And hungry."

"Good," Kärinik said. "The fish I caught last week are almost dry; once they're ready for the market, we'll head to my daughter's village."

She noticed the look on Na'om's face. "It will only be a day or two more, I promise. You need the time to rest if you're going to make it to Xiat."

Na'om nodded. She knew Kärinik was right. At this point, she and Ek' Balam were both too weak to travel anywhere. But she didn't know how she was going to just sit for days at a time. She needed to see Ajkun and Chiman and let them know she was alive, and more importantly, she needed to find Tz' before Satal did any more harm to him.

Two days later, Kärinik was already awake and at work when Na'om went outside to relieve her bladder in the predawn light. The older woman was taking the dried and salted fish off the many racks that filled the small courtyard, laying each stiff fish on a blanket spread out on the ground.

"Can I help?" Na'om asked. She was anxious and excited about leaving later that morning.

Kärinik looked up and smiled at the girl. "I'm almost done, but you could get those." She pointed toward the last wooden stand. "Just add them to the pile here," she said as she dropped another salted fish onto the blanket.

Na'om nodded, and the two of them worked in silence for several minutes until the racks were empty and the cloth was filled. "Help me slide this into the hut," Kärinik said as she picked up one corner and began to pull the loaded blanket. Na'om hurried to grab the other side, and between them, they hauled the bundle indoors. "We'll take as many as we can carry and leave the rest here," Kärinik said as she began to place the fish in her empty pack basket.

Na'om nodded again. Even though she'd been resting as much as possible, she wasn't sure how much weight she could lug. She quickly grew tired just walking around the hut and down to the ocean and back. "From Xiat, how far is it to Mayapán?"

"Several days' walk for most people." Kärinik looked up at Na'om. "And if it takes longer, then that's all right, too." Kärinik paused and looked more closely at Na'om.

"What?" Na'om asked after a moment of uncomfortable silence.

"I'm not sure what to tell my family about you or those designs of yours," Kärinik said. "Or about Ek' Balam," she added.

Na'om held up her arm in the sunlight streaming through the open doorway. She'd grown so used to the patterns that covered her body that she hadn't thought about how others might react upon seeing them. "I'll tell anyone who asks the truth; what else can I do? Unless you have a better idea?"

"No, unfortunately, I don't, but I do think it's best if we keep you as hidden as possible. If we arrive at night, perhaps no one will notice." Kärinik smiled. "Come now, we must eat and head on our way." They quickly had some fresh fish for breakfast. Then Kärinik shouldered her basket before handing Na'om one of three water gourds. "That should last you until we reach Xiat, but I'll bring extra water just in case we need it." She handed Na'om a small empty basket. "We'll fill that with salt once we reach the drying pools."

As soon as the two women and Ek' Balam left the sand dunes and headed into the scrubby brush behind the hut, the air grew hotter and drier despite the earliness of the morning. Na'om looked about her, but could see no definitive trail through the endless creosote bushes, thorny acacia trees, and various grasses that grew in the sandy soil. She followed Kärinik as closely as she could past pools of stagnant salty water where flocks of pink flamingoes pecked about, scooping up small fish in their beaks that they swallowed whole. Snowy egrets and a great blue heron waded along the shoreline, and three turkey vultures soared far overhead, circling a spot hundreds of paces from where they walked. Na'om stopped abruptly when Kärinik pointed to a caiman lying near a lagoon. It was small, only four feet or so in length, but its long teeth sent a shiver down Na'om's back. Ek' Balam growled when he saw the creature, and Na'om had to hold him with both hands so he wouldn't attack.

As the hours passed, it grew progressively warmer, and it took every ounce of strength Na'om had to keep pace with Kärinik. She knew the older woman was walking more slowly than she normally did for Na'om's sake, so she tried to hurry, but she didn't have her normal stamina. They stopped many times so Na'om could regain her breath, and she saw Kärinik glance more than once at the angle of the sun.

"I'm taking too long, aren't I?" Na'om asked as they paused yet again.

"No, no, it's fine," Kärinik said. "You can only go as fast as you can go. We'll rest when we get to the salt flats, which should be the hottest part of the day."

Even though Kärinik was being nice about their progress, Na'om fretted as they walked. She had to get to Mayapán as quickly as possible and find out what had happened. She prayed to Itzamná that Kärinik was right, and Ajkun, Chiman, and Tz' were safely back in Pa nimá, but deep in her heart, she suspected something was terribly wrong. She knew Satal would not rest until she had inflicted as much damage as possible, especially to the council members of Mayapán who had accused Satal of witchcraft so many moons ago. Images of that moment at the cenote just before she had fallen in overlapped with what Na'om saw in her immediate surroundings, and she felt a pang of pain as she wondered if her father, a man she had never met, had survived the attack on the city. *If he's still alive, I'll find him and ask him to help me fight Satal. He promised he would help if I should ever need it; certainly, I can use all the assistance I can get at this point.* She stopped yet again to catch her breath and watched as Kärinik continued forward, oblivious that Na'om had halted yet again. She sighed, drank a few sips of tepid water from the gourd she carried, and started forward once more.

Absentmindedly, she patted Ek' Balam's head as they continued to push through the scraggly brush. A tiny burst of energy swept up her arm and into her body, and from then on, she walked within touching distance of the big cat. Whenever she felt weary, she touched the jaguar's body and gained a bit of strength to continue.

A few hours later, they crested a small knoll, and Na'om looked down to see a patchwork of rectangular ponds in front of them. Fifty paces or more in length and twenty paces in width, each pond was several feet deep and filled to the brim with a deep blood-red liquid. Narrow walkways made of dirt and rocks linked the pools together. As they got closer, Na'om could see the fluid was beginning to dry along the edges of each section, forming great chunks of pinkish-white crystals. "Is this where you get the salt?" she asked.

"Yes, the men flood the pools with water from the lagoon, over there," Kärinik said as she pointed with her hand, "and once it evaporates, the salt is left behind. This is just one of many places to gather it. Some men are always in a hurry to make salt, so they set up along the ocean shoreline and boil the seawater in vast ceramic pots, but that takes a lot of wood and many hours of work. This way is the oldest and the slowest method, but I think it creates the best salt." She bent down, plucked a small crystal from a rock, and handed it to Na'om. "Suck on that for a moment, and you'll taste all the creatures of the sea in it." She nodded to Na'om who removed her small basket. "We'll take some fresh salt with us; you never know when we might need its healing properties."

One lone ceiba tree grew near the salt ponds, and Kärinik moved into its meager shade once she had filled Na'om's basket with salt crystals. "We'll rest a few hours and then continue. It's only another two hours or so to my daughter's village." She removed a small coconut bowl from her pack basket and poured some water into it. "For Ek' Balam," she said as she handed the container to Na'om. "He must be thirsty after all this walking."

"Maltiox," Na'om said as she placed the dish in front of the big cat. He lapped up the water quickly and looked at Na'om for more. "Is there plenty to drink? He needs more." Na'om shook her own gourd, but knew it was empty.

"There's a small amount left; we'll have to be careful so we don't run out, but I think we'll be all right," Kärinik replied as she handed over the gourd. She gave Na'om a small piece of dried fish for Ek' Balam, and the two women split a fish between them, but it was so salty that Na'om didn't dare eat too much as she knew it would only increase her thirst.

The three of them dozed under the ceiba tree as the sun moved across the sky, and Na'om was startled to see the length of the shadows when she finally woke up. She shook Kärinik, and the woman yawned as she placed her pack basket on her shoulders.

"It'll be dark by the time we reach the village, but it'll be easier to get to Alixel's house without being seen," Kärinik said as she led them past the salt ponds and back on to the narrow trail.

Na'om just nodded. Despite the rest, she was tired, and her feet were sore from walking on the hot soil.

"We mustn't mention the cave or talk of the Underworld while the children are still about," Kärinik warned. "Even Alixel might have difficulty accepting your story; she's still terrified of that area, knowing her father disappeared that way."

"Maybe if she knows I survived, she'd be less frightened. It's possible your husband is still alive as well."

"Hmm, well, I don't know that I'll begin to think too much on Chapal's return, but perhaps it would help Alixel and the children. And we must make sure that big cat of yours doesn't scare anyone." Kärinik's stomach growled, and she laughed. "I do hope she has plenty of food on hand."

"Especially avocados?" Na'om said with a smile.

"Yes, avocados and some mangoes would be nice, too. What about you? There must be something you'd like to eat."

Na'om laughed. "Any food is far better than the little I survived on before." She shivered as she thought of the bats and the blood she'd ingested and wondered again how she'd managed to endure for so long on so little.

Most of the oval thatched huts in the village were dark by the time the three arrived, and Kärinik hurried them down the few narrow streets to yet another dark house. She tapped gently on the wooden door and called out. "Alixel, it's me, come quickly and let us in." They waited for a few minutes, and finally a single candle could be seen through the open window.

A slender woman wearing a long sleeve white dress, her long black hair loose about her shoulders, peered into the darkness. "Chuch, what are you doing here? Is everything all right? You're not sick, are you?"

"No, child, I'm fine, let us in, and we'll explain everything."

Alixel stepped away from the doorway and gasped when she saw Ek' Balam. "Chuch?" she cried as she backed away from the cat.

"It's all right, Alixel," Kärinik said. She nodded at Na'om, who placed her hand on the cat's shoulder, stopping him from entering into the room.

"He can wait outside for now," Na'om said and guided Ek' Balam back through the open doorway. "Give me a few minutes," she whispered to the cat. "I'll be back with some food and water as quickly as I can."

With an audible sigh, Ek' Balam plopped down on the hard-packed ground just outside the hut and laid his big head on his front paws.

Another light appeared from an inner room when Na'om stepped back into the house. A young girl appeared, dressed in a small white shirt that hung below her knees. Behind her was a boy, wearing a simple leather loincloth. His short black hair was all mussed, and he rubbed his eyes as he entered the room.

"Chuch? What's going on? We heard voices," the girl said. Then she saw Kärinik. "Ati't! What are you doing here?" she cried as she placed the candle on a small table and hurried over to hug Kärinik.

"Mial, Ukabal," Kärinik said as she squeezed her grandchildren.

"You've both gotten so big since I last saw you."

Na'om stood patiently near the door while the family embraced yet again.

"Chuch, who's the girl?" Alixel said to Kärinik as she glanced over at Na'om.

Kärinik beckoned with her hand, and Na'om moved out of the shadows and into the candlelight. She heard Alixel inhale sharply and saw the children move quickly behind their mother.

"This is Na'om. She has quite the story to tell, but first, it's been a long day, and we're all in need of some food." She sat down on a small wooden stool near the table and pointed to one across from her. "Come and sit, Na'om. You must be weary; I know I am."

Grateful for the invitation, Na'om remained silent and watched as Alixel hurried to gather some food. Her daughter, Mial, placed a ceramic jug full of watermelon juice and several glazed mugs on the table while Ukabal hung near the doorway to the second, smaller room. Alixel laid a plate full of tamales on the table, followed by a bowl of sliced avocados, mangoes, and papayas. Then she added a small plate covered with boiled turkey eggs that she'd peeled and sliced and sprinkled with salt. "It's not much, but I don't want to start the fire as that would just rouse the neighbors," she said as she sat down on another stool. "Please, help yourself," she said as she pushed the platter of fruits toward Na'om.

"Where is Tikonel?" Kärinik asked as she helped herself to another slice of avocado.

"Gone to Mayapán, like many of the other men in the village, to see if he can help those who survived the attack," Alixel replied. "Mothers with small children, the old, and the members of the council stayed to tend the crops and keep the village going." Alixel shook her head. "But we need the others to return to take care of things."

"So, there's no more fear about sickness, then?" Kärinik asked as she reached for a second tamale.

"From what we've heard, the disease has been contained. But I still didn't want Tikonel to go to the city, as I'm afraid he and all the other men will be forced to join the counterattack."

"They plan to retaliate?" Na'om asked as she choked on a piece of dry cornmeal. "Surely they know who they're up against," she added.

Alixel was about to speak, but Kärinik shook her head, stopping her daughter from speaking. She turned to Na'om and whispered, "I doubt they think it's the person you're thinking of, but enough of this talk for now. Let's finish our meal and get the children back to bed."

While Na'om ate the rest of her meal in silence, she listened to Kärinik talking to the children, asking about their schooling and life in the village. She studied Alixel who sat next to her mother. Na'om could see she was taller than Kärinik, but she had the same dimple in one cheek when she smiled and small wrinkles around her deep brown eyes. Her daughter, Mial, stood behind the two women; her hand was placed gently on her grandmother's shoulder, and every now and then, Kärinik reached up and patted it before turning back to the food. Na'om looked from the young girl to the boy, Ukabal, who still stood off to one side. The girl was obviously the older of the two children, and Na'om guessed she had passed her tenth name day and the boy his eighth.

Na'om knew they were all waiting for her to finish eating so she could tell them her story. She felt the three sets of eyes on her skin like tiny moths fluttering nearby and quickly finished her second tamale. "I should give something to Ek' Balam," she said to Kärinik, who nodded her head.

"Bring him inside, but keep him near the door."

Na'om stepped out into the darkness and saw Ek' Balam lift his head. He studied her with his big eyes. She bent down and stroked his head. "So, you know you have to be very calm inside," she said. He blinked twice and stood up. "I'll take that as a yes," Na'om said as she leaned over and kissed him on the soft fur between his ears.

Together, they entered the hut, and Na'om placed her hand on Ek' Balam's shoulder so he stopped just inside the doorway. Kärinik tossed her a dried fish, and Mial stepped forward with a coconut bowl full of fresh water, which Na'om took and put on the floor.

In silence, the group watched the big cat eat and drink; then they all laughed as Ek' Balam lay down on the floor, exposing his belly. "All right, all right, I'll rub your tummy," Na'om said as she sat down next to the cat. His loud purr filled the room.

Ukabal peeked around Kärinik's shoulder at the two of them sitting on the floor.

"Would you like to touch him?" Na'om asked.

The shy boy nodded and edged a little closer.

"Ukabal, no," Alixel said as she grabbed her son's arm and pulled him back to stand beside her. "Chuch, it's time you explained what's going on. Who is this girl, why is she covered with those markings, and how can she be friends with this jaguar?"

Kärinik sighed. "This may take some time," she said. "Send the children to bed, Alixel. Some things are best not heard by the young." As her daughter led the reluctant children back into their bedroom, Kärinik looked over at Na'om. "Do you want to tell Alixel or should I?"

"Do you mind explaining? Suddenly, I'm so very sleepy." Even though she knew it wasn't polite, she curled up beside Ek' Balam, her head on his stomach, and quickly fell asleep to the sound of Kärinik's voice and the occasional questions raised by Alixel.

When Na'om woke, daylight was streaming through the window opening, and Ukabal stood only a few feet away from her. His almost black eyes bore into her, and Na'om felt bombarded by a thousand unspoken questions.

"Where is everyone?" Na'om asked as she stood up and stretched. But the boy didn't answer; he just continued to stare at Na'om and Ek' Balam, who was licking his fur.

"Chuch and Ati't went to the market to sell the fish; they'll be back soon," Mial said as she entered the hut. She took off a straw hat and hung it on a nail embedded in the wall before placing a plate full of fried turtle eggs and a mug of steaming tea on the table. She motioned to the stool, and Na'om sat down.

With the two children watching her, Na'om ate her meal in silence. She was still hungry, but she made sure to leave a few bites of runny yolk for Ek' Balam. Even though her body ached, she was anxious to continue the journey to Mayapán. From the slant of light coming through the open doorway, she could tell a good deal of the day had already gone by, and she fretted about the loss of time.

Ek' Balam bumped Na'om's knee with his big head, and she placed the plate in front of him. The jaguar licked it and sent it sliding across the compacted dirt floor.

Ukabal laughed as Ek' Balam kept nudging the plate with his tongue until it finally stopped on the far side of the room. Only then did Ek'

Balam turn and pad over to Na'om where he sat down next to her. His head was almost level with the top of the table, and she could see him sniffing the air for more food.

Turning to the children, Na'om said, "He won't hurt you, I promise." She placed her hand on Ek' Balam, gently rubbed his ear, and his purring filled the air. The children grinned. Na'om saw a small flute sticking out of the leather pouch Ukabal wore around his waist. She pointed to it. "Do you play?"

Ukabal nodded, and with a shy grin, he pulled the instrument out.

"Play a tune and watch what we can do," Na'om said as she turned to Ek' Balam. She bowed in front of the big cat and held out her hands, palms up. "May I have this dance?" Ek' Balam's purring stopped, but he did place one front paw and then the other in Na'om's hands. She gently lifted his feet to her shoulders and held them there with her hands. She nodded at Ukabal who began to blow into his bamboo flute. As the piercing notes filled the air, Na'om and Ek' Balam slowly shuffled around in a circle, matching their steps to the beat of the music. As Ukabal grew more confident, his pace quickened, and Na'om struggled to lead Ek' Balam in an ever-widening route around the small room. But they stumbled when Na'om felt Ek' Balam step on her right foot with his back paw, and Ukabal stopped playing. Na'om let Ek' Balam's front paws go, and he shook himself and hurried over to corner of the hut to lick his ruffled fur.

"That's quite the trick," Mial said as she helped Na'om to her feet.

"It's been a long time since we've tried that; I think we need some more practice," Na'om said as she examined her foot. She couldn't see any scratches in the skin, but the area was painful to the touch. Just then, she heard voices outside the door, and Alixel and Kärinik entered. They both carried several cloth bags, which they set on the floor.

"Good, you're awake," the older woman said as she hugged Na'om. "It's quite late; do you want to stay here another night or leave now for the city?"

"Let's go today; the longer I linger, the more anxious I get."

Kärinik turned to her daughter. "I suspected as much. We'll take as much food as we can carry and purchase more on the road when we run out. We'll leave as soon as it gets dark and walk through the night. The less people see of you and that big cat of yours, the better." She rummaged in one bag and pulled out a long white skirt and a huipil with long sleeves, which she handed to Na'om. "Put these on; they'll help hide your markings."

Na'om nodded and quickly went into the back room to change. The clothes were soft against her bare skin and fit perfectly. She bundled up her other outfit and laid it gently on top of the salt in her basket.

Just then, there was the sound of someone pounding on the door. Kärinik looked at Alixel. "Who could that be?"

Alixel shrugged her shoulders as she moved to open the door. "I don't know; no one knows you're here." From the open doorway, the group inside the house could see a large crowd had gathered outside the small hut.

"Ch'awinel, what brings you here?" Alixel addressed the shaman of the village. He wore his ceremonial jaguar skin cape and long quetzal feather headdress. The iridescent greenish-blue feathers swayed in the light breeze. She looked beyond him to see that most of the villagers were present, with the crowd filling the narrow street in front of the house from side to side.

"We've come to pay homage to the girl," Ch'awinel replied. He tried to peer around Alixel to catch a glimpse of her.

"So much for leaving after dark so no one sees you," Kärinik said. She turned to look at her grandchildren. "Which one of you told your friends she was here?"

Mial refused to look her grandmother in the eye as she mumbled, "I did. I'm sorry, Ati't."

Kärinik gently pushed Na'om forward. "I was afraid this might happen, but perhaps it's for the best. "We need all the support we can get."

As soon as Na'om stepped forward into the small courtyard, Ch'awinel and the other elders of the village scrambled to prostrate themselves on the ground. "No, no, please, don't do that," Na'om cried as she bent over and gently tugged on the shaman's right arm. "I wish no adulation from any of you."

Ch'awinel slowly stood, but continued to bow deeply in front of Na'om. The tips of the long feathers on his headdress brushed Na'om's leg, and she stepped a pace back. "We're here to serve you in any way that we possibly can," he said.

"Maltiox," Na'om said. She paused, unsure of what to say or do next.

She felt Kärinik step beside her.

"My friend's name is Na'om," she said as she placed her hand on Na'om's shoulder. "She's survived the greatest tests that the gods can imagine and lived to be with us today, but she's still weak from all her trials. She's headed to Mayapán, but under the circumstances, she could use your help in getting there."

Ch'awinel nodded. "Of course, of course." He turned toward the crowd, searching for the village carpenter. He spotted the older man near the street wearing his leather apron over his broad chest. "Josol Che', gather the necessary materials and have your men build a litter, so we may carry Na'om wherever she needs to go. Spare no expense; the village will compensate you for the materials."

Josol Che' nodded to Ch'awinel. "At once, my lord." He pushed his way through the throng with several men on his heels, who also wore leather aprons that hung down over their loincloths.

"Maltiox, Ch'awinel," Kärinik said as she bowed graciously to the shaman.

"Yes, thank you," Na'om said. She was still a bit flustered at all the attention directed her way.

"We want to see the jaguar," a voice in the crowd yelled. "Yes, show us the jaguar and your spots," another voice added.

Ch'awinel spun around, glaring at his neighbors. "Who dares to insult this girl this way? Speak now so I may deal with you swiftly!" The murmuring ceased, and a strange silence filled the air, broken only by the sound of a hummingbird searching for nectar in the pink hibiscus flowers next door.

"It's all right," Na'om said to Ch'awinel as she stepped into a patch of sunlight closer to the crowd. There was a general gasp as the light caught the marks, clearly visible on her mocha-colored skin. Many in the crowd backed away from Na'om, others hid their eyes with their hands, and some fell to their knees, begging for help.

"Itzamná, now what do I do?" Na'om said as she twisted her head to look back at Kärinik and the others still in the doorway of the small hut. In answer, Ek' Balam pushed his way past the women and children and came to stand next to Na'om. Those in the throng who had not budged before now took several paces back, leaving a wide gap between Na'om, the jaguar, and the villagers.

"Please, he means no harm, nor do I," Na'om said as she addressed all the strangers in front of her. "I only wish for food for our journey so I might travel to Mayapán and see if members of my family survived the attack."

"They say Satal, the witch of Mayapán, rose from the dead and led the assault with members of the Underworld by her side," a man's voice called out. "Do you know anything of this?"

Before Na'om could answer, another man said, "If Satal is behind it all, can you defeat her?"

Many in the crowd echoed the question. "Yes, can you overthrow her powers?"

"Can you undo the spell she cast that causes anyone who comes within two days' walk of the city to fall ill, unable to hold down any food or water?" The woman who had spoken began to weep. "My son, he died because of that woman. I would do anything to send her to the Underworld where she belongs."

"Help us, Na'om. We promise to fight for you, just tell us what to do."

Seeing Na'om was completely bewildered with all the attention, Ch'awinel quickly stepped in and addressed the people. "Rest easy, my friends, we will all have a part to play in the counterattack, and when the time comes, you'll be given instructions on what to do. For now, though, go back to your daily tasks. Tend to the corn in the fields, harvest the manioc roots, and process more salt. Tan the leather hides, fletch the arrows, and carve the obsidian knives we'll need for battle. Without supplies, we can gather no army, so we must begin today to prepare for the retaliation."

In small groups of two and three, the people dispersed, leaving Na'om standing next to Ch'awinel. "Thank you for your help," Na'om said as she turned to the priest. "You must tell me more about the counterattack being planned."

Ch'awinel laughed. "My apologies, dear child, I needed to say that to send everyone back to work; otherwise we'd have stood here all day in the hot sun. There are rumors the council in Mayapán is planning a counteroffensive at some point, but I haven't received any official documents to verify it. But now that you're here, you'll lead the men into battle, am I right?"

Na'om laughed. "Me, at the head of an army? I'm just a simple girl. What do I know of waging war?" She shook her head. "I'm afraid you have the wrong person."

"You may not have the battle skills necessary to plan the attack, but as evidenced by your return from the Underworld and the markings on your skin, you certainly have the power to defeat Satal," Ch'awinel replied. "There will be many willing to advise you, but you must decide to fight or not."

Na'om looked from the older shaman to Kärinik to Alixel and the children. Deep inside, she knew the priest was right, but she was still afraid that Satal had the advantage with her ties to Camazotz and the other gods of the Underworld. She also knew that if she didn't try to defeat Satal, then her hold over the city and the surrounding countryside would continue indefinitely. *Perhaps, with Ek' Balam by my side, and an army of trained men behind us, we can finally overthrow the witch.* "I thank you all for your confidence. I only hope that Ek' Balam and I are as strong as you think we are."

Kärinik broke the solemn moment with a smile. "From what I've witnessed, you'll do just fine. Come inside now, out of the hot sun, and rest. We still have a long trip ahead of us."

It was late in the afternoon by the time Josol Che' and four of his men knocked on Alixel's door once again. They stepped aside so Na'om could see the litter they had built. Four long poles provided the main support for a narrow plank platform upon which they'd nailed a simple wooden stool. They'd padded the hard back and seat with leather cushions stuffed with ceiba fluff and attached a sun umbrella that extended up and over the back of the seat to shield Na'om from the hot sun. Only a few inches of wood extended beyond the seat on either side and in the back, but there was plenty of room for Na'om's feet in front.

Kärinik, Alixel, with the children behind her, watched as Na'om circled the litter.

"Goodness, I never expected anything like this," Na'om said as Josol Che' ushered her to sit down. She grabbed the edges of the stool with both hands as the four younger men each picked up one corner of the palanquin, lifting Na'om with ease. She looked at the two men in front of her and realized they were twins. They had identical faces, strong shoulders, and many of the same geometric blue tattoos across their chests. Then she glanced behind her and saw those youths were identical twins as well. The four men set her back down on the ground, and Na'om stepped off the platform, her face flush from the sudden attention.

"Jumumik, let's see if we can pick her up ourselves," one of the twins said to the other. The brothers quickly moved to the front and back of the carrier.

Josol Che' helped Na'om sit back down. "Jututik, are you ready?" Jumumik asked.

"Yes." Both men bent at the knees and strong-armed the litter up onto their shoulders. Na'om clutched the seat again as the platform dipped and swayed, threatening to spill her to the ground. The twins carried Na'om around the small courtyard, out into the street, and back to the hut before setting her on the ground.

"It would be a great honor to carry you to Mayapán, my lady," Jumumik and Jututik both said in unison as they bowed in front of Na'om.

Then the other set of twins stepped forward and bowed. "It would be an honor for us as well," Be Anim and Tik Anim said. "We can take turns with our cousins here and get you to the city as if you were floating on the wind."

"Please, call me Na'om," Na'om said as she motioned for all the twins to stand up. She looked at the older carpenter who stood near the doorway. "Can you spare these men?" she asked Josol Che'.

"My lady, Na'om," Josol Che' said, "We'll all be coming with you to the city. Only a few have promised to stay and take care of the crops and the young children. The village has pledged itself to you; we are at your service." The older man bowed.

Na'om felt the heat rise on her face once again. *Itzamná, I'm not sure I'll ever grow used to all this attention after a lifetime of being shunned.* She looked at Kärinik for support, but the older woman only smiled as she stepped forward.

"I hope the rest of us will be able to keep up with you," Kärinik said as she gave Na'om a quick hug. "These men who have pledged to be your porters are the swiftest runners in the village. They win all the footraces in the annual competitions."

Just then, Ch'awinel appeared with many of the other villagers. He nodded to Josol Che' after examining the litter. "Have you tried it out?" he asked as he bowed to Na'om.

"Yes, it works very well, maltiox. I only need to balance a bit better, so I don't fall out when they lift me."

Alixel slipped inside the hut and returned a moment later with a length of sisal cord. "Perhaps we should tie you to the chair," she suggested.

"Excellent idea, Alixel," Josol Che' said. "I should have thought of that myself." He looked around the small gathering of people. "If you're ready, we should go while there's still a few hours of daylight. We'll stop in the village of Kini for the night and then push on toward Mayapán in the morning."

Kärinik swung her pack basket full of food on to her back. "As soon as we find Tikonel, I'll send a messenger," she said as she hugged Alixel.

"You're sure you don't want us to come with you?" Alixel asked as she stepped away from Kärinik.

"Maltiox," Na'om said as she nodded toward Alixel. "But I think it's safer if you remain here with the children." She looked toward Alixel's young son, Ukabal. "Continue practicing that flute, and next time we see you, we'll dance again." The boy grinned and nodded.

Mial stepped forward and pressed her straw hat into Na'om's hand. "You might need this on the journey."

"Good idea, Mial," Kärinik said as she embraced her granddaughter. She turned to Na'om. "Ready?"

"Yes," she replied as she sat down on the chair. She quickly tied herself to the seat and braced herself as Jumumik and Jututik lifted her into the air. She glanced over into the shade of the hibiscus bush where Ek' Balam was lying, watching everyone from a safe distance. "Are you coming?" she asked as the men stepped into the street. Ek' Balam stood, stretched from head to tail, and quickly fell into place next to Na'om's right side. The crowd of middle-aged women, young maidens, and the older men still fit to walk such a distance left a wide berth around the jaguar as the procession left Xiat, heading south toward Mayapán.

***

As the group from Xiat, with Na'om and Ek' Balam at its center, left the village of Kini, more people joined them, slowing their progress. And as they walked further south, from village to village, the crowds waiting for them grew. Everyone was eager to see the jaguar woman and her loyal companion. Many immediately pledged their allegiance to Na'om and fell in step with those who carried her. Old women lined the dirt pathways, offering the walkers plates of tamales, bowls of stewed fruits, and gourds full of sweet melon juice. Younger women with their toddlers strapped to their backs hurried forward to spread bouquets of purple jacaranda flowers on the ground so the air was scented with sweetness as they passed. Some tried to hand their bundles of blossoms to Na'om, who was quickly overcome by the generosity of the people around her. She hated to refuse such beautiful gifts, but she had no place to put them on the litter. Other young mothers begged her to touch and bless the tiny trinkets and sculptures they held out to her.

"What do they hope to gain if I touch them?" Na'om asked Kärinik who walked just next to Ek' Balam on the right side of the litter. Na'om trailed her left hand out, skimming the bracelets, necklaces, and tiny carved limestone statues with her fingertips.

"Your healing powers, of course," Kärinik replied. "The news has spread quickly of the girl who fell into the cenote and returned to tell the tale. They want protection for their children and for themselves before any other disasters happen. Some believe your appearance is the reason the vomiting sickness has finally stopped spreading." She waved her hand through the air, indicating the clusters of old couples, young mothers with their infants bundled into shawls on their backs, and the adolescents who lined the dusty dirt pathways, peering at the procession as it continued south to the city. "All these people have suffered in one way or another because of Satal's attack on Mayapán. Commerce between the villages and Mayapán almost stopped while those who were ill or wounded regained their strength, so many have had no income for many, many days. Others lost family members in the great battle or were gravely ill themselves. They're all looking to you for help now." The older woman shifted the walking stick she carried to her other hand and continued to keep pace with the twins who carried Na'om.

"With word spreading this rapidly, that means it won't be long before Satal knows I'm alive," Na'om said. Anger and fear twisted her stomach. "I knew the woman was evil, but I had no idea she would cause such pain and misery to so many." Na'om felt the weight of want from all the strangers land squarely on her shoulders, and she slumped a bit in her stiff-backed chair. *Itzamná, I don't think I can do this,* she thought as she brushed more amulets with her hand.

"Remember, Na'om, you're not alone," Kärinik said as she briefly touched the girl on the leg. "We shall stand behind you, no matter what that entails."

Na'om nodded, too overwhelmed with the prospects ahead of her to say anything. As the two sets of twins continued to carry her across the countryside, she thought about the hundreds upon hundreds of people who suddenly expected her to accomplish what a whole army of trained men had been unable to do. *It's not fair after everything I've already been through. All I want is to head home to Pa nimá and find Ati't and then Tz'. I need to tell him that I love him, and continue my life with him by my side. Why should I help these strangers?*

Na'om fussed on her chair as the sun slowly crossed the sky. She wanted to leap down and disappear among the groups of women laden with baskets crammed full of fresh ears of corn or hide behind the men who carried poles strung with haunches of freshly slaughtered deer to another small village marketplace. Or be one of the young boys who lugged baskets of turtle eggs in their arms and bamboo cages filled with live iguanas of all shapes and sizes on their backs. She longed to trade places with any one of them so she could regain the anonymity that had been hers for most of her life. But as she looked about, she saw the deep furrows etched into the foreheads of the old women, the wounds healing on the arms and legs of the men, and the lack of joy on the faces of the children. No one laughed, no one smiled, very few people even talked, and all the angst and resentment she felt swiftly flowed away. She knew the only way to lift the dark cape of depression that pressed down upon everyone was to defeat Satal. She also knew she was the only one capable of doing it.

During the rest of the day, they traveled as quickly as they could, but as the crowds increased, the pace of those walking slowed, so the group was forced to spend another night out in the open. Na'om ached from head to toe from sitting for so many hours on the padded chair, but realized the lack of walking and the abundant food were rapidly building her reserves of strength. After another meal with Kärinik, she lay curled on the ground in a blanket a stranger had provided near one of the many small cooking fires. Ek' Balam circled around her three times before lying down beside her. She reached out to pet him, reassured by his presence. Soon the murmurs of those near her ceased as everyone drifted into sleep. But Na'om and Ek' Balam lay wide-awake, staring up into the night sky. She felt Ek' Balam's body tense as he lifted his head, and she followed his gaze. Several bats flitted above the camp, swooping and dipping high above those sprawled on the ground.

Ek' Balam growled and began to rise, but Na'om held on to his back and pulled him back down. "It's only a few bats, boy, nothing to fear," she said as she stroked his head. But he refused to relax. Even rubbing his favorite spot behind his ear failed to make him purr. His tail swished rapidly back and forth on the ground, sounding like a straw broom sweeping rough clay tiles, and Na'om fell asleep only to dream of Camazotz and the hundreds of bats she'd faced in the Underworld.

She woke in a sweat, despite the early morning dew that coated everyone, and was grateful when Kärinik opened her eyes.

"How long have you been awake?" the older woman asked as she stretched awkwardly. She glanced around and saw that most of the others were beginning to rise as well.

"Since before the sun began to lighten the sky," Na'om said. She sat up, folded her legs under her body, and shivered. "I should have had some of your herbal tea last night."

"Ah, more bad dreams . . . what were they about this time?"

"Bats, a whole sky full of them. Ek' Balam spotted some flying high overhead last night, and I can't shake the feeling that Camazotz sent them to spy on us."

"Perhaps, or maybe they were just bats, out catching the bugs that fly at night. Either way, they're gone now. In two more days, we'll reach the safety of the city." Kärinik hurried to get the embers left in the fire pit burning. "Right now, a hot meal will do you good."

Na'om nodded, but she couldn't shake the idea that Satal had sent scouts out to find her.

The days passed much as the ones before, and it was near dusk by the time they reached the outskirts of Mayapán. Even under the deepening purple sky, Na'om could see signs of the recent battle everywhere she looked. Creosote bushes, tall grasses, even the cornfields had been trampled flat. Several groups of oval huts had been burned, their blackened rafters leaning precariously against crumbling stucco walls, and everywhere hung the musty, rank smell of death that Na'om remembered from her encounters with Camazotz and the gods of the Underworld. The twins slowed their pace as they stepped from the wide dirt path they'd been following onto the sacbé that ran past the city. Throngs of people lined the limestone causeway, and as one person and then another caught sight of Na'om, the murmuring of the crowd slowly ceased.

Lit torches placed along most of Mayapán's walls cast a steady yellowish-orange glow into the dusk, illuminating the destruction below. Several sections of the wall had been torn down, turned into piles of rocks and rubble, and tall bamboo scaffolding had been erected in the worst areas so the stonemasons could rebuild. Many of the copper gates were missing, and the entrances had been filled with interwoven ceiba and lime tree branches, the multitude of spines meant to keep any creatures away. Despite the late hour of the day, a few turkey vultures still pecked at the black splotches and stains that marked the pounded ground and walls, and Na'om quickly looked away. She didn't want to know what the birds were feasting on.

The wave of silence continued flowing in front of them, so that by the time Be Anim and Tik Anim placed Na'om's carrier down in front of the main gates, there was no sound except the last trills of birds as they settled down to sleep.

Na'om stepped off the litter and reached out to touch Ek' Balam on the shoulder. "Back where this all began, eh boy?" she whispered as she stroked his head. She could feel the essence of Satal everywhere, in the air, in the ground, in the silence that surrounded them. Her ears buzzed and her head ached and she knew that Ek' Balam also sensed the witch's presence.

"Na'om!" a woman shouted.

Na'om turned in the direction of the voice. The crowds parted, and Ajkun ran toward her, with Chiman and another woman just a few steps behind.

"Ati't!" Na'om screamed and raced to embrace her grandmother. Tears spilled as the two women hugged and kissed, the crowd around them forgotten. Na'om felt her heart cramping as she took a deep breath of her grandmother's scent. "Sweet honey and spices, just as I remembered," she said, laughing through her tears. "Oh, Ati't, I was so afraid I'd never see you again." She felt a hand on her shoulder and stepped slightly away from Ajkun so she could include Chiman in a group hug.

"Na'om, oh, Na'om, we never expected to see you alive," Chiman said as he wiped at a few tears of his own. "But when we heard the rumors that a girl with a jaguar was headed to the city . . . well, we knew it could only be you and that the last drawings you made in your journal were true."

"But what are you doing here? I didn't expect to see you until I returned to Pa nimá."

"After the attack, messengers arrived in the village asking for healers to come to the city to help the wounded and sick. I needed to know that Alom and the others were safe," Ajkun replied. She smiled, looking at the confusion written on Na'om's face. "People we met and became friends with while we waited to return to the village, after . . . after you disappeared."

Na'om nodded. "There's so much I need to know." She smiled at the older woman who stood near her grandmother, noticing the scar that ran down her right calf to her ankle. A young boy peeked out from behind the older woman's gray skirt. "Noy, is that you?"

"Yes, child," Noy said as she stepped forward to hug Na'om. "I've become good friends with your grandmother." The two women reached for each other's hands and squeezed them.

"And is that Lintat hiding behind you?" Na'om knelt on the ground. "Don't be afraid," she said as she held out her arms.

Lintat dashed around Noy, straight into Na'om's embrace. He ran his fingers lightly over the jaguar markings visible on her hands and reached up to caress the spots on her face. She kissed the boy on the top of his head as she stood back up. "You've grown so much bigger since I last saw you."

Lintat slipped his hand into Noy's, scuffed his bare feet on the ground, but didn't answer.

"He's been a big help in the village," Chiman said as he patted the boy fondly on his bare shoulder.

Na'om turned to Kärinik and introduced her to the small group. She sensed instant friendship among the three older women and smiled.

Na'om placed her arms around the waists of Ajkun and Chiman and scanned the crowd near them. "And Tz', where is he? Is he in Pa nimá or did he come with you? I must see him."

She noticed the quick glance between Chiman and Ajkun. Instantly, she knew. "Satal has him, doesn't she?"

"We think so," Chiman said, the smile wiped from his face.

Suddenly all the questions and doubts that had nagged at Na'om ever since Ch'awinel had said she must lead the counterattack vanished. Now she knew she had no option but to engage in another battle with Satal. *She'll do no more damage to those I love!* But before she had a chance to speak, a man approached and bowed deeply in front of her.

"Na'om, let me introduce you to your father, Yakal," Chiman said as he placed a hand on the man's shoulder, indicating he should stand.

Tears streamed down the man's face as he lifted his head. "By the grace of all the gods, you've been returned to me, to us all." He stepped forward to hug Na'om.

A thousand thoughts raced through Na'om's mind in that instant; the multiple years of longing and desire to know this man, the anger at having been forsaken by him, the fear she'd felt throughout her young life with no father to protect her, how fatigued he looked, his face etched with lines of worry across his forehead. As the emotions churned inside her chest, she stood stiff and wooden in Yakal's embrace, barely wrapping her own arms around him to return his hug. Na'om glanced over Yakal's shoulder and saw the crowds were all still watching. She stepped back hurriedly.

"I'm sure Na'om and her companions are tired and hungry, so let's get them inside the city's walls before it's completely dark," Chiman said as he glanced at the sky. Only a sliver of sunlight remained on the horizon.

In the far distance, Na'om saw a colony of bats swooping about in the blackness and shivered. "We need to talk, but not here, not now," Na'om said. She reached out instinctively for Ek' Balam, and the jaguar pushed Yakal out of the way so he could stand at Na'om's side.

Yakal looked at the group of men and women who had accompanied Na'om. "Yes, of course," Yakal said. He beckoned to Nimal who approached slowly, his eyes concentrated on Ek' Balam whose tail swished back and forth rapidly. "You must get everyone to go home now; the travelers are weary and need food and rest. There'll be more occasions to see Na'om and her cat in the future."

Nimal nodded and waved to several of his guards who stood sentry at the main gates. Three young men in leather battle gear carrying spears hurried to his side. "Get these people moving back to their homes; remind them the curfew still holds." He glanced at the newcomers who had traveled with Na'om and turned to Yakal. "Where shall we house them?" he said with a quick nod of his head.

"In the Temple of the Warriors, along with all the others who are still homeless."

"These people have spent the past few nights out in the open, so anything you can provide will be welcome," Na'om said. The cloud of bats was getting closer, and Na'om stroked Ek' Balam's head as he began to growl. 'It's all right, boy, I see them."

"What's wrong," Na'om?" Ajkun asked. She slipped her arthritic hand into Na'om's and squeezed it.

"The bats, they're coming this way," Na'om replied as she pulled on Ajkun's hand, hurrying them toward the gates of the city. "We need to get indoors, quickly, before they see us." Na'om dropped Ajkun's hand and began to run, with Ek' Balam loping beside her. Chiman rushed to Ajkun's side, wrapped his arm protectively around her, and hurried her inside the walls. Noy picked up Lintat, placed him on her hip, and scurried as rapidly as she could behind them. Yakal, Kärinik, and the sets of twins quickly followed as fear rippled through the group. Those who hadn't left the scene before swiftly did so now, rushing for cover from something they didn't know or understand.

"Shut the gates," Nimal shouted. Six of the sentries on duty swiftly closed the heavy copper doors. They slid the vast wooden bolt through the channels to lock it tightly and took up places across the front of the doors.

Yakal ran ahead of the others and caught up with Na'om. He touched her briefly on the arm. "Come, this way, Na'om," he said as he led her toward the Temple of the Warriors. He hurried up the darkened steps and spoke to the warriors on duty, who quickly stepped aside to let everyone in. More candles were lit, and orbs of golden light soon filled the large main room. Breathless from running, the people filtered in in groups of twos and threes to stand against the painted walls, waiting for new instructions.

"Na'om, what happened back there?" Ajkun said as she gripped

Na'om's arms. She was puffing heavily, yet refused to sit down on the stool Chiman placed near her.

Na'om winced as her grandmother's hands tightened on her forearms. "The bats were sent by Satal and Camazotz to spy on us, I'm sure of it. We must remain out of sight until they're gone."

"Come, child, sit down, you're safe now," Ajkun said soothingly as she pushed Na'om toward the stool. She stroked Na'om's hair with one hand and waved to Yakal and Nimal who were conversing by the open doorway. "Have your men kill any bats that attempt to fly over the city walls. Then hang the bodies from long poles set on the top of the wall as a warning to any others that might come near."

"Of course, Lady Ajkun," Nimal replied. He hurried to speak to his men.

Na'om looked up at her grandmother and smiled. "You've changed; I've never heard you speak with such authority before."

Ajkun laughed. "I've gained a certain amount of respect from those in the city after helping heal many of those wounded in the battle." She took a deep breath and let it out. "I'm not sure I like it, but it is useful from time to time."

After food had been prepared and everyone had eaten, Na'om, Ajkun, and Chiman found a quiet corner where they talked long into the night, filling each other in on much that had transpired during their time apart.

Na'om smiled and felt her eyes well with tears when Ajkun told her that she and Chiman were now a couple. "We've held off on having any official ceremony. I've been praying to Ixchel for your return so you can bear witness to it," Ajkun said as she smiled wearily at Na'om.

"It'll be one of the first things I'll gladly do once I've defeated Satal and brought Tz' home," Na'om replied as she hugged her grandparents.

The threesome finally went to sleep, with Na'om nestled between Ajkun and Ek' Balam, while Chiman lay down next to Ajkun. Na'om dreamt again of bats flying overhead and then of the drying ponds full of reddish salt that she had passed with Kärinik. She meandered among the pools in the darkness and realized the bats refused to come near her as long as she was surrounded by the salty water. She finally curled up on one of the many paths between the salt ponds and fell asleep while bats drifted on the night breezes off in the distance.

Ajkun and Chiman were the first to rouse, but Na'om slept until mid-morning when Kärinik and Noy appeared with mugs full of hot chocolate, and plates of scrambled turkey eggs, fried bananas, and cooked chaya for them all.

Shortly after they'd all eaten, Yakal approached, followed by a group of men. Na'om recognized the heavyset man just behind her father; she'd seen him at the cenote many moons ago. She noticed he was much thinner and walked with a limp, leaning heavily on the arm of his companion. Both men were dressed in matching indigo shirts, new leather loincloths, and leather sandals that laced up their calves.

"Na'om, let me introduce the men from the city council," Yakal said. "This is Kubal Joron," he said as he briefly touched the heavy man's hand, "and Matz' is the man supporting him. This is Nimal, whom you met last night in the dark, and this is your great-uncle, Bitol." The leather breastplates the two men wore on their chests were stamped with the city's emblem, a large circle with the pyramid of Kukulcan in the middle. Their loincloths had been worn smooth by the obsidian knife sheaths they wore at their sides, and each had scuffed sandals on his feet. The four men bowed deeply. "It's an honor, Lady Na'om," they said in unison.

"Please, all of you, enough with the bowing. And, Na'om is sufficient." She looked around the group. "What is it that you want?"

"We must discuss the counterattack against Chichén Itzá," Nimal replied. "The people of Mayapán and of all the regions that are sworn to the city demand revenge." He placed his large hand on the hilt of his obsidian blade. "As leader of the regiment, I wish retribution as well, but my forces were severely depleted in the battle, so I'm at a loss as to how to proceed."

Ajkun looked at Kärinik and Noy. "That sounds like our cue to leave," she said as she started to rise from a leather stool.

"No, Ati't," Na'om said as she placed a hand on her grandmother's arm. "I want you to stay, all of you." She looked from one woman's lined face to the next. "I need your support."

Ajkun sat back down, and the two other women fidgeted on their stools as they waited for Na'om to continue.

"In all the villages that we traveled through to get here, the people pledged their allegiance to me, the old, the young, even mothers with children." She waved her hand to indicate the scores of people inside the temple. "They are just a small sampling of those ready to fight. I believe that, with some training, they can become skilled enough to engage the warriors from Chichén Itzá."

"But what of Satal?" Kubal Joron said. "The witch's personal army of shamans and those from the Underworld is far greater than anything we ever imagined." His face paled, and Yakal fetched him a stool. Matz' helped him sit, squatted next to him, and began to fan Kubal Joron's face with a small cloth he pulled from his sleeve.

Yakal hurried to fill Na'om in on more details of the attack, including his attempt to kill Satal using salt water.

"I'm not surprised by any of it," Na'om said when Yakal was finished. "Trust me, I've seen what the gods of Xibalba can do." She cleared her throat, noticing the dark circles under the men's eyes, the fear that crisscrossed everyone's faces. She looked up at Chiman, who leaned against one of the tall stucco walls. "Have the shamans study the stars to determine the best time for the counterattack."

"They've already started and should have an answer in the next day or two," he replied.

"Good; in the meantime, we shall prepare." She turned to the three older women near her. "I need you to teach every woman and girl the healing properties of the local herbs and flowers and how to properly prepare them into tinctures and compresses. We can't afford to lose anyone else to illness or disease."

The women nodded in unison. "We've already started holding classes every afternoon," Ajkun replied. "But we'll send our best pupils out into the villages to train the others."

"Perfect," Na'om replied. She turned to Bitol and Yakal. "Have every man capable of carrying a load go to the salt ponds and bring back as much salt as he can. If what you say is true about Satal, I'm going to need a vast quantity of it if Ek' Balam and I are to defeat her."

"What do you have in mind?" Yakal asked.

"A purification ritual such as no one has ever seen before," Na'om replied. "She'll be prepared for another attack, so we must do more. If I've learned anything from my time in the Underworld, it's to trust the images I have in my dreams. Last night, I dreamt of colonies of bats that refused to come near me because I was surrounded by the salt ponds. I'll use the salt, along with the strength I possess with Ek' Balam, to defeat Satal, and then I'll bring Tz' home where he belongs."

GLOSSARY

Akab Dzib: The Red House or house of the shamans in Chichén Itzá.

ati't: An affectionate term for grandmother.

balché: A fermented, honey-sweetened drink made from the bark of the *Lonchocarpus violaceus* tree.

ceiba tree: The sacred tree of the Maya. Considered the world tree, its branches reach into heaven and its roots extend down into the Underworld.

cenote: Natural sinkholes that appear in the limestone terrain and are the source of fresh water in northern Yucatán. They are interconnected by a series of underground caves and tunnels, and many of these tunnels eventually lead to the sea. The Mayans considered cenotes the entranceways to the Underworld.

chac mool: A stone sculpture in the shape of a reclining man, whose head is turned 90 degrees from his body and who holds a rounded vessel between his hands on his abdomen. This bowl is used to hold sacrificial blood for the gods.

chaya: a plant high in vitamins and minerals, similar to spinach, used in many Mayan dishes.

Chichén Itzá: A city in northeastern Yucatán, ruled by the Xiu tribe, and childhood home of Satal.

chuch: An affectionate term for mother.

Cocom: The leading tribe of the city of Mayapán and the enemy of the Xiu.

copal: An aromatic tree resin burned as incense during ceremonies for purification.

huipil: A loose-fitting tunic shirt for women, made from cotton, often heavily embroidered around the square neckline.

Itzamná: Supreme god of the Maya; often used to express surprise, agitation, or other exclamations.

jequirity beans: A hallucinogenic bean, toxic in high doses.

Kini: Small village that Na'om passes through on her way to Mayapán.

Kukulcan: The feathered god of the Maya. Many Mayan pyramids are built in his honor.

maltiox: Thanks.

matzaqik: Good-bye.

Mayapán: A city in northern Yucatán ruled by the Cocom.

noy: An affectionate term for grandmother.

Olmecs: The ancestors of the Mayans who lived north and west of the Yucatan Peninsula.

Pa nimá: The village where Na'om was born; a phrase meaning 'by the river.'

Popul Vuh: The sacred book of the Maya, which included creation stories and other important events.

q'inomal: Riches, wealth, used as a toast when drinking.

sacbé: Raised causeways made from white limestone that connected Mayan cities, temples, and plazas.

saqarik: Good morning.

Silowik Tukan: The name of the bar in Mayapán; to be drunk; blackberry.

tat axel: An affectionate term for father; **tat**, dad.

to'nel: A witch who helps.

Tulum: A Mayan city built on the east coast of the Yucatan Peninsula.

tzompantli: A stone wall covered with spikes where the heads of sacrificial victims were put on display.

utzil: goodness, gracious, often used as an exclamation of surprise.

Wayeb: The five unnamed days at the end of the calendar year when the portal to the Underworld stands open.

were-jaguar: A supernatural creature created when a woman mated with a male jaguar.

Xibalba: The Mayan Underworld.

Xiat: Small village that Na'om passes through on her way to Mayapán.

Xiu: The leading tribe of the city of Chichén Itzá and the enemy of the Cocom.

ACKNOWLEDGMENTS

Thanks goes out to the many people who helped me during the creation of this novel.

First, a huge thank you to my husband, Jeffrey Thomas, who has always been more than happy to take over my chores so I might have time to write. I've used him as a sounding board for countless ideas, and I truly am thankful for his honest and thoughtful answers.

A big thank you to my editor, Jennifer Caven, who once again did a wonderful job of highlighting areas in the final draft that needed more work. Although she insisted one character's story arc needed a complete rewrite, which was a difficult task to achieve, this novel is far better for that work. So, thank you, and I hope you'll be ready to work on book three!

Thanks to all my friends and family members who have encouraged me to keep going with this story. Your desire to know what will happen next has helped me continue the writing process on some of the bleakest days.

Thank you, Jenson Aiden, for entering my life this year. You are a joy. The multiple scenes with infants are a direct result of you being born.

Thanks to all the authors who have written numerous books, articles, and webpages on the Mayan people and their way of life. Without my intensive research, the book would lack its level of authenticity.

And thanks to the Mayan people, who continue to amaze and impress me.

ABOUT THE AUTHOR

Lee E. Cart is an award-winning author, editor, and publisher for Ek' Balam Press. Her first novel, *Born in the Wayeb*, was a winner in the 17th Annual International Latino Book Awards, which celebrates worldwide achievements in Latino literature.

Ms. Cart lives in central Maine, but lived in Guadalajara, Mexico for over seven years as a child. The time spent in Mexico created a deep love for the Mexican people and their various cultures.

Ms. Cart enjoys reading, writing, cooking, gardening, and traveling to Mexico, Hawaii, and Ireland. When she is not writing, she can often be found curled up some place snug with a good novel, a cup of hot tea, and a piece of very dark chocolate.

38637159R00218

Made in the USA
Middletown, DE
21 December 2016